Vive Mad la Dauphine

A biographical novel
by
André Romijn
Translated by Kate Ashton

BOOK ONE OF THE MARIE ANTOINETTE TRILOGY

First published 2008 by Roman House Publishers Ltd

English translation Copyright © Kate Ashton 2008

Original title: Vive Madame la Dauphine
Copyright © André Romijn 2008

Cover: Marie Antoinette by Joseph Ducreux, Vienna 1769.

Cover design: Martijn Brinks, APR Group BV, The Netherlands

Editor: Naomi Laredo

www.ma-trilogy.com

ISBN 978-0-9554100 2-4

I dedicate this book to Marie-Thérèse Louise, Princesse de Lamballe, née Savoie-Carignan, whose infinite loyalty may serve as an example to many.

André Romijn, 16 October 2008

Je me hâte de me moquer de tous, de peur d'être obligé d'en pleurer.

I hasten to laugh at everything, for fear of being obliged to weep.
(Pierre-Augustin Caron de Beaumarchais,
Le Barbier de Séville, Act 1, 2., 1773).

Les choses valent toujours mieux dans leur source.

Things are always at their best in their beginning.
(Blaise Pascal, Lettres provincials, 2, 1656).

Opening entry in the journal of the Princesse de Lamballe, 22nd June 1768

prologue

Paris, Le Temple, 19th August 1792

From a pale pool of light cast by the flickering candle, her life stares back at her. Marie-Thérèse, Princesse de Lamballe, reads yet again the first lines she entrusted to her diary, now more than twenty-four years ago. She is no great writer. She has set down her life in few words, and whole days have passed without her penning a single one. At first, just as the abbess of Saint-Antoine had promised, the journal had given the princess something to hold onto. The advice had been sound enough: she should set down her thoughts as a way of working through her grief and restoring her self-confidence. Back then, her life had lain in tatters; writing, said the abbess, would surely help the princess to recover.

She turns page after page, on and on through the years, through her own history. She had recovered – much more fully than ever she dared hope. Running her thumb over the entries, she finds herself now smiling, now sighing; sometimes there is a stab of pain. The emotions of years lie stored away between the stiff pigskin covers of this tiny book. Though insignificant enough in appearance – the leather has faded over time – it is almost completely full, as if bearing silent witness to the approaching end of her life.

On this point the Princesse de Lamballe has no illusions. It cannot go on much longer. Her index finger flicks over one page after another. During this past year she has written less and less, perhaps in an unconscious attempt to keep some pages blank, pristine for as long as possible. But can she really prolong her life with such artless tactics? Is it sensible to try? Would it not be a relief to write the final pages full, commit to them the thoughts that torture her, pronounce judgement upon those who have brought down her world?

Her zest for life is still too strong: it will not allow her to bow finally to her destiny. Yet in every fibre of her being she feels it is all over! Tearing her thoughts away from the coming night, Marie-Thérèse turns back to the years that brought her joy and pleasure. If she closes her eyes, it is not too difficult for her to live them again. She can easily transcend this narrow bed, this small, damp cell. The massive walls of the ancient tower in which she is imprisoned have no power to hold her thoughts. Once again she hears the merry music of André Grétry, birdsong and, loveliest of all, the laughter of a carefree Antoinette. Again the sweet scent of blossom assails her senses, and now her favourite perfume, then freshly laundered silk sheets. Yet she is sitting on a pallet of straw, covered with rough linen and a couple of scratchy horse blankets.

Around her, all is quiet. Are the others asleep? The silence is broken by the mournful, far-off tolling of a bell. Marie-Thérèse counts the strokes, uncertain if she has missed one. It is eleven o'clock, perhaps midnight. She should lie down and try to sleep. Softly, the princess shuts her diary and stows it safely under her pillow. Another evening has passed as an empty page. Marie-Thérèse blows out the candle, plunging the cell into the darkness of the grave. She turns restlessly onto her other side. It is so claustrophobic in here, too close for sleep. How she would love to stretch her legs. But there is nowhere for her to walk, not even a window that she can open.

Sleep must have come to Marie-Thérèse at last, for she wakes with a shock to the sound of screaming and thumping. More footsteps on the stairs ... *Mon Dieu*, not again! She puts her hands together in prayer, pricking one ear to what is going on outside her tiny room.

'Allez, get off your backside!' commands a harsh male voice. There is the sound of a chair being scraped aside, and the Princesse de Lamballe hears a door opening. Then the voice of Marie Antoinette, followed by a loudly weeping Dauphin and the hushing tones of the *Madame Royale*. Marie-Thérèse rises slowly from the wooden bed, dizzy and shivering all over. Fumbling in the darkness, she finds the door latch, lays her hand on the cool metal and hesitates. Then, drawing a deep breath, she resolutely opens the door.

The small space outside is crammed with men, all stinking of alcohol and tobacco.

'Ah, you. Over here,' commands the smallest of them, clearly the officer of the watch, as Marie-Thérèse appears in the doorway. He points in her direction, narrowing his eyes venomously. She catches her breath. So this is it, the end. Then, suddenly, Marie Antoinette is standing between them.

'Don't move,' the Queen of France counters, her tone level but full of outrage. 'The princess is a cousin of the king. She remains here!'

The diminutive officer, a whole head shorter than the queen, is clearly put out by having to look up at her. 'Orders!' he barks. 'Anyone outside the immediate family of the Capets is to appear immediately before the tribunal.' He casts the queen a callous glance, as if he would like to put some distance between them with a kick. But something holds him back. There's time enough yet. With the same filthy look on his face, he turns and beckons to the Tourzels, mother and daughter, the child locked in her mother's embrace.

'Move! Downstairs, both of you,' he yells.

'For God's sake let them pack some things,' intervenes Marie Antoinette.

With a sardonic sneer at the queen, the officer concedes: 'One minute!'

Grabbing the Princesse de Lamballe by the arm, Marie Antoinette pushes her back into the cell, in the same movement snatching the lantern from the table so that the officer and his men are left in semi-darkness. As soon as the two women are behind the closed door, Marie Antoinette drops her mask. Her proud manner gives way to sobs, as the two women fall into each other's arms.

'Oh, I can hardly find the strength to go on,' she weeps. 'How much more humiliation must we endure? Will there be no end to it?'

'I don't want to go,' says Marie-Thérèse in a small, tearful voice. 'I can't leave you.'

Brutal hammering on the door. 'Get a move on!' is the curt command from the other side. The women hold one another more tightly still, until the sound of her son's crying reaches Marie Antoinette. Freeing herself from Marie-Thérèse's arms, she dries her eyes and straightens her back. Slowly, the deposed Queen of France opens the door.

'Be brave, my son,' she calls proudly. 'Remember who you are. I'm coming now.'

The short officer slams his fist upon the table. 'Right. That's enough of the puppet show. I have here a list of names, and top of it is Madame Lamballe. She is to come with me, now, at once.'

Marie Antoinette looks into the man's dark eyes and they blacken even further with hatred. She has been through enough in recent weeks to understand how little it takes for that volatile loathing to ignite into deeds.

'One moment,' she asks in a whisper, her smile serving to defuse the situation slightly.

'Ma *chère* Lamballe,' she whispers, closing the door softly behind her, 'I'm afraid I must let you go. But do not fear. If you are to undergo interrogation, you will almost certainly be back soon.'

By now trembling in every limb, Marie-Thérèse shakes her head emphatically and, gazing at her cousin with overflowing eyes, sobs, 'Oh, I'm so sorry. I'm so terribly sorry that I can't stay with you. I promise you, my thoughts will be with you always, to the end.'

Marie Antoinette swallows hard. 'Don't say such things,

Lamballe. Truly, you will be back here before you know it.'

'No!' a heartrending cry escapes Marie-Thérèse and, like a child, she falls on her knees before Marie Antoinette, burying her head in the queen's lap. Stroking her hair, Marie Antoinette replies with as much self-assurance as she can muster.

'Listen to me, cousin. They really will not hurt you. It is I they are after. Once the hearing is over, I am sure they will set you free. But, I beg you, do not come back this time. Leave Paris while it is still possible.'

There is much more that she would like to say, but, before Marie Antoinette can utter another word, the door swings open.

'What sort of nonsense is this?' shouts the stunted officer, staring contemptuously at the Princesse de Lamballe kneeling submissively at the queen's feet. 'Pick yourself up off the floor, for goodness' sake, woman. Pack your stuff and get downstairs.'

Marie Antoinette helps the princess up. 'Be strong, ma chère,' she gently implores her friend. 'Please, for my sake.' Marie-Thérèse nods and dries her eyes. Marie Antoinette dare not look her in the eye, afraid she too will break down. On a sudden impulse, she pulls a ring from her finger and presses it into Lamballe's palm. 'Wear this as a memento of our friendship,' whispers Marie Antoinette. 'I love you, and I always will!'

Lamballe feels the officer's rough grip on her other arm. 'Right. Time's up,' he commands, but his tone is a shade softer. Marie-Thérèse turns once more to Marie Antoinette and they embrace for the last time.

'My journal.' Lamballe's voice is muffled with terror. 'Under my pillow,' she manages to tell the queen, 'my most private recollections, cousin, they are for you.' A last kiss hangs in the air as, under the triumphant eyes of the officer, two soldiers drag Lamballe away. The friends hold one another in an agonised gaze across the silence, until Lamballe vanishes into the darkness of the hallway.

Madame de Tourzel lowers her head before the queen.

'That's enough of that,' instructs their little boss, affronted.

'Bows are for tyrants. We're all equal now.' With a chuckle he sticks his head into the little room Lamballe has just left.

The journal! remembers Marie Antoinette with horror. Stepping smartly up to Madame de Tourzel, she throws her arms around her children's governess. 'You cannot abandon us,' cries the deposed queen dramatically. Distracted from his exploration, the officer turns his attention to the governess.

'Quick, pack your bag and get a move on!' he bawls, grabbing Tourzel roughly by the hand.

'Take care of Lamballe,' Marie Antoinette entreats the governess, under her breath. A tiny motion of the head shows the queen that Madame de Tourzel has understood her message; then the governess allows herself to be led away.

Soon all is still in the stairwell, the silence broken only by the sobs of the Dauphin. Marie Antoinette goes over to his bed and comforts the boy. She puts her arms around her daughter and kisses her on the forehead.

'You have been such brave children. I'm so proud of you both. Try to sleep a little now.' Marie Antoinette covers Louis-Charles and once more runs her fingers lovingly through his hair. Her daughter has meanwhile crept into bed by herself and pulled the blankets up over her head, as if to shield herself from all the dangers of this cruel world. Marie Antoinette swallows hard again. What will become of her children? She does not know what exactly has been happening on the floor below, but suspects that her husband's valet and gentlemen of the chamber have also been removed.

The guards in the stairwell will not let her go downstairs now. She will have to wait a couple of hours, until daybreak, before she can find out the situation there. Marie Antoinette tiptoes into Lamballe's tiny, empty room and sits down on the bed. With one hand she lifts the pillow, with the other straightens the sheet. Her fingers close upon the little book and she holds it tight against her breast. 'My most private recollections are for you.' She hears her best friend's words and silent tears run down her cheeks. If nothing else, the years have taught her this, the art of noiseless weeping. The face she presents to the world is always that of the brave queen, the proud mother. No one sees her true feelings. No other soul is privy to her weakness. She keeps her vulnerability hidden even from her children.

For an hour or more she sits on the edge of the hard bed, unable to believe recent events, hugging her friend's diary to her. 'Oh, ma chère Lamballe, shall I ever see you again?'

Secretively, the first long fingers of dawn stroke the grey walls of the Petit Tour, temporary home of the deposed King Louis XVI, his sister, his wife and their two children. Marie Antoinette has got up from her friend's bed and returned to the room containing a table and a couple of chairs. She stretches, stiff from long sitting. Her tears are dry; after all, the children may wake up at any moment. On the table before her lies Lamballe's diary. Respect for her friend has prevented Marie Antoinette from opening it, but now the little volume seems to scream out at her to do so. Burning with curiosity, she pulls it towards her and gently separates the covers.

Her eyes run swiftly over one or two passages at random. Thoughts jotted down, each reminding her of better times. Not everything she reads makes sense to her. There were years in which the two women saw little of each other. But, overwhelmed by the sweetness of some of the memories recorded by her friend, Marie Antoinette feels her heart move. Oh, how cruel her world has become! What in heaven's name went wrong?

Reading on, she is suddenly arrested by a line. She stiffens and goes over the words again. My God, did she really put that down word for word? Marie Antoinette checks the date. Pulse racing, she skims further through the pages in search of the other relevant entries. Her heart stops. *Mon Dieu*, why did she never destroy this journal? I warned her! If this falls into the wrong hands, it will certainly be used against her.

The queen reads on, her face flushing, then slams the diary shut. She glances about the room in panic. The safest thing to do is consign the whole book to the fire at once. But it is August; the hearth is clean and no fire will be lit there for a while. She cannot think how else she could safely hide the pages.

She will have to keep them on her person. That is the only solution for the time being. Then she might eat them, or at least chew them small, form the illegible pulp into pellets and stuff them into cracks in the plasterwork. Yes, that is the only way. Marie Antoinette opens the book again and takes one of the pages between thumb and forefinger. She tugs gently, but the page holds firm. The book has obviously been professionally bound. She lets the page slip from her grasp. The more she thinks about it, the more she doubts her decision. Is it not too cruel so to mutilate Lamballe's thoughts? To destroy them forever? Perhaps her friend will return tomorrow; probably they will all sooner or later be released ... and then what? No, out of respect for Lamballe, her most loyal friend, the diary must remain intact for now. But she will read it. That much she is resolved to do. Her curiosity must now be satisfied.

'Mama,' the sleepy little voice of the Dauphin of France calls from behind her. Smiling, she holds out her arms to him. 'Oh, *mon chou d'amour*,' she caressingly intones. As the child settles himself, yawning, into her lap, she slides the diary deep into a pocket of her gown.

Already, long days have passed since the hearing. Instead of returning to the royal family, the Princesse de Lamballe and the ladies in waiting have been imprisoned in La Petite Force. This jail, built a couple of years ago to accommodate the prostitutes of Paris, in no way resembles the many mediaeval dungeons boasted by the city. Only the thick bars at the large windows betray the true purpose of this building, halfway along the Rue Saint-Antoine. Its roomy cells are freshly plastered. The courtyard is remarkably spacious, providing a playground for the children of detainees.

The building is full to bursting. But for a long while now La Petite Force has ceased to offer shelter exclusively to prostitutes. In the courtyard, where by day the inmates are allowed to roam freely, all class distinction has dissolved. While their kids tear madly around, yelling and shouting at their game of tag, whores sit placidly side by side with elderly nuns. Little groups of aristocratic ladies murmur to one another while common Parisians mill around them. Guards stroll lecherously amongst the women, grinning and unsettling the girls with obscene remarks. But, apart from the filthy comments, no one suffers abuse.

Not one of the captives knows what offence they have committed to land them here, and every day more women join their ranks. The Princesse de Lamballe is seated between Madame de Saint-Brice and Madame Thibault. The narrow stone bench is hardly big enough for all of them, but at least the three unhappy women have found a spot of shadow, for the sun is ferocious today. They let the clamour of the courtyard wash over them. For the main part it is gossip and guesswork, but the Princesse de Lamballe, hands clasped tight in her lap, only hopes there is some truth in it. The latest news is that combined Prussian and Austrian forces are advancing steadily. Some even say that Verdun is completely surrounded and about to fall at any minute. Any fool can predict what would happen then. The way would be open for the Duke of Brunswick to bring his men to the gates of Paris. Lamballe shuts her eyes. Might the end of all this horror be in sight?

For of course the king would then be freed immediately. But could the old order be restored? Oh, how would it feel to dance again at Versailles? To walk at leisure in the Petit Trianon and seek again the cool shade of the grotto, hear the croaking of the frogs and the splash of the little waterfall? And ah, what would Marie Antoinette have been through in the meanwhile? May God spare us all!

What would befall the revolutionaries then? Would the king show them mercy? There was a good chance, of course, that the whole rabble would vanish like magic from the streets of Paris, so avoiding their fate ...

'What's your name?' Lamballe becomes aware of someone

tugging at her skirts and finds herself gazing into the mischievous eyes of a little girl, dressed from head to foot in rags and tatters. A rush of sympathy fills Lamballe's heart.

'I'm Charlotte. What's your name?'

With a laugh the princess replies, 'I am Marie-Thérèse.'

'Mama says you're a princess. Is that true?' asks Charlotte with a giggle.

Lamballe nods. 'Princesse de Lamballe.'

'When I grow up I'm going to be a princess too,' states Charlotte with dignity, fingering a soft fold of Marie-Thérèse's gown. A loud pealing of church bells breaks over them. Charlotte runs back to her mother, as everyone looks up in alarm. Could this be the army of liberation?

'Inside!' commands one of the guards nervously. The women allow themselves to be driven back into their cells, dawdling and delaying as much as they dare, listening expectantly for any sound that might betray what was going on in the city. But apart from the bells there is nothing. No cheering, no thunder of cannon and no throwing open of doors with a shout of 'Freedom!'

That night nobody can get to sleep. The Princesse de Lamballe, sharing a cell with Pauline de Tourzel and her mother, hears the bolts on their door shot back, and all three hold their breath. A creak of hinges, and someone steps inside. The three women sit up suddenly in bed, shocked at the intrusion. A lantern is shone over their pale faces and comes to a flickering halt beside Tourzel's daughter.

'You, there,' comes a thick voice. 'Come with us.' The man grabs Pauline by the arm and drags her from bed. 'Mama!' she cries in terror. Another man stands in front of Madame de Tourzel and, as she tries to rush to her daughter's aid, shoves her roughly back down onto the bed. A moment later the men are gone, taking her daughter with them.

Behind them, Madame de Tourzel hammers hysterically on the door, to no avail. The Princesse de Lamballe runs to comfort her, but her words are powerless to help the distraught mother. The whole night long, Madame de Tourzel lies curled on her side with knees drawn up, sobbing incessantly, 'My child, my child. My little Pauline.' Next to the inconsolable mother, tenderly stroking her head, sits Lamballe – livid, terrified, and frantic at her own impotence. Marie-Thérèse dare not even imagine what might befall Pauline, or what her own fate may be. Her shattered nerves leave her incongruously smiling. Next week will be her forty-third birthday; yes, the guards will let her be. She's too old for them.

It is very early morning when she hears footsteps in the corridor approaching their room. A key is turned in the lock and both women get to their feet expectantly.

'Pauline?' whispers Tourzel, her heart full of hope. The bolts are drawn and a handful of armed men step resolutely into the room. The women jump back in surprise; there is no sign of the missing child.

'Your names?' demands one of the men abruptly. These are not the usual guards. The women, confused by this on top of the sleepless night, rap out their names. The man checks his list and nods in apparent satisfaction. '*Allez*,' he gestures to the others, and they all silently troop out of the cell. The two women hear the door being bolted again.

'What in heaven's name does this all mean?' whimpers Madame de Tourzel, her eyes filling again. 'What do they want with us? We've done nothing wrong, have we? Where in the name of the good Lord is Pauline?'

The sun climbs the sky. The higher it rises, the more worried the two women grow. Each takes turns to listen at the door. But all is still. Nobody comes this morning, as they have done every other so far, to bring them breakfast. All remains quiet in the courtyard, in sharp contrast to the noise reaching them from beyond the prison walls. Louder and louder come the roar of cannons and the cacophony of bells. Lamballe and Tourzel hold each other tight, now more in hope than fear. 'Can that be the army? Are we about to be freed?' The noise from the street is now deafening, but it is impossible to make out what the mob is screaming.

Suddenly the cell door is flung open to reveal the armed men of this morning. One silently beckons at the two women. Hand in hand, they follow him in trepidation along the corridor to the staircase. Once on the ground floor, the frightened women are led into the courtyard, where they find the other ladies in waiting assembled. With relief they fall into one another's arms. The ladies Thiébault, Bazire, Navarre and de Saint-Brice all burst into tears when the Princesse de Lamballe gives them the news that Pauline has been taken away.

The din penetrating the prison walls increases, now and then punctuated by a piercing shriek. What on earth is going on out there? The question is upon everybody's tongue, but no one dare ask it out loud. Each keeps the dreadful speculation to herself, while more and more prisoners are being herded out into the courtyard.

At least an hour passes in which nothing seems to happen. Then a guard appears and, smirking, produces another list. Everyone hearing her name must step forward at once, 'over here, right away. Understood?' Behind him, two of his mates with sabres drawn guard either side of a door that leads to the other prison, La Force. The guard, obviously barely literate, begins with difficulty to articulate one name after another. 'Mademoiselle Trudaine. Madame Tronchin. Madame Ville ... er, Villedieu.'

There is rustle of anxiety amongst the women in the courtyard. What is going on? What are they being called up for? Lowering his list, the guard rasps over the top of it, 'What are you lot making such a fuss about? Routine hearing! Nothing a good republican need worry about at all.' He gets back to the job in hand, tracking down the names with a clumsy forefinger to find his place, and resumes: 'Madame Simon. Mademoiselle Suarda. Madame Masson ...'

'Mercy!' A pathetic wail goes up from the courtyard.

'Have courage,' someone else replies, her voice weak with

exhausted hope. One by one, the women are summoned and dispatched through the gates to La Force. The Princesse de Lamballe leans back against the wall, her eyes closed. She prays. Every one of her friends has now passed through that gate. Each time a new series of names is read out, Marie-Thérèse holds her breath. Surely they will not harm her. After all, she is *Surintendante* to the queen. Her breath comes quick and shallow. This stifling cattle-yard! It must be even more humid today than it was yesterday.

Trying to shut her ears to the bloodcurdling shrieks and hubbub all around her, Lamballe does not at first hear her name. 'LAMBALLE,' it comes again, for the third time, and so laden with menace that it brings the princess to her senses. The brute with the list glares at her and spits at her feet. Taking a deep breath, she walks with as much dignity as possible towards the doorway. A shove from behind almost makes her stumble. Incensed, she turns to stare into the insolent features of a young whelp of a man. 'One, two, one, two ... quick march,' he grins, brandishing his sabre. The princess turns away in disgust. What utter degradation to be treated thus! The child with the sabre cannot be more than fifteen years old!

The long passage is dim, but at the end she can see light. Lamballe finds herself in an airless, dingy room, packed with men. Despite the lanterns, it is hard to make out what is going on. The place looks like a tavern with a party in full swing. A dense cloud of tobacco smoke hangs over everything, assailing the nostrils along with the stink of cheap wine and another, sharper smell that she can't quite place. Rubbing her stinging eyes, she looks round for a familiar face. But these are all common men, beasts from the street, with unshaven faces, an unholy glint in their eyes and black, dilated pupils. Their accents are loud and vulgar, the room filled with their vile belching and drunkenness.

The princess is feeling more uncomfortable by the minute. What is she doing here? The only exit within sight is guarded by a group of men, all waving their sabres wildly in the air and drinking from the bottle. She can see now that the reprobates are leering at a woman standing with bowed head before the large table. The Princesse de Lamballe does not know her personally, but recognises one of her fellow captives.

A man sitting at the head of the table slams the butt of his pistol down on the surface. 'SILENCE!'

He must be one of the ringleaders, for everyone responds almost immediately to his command. He consults the men sitting on either side of him and then clears his throat. Focusing gravely on the woman before him, he pronounces, '*Elargissez* Madame. You are acquitted.'

The woman looks up and turns about, relief in her face. She is led to the exit, where the swaying guards step aside to let her pass, moving to open the door. Perhaps all my fears have been unfounded, thinks Lamballe, watching the courtesy with which the men make their sweeping bows. But as the door swings wide, a flood of brilliant sunlight pours in, carrying with it the sickening stench of the slaughterhouse. A scream escapes the woman, and she tries desperately to turn back, but the rollicking guards push her outside. Her petrified shrieks pierce Lamballe to the marrow. Then they cease. Open-mouthed with horror, the princess stares at the door.

Seconds later the men stagger back inside, grinning moronically and wiping their dripping blades on the filthy rags that hang from their belts.

It cannot be true!

Marie-Thérèse forgets to draw breath. Darkness falls.

A sharp sensation in her nose brings the Princesse de Lamballe to herself. Calls echo in her ears, but do not reach her consciousness. Contours slowly sharpen, until she once more knows where she is. At the gates of hell.

'*Mon Dieu*,' she murmurs, still faint with shock. Disdainfully she brushes aside the hand holding the smelling salts under her nose. Shakes her head, as if to rid herself of the nightmare. It is not possible. She is hoisted roughly to her feet, and two men raucously frogmarch her to the tribunal table.

'Name?' demands the ringleader.

The princess gives him a look of contempt.

'Come on, speak up!'

She straightens. What more has she to lose? 'Marie-Thérèse Louise de Savoie-Carignan, Princesse de Lamballe,' she replies in loud, clear tones.

'Ha! You must mean Marie-Thérèse de BOURBON-Lamballe,' sneers her interrogator. There is a burst of laughter. Lamballe does not flicker. 'What is your function?'

'*Surintendante* of the Queen's Household.'

'Were you aware of the conspiracy of tenth August?

'I have no idea what you are referring to. I know of no conspiracy.'

There is a flurry, murmuring behind the table.

'Will you swear on the principle of freedom and equality for all, and upon your hatred for the king and queen?'

Lamballe's brow furrows. What an extraordinary request! 'With the first two assertions I have no difficulty whatsoever, but I cherish absolutely no hatred for the king or queen.'

'Swear, or it will be the death of you!' She feels the hot breath of one of the men in her ear, and gags at the stink of alcohol.

'*Allez*, swear your hatred for the royal family!' comes the bellicose command from behind the table.

Marie-Thérèse suddenly feels overwhelmed with fatigue, too tired even to form a reply. All the accumulated exhaustion of months of terror and threats, which now seem to be coming to an end at last. And shall she save her own life by betraying her best friend? One by one she scans the hazy faces of the revolutionaries, each so certain of the justice of his cause. Where do they get their sheer brute self-assurance? The audacity of them! Another paw in her back: 'Swear.'

'Never!' She pours all her remaining life force into that one word. 'I must die sooner or later, whatever happens. I have

NOTHING more to say to you.'

Roused to a passion, the ringleader gets to his feet, shoving his chair back from the table. The dirty upper-class bitch! 'You are acquitted, Madame,' he hisses. The Princesse de Lamballe feels the forked words enter her flesh, banishing any remaining illusion.

Her two guards hustle her to the door, where the others bloodthirstily await her. The burst of daylight suddenly bathing her face makes her momentarily close her eyes. Another shove in the back, and she is standing on the top step. The gutters of the Rue Saint-Antoine are running red. Before her looms a ghastly mountain of mutilated bodies, women and children. At her feet lie heads, hacked off, their dead eyes transfixed in terror. Foragers, intoxicated beyond any vestige of respect, rummage about amongst the gruesome remains, tearing rings from fingers.

With a dull stab of dread, Lamballe recognises the broken face of little Charlotte. It is unbearable to behold. Her gaping mouth stretched in a stiff rictus of amazement, the child lies naked in a pool of blood. The Princesse de Lamballe feels her stomach heave.

She turns about, incensed. 'Monsters!' she tries to shout, but the curse dies on her tongue as a sabre crashes down upon her skull. She is dragged down into the deep, and panic fills her. She can feel blood, her own warm blood, flowing down her face. Cries of *'Vive la Nation'* fill the air around her. She tries to find her feet, but another blow falls. Groaning, she sinks to her knees among the corpses. She is tired, so very tired. It is enough.

The next assault she does not feel. Encountering no further protest, her life ebbs from the Piedmont princess. Still firmly clenched in her right fist lies Marie Antoinette's ring. The clothes are ripped from her body, and her jubilant murderers spit upon its nakedness.

'I know what!' yells one, reeling drunk. And, taking hold of her long hair, he yanks up the dead princess's head and slices through the lifeless white neck with his butcher's knife.

'There,' he announces proudly, holding aloft the spurting, gory trophy. His mates snigger, but are not unduly impressed. They have already kicked so many decapitated heads along the gutters!

'Oh, wow, what an original idea!' scoffs one. 'Pack it in, you. Let's get over to the Temple, show Marie Antoinette how we deal with her sort.'

'The Temple?' It takes a while for the message to penetrate the drink-sodden brains around him.

'Come on, lads, we're going to pay a visit to the Temple, let the Austrian bitch say a proper goodbye to her bosom pal. Let's go. Maybe the queen will want to kiss her lovely lips!'

Cheers break out among the men. This should be fun. The idea takes hold, despite their paralytic state. They manage to mount the head of Marie-Thérèse, Princesse de Lamballe, on a pikestaff, and anyone still capable of walking stumbles along behind it in obscene procession.

'To the Temple!' they shout in baleful triumph. 'Yeah! Kiss her lips, your ladyship!'

A faithful few remain behind to perform their duty to the new republic by slaughtering in its name the next 'exonerated' victim, to roars of *'Vive la Nation!'* from the chorus of glassy-eyed carousers.

Yesterday we talked to each other properly for the first time. Best of all, we danced together. But I did feel awkward, because the Dauphin didn't look at all happy about it. I couldn't have insulted him, could I? Antoinette wants us to be friends. I like her very much, and I think she's very lonely. Can I be a good friend to her?

From the journal of the Princesse de Lamballe,
13th February 1771

For two long days it has been snowing. Tiny flakes, much smaller than she was used to at home, pirouetting slowly down. Antoine presses her nose against the windowpane and giggles as the cold makes her skin tingle. The world outside seems deserted. There is no sound; even the birds are still. She can't see to the end of the terrace: the horizon is obscured by tumbling masses of white swansdown. The light from the window casts a golden glow across the crystalline blanket. She sighs.

The snow is her only friend here. She presses her face still harder against the glass and imagines herself back in the safety of her parents' house. Oh, if only she could talk to father! The snowflakes softly floating against the pane seem to be doing their best to comfort her, to make her feel at home in this totally alien world. Dreamily, she gazes at the ever-shifting kaleidoscope of white crystals. It seems an age since the winter sleigh rides she enjoyed with her sister. She misses Caroline and wonders how she is. Does she ever think about her little sister, or is there no place for Antoine in the life of the Queen of Naples and Sicily?

She misses her friends, too, Charlotte and Louise. How far away they seem! Oh, to see them again, if only for a moment – just one hug! She feels trapped, for she knows there is no way out of her situation. Twilight begins to fall and Antoine shivers. Yet, despite the chill creeping over her shoulders, she remains staring out into the snow.

'Oh, *Madame la Dauphine!*' comes a sudden shrill exclamation from nowhere. 'For God's sake, let us not catch cold.' One after another the shutters are being closed. Disturbed from her daydream, Antoine rises to her feet and takes a backward step into the room. The Comtesse de Noailles has abruptly reclaimed the young princess from the white world in which she feels at home.

After more than six months at court, Antoine is still not used to her title of *Madame la Dauphine*' or being addressed as Marie Antoinette. But one thing she is already sure of: she will never, ever get used to the Comtesse de Noailles, her *Dame d'Honneur*, who right from the start has lectured her incessantly in the thousands of unwritten laws that govern life at Versailles. The whole livelong day, from dawn to dusk, proceeds according to a prescribed, monotonous ritual that may not be departed from for an instant. Every move, every smile and nod has been stripped of spontaneity. Marie Antoinette has hated the straitjacket of this protocol from the minute she arrived at Versailles.

'What's the point of it all? Whoever dreamed it all up?' she would ask one of her ladies of the bedchamber, knowing all the while that the only reply would be a surly look from Noailles. It was not long before Marie Antoinette had gleefully re-christened her official Mistress of the Household '*Madame l'Etiquette*'. It was one of the few flights of fancy she could indulge in here.

Marie Antoinette lets herself flop into the armchair nearest the hearth. Now, with the warmth of the flames caressing her arms, she notices for the first time how cold she is. The Comtesse de Noailles carefully lays a log upon the glowing ashes and pokes them until sparks fly up the chimney. The crackling makes one of Marie Antoinette's little dogs start and spring into the princess's lap.

'Oh, did it frighten you, my little Poppet?' croons Marie Antoinette. The animal rubs itself against her bodice and decides that this would be a nice place to go back to sleep, with Marie Antoinette's soft fingers stroking its head.

'In half an hour it will be time to get you dressed, Your Highness,' cautions *Madame l'Etiquette*, a flutter of excitement in her voice. This evening she is giving a Carnival ball in her salon at which the princess and the Dauphin will be guests of honour. Marie Antoinette smiles her most amiable smile and shuts her eyes.

A ball; she wonders who will turn up this evening. All the same old faces, very probably, so this event in her own and her husband's honour will end up just as predictable as every other evening. Oh, how dreary she finds everything here; not a bit how she had expected it to be! Her mother had made it all sound so lovely. The future Queen of France, the Palace of Versailles! She would be the envy of every princess in Europe. Huh! They should see what her life was really like; then nobody would want to swap places with her! Marie Antoinette is well aware that her marriage is no more than a business contract between her mother, Maria Theresa, Archduchess of Austria, and Louis XV, King of France.

The wedding was the crowning diplomatic achievement of the Duc de Choiseul, the French Minister for Foreign Affairs. The Church's blessing of the nuptial pair would bring years of hostility between these two great European nations to a decisive end. But French contempt for the Austrians ran deep. This was the first time in many centuries that a French dauphin had taken an Austrian wife. The fact that Marie Antoinette was the daughter and granddaughter of rulers of the Holy Roman Empire served only to underline the frustration of the French, for since the death of Charlemagne no French sovereign had succeeded in winning the title of Emperor. It was a matter that King Louis XV had thought long and hard about. After all, his predecessor, Louis XIV, had warned him in his will about the might and ambition of the Holy Roman emperors. But times had changed, and although his subjects had yet to accustom themselves to the idea, the French king was convinced that this marriage would be good for France.

Marie Antoinette has her own thoughts on the subject. In her eyes, this brand new husband of hers, Louis-Auguste, Duc de Berry, Dauphin and future King of France, is nothing but a baby. He may be a good year older than she is, but his behaviour is so childish!

For weeks after their wedding he hardly opened his mouth. At first she was afraid that he found her ugly and didn't like her. But she soon realised this wasn't so. It took hours of gentle coaxing to discover what lay behind the Dauphin's mute smile. A good six months on, Marie Antoinette is slowly beginning to win his confidence. Bit by bit, the Dauphine has learned that not everyone is happy with the choice of a bride for the Dauphin, including the bridegroom himself. The young Louis-Auguste, however, had been the very last to be consulted in the matter. He simply had to accept in silence the decision of his grandfather, Louis XV, 'Most Christian King of France and Navarre'.

The descriptions of Marie Antoinette reaching the French king were so attractive that he had seriously considered marrying the young princess himself. But all his mental peregrinations on the subject had been dispelled the previous spring, when he first saw the Empress Maria Theresa's daughter in the flesh. He had to chuckle at himself! Marie Antoinette, for all her charms, was no more than a child of fourteen, her breasts hardly budding! He'd had them younger, of course, and very nice it was too. But that was all in the past. Certainly the child was very touching. He admired her open face and sparkling blue eyes. Yes, she would undoubtedly turn into a fine woman one day; but could she ever hold a candle to his heavenly mistress, Jeanne du Barry? No, he thought not.

By the time Marie Antoinette was introduced to the young Dauphin, his head was so full of preconceptions that Louis-Auguste barely heard a word she said to him. Marie Antoinette did not let it trouble her. He was a shy boy, that much was obvious. He looked different from what she had imagined. She was pleased that he was taller than her, despite her own above-average height; but Louis-Auguste was also quite heavily built, if not as fat as his younger brother, the Comte de Provence. But she had not had time to assess the Dauphin properly, for a host of other people were being introduced to her, so many that she was hardly able to memorise more than one or two names. This first encounter between the betrothed pair was soon over, and the company continued its journey via Compiègne to Versailles, the court where she was to spend almost all the rest of her life.

She recalls as if it were yesterday how, as her carriage approached along the Avenue de la Place d'Armes, the former hunting lodge of the Sun King revealed itself to her. She did not like the look of it. After all the fine stories that had been told her about Versailles, she had expected a far grander palace, and one with much higher walls. But once inside, Marie Antoinette understood what all the fuss was about, and she too was enchanted by the flamboyant style of Louis XIV's architect. When a few days later she viewed the castle from the grounds, she could not understand why they had not brought her carriage round this way instead. For the visitor catching the first glimpse of the château from the gardens to the west is understandably struck by the sweeping grandeur of the famous palace.

On first sight, at least. But as she roamed the many pathways it soon became plain to Marie Antoinette how badly neglected the palace gardens were. So different from home! In the great park, parched trees and dead shrubs stood sadly between the sunken terraces. Some flights of stairs had steps missing, swept away by years of rain and lack of maintenance. Pools were choked with rotting vegetation, not just last autumn's leaves, but the detritus of many seasons past. Silted halfway to the brim, they seemed to symbolise the reign of Louis XV. In summer the stench was unbearable, and only the swarms of mosquitoes hanging above the rank water seemed at home there. Greek gods, once the glistening centrepieces of proudly leaping fountains, glared more forbiddingly than ever across their foetid, fallen kingdoms as if in silent protest at their own decay.

Once her eyes had recovered from the dazzle of such a sumptuous surfeit of gilt in stateroom and salon, the young princess saw how uncared-for the palace was, too. Statuary and windowsills were crumbling away, as if no one could care less about the state of the immense edifice. But what really disappointed and even disgusted her was the daily stream of visitors through Versailles. In contrast to the privacy Marie Antoinette had known at home, the imperial palace of the King of France was open to the public.

Every day, hundreds of Parisians and foreign tourists would flock into the place and stand staring like sheep while the royal family sat at table during the *Grand Couvert*. Hawkers swarmed around the chateau and pedlars at wooden stalls pressed their wares on every passer-by. Everything was for sale: souvenirs, the *Gazette de France*, and even the very latest publications from the pen of Voltaire passed clandestinely over the counter, so that the court looked more like a market than the palace of the 'Most Christian King' of the greatest country in Europe.

Parades of brightly coloured uniforms would march past: soldiers of various regiments, each with their own duties. But nothing impeded the passage of visitors. Only the private quarters of the royal family remained safe from curious eyes, protected by members of the Swiss Guard. The antechambers surrounding the rooms once occupied by the king's late queen, Marie Leszczynska, and now allocated to Marie Antoinette, were littered with the bodyguards' weaponry and camp beds, stacked behind screens. Their filthy socks hung steaming before the open fire. Cats with matted fur sidled from chamber to chamber, keeping the palace more or less free from rats and mice. As for the fleas that teemed beneath their coats, the cats seemed to ignore them. The soldiers too were apparently immune both to fleabites and to the stink with which the spraying toms marked out their territory. Mother had not mentioned any of this!

At mealtimes, Marie Antoinette could hardly swallow a mouthful under the gaze of all those strange eyes, while in the background the maddening whispered commentary never ceased. Yet the Dauphin seemed completely oblivious to it all. His enormous appetite never suffered, at any rate. Whose idea had it been in the first place to allow people in like this? The awful clamour all the time and, worst of all, the stink! In summer, when the windows were open and the wind changed direction, it really became unbearable. Every staircase and courtyard reeked horribly of urine; but where else were people expected to do their business?

It might have been possible to put up with all of this, were it not for those silly rules. The Comtesse de Noailles, the personification of court etiquette, made her life insufferable. The countess's reprimands very often seemed to Marie Antoinette more like bullying, and she seriously suspected *Madame l'Etiquette* of dreaming up new instructions on the spot, just to annoy her.

The young princess lapses deeper into boredom and sinks deeper into her armchair. Disturbed by the movement, her lapdog yawns, scratches behind its ear and sleeps on. Marie Antoinette returns to her musings. Is there anything she likes about this place? The aunts, perhaps? *Mesdames de France*, as everyone calls the unmarried daughters of the king, aunts to the Dauphin. The eldest, Madame Adélaïde, is always particularly kind to her and Marie Antoinette knows she can go to her with all her problems and difficulties. But are the aunts entirely trustworthy? The youngest of the three, Sophie, is the quietest and often seems quite jumpy. Victoire is nice, but it is Adélaïde who has the strongest personality. There is a fourth aunt, Louise, but she withdrew years ago to the Carmelite convent in Paris.

Marie Antoinette always gets the same unsettled feeling deep inside when Adélaïde addresses her so sweetly. But surely there must be someone she can trust? The king himself, *Papa Roi*, is of course enormously kind to her, but he is the only friend she feels she has at court. She has felt unwelcome here from the start. For ages the Dauphin did his best to avoid her. Their first night didn't go at all as she had anticipated. He didn't lay a finger on her – although she has to admit that she did little to encourage him. She didn't like him that much, after all. But this whole business has nothing to do with liking each other. Her mother's letters leave her in no doubt whatsoever concerning her role in the vital political rapprochement between Austria and France, a settlement that can only be sealed by the birth of an heir.

It is almost ten months since her arrival in Versailles and not once has the Dauphin tried to make her his wife. It unnerves her. Is there something wrong with her after all? There is no one who can confirm or dispel her fears, no companion with whom she can really share her deepest feelings; and evening after evening she waits patiently for her husband. Oh yes, sometimes he does come to her bed and slips cautiously in between the sheets. But when she wakes the following morning, it is always to find him gone. She feels disappointed one minute and relieved the next. It's so confusing!

Before she left Vienna, her mother had given Marie Antoinette a brief lecture on her wifely duties. The girl had hardly understood a word of it, and she cannot imagine how the adults here can simper so coyly and speak romantically about such things. As far as she is concerned, the Dauphin is welcome to stay away. But time and again she is stung by the impatient tone of her mother's letters, and she knows that sooner or later she must fulfil Mama's expectations of her. Yet, for this to happen, surely Louis-Auguste must change his ways too.

Without being able to put her whole heart into it, she has made shy attempts to win his. Whole weeks passed before he began to grant grumpy answers to her questions. Then, to the court's amazement, his constant rude behaviour gradually changed for the better. To her own delight, Marie Antoinette discovered that he was also capable of being friendly. As she got to know the Dauphin better, trying all the time to find new ways into his inner world, she uncovered beneath the boy's sullen exterior an unhappy but gentle soul.

Louis-Auguste's parents had died far too young. He still missed his mother dreadfully, whilst his grandfather, *Papa Roi*, hardly gave him a second glance. All the king's attention was devoted to his younger brothers, while the Dauphin grew lonelier by the day and more and more convinced that there was no one left who loved him. The young crown prince had been placed entirely in the care of his governor, the Duc de La Vauguyon. It was an open secret that this gruff Breton utterly opposed the alliance with Austria, and thus also his pupil's marriage with Marie Antoinette. What sort of tales the Duc de La Vauguyon had told the Dauphin, Marie Antoinette couldn't yet be sure. But apparently the boy had the good sense to see through his mentor's manipulations and trust his own judgement.

To the governor's great annoyance, the Dauphin was showing signs of thawing. But how on earth, and why? Did the young man see something of his mother in the Dauphine's eyes? Perhaps it was the way she laughed. Might there after all be someone capable of loving him? Or was this just a trick, a ruse to win his confidence? Despite his governor's warnings, Louis-Auguste's instinct told him that he could trust his new bride. She was the first person since the death of his mother to whom he found it possible to show his feelings, however warily.

'Why are you so rejecting of me?' she had asked him outright.

How confrontational! He dared not meet her eyes. 'It has nothing to do with you. I can't love anyone because no one loves me.'

Those few whispered words were enough for Marie Antoinette. Still waters run deep, she thought, and her young heart went out to the crown prince. From then on, whatever it cost her to get him talking, she would do everything in her power to engage him in conversation. One thing that soon became apparent was her husband's loathing for the Duc de La Vauguyon. Yet there was nobody willing or able to change Louis-Auguste's situation. The poor, poor boy!

Her little dog suddenly opens its eyes wide and darts a look about the room. Ears pricked, it springs from its mistress's lap and rushes yapping to the door. 'Shush, shh, *mon chéri*,' Marie Antoinette calls out reassuringly. The princess pulls herself upright in the chair. It will be Jean-Marc, on his usual early evening rounds. The door opens to reveal the muzzles of two huge canines, who bare their teeth over the head of the yelping lapdog. It is obvious that they don't consider the little thing worth bothering about; it doesn't count as one of their kind at all. Laughing, Marie Antoinette gets to her feet and picks up her precious pet. 'Come in, Jean-Marc, the coast's clear now,' announces the princess. She strokes the growling lapdog's curls while the chained intruders sniff in every corner of its territory.

Every day, after the visitors have been expelled from the chateau, this round of inspection is conducted throughout the extensive chambers, halls and salons. Jean-Marc's dogs regularly sniff out a 'stowaway' hidden in a vestibule or storage cupboard. Most of them are visitors who have not managed to arrange lodgings for the night and so have found a bed in a comfortable corner. But often enough the dogs discover a petty thief hoping for some rich pickings. Marie Antoinette shudders at the thought that anyone can simply walk into her bedroom. That is what comes of opening the palace to the public. Her mind set gratefully at rest, she wishes Jean-Marc a good evening and offers his trusty hounds a biscuit.

Poppet jealously licks the last crumbs from the floor. The gentle tinkling of the exquisite clock on the mantelpiece – a wedding present from the Princesse de Lamballe – alerts Marie Antoinette to the fact that she has only fifteen minutes before her ladies of the bedchamber arrive to dress her for the ball. Just a few more moments to herself before she must resume her role.

The first day she thought it wonderful – a whole household at her command! The king himself had appointed the holders of the highest positions. At the head of the household the diligent Comtesse de Noailles, followed by the Duchesse de Cossé-Brissac, *dame d'atours* – Mistress of the Robes – to the Dauphine. Then Marie Antoinette had at her disposal twelve *dames pour accompagner Madame la Dauphine*. Every one of these ladies in waiting was from an old-established noble family whose connections with the court went back many generations. Also at her service were sixteen *femmes de chambre* – ladies of the bedchamber, ready to act upon her every whim, though very skilled in delegating their least favourite tasks to the *femmes rouges*, the crimson-uniformed women who did the real work, including cleaning the Dauphine's apartments.

Marie Antoinette also had at least a hundred officials and other courtiers allocated to her, each with their own responsibilities, such as keeping track of her finances and domestic arrangements. For behind the scenes a further two hundred staff were kept busy in the kitchen and linen-room, and in addition the Dauphine had her own maids, a handful of doctors, a fencing instructor, a clockmaker and several priests. All with a single aim: to provide the very best service for Madame la Dauphine, the future Queen of France.

Marie Antoinette could not move a muscle without one of her ladies in waiting, a courtier or an attendant catching her eye and rushing to her aid. She had begun increasingly to treasure those rare moments when she could be by herself, fly free of the golden cage that was Versailles for a few minutes. A deep sigh escapes her. She hopes the evening ahead will be a pleasant one. After all, it is Carnival. The door sweeps open almost noiselessly and two ladies of the bedchamber glide through. It is time.

Just as she feared. No new faces – at least, no young ones. A few familiar old hags, distant relatives of the Bourbons: Rohans, Mortemarts and Noailles or related to them by marriage. Bleached-out bags of old bones who look to Marie Antoinette as if they have been haunting the corridors of Versailles since the days of the Sun King. Up to now she hasn't even bothered to commit to memory the names of most of these ancient countesses. Why should she? They are all half deaf and unbelievably dull. Purely to please Noailles, she does manage to cast a sweet smile in the direction of the musty old harpies huddled in a corner, who receive her gesture as greedily as if it were a gift.

Four musicians are lackadaisically playing their way through some pieces by Rameau. Nobody is dancing yet, just gossiping, playing cards and exchanging desultory laughter. Nodding in greeting, Marie Antoinette walks up to her husband, sitting paralysed with boredom next to his younger brothers. The youngest of the three, Charles-Philippe, Comte d'Artois, springs enthusiastically to his feet at the sight of his sister-in-law. With his black hair, dark eyes and fine features, Artois in no way resembles his podgy brothers. Only the characteristic Bourbon nose betrays their common paternity. Artois is tall for his age, but he is also slender and elegant.

Louis-Stanislas Xavier, Comte de Provence, just two weeks Marie Antoinette's junior, is even fatter than his elder brother the Dauphin. This, in addition to a congenital hip condition, keeps him in his seat. From the depths of his double chin he offers a hello to his sister-in-law. Artois, in contrast, enfolds her in a bright embrace and then gallantly offers her his chair. This Marie Antoinette accepts, as far as the tilting hoops of her crinoline and the pinching corset allow. Looking his wife straight in the eye, Louis-Auguste gives a short, embarrassed laugh, and then resumes his examination of the parquet floor.

'Come on, let's have a dance,' invites Artois with a grin. Marie Antoinette demurs. 'I'd rather wait a bit.' She wants to see who else is here before she makes her public debut on the dance floor. She knows that she has nothing to be ashamed of now; she has even managed to master the quadrille. But she hates the idea of being laughed at. First check who might be watching. The old aunts, of course; sitting neat as crows in a row, all silently squinting into the middle of the room. As her glance passes, they return a whole line of beaky smiles of 'surprise'. Fancy Marie Antoinette noticing them! Behind them sits the Comtesse de Narbonne, deep in conversation with the woman next to her. The Dauphine lets her gaze roam further round the room, soon noting with a sinking heart the absence of a single interesting face.

At least 'that creature' is conspicuous by her absence this evening. That's something to be thankful for. Why does the king humiliate himself by keeping company with that cheap whore? No one had prepared Marie Antoinette for the presence at Versailles of the Comtesse du Barry. During her first dinner with the king and his family, the young Austrian princess had admired the lady with the golden locks. She looked very nice. But who was she? When Aunt Adélaïde later told her that Madame du Barry was nothing but a common streetwalker who had worked her way up from the gutters of Paris, Marie Antoinette had been thoroughly shocked. She knew how Mama felt about such women and how much she would have disapproved of her daughter keeping company with a prostitute.

And Adélaïde had not spared her the details: how *la Barry* had slept her way up the social ladder, and how with her flattery and childish ways the *maîtresse en titre* could twist the king around her little finger. It was almost certainly down to that *créature*, too, that on Christmas Eve the king had quite unexpectedly sacked the Duc de Choiseul and banned him to his country house at Chanteloup. This liberal statesman and architect of the Franco-Austrian alliance, broker of the marriage between Marie Antoinette and the Dauphin of France, had been succeeded by the corrupt and hated Duc d'Aiguillon. Choiseul's dismissal and the appointment of *la Barry*'s friend d'Aiguillon had split the court into two camps, increasing the power of those who opposed the alliance.

Marie Antoinette, as yet barely conscious of the political scheming going on all around her in the chateau's salons and apartments, simply misses Choiseul. His face, apart from those of the Abbé Vermond and the Austrian ambassador, the Comte de Mercy-Argenteau, is the only one she knows here. It was Etienne-François Choiseul who, back home in Vienna, had prepared her for her future life as Dauphine; Choiseul who recommended the Abbé Vermond for the role of tutor to the young princess. It was the hairdresser who did Choiseul's sister's hair who adjusted Marie Antoinette's style to suit the tastes of the French court; Choiseul who accompanied her on the long journey from Vienna to Versailles and who was her only friend during those first few months, the one person she could rely upon.

Not only does she miss him personally, she is denied the

company of the many noblemen and women, friends and family of Choiseul, who now stay away from court in solidarity with him. One way or another, court balls and festivities are now less well attended, whilst rumours are rife that half the aristocracy of France is spending its time at Chanteloup, dancing and merrymaking into the small hours. But such disloyalty to the king costs dear: Louis XV takes sardonic pleasure in systematically stripping the marquesses and counts one by one of their position at his court. That will teach them who matters in this country!

Adélaïde keeps a sharp but unobtrusive eye on Marie Antoinette. She never misses a trick, noting the name of everyone the princess speaks to. Adélaïde is not among those who lament the absence of the Duc de Choiseul, not in the least. Like her dead brother, she is a fervent opponent of Choiseul and his politics. At first, Adélaïde too was against the alliance and Marie Antoinette's arrival on the scene, and she was the one who contemptuously dubbed the Dauphine l'AutriCHIENNE – the Austrian bitch! Adélaïde's ingenious pun was still a rich source of amusement among the maiden aunts. Always, of course, behind the subject's back. But the moment it dawned on Louis XV's eldest daughter how she might use the naive Dauphine to get the better of that dreadful woman du Barry, there was a change in her attitude. For the time being, at least. Using all the charm at her disposal, Adélaïde soon had the Dauphine in the palm of her hand. With a smile that would not have shamed Aesop's sly fox, she even thrust upon Marie Antoinette the key to her boudoir. 'Do not hesitate, Madame; whatever may be troubling you, come to me, day or night.' The crown princess gratefully accepted her gesture.

The banishment of the Duc de Choiseul had caused a tremendous shake-up at Versailles. One faction, the Barriens, stood in direct opposition to the supporters of the deposed minister. As it was impossible to adopt a neutral attitude at court, Adélaïde was forced against her will to join Choiseul's camp. Her sister Victoire, who could not be bothered with politics, took the easy option and followed her sister's line. Bored to distraction by all the gossip, Victoire mindlessly stuffs her face with one delicacy after another and chews away, contented as a cow on the cud. Victoire is well over thirty and, like her sisters, unmarried. She stopped worrying about her figure long ago. And the knight on a white charger who never turned up to claim her hand? She has devoured her yearning for him, too. Not without reason has her father the king scornfully nicknamed her '*Coche*', his little sow.

'Let's dance,' says Marie Antoinette suddenly, tapping Artois furtively on the arm with her fan. Her brother-in-law turns round from flirting with the much older Comtesse de Ghérac. Unlike his brothers, Artois has a keen eye for the ladies. Not yet fourteen, he has discovered early in life that being the king's grandson gives him a fair crack of the whip when it comes to the fair sex. Radiant, he escorts his 'sister' to the middle of the salon and, amid enthusiastic applause, leads her in the dance. Making supple passes with his slim body, he moves close about her, revelling in all the attention he is attracting. The Dauphin watches indifferently. Louis-Auguste is no dancer. Although he has taken lessons in an attempt to please his wife, he will never be as light on his feet as his little brother. And the truth is, the Dauphin doesn't even enjoy the pastime. Artois is more than welcome to do the honours for him. What Louis-Auguste doesn't seem to see is the hungry look in his younger brother's eye. Secretly in love with Marie Antoinette, Artois suffers frequent pangs of jealousy and wishes he were in the crown prince's shoes. Then, no doubt, the Dauphine would have been expecting long ago!

The young widow Marie-Thérèse Louise, Princesse de Lamballe, stands tremulously in the doorway, smiling shyly. Everyone looks up, for the Italian princess is a lovely sight. Beneath her head of thick blond hair, beautifully set by her stylist, her large blue eyes set off a flawless, creamy complexion. A mourning gown of black taffeta enhances the effect and, although her forehead may perhaps be a shade on the narrow side, her lustrous skin and small mouth are enough to make her the envy of many a lady at court. The princess is welcomed by her hostess for this evening, the Comtesse de Noailles, who takes her arm and conducts her into the salon.

Marie Antoinette makes a graceful turn, bringing the dance to an end, and claps her hands with pleasure. Artois bows gallantly, urgently requesting under his breath, 'Another?'

'Perhaps later,' she responds, her surprised eyes meanwhile meeting those of the Princesse de Lamballe. '*Cousine* Lamballe, how lovely to see you again. How are you?'

Marie-Thérèse bends her neck to her cousin. 'Much better, *cousine*, much better. How graceful you looked on the dance floor!'

Marie Antoinette smiles broadly. Everyone knows what a wonderful dancer Lamballe is, and although the compliment seems sincere and gives her pleasure, she is not quite sure if it is truly meant. Marie Antoinette takes Lamballe's arm, displacing Noailles. 'Come and sit with us,' she invites the princess warmly. They make their way over to the Dauphin, while people stand aside and offer their own chairs to the two princesses as they pass with arms linked. But the Dauphine leads her cousin back to her former seat. Artois has found another dancing partner, so Lamballe can take his chair. Cordially, Marie-Thérèse greets first the Dauphin and then his brother, the Comte de Provence. Each rather stiffly returns the formality.

Lamballe turns back to Marie Antoinette. 'I love the way you've done your hair.'

'Thank you,' replies the Dauphine. 'I want to grow it long, but it takes such an age. I envy you yours, it's so long and thick.' She reaches out and caresses a lock between finger and thumb.

'But the colour of yours is so much more beautiful than mine,' returns Lamballe. Marie Antoinette shrugs her shoulders in response and continues with a smile: 'How nice that you came this evening. Where have you been hiding these past few months?'

Lamballe shifts her chair closer to the princess. 'Château Rambouillet. In the main, I've been keeping my father-in-law company. Poor man, he's so lonely. Now that his daughter is married too, I'm the only family he has left.'

Marie Antoinette tries to recall the face of the Duc de Bourbon-Penthièvre, by all accounts the richest man in France. As a *Prince du Sang*, a member of the royal family, he had honoured her wedding with his presence and she recalls a charming man with a kindly face marred only by the melancholy in his eyes. The Duc de Bourbon-Penthièvre had by then buried his wife and all his children bar one daughter. The most difficult loss to bear was certainly that of his son, the Prince de Lamballe. A reprobate he may have been, but the young man was still his heir. His only son and heir, in whose veins had run the blood of the Sun King.

It was said that the Princesse de Lamballe had herself been inconsolable at first. Her marriage had lasted just over a year, and before reaching the age of nineteen she was already a widow. Her short marriage, which had begun like a fairy tale, had ended in disaster. Three weeks after the wedding the bridegroom, a notorious womaniser, had already had his fill of his exquisitely mannered Italian princess and deserted her for the Bohemian company of his Parisian theatre friends. A carriage accident in which his leg was crushed had been the beginning of a slow and painful end for the faithless prince. The young widow was quick to forgive her young husband his sins, but her mercy was not enough to save his life. Despite amputating the leg, the best doctors in France were unable to alleviate his fever or save the bastard great-grandson of Louis XIV from suffering a hideously painful death. For the next few months, the devastated Princesse de Lamballe had taken refuge in the convent of Saint-Antoine, where Abbess Gabrielle Charlotte de Beauvau cared for the despairing girl and gave her back the will to live.

Louise Marie Adélaïde, the last surviving daughter of the Princesse de Lamballe's father-in-law, had been married two years previously to the delightful young Duc de Chartres, son of the Duc d'Orléans. Directly after their wedding, the couple had moved to the Palais Royal in Paris. Bereft, the Duc de Bourbon-Penthièvre had begged the young widow Marie-Thérèse to stay at his side. She would lack for nothing, if only she would consent to keep him company.

During Lamballe's long months of absence from Versailles, her story had completely slipped Marie Antoinette's mind. But now the sad tale comes flooding back. And, watching the young widow's face as she recounts her travels with 'Papa' from one of his vast estates in Brittany to the next, it slowly dawns on Marie Antoinette who she reminds her of. She looks like my sister, thinks the Dauphine. Even the voice is similar, apart from the Piedmont accent of course. Long years abroad have not eroded the lilt that betrays where Marie-Thérèse spent her childhood. The Dauphine closes her eyes for a moment and imagines herself back in her own room in Vienna, where she shared so many happy hours with her sister, the best friend she ever had. Oh, she misses her so!

'How old are you exactly, *cousine?*' Marie Antoinette asks suddenly. Lamballe stops in mid sentence, blinking in astonishment. 'Twenty-one,' she whispers from behind her fan, as if half-ashamed of the admission.

'Oh my goodness, you look much younger!' exclaims the Dauphine. Lamballe decides to take this as a compliment. She blushes.

The musicians strike up a minuet and a sparkle comes into Marie Antoinette's eyes. 'Would you be so kind as to lead me in this dance? You're so good at it, and I'd like to learn from you.'

'Are you sure, cousin?'

'Absolutely! Come on!'

A sudden hush descends upon the salon as a hundred pairs of eyes are turned upon them. Seeing the two laughing princesses dancing together, the old witches shake their heads disapprovingly. Where will all this end?

Lamballe, leading lightly across the floor, finds less and less to correct in her cousin's technique. 'You see, you just have to relax and let yourself go. Don't think, just move to the music ... la la, la la!'

'Oh, I like this! It's a lovely feeling,' giggles the Dauphine. The tempo increases and Marie Antoinette discovers that, whereas hardly a week ago she was still struggling with a certain pass or deceptively simple-looking turn, she is now gliding self-confidently across the floor in Lamballe's wake. Whatever people might be making of it, the applause at the end of the dance lasts a long time. Marie Antoinette gestures to the musicians to keep playing, until twenty minutes later both princesses, with fiery faces, are forced to resume their seats.

'Oh, Lamballe, that was fantastic!' declares Marie Antoinette, fanning herself furiously to prevent the sweat matting the powder on her face. Lamballe cannot speak. She has stopped just in time, before dizziness overcame her. Is it the heat or the excitement? She takes some deep breaths, recovering a little with each one. Thank goodness she soon stops feeling so strangely light-headed and sick. Once the buzzing in her ears stops too, she feels quite normal again. Odd, this has happened to her on a few occasions now. Surely she can't be ill?

She takes another deep breath, this time of relief, and dabs with her handkerchief at the perspiration she can still feel springing from her forehead. Looking up, she finds Louis-Auguste's solemn eyes upon her. He looks away quickly, but not before a pang of guilt runs through her. What could he be thinking? Surely he isn't jealous of me for dancing with his wife, she thinks. Everyone knows that dancing isn't the Dauphin's strongest point. Oh, how stupid of me! I should never have allowed myself to get so carried away.w

Artois has exhausted himself on the dance floor, meanwhile, and comes over to the princesses. 'That was terrific, sister,' he teases the Dauphine. 'You may dance like that with me any time you like.'

'Only if you can lead as well as the Princesse de Lamballe,' retorts Marie Antoinette in the same spirit, winking at her cousin.

Artois is already on the lookout for someone else to collar for the next dance. Certainly not Lamballe: she is far too serious for him. The Comtesse de Ghérac is making eyes at him from behind her fan. Here we go!

'Isn't it about time you were put through your paces on the dance floor?' The Comte de Provence challenges his brother with a nudge. Louis-Auguste gives him a dirty look and suggests he mind his own business.

'Ooh-er, listen to His Highness! If you could only dance as well as you blow your own trumpet ... ta-rah, ta-rah ... ouch!' The Dauphin has managed to land a timely kick on his brother's shin beneath the table. 'Brute!' puffs Provence, his fat neck slowly turning crimson.

'Come on then,' returns the Dauphin, raising his strong young huntsman's fists in his brother's face.

'Oh, do stop it, you two,' Marie Antoinette breaks in, irritated. 'Can't you behave like grown-up princes?' They both lean back obediently in their chairs.

'He's nowhere near grown up,' mutters Provence, nodding heavily in his brother's direction.

'Oh, for goodness' sake, Provence,' responds the Dauphine with disgust. 'Where does all this get you?' Provence gives her a sulky pout and shrugs his plump shoulders.

'I'm going to bed. It's far too late already,' announces the Dauphin, standing up. Marie Antoinette is about to get to her feet too, but Louis-Auguste, terrified that she will try to kiss him, signals her to remain in her seat. Without bothering to bid company or hostess goodnight, the crown prince makes for the door with long, clumsy strides. His brother Provence is sitting bolt upright with a triumphant gleam in his eyes, but Marie Antoinette turns her back on him.

'I'm so sorry, *cousine*, if I've upset the Dauphin,' whispers Lamballe in distress.

'Of course you haven't, my sweet. There's nothing the matter with him.' Marie Antoinette flips her hand to show hopeless it is to expect anything more from mere boys. 'They're always like that, picking fights with one another over nothing.'

'Are you quite sure the Dauphin wasn't offended by my dancing? Maybe I went on too long?'

'No, of course not! Dearest Lamballe, please don't worry about the Dauphin. He's really awkward sometimes, but honestly, deep down he's quite nice. You see, I'm getting to know him now. Soon he will have no more secrets from me!'

'Oh, that's all right then,' breathes Lamballe, relieved. She is a good deal more at ease now. 'And how are you finding life at Versailles? Do you feel quite at home?' she asks the Dauphine. 'It's months since last we met, after all.'

Marie Antoinette gives Lamballe a look of mock severity. 'Yes, indeed it is, *cousine*!' she swiftly retorts. 'You should have come to see me much more often. But still, you want to know how I like it here? Whether I feel at home? I know I should say yes. But just between the two of us,' she leans closer to Lamballe, 'I don't!'

'Oh, how awful for you!' exclaims Lamballe, genuinely shocked, and holding her fan wide open before her face so that the bystanders cannot make out what she is saying.

'It's the fate of a Dauphine,' Marie Antoinette laconically replies, adding archly, 'But I suppose I shouldn't complain. According to my mother, I'm the envy of all the young women of Europe.' Her scornful tone speaks volumes.

Marie-Thérèse, Princesse de Lamballe, stares sorrowfully straight ahead and thinks back on her own short-lived marriage. 'I think I know what you mean, *cousine*. I've felt the same, and I don't know myself what is meant by "home".'

'But of course. You're away from your own home, too, aren't you?'

'Turin,' says Lamballe quickly, with a tremor of homesickness. 'And, like you, also thanks to the Duc de Choiseul. But in the end I stayed on here after my husband's death. I may be niece to the King of Savoy, but my father is not so wealthy. Here I have everything my heart desires ...'

'Except a husband,' Marie Antoinette bursts in again.

'Yes, except a husband,' says Lamballe, sighing and picking at a thread in her black taffeta. 'But now that I know what marriage entails and how false a husband can be, I think I can resist the desire to repeat the experience for now. The Prince de Lamballe made me very unhappy.' She gives Marie Antoinette such a tragic glance that the Dauphine swallows the quip she was about to utter and instead lays her hand tenderly on her cousin's.

'Poor, poor Lamballe. Have you many friends?'

Marie-Thérèse catches her breath. 'Not really. My sister-in-law is my best friend, but since her marriage to the Duc de Chartres I see far too little of her.'

'Ah.'

There is a moment of silence between the two princesses, broken at last by Marie Antoinette. She giggles as if a brilliant plan has occurred to her. 'I tell you what, Lamballe, why don't you be my friend? We have so much in common. Both of us are foreigners here, and you know, since de Choiseul was thrown out of court I've lost my last friend here too. Oh, I'd so love you to agree to be my friend! Do you know, you look a tiny bit like my sister, and I miss her so terribly. There's no one here I can trust, and I'd so like somebody I could speak freely to without having to weigh every word ...'

On and on gushes Marie Antoinette, as if some inner floodgate has been opened. The Princesse de Lamballe proves to be a good listener, but while she nods and laughs she is wondering privately whether tomorrow Marie Antoinette will think better of her openness. The gentle Lamballe's faith in human relationships has been tested to its limit. And, after all, she hardly knows the Dauphine yet.

Aunt Adélaïde thinks she has seen quite enough. And she does not like the look of it either, all that chit-chat behind the fans. What can they be talking about? Her, perhaps? She gets impatiently to her feet and crosses the room to the two princesses, determined to put an end to their whispering. 'May I invite Madame la Dauphine and the Princesse de Lamballe to join me in a game of cards?' she requests in honeyed tones.

Her flow of confidences interrupted, Marie Antoinette casts a vaguely irritated upward glance at her aunt. She really isn't in the mood for a boring game like that. 'Perhaps later, aunt,' she politely replies.

'May I draw your attention to the fact that it is rude to the other guests, and particularly to your hostess, for you to remain engaged in conversation with the same person for the entire evening?' Her tone has now changed to one of clear reprimand.

Marie Antoinette looks back at Lamballe. 'You see what I mean,' she says, her blue eyes twinkling. Her cousin answers with a laugh.

'Come then, aunt,' continues the Dauphine, 'where would you have me?'

Adélaïde's face cracks into a grin, like a cat that has got at the cream, and she shoos the pair across to the little card table. The players duly greet the newcomers, the cards are shuffled and dealt, and the game proceeds.

'Oh, what fun!' exclaims Marie Antoinette in a show of delight that would be transparent to anyone who really knew her. To them it would be plain that the one game she truly excels at is playing her role.

I've heard that the villagers of Rambouillet call me La Bonne Lamballe. 'Goody-goody', just because I support my father-in-law in his charitable work. Charming of them. Papa is quite worried. Maupeou's new parlement seems to be unpopular with everyone, and there's more and more unrest in Paris. Papa and the Comte de la Marche seem to be the only Princes of the Blood who haven't turned against the king. But who is in the right?

From the journal of the Princesse de Lamballe,
20th February 1771

2

Brilliant sunshine streams into the bedchamber. This, and the clatter of the shutters being thrown open, conspire to prevent Marie Antoinette from sleeping on. Still, she does her best, turning over and ignoring the Comtesse de Noailles's 'good morning'. But she gives in when her dog leaps onto the bed and begins licking her face all over. As always, she has had the vast bed to herself all night; Marie Antoinette stretches and swings her legs over the edge. *Madame l'Etiquette* claps her hands twice and the ladies of the bedchamber come swarming in to help the Dauphine dress. As if she couldn't manage that herself – but protocol is protocol.

Breakfast over, she goes to pay her daily courtesy visit to the aunts. On her way through the gallery she sees that the snow from yesterday is already melting away. What a pity!

'Oh, good morning, Papa,' she greets the king, who is standing near a window in lively discussion with his daughters. Louis XV turns at the sound of her voice and beams at the young princess. He welcomes her warmly, kissing her brow. 'My sweet little Dauphine! Coffee?' he enquires affably, without waiting for a reply.

Louis XV loves to make coffee for anyone who will give him the opportunity to do so. He expertly mills the special, freshly roasted beans himself. With a serious expression, he then prepares the beverage in the small coffee machine that he brings with him to his daughters' apartments every morning. At last he ceremoniously hands Marie Antoinette a tiny, aromatic cupful.

'Merci, Papa.'

The king sits down at the table, slapping his knee. 'Come here, my princess. Tell your Papa what you got up to yesterday evening.'

Marie Antoinette assumes her perch while Adélaïde looks on with satisfaction. She knows how her father adores Marie Antoinette. Ever since the Dauphine began her daily visits to the aunts, Louis has been coming to their chambers more often too. 'A perfect arrangement,' calculates Adélaïde with loathing. 'The more time the king spends here, the less he spends with that du Barry woman.'

'I have a new friend, Papa,' Marie Antoinette tells him between sips of coffee.

'Well, I never. And do we know her?'

'Oh, you're bound to, Papa. She's Marie-Thérèse, the Princesse de Lamballe.' Without altering his expression, Louis glances at Adélaïde. Of course he knows Lamballe. His own daughter had tried to make a match between himself and the attractive widow from Turin. Adélaïde has left no stone unturned in her attempts to marry her father off to a woman of good family. Oh yes, Lamballe is young and beautiful all right. But so blessed prim and proper! No, he had just become acquainted with Jeanne and discovered that there was a woman who knew exactly how to please a king.

Louis blinks a few times, as if deep in thought. 'Yes, indeed I do know the Princesse de Lamballe. A charming young woman and, what is more, one of means.'

'Surely that is of no account, Papa!'

The king shakes his head sagely and smiles at his young protégée. 'Child, child, you have so much to learn in life. The fact that Lamballe is a not only a Princess of the Blood but also in possession of her own fortune means that her friendship may be trusted. She's not trying to use you to better her own position. She has already reached the top.'

'She could have been Queen of France of course,' remarks Adélaïde sourly.

The king glares at his daughter. 'Put that idea right out of your head, *ma petite Chiffe!*' His blazing eyes silence any attempt she might have made to reply.

Marie Antoinette, innocent of what has happened in the past, cannot fathom the cause of the king's sudden irritation. She fidgets uncomfortably in his lap and wishes she could get down.

'Do you have any objection to my befriending the Princesse de Lamballe?' she asks him timidly. To her surprise, his response is a guffaw of laughter and a bear hug. 'No objection whatsoever, my child. As far as I'm concerned, I think her the very best friend you could find at court.'

Over Marie Antoinette's head he casts a sardonic glance at Adélaïde, who lowers her eyes in defeat. Gently pushing Marie Antoinette away from him, the king makes to stand up. 'I must be going, children. Duty calls. The State has need of me.' As she slides from his knees, he gives the Dauphine a playful slap on the backside.

'Papa!'

'Duty calls' – what rubbish! Adélaïde's thoughts are in turmoil. The last thing her father concerns himself with is governing France. She watches incensed as he makes a regal exit, complete with coffee machine.

'It's time for your *toilette*,' his daughter snaps bitchily at Marie Antoinette. Now that her father has returned to his mistress, she can do without the crown princess hanging round her neck.

'Oh, is it that time already?' replies the Dauphine brightly. Forgetting etiquette, she gulps the last of her coffee and skips off in her little silk pumps to her own apartment, leaving her aunts shaking their heads.

Halfway there, Marie Antoinette wonders what she is rushing for. The *toilette* is nothing to look forward to. *Madame l'Etiquette* will once again try to lace her so tightly into her corset that she can hardly breathe, the hairdresser will spend hours fiddling with her coiffure, and throughout the whole procedure she will have to smile while half the court stares on. Every living soul holding right of 'entrée' will show their face during the course of the morning. And Marie Antoinette must greet the courtiers correctly according to their rank or position. Quite often she makes an error. Someone gets a nod of the head, whilst protocol demands that this individual be bowed to from the waist up. What a pain it all is! And the Comtesse de Noailles goes on indefatigably correcting her.

Marie Antoinette is dressed at last, face powdered and richly rouged. She is ready for public exhibition. At twelve o'clock on the dot the gates and doors of the chateau are thrown open. Louis-Auguste is back from the hunt in time to take his place at table beside his wife. And the public is once more treated to its daily gape at the menu and the heirs to the throne of France.

It is late afternoon when the Abbé Vermond strolls into the Dauphine's private quarters. He finds Marie Antoinette slouched in a chair, gloomily gnawing at her fingernails.

'How lovely Madame looks today,' teases Vermond, in the hope of rousing her from her lethargy and perhaps even raising a smile. It saddens him to see her like this. Marie Antoinette almost always gives an impression of gaiety when other people are around, but he recognised long ago that this was a façade behind which she hid her true feelings. She doesn't need to put on a show for the priest; like her, he has no friends at the court of Versailles. They also share their contempt for the absurd rules and regulations that keep a stranglehold on its inhabitants.

Jacques-Mathieu de Vermond, a humble priest in his mid-thirties, was taken entirely by surprise by the order to leave for Vienna. On the recommendation of the Archbishop of Toulouse, the Duc de Choiseul had appointed him to make of the Austrian archduchess a future Dauphine of France. After a year of Vermond's tuition Marie Antoinette was more or less equipped for her new role, though it was a matter of great regret to the priest that the young princess's basic education was so poor.

Luckily, she showed a reasonable aptitude for the French language. Enough, anyway, to lift her above the dreadful French, full of mutant German and Italian phrases, gabbled at court in Vienna. Her love of history had helped consolidate her knowledge of the French royal family, which could also be judged adequate.

But Vermond was far from satisfied with her progress. The priest soon learned that there was no point in bombarding her with dates, facts and figures. Fortunately, he was a gifted storyteller. In his soft, melodious voice he could relate the events of the past so that the history of France came alive before her eyes. At such moments she would hang on his every word, and, although certainly no swot, the most charming student he had ever had stored away in her radiant head every scrap of information he presented to her.

On the eve of her departure for France, Marie Antoinette had taken sorrowful leave of the abbé. She continued to miss her down-to-earth mentor until, a couple of months later, the Duc de Choiseul found a way of remedying the situation. The minister was honoured to be able to fulfil the request of the crown princess and officially appoint Jacques-Mathieu de Vermond *lecteur de la Dauphine*.

Not everyone at court was as pleased as she was. Even the king had had to think twice before granting his permission. After all, this brought yet another Choiseul pawn into the game.

Choiseul's banishment left Vermond feeling less and less comfortable. And with good reason! He had overheard the murmuring in corridor and gallery ... 'What does the Dauphine need a Reader for, when she never opens a book?' was the echo on the stairs. 'He's one of Choiseul's spies who's trying to get a hold on the Dauphine ...' The whispers bounced from wall to wall and back again. Louis-Auguste was no happier about the priest's presence: Vermond must be close to Choiseul and thus against the Dauphin! He vividly recalled his father speaking with hatred of Choiseul, a rank-and-file soldier who had risen to his elevated position only thanks to Madame Pompadour. The Dauphin was still fully persuaded by his father's assessment of the situation. Louis-Auguste determined to ignore the priest as far as possible and, if he did have to address him, to watch every word he uttered in the presence of the spy.

The Abbé Vermond took the rumours surrounding him for what they were. Fortunately, he enjoyed the support of the Austrian ambassador, the Comte de Mercy-Argenteau. The ambassador regularly discussed with him Marie Antoinette's progress, which remained a source of constant worry to her mother, Maria Theresa. Now that Vermond's position had come under threat, however, Mercy had little difficulty in recruiting him into his small band of spies keeping watch on Marie Antoinette. At the personal request of the Habsburg empress, Mercy drew up a detailed daily report on the Dauphine's every word and deed, dispatched the same day to Vienna by secret courier.

Jacques-Mathieu de Vermond takes his place behind the desk and opens one of the books in the pile before him. 'Le Siècle de Louis XIV, by Voltaire,' he dutifully declaims. He leafs studiously through the pages, looking for the chapter that will provide the best introduction to this afternoon's lesson. Marie Antoinette listens to the rustling of the pages with aversion and sighs loudly.

'I'm not in the mood today,' she announces.

The priest shrugs indifferently. How often has he heard her say this before? Ignoring her, he continues his quiet search.

'Seriously, I mean it,' simmers the princess. Perhaps the priest didn't hear her properly. 'I won't be able to learn a thing today.' She sinks still lower in her chair. Any further and she will slide to the floor.

Vermond smoothes down a page and lays the palm of his hand on it. 'What is upsetting you today?'

'I'm not upset!' she snaps.

'But you look so downhearted, and I can only suppose that you are upset.' He pauses, waiting for her response. 'Or are you perhaps unwell?'

She gets to her feet and looks past him, slowly passing a hand over her abdomen.

'My God,' thinks Vermond, 'could she be pregnant at last?' He feels his features relax. Marie Antoinette frowns, raising her left index finger and pointing down at where her right hand still moves gently back and forth over her tummy.

'You could not be …?'

Before he can finish his sentence, she spits back at him: 'Forget it, priest! Honestly! How in heaven's name could that be? The person in question has never yet laid a finger on me.'

The smile vanishes from Vermond's face. It was too good to be true. A pregnancy would solve all the problems at one fell swoop.

'I must have eaten something that didn't agree with me, that's all.'

'I'm sorry,' says the priest.

'Me too. I know for sure that the minute I'm pregnant people will start treating me with some respect. The only thing they're interested in is the state of my womb. Vile!'

'Madame, surely you don't believe that. People hold you in great esteem, as a person, I mean.'

Marie Antoinette snorts contemptuously. 'Nice of you to say so. But give me an example.'

The priest feels the colour rise to his cheeks. She is quite right. He sniffs and raises his eyebrows, extending both hands palm upwards, in an expression of helplessness. What can he say? 'This is Versailles.'

'Voilà! The only thing that really interests people is that terrible creature. And just as she has always done, *la Barry* lets herself be vulgarly used. Everyone knows she is the gateway to the king. *La favourite* is his eyes and ears, and whoever can worm their way into her good books gets in with Papa. I'm not stupid, you know, I can see what's going on.'

Vermond finds himself, not for the first time, astonished by his pupil. One minute she is playing dolls and romping with her ladies in waiting's toddlers, and the next she displays an entirely adult insight into the true workings of the court.

'You are completely correct in your assessment, Madame. But in the last analysis, it is the king who decides. It is he who makes all the decisions, and that is my greatest concern. The talk in the corridors is not only that my own position is in jeopardy, but yours too!' Marie Antoinette levelly returns his stare. 'The Duc de La

Vauguyon is doing all he can behind the scenes to destroy your marriage. It is said that you are infertile and there is no hope of an heir. As long as this is the case, the alliance between France and Austria remains extremely fragile.'

The Dauphine dismisses his concerns with a wave of her hand. 'Oh, I've heard all that old stuff before. But as long as *Papa Roi* is making all the decisions, nothing will go wrong. The king adores me, you know,' she adds with pride.

Vermond stands up and goes over to the window. Gazing out across the courtyard as if to assure himself that nobody is listening in, he resumes: 'As long as you continue to "pleasure" the king, all is well. But Choiseul's departure exerts huge pressure upon your situation. Perhaps much more than you think.'

Marie Antoinette considers for a moment. 'Perhaps I wouldn't even mind a divorce. Then I could go home.' She opens her arms in an all-embracing gesture of displeasure. 'I certainly wouldn't miss any of this.' Vermond is silent.

Marie Antoinette mentally reviews the possible consequences. Would she ever dare show her face again at her mother's door? She imagines the carriage drawing up outside Schönbrunn and her mother, Maria Theresa, Empress of the Holy Roman Empire, waiting imperiously at the top of the long flight of stone steps, the wind whipping the black skirts of her mourning dress. She sees her mother's raised forefinger and hears her roar: 'You have failed, Antoine, and brought shame upon our house. Go! Get out of my sight!'

A wry smile plays about Marie Antoinette's mouth. There is no way back. Her mother would banish her, most probably to some remote convent in the dark mountains on the farthest frontier of Hungary. Shaking her head slowly, she sobs, 'I shall never return home again.' Her protruding Habsburg lower lip is quivering.

'Your relations with the king would be inviolable were you to become pregnant,' advises Vermond. Marie Antoinette's expression changes to one of impudence and she murmurs, 'Yes, I should dress up, just for the fun of it.'

'What did you say?' The priest gives her a quizzical look and the princess bursts out laughing.

'Well, everyone is so obstinately fixated on my belly. I only have to rub my stomach and even you think I must be expecting. Pah! What a joke if each day I were to put a little more padding under my dress. I'd soon find myself the centre of attention!' She collapses in giggles.

But Vermond is not amused. 'How long do you think you could keep that up? The moment people realised you were making a cheap joke at their expense, they would lose all respect for you.'

'Respect? Be honest, Vermond!' She flops back into her chair. 'You know I have none to lose!'

Jacques-Mathieu de Vermond compresses his lips and sighs. She has indeed none to lose. But neither is she going the right way about redeeming the situation. 'Respect has to be earned, Madame. And that you will not do unless you alter your behaviour.'

'What do you mean by that, Vermond?' she demands sharply, stung by the implied insult.

'I'm sorry to have to say this, Madame, but rushing around your salon playing tag with other people's children is not what people expect of a future queen. You know that I am always candid with you. This is such a moment. For example, the way you are slumped in your chair just now like a sack of flour; such comportment in the presence of other people would not command the least bit of respect.'

The princess levers herself upright, her expression sulky. 'This is how I always sit when others are around,' she archly retorts.

'You know precisely what I mean,' parries Vermond.

The princess slams her fist down on the arm of her chair. 'What exactly do you expect of me?' she demands.

The priest returns to the open book. 'Well, I think for a start we shall do some lessons today,' he responds with a bright smile.

'Oh, no,' she protests, clapping her hands over her ears.

'Respect?' enquires Vermond, his tone grave now. The Dauphine grimaces, but knows when she is beaten.

'I'd like to relate something about your favourite king, Louis XIV. One thing I don't have to tell you is the great respect with which this forefather of yours is regarded.'

'Well, that stands to reason,' scoffs the princess. 'He was the Sun King.'

'Of course, but he was not born so. He had to fight for his title, and often against the tide. But it's interesting to learn how he went about this. You may profit from it. Look here, in those days France was still in a very unstable state. Religious rivalries, jealousy and greed led to one outbreak of civil conflict after another. By taking a firm stand against these, Louis XIV was able to end them. Thanks to the Sun King, we now live in a more or less united land. But the king certainly faced his fair share of challenges.' Vermond beams as though he had survived them all personally. He picks up another book and leafs through it until he comes to a large engraving. Louis XIV gazes proudly, even arrogantly, out at the reader. 'Just take a look at that,' instructs the priest, showing the print to the Dauphine. Clad in his robes of State, the king seems to exude power. 'Not to be compared with our present monarch,' mumbles Vermond, tracing the ermine-trimmed mantle with his finger. 'One's manner of dress and presentation is most important, especially at court ...' He looks witheringly at Marie Antoinette's simple dress. Her hem has come down on one side, probably during one of her cavorting sessions with the dog, and the frayed edge is grubby from trailing on the floor. 'Another difference between the two of you,' concludes the priest.

Marie Antoinette is silent. What is Vermond thinking of? Does he imagine I'm going to start parading around got up like that? No thank you!

An enigmatic smile appears on Jacques-Mathieu de Vermond's face as he places his chair right in front of the Dauphine. 'In the spring of 1655, when Louis XIV would have been sixteen years old, there occurred an interesting encounter. The whole *parlement* had gone into a huddle at the Palais de Justice. The purpose behind this secret gathering was to discuss the seventeen edicts recently enacted by Louis XIV. Most of these concerned funding for the war against Spain, and opinion was apparently divided, for the hundredth time, over what the king had done. Well now, Louis XIV had got wind of this and didn't intend to allow the *parlementaires* to form their own government. Now comes the crunch: neatly attired in his *justaucorps*, the royal hunting outfit, he galloped to Paris and burst into the meeting.'

Marie Antoinette is all ears. It enthrals her to be whisked away into the past like this. Softly, Vermond continues his tale. 'Every single member of the *parlement* was struck dumb and felt himself betrayed. They had been caught in the act. How had the king come to hear of this meeting?

'It didn't take them long to recover themselves. What did they have to worry about? Louis XIV was a mere child, after all. But the boy was fast becoming a man. The king surveyed the scene in silence for a moment. His riding coat and breeches set off a powerfully muscled young physique. Despite his small stature, this was clearly not someone to meddle with. In his right hand he held a small whip, which he now tapped softly against his boot whilst scanning the faces of the *parlementaires*. His eyes blazed. The only sound in the room now was subdued whispering. A sudden whip-crack on the table and everyone sat bolt upright and silent in his seat.

'Louis XIV strolls calmly to his place and takes the king's chair. "It is common knowledge," he proceeds in a clear voice of authority, "what problems your little gatherings cause in MY State." The whip taps threateningly against the wooden arm of his chair. "Everyone knows the dangerous situations that have resulted from your meetings." He stares round the ring of faces. "I understand that what is under discussion here are the edicts recently enacted by myself. Well, I am here to end these discussions!" With this he jumps to his feet and points his whip at the chairman of the meeting. "Monsieur le *Premier Président*, let this be a final warning to you! Bear it in mind now and for all time: I am the absolute ruler of France. Not you men, but I MYSELF am the State!"

'Without a backward glance at the bemused *parlementaires*, he strides from the hall. Behind him the men exchange mute stares. All the wind has been taken out of their sails and they have no idea what to do next. It is unheard of – such a thing has never happened before. But the might of an absolute monarch in the making has them in its power. Shaking his head, the chairman disbands the meeting. The edicts thus remain intact. The little king can only grow in stature from now on.'

Marie Antoinette's cheeks are glowing. Wow, what a man! How different from his grandson, the present King Louis XV, so introverted and averse to decisive action.

'What can we learn from this, Madame?'

The Dauphine thinks hard, but is still too much under the spell of the Sun King to formulate words. Her ears still echoing to the thwack of his whip, she shakes her head.

'His message was clear,' extrapolates Vermond. 'He, and he alone, was the boss – despite the fact that Louis XIV was actually taking a huge risk just then. One of the *parlementaires* might have stood up to him, someone capable of taking the king's place. Had that happened, we would not be here now. Louis XIV sensed from the outset that everything depended upon a show of strength on his part. He liked to dress in his hunting costume and wearing it made him feel strong. To be mounted on a prancing stallion gave him the same sense of power that being fully garbed in robes of State would later confer. Versailles, splendid yet sufficiently far removed from the intrigues of Paris, became the base for his absolute sovereignty. Such an example may serve us well. Just consider the Comtesse de Barry. She may be of humble origin ...'

'She's nothing but a tart,' Marie Antoinette breaks in.

The priest swallows hard and continues. 'She may be of humble origin, yet she has become the most significant woman at court, and everyone holds her in high regard. What do you need to do to earn that same respect?'

'Oh well ... that's impossible,' sighs the princess, immodestly lifting her small breasts in her cupped hands and gazing down on them with a disgruntled air. 'The only thing *Papa Roi* has any respect for is a well-filled bosom. And I haven't even the pimples of a common dressmaker's daughter.'

The unfathomable smile returns to the priest's face. 'You are still young, but time is on our side. Think about it. Where does the king spend most of his life, apart from with his mistress?'

'I should know! Just like Louis-Auguste, out hunting!'

'*Voilà, Madame*,' replies Vermond in triumph.

The princess stares uncomprehendingly at the priest. 'What do you mean exactly?'

'Well, might you give the king pleasure, perhaps, by accompanying him on the hunt?'

'Well, of course,' rejoins Marie Antoinette quickly. 'That should be obvious.'

She had already remarked a few months previously that she would like to ride to hounds, but properly, not in a carriage or lurching along on a donkey. The king had laughed heartily at the idea, and so had Louis-Auguste. But she was serious! Naturally, this provided yet more grist for the gossip mill. But once the king saw that Marie Antoinette was in real earnest, he allowed her to ride out with him at the end of October, mounted as she wished. Of course, a footman had to hold her animal on the halter. A horse, after all, was not a donkey. But it delighted the king to find the princess still laughing in the saddle at the end of the day. The idea of having his granddaughter gallop through the forest at his side appealed greatly to him. The same week, Marie Antoinette had celebrated her fifteenth birthday. He had made her a royal gift of stables stocked with English thoroughbreds, and she soon acquainted herself with the art of dressage. Now, with spring on the way, she was looking forward to taking one of her horses out into the countryside. Riding suited her, and she had little trouble mastering the finer points of command and control.

But it was not long before she was confronted by her mother's concern and disapproval. The letters from Vienna seriously questioned the wisdom of her equestrian activities. And could spending all that time in chilly stables really be good for her figure?

The hunt! Now it really begins to dawn on her how much *Papa Roi* would love her company in the field. What's more, it will also enable her to spend a good part of the day with her husband. But what will Louis-Auguste make of it? Doesn't he use hunting just as a way of escaping her? Oh, how jealous that creature du Barry will be, she who apparently refers to the Dauphine as '*la petite rousse*'. What a slap in the face for the mistress, to see her lover riding off for the whole day with the young princess! And what will the rest of the court make of it? The Dauphine on horseback at the king's side! The magnificent picture conjured up in her mind's eye makes her discontented, and she picks at her skirt, pulling a face. Naturally, she will have to dress up like Louis XIV. Until she becomes a real woman she can never compete with Papa's mistress. But were she to appear like the living image of Louis XIV, neat and elegantly turned out in a specially cut *justaucorps*, she would surely steal the show, captivating king and courtiers, and even Louis-Auguste himself! Yes, that's what she must do.

'I have an idea,' she says, her eyes sparkling.

'Go on, surprise me!' says Vermond, knowing what is coming. It warms his heart to see her happy again, for however short a while.

I shall be glad when spring comes. The weather is really too bad for travelling. It has been raining for days and the road to Paris, like the park, has turned into one great sea of mud. I'm bored stiff here and would rather have stayed in Paris. But, what with the unrest there, Papa preferred me to stay safely at Rambouillet. I wonder how things are with Antoinette.

From the journal of the the Princesse de Lamballe,
27th February 1771

3

Steering a course between Scylla and Charybdis: that would be the Austrian ambassador's best description of his position at the court of Versailles. Florimond Claude, Comte de Mercy-Argenteau, is aware of the forces constantly trying to sabotage the alliance with Austria. Behind the scenes, its opponents are desperately trying to come up with the perfect case to undermine the marriage between the Dauphin and Marie Antoinette. What a triumph that would be for them! The ambassador follows the plotting and bickering between the two camps – the Barriens and the followers of Choiseul – with suspicion but as yet no real concern. After all, the king will hear nothing of it. His relationship with Austria is important to him and, what is more, the Dauphine is absolutely no plain Jane. Neither is it her fault that the marriage hasn't yet been consummated. It is time his grandson grew up. But with his usual laissez-faire attitude, King Louis XV lets the whole business, like many another, slide.

Lacking any strong direction from above, the various factions at court continue to pursue their speculation and intrigue. The Comte de Mercy is driven to distraction by the king's sitting on the fence. It is precisely this ambivalent behaviour on the part of Louis XV that raises petty scheming to a game of high stakes, whereas a clear signal from him could put a stop to it once and for all, making life a great deal easier for the ambassador.

The loyal Florimond de Mercy has spent his entire career in the service of Maria Theresa, Empress of the Holy Roman Empire. Five years ago, Marie Antoinette's mother appointed him ambassador to France, and the Dauphine's marriage to Louis-Auguste has hugely enhanced his position. The Viennese empress showed her faith in him by personally placing Marie Antoinette under his guardianship. But he is much more than that. Unbeknown to anyone, Mercy also acts as the eyes and ears of Maria Theresa. It is barely a year since Marie Antoinette came to Versailles, yet Mercy has managed to establish a dense network of informants. His spies keep him fully appraised of what goes on in the salons and private apartments. The empress expects a daily report from him, a commission Mercy at first resisted but which has gradually become routine.

There is squabbling aplenty at Versailles, quite enough to fill a page or two every day. Trickier is separating fact from fiction. A molehill can turn itself into a mountain overnight, and Mercy entrusts nothing to his report until he is convinced of its veracity – although he is not above embroidering a little here and there when it suits him. The ambassador is fully cognisant of the weighty responsibility resting upon his shoulders. In his reports Mercy repeatedly expresses his rather low opinion of Louis-Auguste. Unconsciously, perhaps to strengthen his position further, the ambassador paints the future King of France as a weaker character than he really is. It is this advice from her confidant that forms the basis of Maria Theresa's letters to her daughter.

The empress regularly consults Mercy concerning the content of this correspondence, and he has thus made himself completely irreplaceable. Of course, his post precludes him from openly taking sides. But with the intuitive ease of a natural ambassador, de Mercy makes it his business to stay on good terms with one and all.

Florimond de Mercy looks younger than his years. No one would think he was a man well into his forties, so deceptive are his rosy complexion and the darkly sweeping eyebrows that emphasise his brilliant blue eyes. Women find his small mouth with its beautifully shaped lips, almost always sealed, irresistible. Mercy is a good listener and does not speak without first carefully weighing his words. Rather taller than average, this nobleman born in the lowlands of Austria might be expected to stand out in a crowd.

Remarkably enough, the reverse is true. Mercy has a talent for melting into the background.

At receptions and balls he is never to be found swapping amusing anecdotes in the company of other men. It is as if he considers himself above such things. Instead, he wafts from salon to salon like a butterfly on a lazy summer breeze, never pausing long enough to engage anyone in conversation. As a result, no one really takes him seriously. Only Louis-Auguste's youngest sister, Madame Elizabeth, seems to have the perspicacity to see what he is really up to, and in her childish innocence she refers to him openly as 'le vieux renard' – the old fox.

The count does not get involved in politics or play power games, but behind his benign façade lie watchful eyes. His hawk-like view takes in everything that goes on around him, in particular every detail regarding Marie Antoinette. It has become clear to him that the relationship between the Dauphin and Marie Antoinette is unlikely to produce an heir in the near future. Of more current concern are the recent events in Paris. The disbanding of *parlement* has not gone down well with the citizens of France. Even members of Louis XV's own family, the Princes of the Blood, have turned against their king. The country must be as good as bankrupt, and all things considered Mercy can see the necessity for the reforms put forward by Louis XV and Chancellor Maupeou. But until recently every proposed change to the tax system had been rejected by *parlement*. Now that it has been dissolved and its former members banished to the provinces by means of a *lettre de cachet*, the way is clear for modernisation.

Faced for the first time with having to pay taxes, the privileged classes feel under threat and are standing in the way of change. Heated discussions are the order of the day, and the words 'despot' and 'tyrant' are being bandied about. Because Louis XV has been known so often to back down under pressure, Mercy is afraid that the monarch will once again renege on his decision. The reputation of the Most Christian King of France has already suffered enough blows; one more and it will be dented beyond repair, saddling

Louis-Auguste with a most unwelcome inheritance.

All things considered, these are not easy times for the ambassador. The pressure from Vienna continues unabated, with Maria Theresa repeatedly expressing her concern at the continuing failure of Marie Antoinette to conceive. The absence of an heir apparent is making the prospect of a new dynasty uniting the two great powers seem ever more remote, especially since the announcement of a betrothal between the Comte de Provence and Princess Marie Joséphine Louise of Savoy. If the Dauphin's younger brother manages to get his bride with child promptly, this could put the whole alliance in jeopardy. And with it his own career, as Mercy understands only too well! The ambassador has racked his brains to find the best way of persuading Marie Antoinette to take her relations with her husband more seriously. The Dauphine has promised to do her best, but the desired result is not forthcoming. Mercy clearly cannot make a direct appeal to the Dauphin – which is a shame, for the boy could certainly do with some encouragement.

The Comte de Mercy looks up on hearing Marie Antoinette's exasperated sigh as the Comtesse de Noailles is lacing up her corset.

'Not so tight,' complains the girl.

It has taken months for the Dauphine to capitulate. At one point she categorically refused ever to wear stays again. The stiff bodices strangled her half to death! Especially in summer, she could hardly draw breath or eat, let alone have a good romp. But there was nothing for it; she had to wear them. Luckily, the threatening tone of her mother's letters was softened a little by the arrival of some custom-made Viennese corsets, far less stiff than the French whalebone variety. Maria Theresa, herself rather broad in the beam, was having palpitations at the thought that her daughter might lose her waist before she was twenty. That she might end up looking like one of those fleshy strumpets trading in Graz market! In the meantime, Mercy reports almost daily on how the Dauphine is following her mother's advice, which is most reassuring.

Less so is the state of Marie Antoinette's financial affairs. Her household budget is overseen by one of the king's accountants, Monsieur Pommery. Mercy has never liked the man, although of course he never lets this be known. Slippery as an eel, Pommery always pretends to be less clever than he really is. Mercy sees right through the charlatan, who keeps him waiting for answers to his critical questions whilst putting on a show of considering them deeply. A lot of money seems to be going on ill-defined appointments or under the heading 'miscellaneous', and Mercy is convinced that a good proportion of it is disappearing into Pommery's pocket. The ambassador checks the accounts regularly and advises Marie Antoinette to do the same.

'But Mercy, all those numbers. They honestly mean nothing to me. You tell me what to do,' sighs the princess. She has absolutely no head for figures. Her hairdresser has meanwhile applied a new layer of pomade and is now busy combing the gleaming curls into a new creation.

Mercy's index finger creeps on down the columns of the cash book. The amount budgeted for the princess's personal expenditure has hardly been touched again this month. 'What would you like to do with it, Madame?' Mercy politely enquires.

'I can't hear you,' is the muffled response. The princess's head is completely enveloped in a cloud of white powder from the hairdresser's bellows, and her face obscured by a funnel to prevent the stuff getting into her eyes or nose. The perfumed rice-flour sticks directly to the pomade, which, despite its sickly scent of summer roses, still emits a whiff of paraffin. As the air clears, the Dauphine lowers the funnel and peeps gaily over its rim at the ambassador, 'You were saying?'

Mercy reiterates that there is money left over.

'Oh, could that be given to the youngest servants? I hear they haven't had any wages for months.'

Mercy, restraining himself despite his annoyance, turns to the accountant, who is busy polishing his glasses. He looks up, blinking like a mole, and with his mouth half open gapes stupidly first at the Dauphine and then at Mercy.

'Is it true that these people have not been paid?' asks the ambassador in measured tones.

Pommery shrugs indifferently. 'I wouldn't know, Your Excellency. The lowest echelons of staff come under another department. Not my job.'

The continual offloading of responsibilities so typical of Versailles is abhorrent to Mercy. How can he tackle this particular instance discreetly?

'Don't make things so complicated, Mercy,' pleads Marie Antoinette. The hairdresser applies the last touch of rouge: two perfect spheres, one on each cheek. Mercy is not impressed; to him she looks like a porcelain doll. 'I honestly have no idea what to do with the money,' pursues the Dauphine, staring into the mirror the stylist holds up to her. 'Please share it out among those poor people, then at least they'll have something to be going on with.'

'Of course, Madame,' nods the Comte de Mercy, returning the ledger to Pommery.

'Consider it done,' blusters the official, making off as fast as his legs will carry him.

In the distance, the chapel bell chimes twelve. The gates of Versailles swing open to admit the usual swarms of onlookers, greedy for a glimpse of royalty. Like an actress about to play the leading lady in one of Racine's plays, Marie Antoinette rises to her feet and glances one last time at her reflection. Brushing an invisible speck from her cheek, she straightens her back. 'I am ready,' she dutifully declares, nodding at the servant to open the door for her. Outside, the pushing and shoving crowd is rewarded with the charming smile of Madame la Dauphine.

How can I be a proper friend to her when she's still playing with toddlers? She hardly notices my existence when she's horsing around like that. But then, what was I like at fifteen? And her joie de vivre is contagious. That alone makes her better company than Papa, who never stops grieving for his dead wife and children - even now, when spring's on the way again.

From the journal of the Princesse de Lamballe,
13th March 1771

4

The Comtesse de Noailles looks despairingly around Marie Antoinette's apartment. The Dauphine is taking lunch, hence the temporary peace and tranquillity. 'What a shambles,' sighs Noailles. With seven children of her own, she is used to a certain degree of disorder, but Marie Antoinette is the end. The *Dame d'Honneur* rights a small table that has been overturned, picks up the clothing and toys littering the floor, and shakes her head sadly on discovering in a corner the shards of a Chinese porcelain vase. The Dauphine's salon looks more like a playground than the apartment of the future Queen of France.

Anne-Claude-Louise d'Arpajon, Comtesse de Noailles, sinks into a chair and thinks back to when her daughter Louise was the same age as Marie Antoinette. A decade has passed since then: how time flies! As far as she can recall, Louise behaved in a much more adult fashion than does the Dauphine. She certainly never made this kind of mess! What sort of upbringing has the Austrian archduchess had?

Sometimes the *Dame d'Honneur* finds things getting too much for her. After all, she is forty-two now. It was a great distinction to be asked by the king to take on her present task, but back then she had no idea of Marie Antoinette's character. The countess is sure that the Dauphine deliberately refuses to take her seriously, that the princess laughs at her behind her back and does things on purpose to needle her. She wonders what has she done to deserve it. On several occasions she has seriously considered handing in her notice; she simply doesn't have the energy nowadays. But her husband, more interested in his wife's generous honorarium than her state of exhaustion, advised her strongly against it. 'What would the king make of that?' he anxiously enquired, 'and what would it mean for our position at court? No, it's out of the question!'

'Comtesse de Noailles?' The deep voice comes from the doorway, where a manservant of Louis XV is bowing to her. 'The king commands your presence. He wishes to see you directly!'

'*Sacrebleu*,' whispers the woman to herself, shocked. She feels her heart miss a beat. She has been dreading this for so long, the moment when she must account for the Dauphine's behaviour. Her mouth goes dry and she longs for a glass of water. If only she did not have to get out of her chair! But the servant is waiting impatiently. When the king says 'directly', he means right now. Taking a deep breath, she straightens her back and, with head held high, accompanies the messenger through the great gallery towards Louis XV's chambers. With a friendly smile, the Swiss Guardsman holds the door open for her.

She looks about her; there is no king, no soul in sight. The doors close behind her. A wave of nausea sweeps over the countess. Should she sit down? At that moment a small door in the corner opens, the one leading to the *petits appartements* on the floor above, the rooms of *la favorite*, Madame du Barry. The Comtesse de Noailles respectfully greets the king as he enters, straightening his finely embroidered waistcoat.

Louis XV returns her salutation and offers her a chair. 'Comtesse de Noailles, take a seat. Coffee?' Noailles dare not refuse his amiable offer, although she does not really like the black beverage. 'How is our Dauphine getting on?' enquires the king, busily grinding his coffee beans. Here we go! The countess knows the king well enough by now: first the niceties – he never comes straight to the point. Now she is sure to be punished for the chaos in Marie Antoinette's apartment. 'Very well, Sire,' she says, as cheerfully as possible. 'The Dauphine is feeling more at home by the day, and I have the impression that her relationship with the Dauphin is becoming closer.'

The king nods. 'Excellent, for that is just what I want to talk about!' Muttering to himself, Louis pours the freshly milled coffee smoothly into the apparatus. Apparently all is not as he wishes; the water is not hot enough. '*Sapristi!*' he shouts, giving the machine a bad-tempered slap. The king does not enjoy this sort of conversation; he does his best to avoid any sort of conflict, because it always puts him in a bad humour. But there is no getting out of this one, for du Barry simply will not stop nagging him about it. The king calls a lackey to take over the coffee-making. There must be something wrong with the burner.

'My apologies, Madame,' mumbles the king in irritation. The Comtesse de Noailles nods sympathetically. If only he would come to the matter in hand! The coffee is the very last thing on her mind. The king clears his throat and stumps nervously around the room. 'Yes, well now. How should I put it? Something is amiss, Madame, and we are not happy about it.' Noailles clenches her fists together in her lap, terrified of what is coming next. 'Sire?'

'So the relationship between my grandson and the Dauphine is improving. Fine and dandy. But all the pair are required do is produce a male heir. We are nearly a year on from the wedding, and if I am not mistaken my grandson still has not once tried to make our princess his wife. Now, we don't mind if they make some youthful blunders and take their time. But,' the king leans forward over the table and wags a warning finger at Noailles, 'the fact that he lets people fill his head with a lot of nonsense that makes him forget his manners – that is something we most certainly do mind about!'

'Sire?' repeats the countess, mystified.

'We are receiving complaints, dissatisfaction concerning my grandson's arrogant and displeasing behaviour. It appears he no longer shows any respect for his governor, avoids the Comtesse du Barry, and looks down on my chancellor, Maupeou, and the other ministers. It can only be the Dauphine who is encouraging such misconduct. She is the one leading him astray. With the utmost respect, the Dauphine is a charming princess. But, at her age, what does she know of life, and what of politics? Absolutely nothing! Marie Antoinette must on no account meddle with gossip and intrigue. Let her simply get pregnant. We wish to hear no more complaints, do you hear? We desire a complete end to them, Noailles.'

Marie Antoinette's *Dame d'Honneur* stares wide-eyed back at the king. Has she understood him aright? Is this discussion really about the behaviour of the Dauphin? Can't the king speak to his grandson himself? 'Sire, I find myself bewildered, amazed. What can I say? As far as I'm aware, Madame la Dauphine concerns herself not a jot with politics. On the contrary, I only wish she were a little more adult in her interests.'

'Agreed,' interrupts the king. 'She is most charming, but still very childish nevertheless. She opens her mouth without thinking about the possible consequences. That's fine as long as she is in the privacy of her own quarters. But she needs to be kept in check when others are around, especially my grandson.'

'I shall speak to her, Sire. But I assure you that no one in my household says a word against your ministers, and certainly not against the Comtesse du Barry.'

The king stands up and stretches his back. 'Noailles, you know perfectly well where it all comes from,' admits Louis XV. 'We are also deeply disappointed in the conduct of *Mesdames*. It would be all to the good if Marie Antoinette saw less of my daughters; she is far too easily influenced.'

The countess nods in submission. But is it not for the king himself to bring his own daughters to task? Why does the man always skirt round his problems? It only exacerbates them. 'Once again, Sire, I am extremely sorry, but I shall address the Dauphine on the matter.'

'Excellent.' Louis XV breathes a sigh of relief. That's one more thing out of the way. 'You may go.'

'I don't believe it,' rages Marie Antoinette between her sobs. 'How humiliating! Why doesn't he dare to say things to my face?' She buries her tear-stained face in her skirt. How could anyone be so mean? Just wait till Mama hears this! What a vile country!

Having delivered the king's message to Marie Antoinette, the Comtesse de Noailles has taken a place by the door, unnoticed by the weeping Dauphine, who is overcome with mortification. If only she could just run away. Far from here, from all the scheming and treachery.

'I've told you before,' remarks the Comtesse de Noailles in a flat voice. 'You may be the Dauphine, but you cannot permit yourself to do as you please. You must adapt to the rules of the court.'

'Go away!' screeches Marie Antoinette.

'If I may be of no further service to you.' The countess leaves the room. In her heart she sympathises with the snivelling child left alone in the huge chamber. No one knows better than her *Dame d'Honneur* that Marie Antoinette lacks any real friends; that she, like everyone else, is a prisoner at Versailles. But is that not simply their fate?

For long minutes after she has gone, Marie Antoinette continues weeping. Her lapdog scampers and whines nervously round and round her feet, finally jumping up onto an armchair. Closing one eye, the little animal tries to ignore her mistress. When she has shed enough tears, Marie Antoinette gets to her feet. She is angry. In fact, she is furious. She cannot get over how unfair and cowardly it is of the king not to have spoken to her directly. He always behaves so sweetly towards her. But does he really mean it? Her blood boiling, she looks in the mirror and sees a mess. Her eyes are red and swollen with crying and her whole face smudged with rouge; she has even smeared some on her skirt.

Rushing to her privy, she slams the door behind her and locks it. Tearing off her clothes, she sits down on the commode, wearing only her chemise. Here in the tiny room with its white marble tiles she slowly comes to herself, dries her tears and thinks about what has taken place. What would Louis XIV have done in her position? Must she just passively accept these allegations? Is that what *Papa*

Roi desires of her, that she meekly bows her head under it all? But to do that would imply that the king was in the right, which is surely not true. She makes up her mind, washes her face and returns to her bedchamber. It is empty. She walks through to the next room, summons a lady of the bedchamber and then sits down at her dressing table to repair the damage.

Instructing Amélie to bring a fresh gown and corset, she redoes her face herself, applying less rouge than is the current fashion. Her complexion is still red enough as it is. 'That one,' she tells the lady of the bedchamber, indicating one of the two dresses Amélie is holding up for her inspection. Marie Antoinette opens a drawer and chooses her most beautiful earrings. 'Tighter,' she commands Amélie, who in surprise pulls again at the laces of her corset. Marie Antoinette slips lithely into the eggshell-blue gown and, as she waits impatiently for all the tiny buttons to be fastened, casts a final glance in the mirror. Then, snatching up her fan from the table, she sweeps out of the room, leaving an amazed Amélie staring after her.

'I wish to speak to my Papa,' orders Marie Antoinette. The bemused gentleman of the bedchamber to Louis XV looks respectfully up at the tall princess. 'Madame, it is not usual to disturb the king at this time of the evening. He will undoubtedly take supper with yourself and *Mesdames* later.'

Marie Antoinette looks down at the man, her eyes flashing. 'I wish to see *Papa Roi* NOW. Or shall I just walk straight through?' The gentleman of the bedchamber gasps. That would be sacrilege! 'No, no, Your Highness. A moment, please. I shall go and enquire immediately.'

Marie Antoinette taps her fan impatiently against her left upper arm. Stepping in front of a mirror, she silently rehearses what she is going to say. She decides that she can make herself look taller and more authoritative by thrusting her chin out and tipping back her head a little. Her heart is thumping. There's no way back now. How will the king react? Well, she doesn't care; her pride is too badly wounded. She is still livid, but has her rage under control.

'My child, what is the matter?' The king's voice comes from nowhere. She didn't hear him approach and is caught by surprise.

'Papa, I understand that I have displeased you. I'm very sorry and it has made me very unhappy. I don't even know if I may still call you *Papa Roi*.'

Louis XV recoils a step. What has that woman told the girl? He had intended the Comtesse de Noailles to discuss the problem with the Dauphine so that he didn't have to. Now here she is in front of him. Must he do it himself after all? He passes his hand across his mouth in discomfort, mumbling, 'I thought something dreadful must have happened.'

'Indeed, Sire, it is dreadful. It is dreadful that I must hear from someone else that I have upset you, that you are put out by Marie Antoinette, the wife of your grandson. It is most disappointing that you think my behaviour childish. That I apparently stir up the Dauphin against the ministers. That I would seem to be the source of discord, the source ...'

'Enough!' orders Louis XV. His face is flushed crimson. No one, none but Richelieu himself dare address him so – Louis XV, the Most Christian King of France.

He glances awkwardly at Marie Antoinette, avoiding her eyes. She stands proud and upright before him, Archduchess of Austria, her Habsburg lip aquiver with rage and her small bosom heaving.

'*Diable!*' thinks the king. 'She is more of a man than my own grandson!' Louis-Auguste would never take it into his head to accost his grandfather and speak to him thus. The king has badly underestimated his princess. But what now? What report will Marie Antoinette give of this in her next letter to her mother, and how will Maria Theresa respond to the incident? Damn it all! He hates confrontation. If he suspects his daughters are about to read him the riot act, he simply leaves the room and avoids them for a week or two. But this is different. He shakes his head ruefully and laughs out loud.

'My daughter, what a terrible misunderstanding. I have no idea what Madame de Noailles has told you, but it seems to have been taken quite out of context. The truth is that I hold you in very great regard and consider my grandson most lucky to have married such a wonderful woman. Of course there is gossip, but you must take no notice of it. I know that my daughters confide all sorts of things in you. But believe me, you must take it all with a pinch of salt. Truly, Madame! I have the utmost faith in you.'

He bows, grasps her hand, raises it gallantly to his lips and plants a soft kiss there, and like the many other female hearts he has stirred in the course of his long life, Marie Antoinette's too is touched by his tenderness.

'Papa,' she sobs, blinking away a tear. 'I'm so very sorry.' Her anger has melted way, but in its place is shame. Has Noailles told her the truth? Why should she lie? 'I'm truly sorry, Papa, and I shall change my ways.' The king brushes aside her apology and embraces her, happy that the situation has not escalated further. 'I'm sorry I disturbed you.'

'My sweet, you are always welcome.' He kisses her hand once more and lets her go. She is still a child, thinks Louis XV, but not for much longer. Soon she will be a grown woman, and then Louis-Auguste will have his hands more than full. That, however, will be his problem, reflects the king, fleeing with relief back up the little staircase.

Marie Antoinette makes her way back to her own apartments with mixed feelings. Who is telling her the truth? Why should Noailles make up such a story? With each step it becomes clearer to her that everyone at court turns everything to his or her own advantage. Versailles is bogged down in lies. And even *Papa Roi*, who should remain aloof from such intrigues, has fouled his hands with them.

I hope the hunt rides out tomorrow, because I'm dying to see how the king reacts to Antoinette. But since yesterday's lit de justice empowering Maupeou's parlement, things have been more unsettled than ever. Papa says there are soldiers everywhere. The situation is so dangerous, I imagine the king has more important things than hunting on his mind just now.

From the journal of the Princesse de Lamballe,
14th April 1771

5

The days are growing longer and spring is unmistakably in the air. The buds on the naked shrubs and the bare branches of the parkland trees are on the point of bursting into green. Bluebells turn the woodland floor azure, the first flush of colour as nature shrugs off winter. Birds chitter-chatter, paying court to one another and curiously inspecting last year's nest. After months shut fast, creaking sash windows are pushed up to let the fresh spring air into the stuffy corridors and stale salons of the palace.

Marie Antoinette has already been out riding a few times with her riding instructor. So different from that cramped manège. At last she can give her horse its head, share its sense of freedom as they gallop through the rustling lanes, the wind rushing in her ears. Although Marie Antoinette is trusted well enough to go where she pleases, her instructor is always close behind. François is careful; he would never forgive himself if anything should happen to the Dauphine. She seems to have her animal well under control and rides as confidently as any young fellow who has been in the saddle all his life, but François has learned over the years that accidents happen when you least expect them. Even the best riders can come off their mount, and the riding instructor breathes a sigh of relief every time they arrive back at the stables unscathed.

'However tempted you may be, make sure you never commit yourself one way or the other,' the Comte de Mercy warns the Dauphine, who seems more interested in her new riding costume. 'Whatever you do, be good enough to take no sides,' continues Mercy irritably, fearing his advice is falling on deaf ears.

Marie Antoinette swings through a semicircle, carrying her nimble tailor round with her as he finishes pinning the last seam. 'What do you think? Isn't it beautiful?' asks the Dauphine of the ambassador, letting her hands glide from her waist down over her hips. Mercy has noticed that her figure is at last beginning to acquire feminine curves. He follows her hands. 'Breeches indeed!' the ambassador remarks nervously to himself. 'I don't believe I'll be including this in any of my reports to her mother.' He is quite sure Maria Theresa would disapprove, though he has to admit to himself that the effect is most seductive.

Beneath the table her little dog growls with pleasure as it mauls a cushion to pieces. The monster! But the ambassador knows better than to mention it; there would be no point. Distracted by the orgy of destruction, Mercy shakes his head. 'Yes, certainly, Madame, most becoming,' he truthfully returns, 'but have you understood my words? Are you listening to what I have to say?'

She nods half-heartedly, caressing the soft fabric that hugs her body like a second skin. 'Mercy, I don't even know what has been going on. How would I have the slightest idea which side to choose? Oh, well then, go over it all for me again.'

It is increasingly clear to the ambassador just how dangerous the situation has become. Under no circumstances must Marie Antoinette ally herself to one side or the other. Perhaps he should simply tell her nothing. But, mentally summing up the possible consequences, Mercy quickly dismisses this option. It is precisely her ignorance that leaves her vulnerable to unwitting and unwilling involvement in some drama or other.

'All right then,' he begins decisively. 'Yesterday King Louis and Chancellor Maupeou convened a *lit de justice*, an enforced sitting of *parlement*, at which the old institutions were permanently dissolved and a new Paris *parlement* installed. The reasons behind this are somewhat complicated, but are principally concerned with the court case against the Duc d'Aiguillon. The fact that the king revoked the allegations made by *parlement* set the king above the law – although I am of the opinion that Chancellor Maupeou misused the dispute between king and *parlement* for his own gain, to bolster his own prestige. Be that as it may, the whole business turned into a sort of power struggle, with each party trying to justify its position. In the end the king applied his absolute jurisdiction – the Princes of the Blood prefer to call it abuse of power – and the Paris *parlement* was disbanded. Each member of the new government has been handpicked by Maupeou and will not turn against the king. I cannot judge the rectitude of the king's conduct, but it will certainly be easier now for him to introduce certain reforms. Whether the ex-members of *parlement* and their followers will accept this lying down, I doubt.'

'Oh, how complicated it all is. But tell me, Mercy, who is actually in the right?'

'That is a good question, Madame, but one to which I can give no good answer. That's why I advise you to arrive at no conclusions yourself. Take care to show no favouritism, and keep out of politics entirely. It's quite possible that the king will change his mind tomorrow and *parlement* will be honourably reinstated. I shouldn't even be surprised to see the return of the Duc de Choiseul.'

'Oh, but that would be fantastic!'

'Madame, I warn you, express no opinion!' replies Mercy sharply. 'Choiseul is adamantly opposed to Maupeou and d'Aiguillon. Maupeou and d'Aiguillon don't get on, but Maupeou enjoys the full support of the king and d'Aiguillon that of Madame du Barry. May I remind you once again that your position at court is not yet secured.' The ambassador points at her flat stomach.

'That is quite plain to me. But for the rest, I still can't make head or tail of it, Mercy,' confesses Marie Antoinette, allowing herself to be helped on with a waistcoat. The tailor mutters his satisfaction, stroking a pleat flat here and there. 'And what are the objections to the reforms?' she asks.

Mercy considers for a moment. Hasn't he told her enough already? Yet her question is a fair one. 'The State coffers are almost empty,' responds the ambassador, pausing again for thought. 'The ordinary people can no longer afford to pay even the level of taxes currently demanded of them. The proposed tax reforms were meant to change all that, but the aristocracy is against them. It is their privilege as the ruling classes of France to be exempt from taxation. Most understandably, they wish to defend that right.'

Marie Antoinette's brow furrows. 'I think it's a very good idea of Papa's. But why did he have to disband *parlement*? Isn't it their job to represent the people? They of all people should have backed Papa.'

'It's not as straightforward as that,' answers Mercy, searching for the right words. 'The *parlement*, despite its name, doesn't represent the people. It's more like a court of law and an enforcement agency. The magistrates are all noblemen, and I'm afraid that the majority of them put their own position above the common good.'

'Oh, I had no idea.' Marie Antoinette gives this careful consideration before putting her next question: 'Who does represent the people, then?'

Mercy can hardly control his mirth. 'To be completely honest, Madame,' he says with candour, 'no one.'

'But that's not quite true,' parries the Dauphine. 'The fact that the king disbands *parlement* and dispatches those who oppose his reforms shows that *Papa Roi* supports the people. Does it not?'

Mercy smiles. If only politics were that simple. 'Yes and no,' is his reply. 'The thing is that the people are on the side of *parlement*. What is more, everyone assumes that it is not the king but *la favorite* who makes all the political decisions. That's why it is so dangerous to take sides. If you support the king, you also support Madame du Barry and are against *parlement* and the people. Public opinion will then turn against you. If you support the Princes of the Blood, you are against the king.'

Marie Antoinette gives the ambassador a horrified look. 'How dreadfully complicated it all is. Surely it can't be true that the king does whatever that awful person tells him to do?'

Mercy shrugs his shoulders. 'You understand my concerns. Do

not allow yourself to be won over by anyone. Smile and remain silent.'

She turns sideways on to the mirror and examines her silhouette. Not yet happy with what she sees, she whispers something to her tailor, who meticulously re-pins the fabric around her bust. The deep décolletage and the cut of the neckline now thrust her breasts pertly upward and outward. She giggles. 'That's more like it,' she compliments the tailor.

'What is actually the purpose of this costume?' enquires the bemused Mercy; Carnival is over, after all.

'Do you like it?' asks Marie Antoinette, head on one side and hands planted in a manly pose upon her hips. Mercy doesn't know what to make of this charade. 'On what occasion do you plan to wear it?'

She taps her tailor lightly on the arm and points to the corner of the room. The man goes off without a word, returning with a flamboyant chapeau. With a flourish she sets it on her head, one hand stroking the enormous plume. 'There!' she cries in triumph. 'I should really have my boots on too, but *voilà*!'

Mercy smiles and runs his tongue over his lips. Dressed as a man, the lass has turned herself into a most seductive lady. 'You look like a musketeer,' is his dry comment.

'Very good, Mercy. Yes, that sounds fine.' She bursts out laughing again and sweeps off her hat. 'I'm intrigued to know what the king will think of it.'

'The king?' Mercy asks suspiciously.

'Yes, tomorrow I'm going to hunt with him for the first time, and I couldn't be better dressed for the occasion.'

Mercy feels his blood run cold. What is she up to now? 'To hunt, you say?' It begins to dawn on him what the purpose of the riding habit might be. 'You are surely not planning to ride to hounds?'

'I most certainly am, Mercy. Do you think the king will admire me?' This is one question Mercy does not have to think twice over. The king would admire any woman looking like that. But what is the aim of it all?

'Would your mother would approve of this, do you think?' Comte de Mercy resumes cautiously.

'Oh yes, I'm sure she would. Mama desires me to stay on good terms with the king and to spend more time with the Dauphin. Well, Mercy, I'm adapting myself entirely to her wishes. It will be a great pleasure to her, don't you agree? For the need to adapt, my dear Mercy, is precisely what you and mother are constantly trying to din into me.'

'That was most pleasant,' the king compliments Marie Antoinette, his eyes running hungrily for the hundredth time today over the Dauphine's trim little frame. Blushing, she gives him a dainty nod of the head and glances stealthily at Louis-Auguste. It works! thinks Marie Antoinette, thrilled. The Dauphin has even exchanged a few words with her this morning, and has spent most of the time riding beside her. Not that he paid much attention to her cleavage; he left that to *Papa Roi*. Louis-Auguste is more impressed with his wife's stamina in riding out the whole hunt. She seems entirely unaffected by the exhausting gallop and here she is at the end of the morning, still sitting fresh as a daisy in the saddle. Just like a man.

For Marie Antoinette has even spurned the traditional ladies' saddle. Her breeches are not just for show! The comments of the other riders this morning did not escape the ears of the princess. All the usual criticism: 'Shouldn't be allowed.' 'She's riding like a man.' 'Look at her costume, scandalous!' But the noblemen's glances spoke louder than their words, especially when she pouted so charmingly at them. Scandalous, indeed! But in the meanwhile they rode as close as possible, or as the king allowed, for Louis XV was not to be dislodged from her side. There was little game bagged that morning; too much distraction.

Marie Antoinette slips nimbly from the saddle and brushes a damp strand of hair from her face. Ignoring her aching legs and buttocks, she walks with a smile and swaying hips through the portico, under the stare of Louis XV. This morning's ride has taken at least ten years off him. As the stable lads lead their sovereign's horse away, he leaps up the stairs two at a time. Where is du Barry?

Marie Antoinette throws herself on the bed without taking off her muddy boots, and nervously unfolds the pages. Every time Mercy delivers a letter from Mama, it eclipses the rest of the world for her. Her correspondence with her mother is like an umbilical cord tying her to home. But, despite her excitement, few of the letters bring a smile to the princess's lips. As usual, Maria Theresa vehemently insists on the need for an heir. Her daughter skims over these passages. Has Mama any news for her? With her finger, Marie Antoinette traces each line entrusted to paper in her beloved Vienna.

'My dear daughter, I should be very much obliged if you could write to me regarding your first impression of your new sister-in-law. I understand she will give you no cause for jealousy. It seems that her figure is not good, she is shy and lacks any great charm ...'

Marie Antoinette is keen to meet the Comte de Provence's bride. Will she be pretty and so distract the king from herself? Will his new granddaughter be quick to present the king with a grandson? The Dauphine shudders at the thought. Marie Antoinette is well aware that, as the wedding approaches, the mood among the Barriens is growing more optimistic by the day. Impatiently she reads on. Oh, what a misery Mama can be! How does she know what's going on at Versailles? With a sinking heart the princess folds away the epistle. All those reprimands, the endless scolding ... after all, she is no longer a child. With a sad sigh Marie Antoinette stows the letter away in her writing table, making sure the drawer is firmly locked. For, although she keeps all her mother's letters carefully under lock and key, she is still not fully convinced of their security. True, she has never caught anyone red-handed, but she often has the impression that someone has been rummaging among her things.

'I wish to bathe,' she tells her lady of the bedchamber, unbuttoning her mud-spattered waistcoat.

What a nonsense, thinks the maid, filling the tub with warm water. 'Typical Austrian! Fancy taking two baths in one week!

How exciting! In a couple of days I'll be meeting my niece again. Who would ever have thought she would marry the brother of the Dauphin? It's nearly five years since I saw Joséphine. The last time she was still a child. She never made much impression on me, but she's probably changed.

From the journal of the Princesse de Lamballe,
12th May 1771

6

Her handkerchief screwed into a tight ball in her hand, the Comtesse de Noailles tries to control her tears. She is sitting red-eyed and quite alone in the carriage. The empty place beside her is the reason for her grief. At any moment the train of coaches will set off on the first stage of its mission to remove the royal family and all their court to Fontainebleau. The grooms are slamming the coach doors; dogs are barking and running left, right and centre in their excitement; the horses are champing at the bit and stamping their hooves impatiently on the cobblestones. Despite the coachman's familiar, soothing words, they sense that the great cavalcade is about to depart and the thrill is too much for the noble beasts.

The king and his entourage are approaching at a trot. As usual, he plans to ride to Fontainebleau. He pauses a moment beside the carriage carrying Madame du Barry, who has already stuck her head gaily out of the window and greets her lover as if they have been apart for years. The king trots on, straight past the coach in which his daughters sit knitting. Drawing level with the next carriage, he leans forward to peer in through the open window. 'Ah, bridegroom!' he shouts cheerfully at the occupant, 'Good and ready, are you?'

His grandson, the Comte de Provence, smiles nervously back. Not usually tongue-tied, today he is stuck for words. His brothers Louis-Auguste and Artois are both in the saddle, riding behind the king, but the Comte de Provence prefers to recline comfortably against the carriage's well-padded upholstery of studded morocco leather. His congenital hip problem makes riding a painful pastime, but lack of exercise and overeating are beginning to turn Louis-Stanislas Xavier into the image of his grandfather August III, the late King of Poland.

The king trots alongside the leading coach. Where is his granddaughter's warm smile? Marie Antoinette usually leans half out of the carriage to greet him. A little disappointed, Louis XV looks in, only to be confronted with the tear-stained face of the Comtesse de Noailles.

Shocked to see him, she stammers, 'I'm so sorry, Sire.'

'Where is the Dauphine?' demands the king gruffly.

'It's not my fault, Sire. It was impossible for me to dissuade her. I ...' Marie Antoinette's *Dame d'Honneur* covers her sobs with her handkerchief.

This show of female emotion only annoys him further. 'Speak up, Noailles, what's going on?'

Before the countess has time to answer, he hears a horse cantering up behind him to the applause of onlookers. The King of France turns, his features melting. Hurrying towards him is the familiar sweet smile beneath a broad-brimmed, plumed hat.

'Mon cher Papa,' calls out Marie Antoinette with warm affection, drawing up beside him. Nodding, Louis XV sees the reason for Noailles's tears. It is, of course, completely unfitting that his granddaughter should choose to ride to Fontainebleau. But what of it? A single glance shows *Papa Roi* that the princess is looking a picture again today, and he follows the example of the rest of the entourage, clapping softly. The Comtesse de Noailles blows her nose. What is the world coming to, when the king himself breaches protocol?

Two coaches behind, the blind is jealously tugged down. Madame du Barry rams her back against the cushions and grinds her teeth. This is the first time she has seen *la petite rousse* done up like that. What can the child be thinking of?

Louis-Auguste, surprised at the universally friendly reception accorded to Marie Antoinette, smiles broadly and spurs on his horse. 'And a good morning to you, my Dauphine,' he says, so cheerily that even the king looks amazed. Marie Antoinette returns his smile, cooing, 'Oh, what a gorgeous day for a ride. If it stays like this the wedding will be an unforgettable occasion.'

Louis XV is feeling better by the moment. It is indeed a wonderful day, and tomorrow the Comte de Provence is to be married; all in all, a welcome enough distraction. These last months have been tense, but despite the protests it looks as though Maupeou will get his reforms through unhindered. Now for the wedding! Perhaps this grandson will prove capable of getting his wife with child. Yet, witnessing the heartfelt way the Dauphin has just greeted his wife, Louis XV feels his hopes rekindling. Might the boy be waking up at last?

Spurring his horse forward, the king orders the couple to ride with him. Holding his reins in one hand, Louis XV waves to the master of the hounds to start the procession of carriages. At the sound of the horn the last attendants leap up onto the boxes and the colourful caravan gets underway.

'I should much appreciate your taking a seat in the carriage tomorrow when we ride to meet Provence's bride,' says the king to Marie Antoinette, in a voice low enough to prevent any eavesdroppers from hearing. His tone forbids any further discussion on the subject. The king turns about in the saddle, not to ensure that the coaches are following in his wake, for that is undoubtedly so, but more in frustration at their sluggish pace. He tightens his girth further and asks Louis-Auguste and Marie Antoinette to do the same. A boyish, mischievous smile flits across the face of the sixty-one-year-old monarch as he looks first at his grandson and then at his granddaughter-in-law, raising his eyebrows towards the horizon.

The three set off almost simultaneously at a mad gallop, scattering clods of earth on every side and soon disappearing from view. The other riders are left staring at their trail as it passes over the next hill, until the sound of their monarch's voice reaches their ears ... '*Tya-Hillaut!!*'

The Comtesse du Barry is angry as much as worried. The fact that the Dauphine thinks she can turn a few men's heads doesn't really bother her. But she is shocked at the way her lover has fallen under the spell of a mere child. It pained her to see with her own eyes how Louis XV devoured Marie Antoinette with his. And the way he careered off just now like a young tearaway! It only proves that the old man is showing off in front of his granddaughter. He needs to watch out or he'll break his neck. What a stupid risk for a king to take just before the wedding!

Meanwhile, her carriage lurches on its way towards Fontainebleau. The future wife of Louis-Stanislas Xavier is causing Jeanne du Barry more concern than she had reckoned on. What if the bride is a ravishing beauty? That would give her something else to worry about. The Dauphine has been enjoying a lot more of her grandfather's attention lately. Before his mistress knows it, Louis XV will be spending all his time with his granddaughter. And imagine what might happen if the princess from Piedmont turned out to have a character like Marie Antoinette's! Du Barry would have to fight on two fronts. The future Queen of France has not yet acknowledged her presence in public. If she has to contend with the new bride turning against her too, she will soon find herself a standing joke at court, and surely she doesn't deserve that.

For tomorrow, though, nothing has been left to chance. Nothing can go wrong. Louis XV has given her the privilege of organising the whole wedding. She has gone through every detail with the Duc de Richelieu and the master of ceremonies: the fireworks, the choice of artistes and music. She has even chosen the jewels to be presented to the bride by the king: superb gems, but not to be compared with those she herself will be wearing. Oh yes, she will glitter, literally, in her newest gown, set off by the most brilliant precious stones. Jeanne du Barry has made sure that, however lovely the princess may be, her beauty will be as nothing beside her own. The Most Christian King of France must, after all, be confirmed in his belief that his mistress is the one and only belle of the ball. Yet, although she knows she has left nothing to chance, her faith in her arrangements becomes more and more shaky with the rocking of the carriage.

Louis-Stanislas Xavier, Comte de Provence, brushes an imaginary bit of fluff from his silk waistcoat. It isn't particularly warm this May morning, yet the bridegroom's forehead is beaded with sweat. Every step the horses take brings him closer to his future wife, and there is no way back. There never has been, for it is the king who has decided whom he would wed, just as he had done for his elder brother. Louis-Stanislas has never set eyes on the daughter of the King of Savoy. A portrait is all he has been allowed to see of Marie Joséphine, and that was very promising: dark eyes and black hair. But the Comte de Provence has seen enough portraits by now to know how painters can flatter their sitters. He inserts a finger between his neck and cravat in an attempt to loosen it, irritated to find that this morning it has been tied far too tight.

'Don't you worry, my boy,' laughs the king, who is sitting next to him. He gives his grandson a slap on the knee. 'I wish I were in your shoes. Ah yes, I remember it well. I was all of fifteen years old when I married your grandmother, here in the very same chapel at Fontainebleau. My God, what a time ago that seems!' The king sighs and thinks back on his wedding, some forty-six years ago. He had fallen in love at first sight with his Polish princess, almost seven years his senior. Theirs had been an instant and mutual attraction, very unusual in a marriage arranged purely for strategic reasons. 'Oh, what a night that was,' reminisces Louis XV, well remembering how they made passionate love into the small hours of the morning, their ardour hardly cooling over the following nights. 'She gave me five children in as many years,' murmurs Louis XV to himself, and falls silent, gazing at the centuries-old trees lining their route. 'They stood here back then too,' he muses sadly. He is assailed by old memories.

The twins Elisabeth and Henriette were his first-born daughters. He can hardly recall their faces; they have both been dead so long. Then there was Louise, who never even reached the age of five. He can still remember her voice. Only she could whisper 'Papa' with so much affection. Ah, and Thérèse – was she seven or eight when she began to sicken? He's no longer sure; it was so long ago. At her fourth confinement his wife presented him with Louis, the father of his grandsons. Oh, how great was his joy at the birth of that first son, the Dauphin. But his second son didn't live to see his fourth birthday, and all that survive now are four manipulative daughters and a handful of grandchildren, the eldest of whom still hasn't learned how to get his wife with child. Louis XV has barely had time to work himself up into a really bad mood about it all when the carriage jolts to a halt, banishing the ghosts of the past. Life goes on!

It is the perfect spot for a first encounter. The avenue is more than broad enough to draw alongside, but the two caravans of coaches have stopped a respectable distance apart. From above comes a crescendo of excited twittering from birds witnessing the events taking place below. The grooms open the doors of the coach and the king steps down, followed by Louis-Auguste and then his brother, the bridegroom. The king straightens his back and inhales a deep lungful of fresh spring air. Family and courtiers are ranged behind Louis XV, all gazing expectantly towards where the contingent from Turin are assembled a little further down the avenue. The two parties shuffle cautiously towards one another, respectfully but apparently not without suspicion.

A small figure then separates itself from the Italian group and walks hesitantly towards the French king. As the bride nears, Louis XV runs an experienced eye over the princess from Piedmont. He manages to retain his smile, but it is fast losing all spontaneity. With every step she takes, Marie Joséphine, daughter of Victor Amadeus III, King of Savoy, makes it plainer to the French king that his new granddaughter will not be joining the ranks of Versailles's most beautiful princesses.

Princess Marie Josephine moves without the slightest grace, a quality which might have compensated for her very mediocre figure. Her face, accentuated by heavy eyebrows and a long but broad nose, is almost expressionless. For courtesy's sake, Louis XV embraces the princess. But not for long – her breath is so bad that he lets her go after a second or two and, making no further effort to engage her in real conversation, leads her towards his grandson. The Comte de Provence smiles a bloodless smile. The king takes another relieved step backwards, as do Madame du Barry and Marie Antoinette. Unbeknown to each other, both women are mightily relieved to discover that the bride from Savoy will pose no challenge to their own position.

Her self-confidence quite restored, the Comtesse du Barry laughs merrily and begins chatting unrestrainedly with everyone in her vicinity. Marie Antoinette feels all the tension draining from her and could almost shout for joy. But she has learned to behave properly by now, so instead, with a warm smile and sweet words, she courteously bids her new sister-in-law welcome.

Louis XV feels a burden drop from his shoulders. Etiquette demands that he share a carriage with his grandson and the bride as they continue to Fontainebleau, but he cannot face it and graciously hands the pair into the coach, personally shutting the door behind them. For a moment the king debates with himself whether to join the Dauphin and Dauphine in their carriage. But with protocol already having been thrown to the winds, he decides he may as well be hung for a sheep as a lamb, and heads instead for du Barry's carriage. Next to her sits an old friend of the king, the aged but still vigorous Duc de Richelieu, with his nephew the Duc d'Aiguillon. The latter, surprised, shuffles along the seat to make room for his monarch.

'My poor grandson,' Louis XV sighs in sympathy. 'He has my permission to imbibe some courage this evening.' He winks at each of the men in turn and they all roar with laughter.

Snug as a she-cat on heat, Jeanne du Barry curls up close to her lover. 'You see,' she tells herself contentedly, 'nothing can go wrong today.'

I arrived safely this afternoon at the Hôtel de Toulouse. It's beautiful weather for the city, and I've seen no sign of any unrest. Louise is coming in a minute to take supper with me. She grabs any opportunity she can to escape the Palais Royal. Her marriage with the Duc de Chartres brings her no joy. But what marriage does?

From the journal of the Princesse de Lamballe,
17th May 1771

7

After the gargantuan wedding feast, life is returning to normal at the court of Versailles. For days, people could not stop talking about how impressive the spectacular firework display had been. Ambassadors and foreign guests were amazed by the lavishness of the festivities, which had seemed more like the wedding celebrations for a crown prince – an opinion frankly shared by Joseph-Marie Terray, the Minister of Finance. He is not at all sure where he will find the money to pay all the bills. A more modest nuptial ceremony with fewer frills would have been more fitting. 'But,' the king had assured his minister, 'such a wedding takes place but once.' Terray did not have the nerve to contradict Louis XV.

As always, the Minister of Finance is scrimping and saving, making the best of the resources available to him. But he feels like a drowning man; it is more and more difficult to keep his head above water. The interest on the debts is huge, and for the time being new loans offer the only relief. Those who shout loudest get paid first. The same goes for the court personnel, who have been patiently waiting for months for their wages. Servant, cook and stableman watched the fire-spewing fountains with a mixture of delight and frustration; as each explosion of sparks outdid the last in magnificence, so every rocket screamed of more delay to their pay. When would they get their money at last? There is plenty of whingeing behind the scenes, but nobody dare ask the king to his face.

In the meantime, the intrigue, gossip and eternal whispering continue regardless. The talk at the moment is of the Comte de Provence and his new wife. How long before the young bride falls pregnant? Any delay will not be down to Louis-Stanislas. In the aftermath of the wedding night, everyone had to hear from the Comte de Provence how the Savoy princess had brought him to climax four times. It pained Marie Antoinette to hear this. Should she have taken more initiative on her own honeymoon night? The Dauphin's response to his brother's triumphant exhibitionism was cool. He knew him better. And indeed, it was not long before gossip began to circulate regarding the new bridegroom's performance.

'You were right,' Marie Antoinette tells her husband excitedly. 'Marie Joséphine told me personally this morning that your brother has never once laid a finger on her.' Louis-Auguste looks up for a moment from his book. 'Typical of Tartuffe,' he says, using his own derisive nickname for his brother, 'to imagine people believed him, too.' The Dauphin carries on reading.

Marie Antoinette shakes her head. What is the matter with the boys? Perhaps they suffer from some abnormality, or an illness? Louise-Auguste often complains of feeling sick, but in her opinion that's because he eats so much. Unbelievable what he can put away. It's no wonder he has trouble with his stomach. But it's a shame he uses his regular bouts of sickness as an excuse not to sleep with her. Louis-Auguste keeps promising to pay her a nocturnal visit soon, but she has pretty well given up hope of that by now. How often has he given his word? Yet up to now the Dauphin has never made any real effort to consummate their marriage. The only difference between him and the Comte de Provence is that the Dauphin doesn't brag about his prowess.

It's a pity he has no mother now, thinks Marie Antoinette. A mother like Mama, who goes on and on endlessly about the lack of an heir. She wonders how much the king worries about it all. As things are, Louis XV is as sweet to her as ever, and it's plain that after Madame du Barry she is still the king's favourite. The unbeautiful Marie Joséphine, Comtesse de Provence, will never take the Dauphine's place in his affections. But Marie Antoinette does have cause for concern regarding her sister-in-law's interests.

A cartload of books has arrived. Servants puff up and down, filling the shelves of the huge bookcases in the young couple's new apartment. The Comtesse de Provence is a well-read woman, and remarkably enough this seems to appeal to Louis XV. At least, Marie Antoinette is amazed to see the king walking along the shelves, attentively scanning her sister-in-law's collection, his fingers gliding softly over the beautifully worked spines of publications covering every subject under the sun. The Dauphine has seen how he quietly removes a volume from the shelf now and then, leafs through it at his leisure and then replaces the book with a confidential smile and approving nod at his new granddaughter. It comes as a surprise to Marie Antoinette that the king takes an interest in such things.

Even more surprised is the Comtesse de Noailles when she receives instructions from the Dauphine to create a library out of the old artist's studio that once belonged to the dead queen. But what does the Dauphine, who has hardly opened a book in her life, understand by a library? The next morning a carpenter is set to work, and in no time at all the long wall of the room is lined with a rudimentary bookcase. That should do for someone who hardly knows the inside of a book from its covers, thinks the countess. But here Madame l'Etiquette is sorely mistaken.

'What is this?' demands Marie Antoinette, clearly irritated and unimpressed by the empty planks, devoid of any decoration. It looks to her like pretty rough and ready handiwork.

'Your library, Madame,' snaps Noailles. Actually, she had hoped that the Dauphine would have forgotten the whole idea by now.

'It reminds me of the saddle room, though I must say this is a sorrier sight. Who in heaven's name did you get to knock it together?'

The Comtesse de Noailles feels an upsurge of the old familiar ire, but as usual controls it. 'One of the joiners,' she curtly replies. Marie Antoinette turns on her. 'Joiners!' she bawls. 'I asked you to build me a library. This is a chicken coop! Do you think this fit for the future Queen of France? It's a travesty, Noailles. A travesty! I am not satisfied. Have it dismantled immediately, and send me Gabriel, the architect. I shall arrange it myself.' With a wave of the hand she dismisses her *Dame d'Honneur*, casting a final disdainful glance at the botched job.

Marie Antoinette surveys the sketches Ange-Jacques Gabriel has made for her. She is content; he has incorporated all her ideas. At least this man understands me, she reflects.

'What do you think, Vermond?' the Dauphine asks the priest. 'It's absolutely beautiful,' he responds in all honesty. 'The detailing particularly appeals to me,' he adds, indicating the handles and keys embellished with the two-headed eagle, emblem of the House of Habsburg.

Marie Antoinette smiles. 'Very good, Gabriel. I should like to have use of it as soon as possible. When can you have it ready?'

The architect carefully calculates the work involved and promises to have it completed before autumn. The Dauphine looks crestfallen. 'I shall do my utmost, Your Highness,' Gabriel responds, the full weight of his experience behind his words. Like his father before him, Ange-Jacques Gabriel is *Premier Architecte* to the palace. Almost without exception, his clients change their minds halfway through a project and demand that all their new ideas be embedded in the original design. It wouldn't be the first time if he had to start all over again and found himself, years later, still working on the same job. But Marie Antoinette knows her mind and makes no changes to his drawings. She is confident that she has found a new way to delight the king.

In his private apartment, far removed from courtiers and power struggles, Louis XV can be himself. France is sweltering in the height of summer. The afternoons are too hot for hunting, and the sovereign takes this time to be alone. But not entirely, for Jeanne du Barry lies naked beside him, running her fingers softly over her beloved's chest. His eyes are closed and his quiet breathing suggests sleep. But the smile on his lips betrays the after-effects of the supreme moment he has just enjoyed. Du Barry revels in her triumph. She has not lost the art of surprise in love, and despite his age he knows how to please her too. She enjoys his body, slim, muscular and showing hardly a wrinkle. His hair is growing greyer, which only adds to his majestic appearance. She loves her king truly and with all her heart. Nestling closer, she licks the salt sweat from his chest, and he murmurs something inaudible as he descends into a deep slumber.

Louis XV counts the slow chimes of the church bell: four o'clock. He sits up, yawns deeply and rubs the sleep out of his eyes. The worst heat of the day is over, and the intermittent breeze wafting in through the open windows feels almost cool. His mistress lies prone beside him, deep in dreamland, her golden curls half obscuring her face. Tenderly he brushes aside her dishevelled locks and admires her sweet features, her slightly open mouth with its infinitesimally curled upper lip. Her sleeping face is that of an innocent young girl. The king smiles to himself. Innocent? She's the best mistress he has ever had, and he doubts he will ever tire of her. She gives him the illusion of eternal youth and, despite his doctors' advice to take things more gently, is the best medicine against the occasional minor complaint.

Stroking her cheek gently with his finger, he considers whether to wake her. The sheet half draping her back and provocative buttocks seems to be encouraging him in that direction. He knows that he has only to allow his hand to glide down over her shoulders, slowly descend to where the skin grows softer, downy as a ripe peach, and he is lost. Tonight, he resolves, and gets out of bed. He dresses slowly.

Nobody can see him as he stands looking down from the window; only the swallows that nest in the guttering, screeching on the wing. As always, people are hurrying about their business, both familiar and unfamiliar faces: scroungers, tourists and a handful of noblemen up from the provinces to ask a favour of their king – the usual uneventful afternoon. As he puts on his cravat he hears Jeanne du Barry yawn behind him and, turning, looks into the sleepy eyes of his beloved. She laughs and stretches out her hand to him. 'This evening, my darling.'

'Mmm,' she groans softly in protest.

'You'll be the death of me,' he teases.

'Oh, don't say that,' she croons. 'You know it makes me unhappy.'

Louis XV takes her hand and kisses it. 'I think you are the happiest woman on earth. Aren't you?' She sits up, crossing her arms over her breasts and staring up at the ceiling with a frown. 'Aren't you?' repeats the king, resting one knee on the bed and tickling her. 'What more could you desire from the King of France?' he mocks, knowing that her wardrobe is full to bursting with the most gorgeous gowns, embroidered with the whitest of pearls and encrusted with diamonds. Her jewellery collection already represents a considerable capital investment, yet almost every day the king showers her anew with precious gifts. She has almost everything her heart desires. Almost, for there is one thing the king is apparently incapable of giving her. She looks at him without speaking.

'Oh no,' answers Louis XV emphatically. 'I have tried, but marriage is not possible.'

She shakes her head. 'I know that, but there is something else. I will stay with you until your dying day, if that is what you wish. I don't need to be a queen for that. But there is one other thing that would make me truly content.'

Sensing where the conversation is heading, the king swiftly pulls his shoes on. 'You would find at your side an entirely happy woman were the court to respect my place here.' Louis XV sighs. He doesn't understand either why his daughters despise du Barry. He's a widower, after all, so what is all the fuss about? The worst of it is that their prejudices are contagious. It's especially sad to see Marie Antoinette so completely under the influence of *Mesdames* that she now shares their aversion to du Barry. The king knows his mistress has become the focus of gossip, but he's the last person who dare mention it. His whole life has been one sustained attempt to avoid conflict, especially within his own family.

'It would make me the happiest woman in the world if the Dauphine were to give me a kind word. I've done nothing to hurt her, after all, have I?' asks the countess, with a sob that guarantees her lover's prompt retreat.

'I'll come back to that,' he patters, but his *maîtresse en titre* has heard it all before. It is high time she took the initiative herself, for left to the king nothing will ever change.

Weeks pass before Madame du Barry sees an opportunity to further her ambition. The court has withdrawn to Louis XV's hunting lodge at Compiègne for its summer retreat. A rota has been arranged so that people can take turns to hunt without getting under one another's feet; there are so many people down this year. Etiquette is less strictly adhered to here than at Versailles, giving Jeanne du Barry a chance to work out her plan. She fully appreciates that it is as impossible for her to address the Dauphine directly as it is to expect Louis XV to instruct Marie Antoinette to treat her with respect from now on. But among the guests at Compiègne she has met the Comte de Mercy-Argenteau for the first time.

At first she did not realise who he was, this man who blended so unobtrusively into the crowd. But his easy manner with the Dauphine did not escape her, and everything fell into place the moment she heard that the Comte de Mercy was the Austrian ambassador.

The same evening she unfolds her plan to Louis XV. He carries on silently picking the last bits of meat from a bone. Only when he is finally wiping his fingers on the tablecloth does he turn to look at her. Full of nervous anticipation, *la favourite* awaits his reply. 'Women are dangerous when they get involved in politics,' he dryly remarks, sipping a fruity burgundy.

'Politics, Monsieur? Moi?'

With a regal wave of his hand, Louis XV brushes the subject

from the table. Du Barry dons her best pout to register her protest, eliciting a chuckle from Louis XV.

'Go on then. But if it all goes wrong, the king knows nothing about it!' She throws her arms around his neck in gratitude and whispers sweet nothings in his ear – which he finds a great deal more to his liking.

Today was lovely, although the hunt was rather chaotic. We had a collision with the Comte de Pontargis's carriage. Luckily, no one was hurt. The Comte looked furious but dared not say anything to us, even though his coach was very badly damaged. Antoinette thought it was hilarious. Tomorrow will be even more hectic. Where on earth are all those guests to sleep?

From the journal of the Princesse de Lamballe,
27th July 1771

8

It is the morning of Sunday 28th July, and final preparations are underway for the *Grand Couvert*, the public dinner. In addition to the royal family, many foreign guests will be present: ambassadors, of course, but also distinguished members of the aristocracy, *Cordons Bleus* or Knights of the Holy Ghost, and eminent clerics. Conspicuous by their absence will be the Princes of the Blood. This special Sunday dinner is in honour of the newly married couple, and the Comtesse de Valentinois, the bride's lady of the bedchamber and close confidante of Madame du Barry, has effortlessly managed to extend an invitation to the Austrian ambassador.

The Comte de Mercy wends his usual easy way through the busily chattering crowd, picking up snippets of conversation – as usual, hardly ever worth listening to. 'Your Excellency.' He at once recognises the voice of the Duc d'Aiguillon, Minister for Foreign Affairs, someone whom he neither could nor should ignore. The Comte de Mercy turns in friendly surprise and with perfect ambassadorial courtesy returns the minister's salutation. He is introduced one by one to the ladies in the Comte de Provence's entourage, greeting the women cordially, each according to protocol, until he comes to Madame du Barry. Up to now he has always managed tactically to avoid meeting her.

'I've heard so much about you,' purrs the *maîtresse en titre* enthusiastically.

'Madame,' smiles the ambassador with a neutral nod.

'How is it possible that we have never met before?' Madame du Barry babbles happily on. Mercy makes a gesture of helplessness: how indeed? He instinctively feels on his guard, uncertain whether this meeting is coincidental or contrived. He inclines to the latter view, for as she talks the king's mistress is already shielding him with her body from the remainder of the group. Extremely impolite. And when Mercy notices the Duc d'Aiguillon watching him out of the corner of his eye once too often, the game is up – although he cannot yet guess the motive behind this conversation, confined as it is to trivialities.

As always, Mercy gives highly polished answers to each remark, asking his own inconsequential questions every now and then, to which the lady replies readily and with evident pleasure. The point of it all continues to elude Mercy, until d'Aiguillon rejoins the discussion. Or rather interrupts it, for the minister lays his hand confidentially on the ambassador's shoulder and whispers in his ear: 'The king would like a private word with you.'

'But of course,' replies the ambassador softly. 'Where and when?'

To Mercy's discomfort, the Duc d'Aiguillon glances around like a conspirator, a precaution that apparently comes quite naturally to him. 'The day after tomorrow, after the hunt, in Madame du Barry's apartment.'

Mercy frowns: why not in the State apartments? 'Is that a good idea?' the ambassador queries with care.

The Duc d'Aiguillon stares back at him in amazement, and then breaks into a smile. 'Ah, it is not what you think. The truth is that the king's apartment is not suited to receiving visitors. And Madame receives many guests in her apartment. You must know that over recent days the ambassadors of Holland, Sardinia, England and even Venice have requested the honour of such a visit to the Comtesse. Regard it as a mark of recognition of your personal standing and of France's relations with your country. Consider: it is the king's wish that you be received there.'

Mercy nods his head. All is plain to him. 'I go where your king desires.'

D'Aiguillon claps the ambassador contentedly on the shoulder and takes his leave. At the same moment, the Comtesse du Barry extracts herself from the group she has been conversing with and, having nodded a polite goodbye to the ambassador, leaves the room arm in arm with the minister. Without moving his head, the Comte de Mercy swiftly takes in his surroundings. Is he being watched? Having reassured himself, he casts around for a safe route whereby he can get away without being stopped and talked to. Having found it, he makes a dignified exit and goes outside to mull over the remarkable request that has just been made of him.

For a start, he is affronted to hear that there are ambassadors who wish to visit Madame du Barry, and in her own apartment, of all places. Such indecent curiosity regarding the *maîtresse en titre* really should be far beneath their dignity! But, now that he has met her for the first time, he has to admit that she hasn't made a bad impression upon him. Perhaps she is no intellectual, but in this she differs not at all from the other women parading themselves around here, all decked out in finery from top to tail but entirely empty-headed. She's well spoken, if a little unsophisticated at times. But she moves gracefully and behaves in every way as might be expected of a genuine Comtesse.

La Barry is extremely attractive, and Mercy can easily understand what the king sees in her. But why this invitation? What lies behind it? The ambassador, now strolling in the shadow of an enormous oak tree, has an uncomfortable premonition. The only reason he can think of is Poland. Damn it! Could the king have got wind of that? Negotiations between Russia, Prussia and Austria over the partition of Poland are still at a very early stage, and highly confidential. The Comte de Mercy knows the French king has an extensive network of spies. They are active even at Versailles, where all the post is censored. But Mercy entrusts nothing to paper unless he knows it will be delivered to the addressee in person by an Austrian courier. Naturally, if Louis XV is aware of the Polish plans, he has every reason to be furious with Austria and, of course, her ambassador. But how could he know?

Mercy feverishly traces all the possible consequences. If the king is aware of the situation, what might be the outcome for

Madame la Dauphine? He cannot bear to think of it. It cannot be. After all, were this the case, the King of France would surely have summoned him immediately. The manner of this approach doesn't rhyme with a crisis situation. On the other hand, Louis XV hates conflict and avoids all confrontation. But who, then, has informed him about the Polish question?

The Comte de Mercy is back among the diners and drinkers, with his ears pricked and more than ever on his guard. Each time he sees flushed faces, heads bent together in conversation, he slips alongside and casually loiters long enough to pick up what they are talking about. But it is always some other subject, mostly the radical reforms being put forward by Maupeou. 'Tyranny', 'despotism' and 'abuse of power' are the catchwords of the day. 'Poland' is on no one's lips.

The next morning the hunt gathers and sets off again, waved out by those who are staying behind. The Comte de Mercy, who has had a sleepless night, sees how Marie Antoinette rides out with the Dauphin, full of bravado. 'It's just as well her mother can't see her like this,' thinks the ambassador with amusement. But never mind, yesterday's accident could have been a great deal worse.

'What a beautiful day!' The sultry tones of the Comtesse du Barry catch the ambassador unawares.

'Madame,' he cordially returns her greeting.

Her smile reveals a perfect set of teeth, a privilege in a woman of her age. 'I much enjoyed making your acquaintance yesterday, Your Excellency,' Jeanne du Barry tells him candidly. 'It's just as if I've known you for years, and I anticipate with pleasure our next encounter.'

'Most kind of you, Madame. The king wishes to receive me tomorrow. In your apartment, so we shall probably meet again sooner than you had expected.'

'Oh, that will be wonderful,' she replies warmly, laying her hand briefly and furtively upon his chest and giving him an intense, cornflower-blue stare. 'I look forward to it,' she whispers with her sweetest smile. She moves away, leaving the Comte de Mercy, who was not born yesterday, blushing slightly. Like Circe, just by speaking to him she has left him as good as spellbound. It is a couple of seconds before Mercy recovers his clear head. One thing is certain: unless he is very much mistaken, the interview with the king cannot be about Poland.

The air hangs heavy in the apartment, although all the windows stand wide open. The sun is sinking behind the ring of trees, and inside dusk has already fallen. The Duc d'Aiguillon bids the Comte de Mercy a warm welcome and leads him into Madame du Barry's presence. 'The king is still getting dressed,' apologises the minister. 'His Majesty will arrive at any moment.' A number of men stand talking to the *maîtresse en titre*, but on catching sight of the Austrian ambassador she excuses herself and greets the Comte de Mercy like an old friend. Dressed in a simple, almost transparent white gown, she looks like a Greek goddess.

D'Aiguillon has unobtrusively escorted everyone else from the room, leaving the ambassador and his hostess alone. Du Barry takes her place on the sofa and softly pats the cushion next to her, inviting him to come and sit there.

The dress suits her very well, which puts the Comte de Mercy ill at ease. The salon is full of armchairs and sofas. It's surely not proper for him to sit right next to her. But neither does he wish to offend the king's mistress. Certainly not until he knows what the king wishes to discuss with him. Mercy coughs and sits down as close to the far end of the sofa as he can without slipping off.

'It's such a lovely idea of our king to have invited you here,' smiles du Barry. 'We'll have a chance to get to know one another better, undisturbed.'

'Most certainly,' agrees the ambassador, uncertain, however, how far he shares this ambition.

'You know,' she continues warmly, 'I'd like to take you into my confidence. As an ambassador you are so skilled in the art of getting on with people. And I have so much to learn in this regard!'

'Madame can in no way be inferior to an ambassador,' says Mercy flatteringly.

'Oh, how kind of you to say so. But you must know that's not true. I find it so distressing that there are still people within our circle who harbour an intense dislike of me, whose attitude may even be called hostile, whilst I do my utmost to remain on good terms with everyone. You see, Your Excellency, evidently I'm not such a good ambassador.'

'I cannot imagine that you have any enemies.' Mercy is lying through his teeth. The woman leans forward a little towards him and he inhales her perfume, the seductive scent of jasmine.

'Oh, but I have, Your Excellency. And you know what is worst of all? There are those who do not know me or whom I have never personally met, whose heads are nevertheless so full of prejudice that I can do no good in their eyes. How should I deal with this, *Monsieur l'Ambassadeur*? Might you be able to help me?' She gives him such an imploring look that it would be difficult to refuse.

'But of course, Madame, with pleasure. But I don't believe that I can be of much service to you. You seem to me to be the most amenable of persons. Who could have a bad word to say about you?'

Du Barry sighs and stares forlornly into space. Mercy cannot imagine how Marie Antoinette would react were she to find her trusted counsellor in the company of the *créature*. He considers her request. How much of it is meant in real earnest, and how much is play-acting? The Austrian ambassador is not in a position to answer his own question, for he has never yet been able to fathom the mysteries of the female soul.

'I have heard,' continues the lady, 'that people say I speak ill of the Dauphine. Yet a bad word about Her Highness has never passed my lips. It wounds me to think such rumours reach her ears, for I see how Marie Antoinette looks at me, or rather ignores my presence. And I should so like to be on a good footing with her, if only to prove the malicious gossipmongers wrong.'

Mercy feels himself in a tight spot. How sensitive is this matter for the king? With the Polish situation looming large at the back of his mind, Mercy wishes to avoid Louis XV finding the slightest pretence for turning his back on Austria. The idea of the alliance falling apart and Marie Antoinette being sent back to her mother sends cold shivers running down his spine. It would mean the inevitable and immediate end of his career. 'I don't believe the Dauphine means ill. I know her well and she is incapable of hating anyone, or of harbouring resentment for long.'

Fortunately the diplomat need not prolong his apologies, for a hidden door in the wall opens and Louis XV, King of France, enters the room. The Comte de Mercy immediately gets to his feet to pay his respects, and almost without a word of farewell Madame du Barry withdraws, leaving the two men alone together.

'You summoned me, Sire,' ventures Mercy, businesslike and without a trace of nerves.

The king laughs rather bashfully. 'Indeed I did, Mercy, indeed I did.' He wanders reluctantly to the open window and looks out. There must be no eavesdroppers. Reassured, he turns back into the room. 'Listen, Mercy, until now you have acted as ambassador only for the Archduchess of Austria. I now wish to request you temporarily to perform the same function on my own behalf.'

Mercy frowns, at once throwing the king into a frenzy of doubt. Louis XV scratches behind his ear, searching frantically for the right words.

Mercy at first waits in silence, but eventually takes pity on his monarch. 'How may I be of service to Your Majesty?'

The king is now rubbing his nose. 'This is a delicate problem, Mercy. I'm not really sure how to formulate it. It's like this, about my daughter-in-law, Marie Antoinette.'

'Has she misbehaved?' asks Mercy in consternation.

'No, oh no. That's not it at all. No, she is absolutely wonderful. I love her with all my heart. She is young, charming, energetic, and she knows just how to make me laugh. But, you see, a young woman of such lively character really needs a husband capable of keeping her on track in life.'

'My God!' thinks Mercy, appalled. A divorce, after all! Does he indeed plan to send Marie Antoinette home, and is this evening the calm before the storm breaks over Poland? 'What is Your Majesty's wish?' he asks the king in measured tones.

The king waves his hands about helplessly. 'It's tragic to see such a child falling under the sway of certain persons at court, and her spirit thus being poisoned with gossip and preconceptions. The result is that she hurts certain people, do you see. Persons who are dear to me and who are not deserving of such treatment.'

Without the name of the king's mistress having been uttered, all is now clear to Mercy. Yet can this whole business simply be about the need for the Dauphine to accept the *maîtresse en titre*?

'Please excuse Marie Antoinette,' answers Mercy. 'I know that her behaviour is inadvertent. The Dauphine respects the king and is under emphatic instructions from her mother, the empress, unfailingly to comply with Your Majesty's every wish and so contribute to the king's happiness and peace of mind. If she has behaved in any way displeasing to Your Majesty, the slightest word from the king will suffice to correct her. She is, after all, still young and, as Your Majesty says, in need of some instruction. What is your advice, Sire?'

The king scratches the back of his head. If only life were that simple. He knows perfectly well that his embittered daughters take immense pleasure in inflaming Marie Antoinette's antagonism to Jeanne. The Dauphine is putty in their hands; they can do with her what they will, and relish the pain it causes their father. What advice can he possibly give? The last thing he wants is another confrontation with Marie Antoinette. His recent meeting with her, when he had been put properly on the spot, is still all too fresh in his mind. Oh, how he hates this sort of thing! He would far rather brush every quarrel and contretemps well out of sight under the carpet.

'Listen Mercy, I'm going to tell you something man to man,

and I hope you will fully respect the enormous faith I'm placing in you. I don't wish to appear like the big bad wolf in my granddaughter's eyes. I'm only too well aware that it is my own daughters who provoke Marie Antoinette to the point where she comes over to certain persons at court as blunt, arrogant or brazen. Of course she doesn't mean to be so, but try explaining that to everyone. What I want is very simple. I wish everyone close to me to be treated with equal dignity. When the Dauphine becomes queen she may do and say as she pleases, but until then I am king and I will have things done according to my wishes! I should greatly appreciate it if, in your capacity as my special ambassador, you might effect this.'

Mercy nods, and no mention of Poland! 'I shall arrange this for you, Sire.'

Relieved, Louis XV shakes the ambassador by the hand and calls Madame du Barry into their presence. Her entry, almost simultaneous with that of d'Aiguillon, is so prompt as to betray her previous presence at the keyhole. The whole scenario is now as clear as daylight to Mercy and he knows precisely what is expected of him. He must take the first possible opportunity to speak to Marie Antoinette.

What a drama! What a comedown! Surely no one could have meant it to turn out like this? Poor Antoinette! How can she go on resisting all this manipulation? I only hope she keeps her faith in me.

From the journal of the Princesse de Lamballe,
12th August 1771

9

'For reasons that I cannot alas explain, it is of *huge* importance,' the Comte de Mercy stresses the word, 'that you treat Madame du Barry in the same way as all the other ladies at court. The sooner you acknowledge and address her in public, the better.'

Marie Antoinette stamps impatiently up and down her salon. 'The sooner the better, you say. For whom?'

The Comte de Mercy had known that this would not be an easy encounter. 'You are aware that this is your mother's wish, and I can assure you that it is now also that of the king.'

Marie Antoinette taps her fan nervously on her palm. 'I don't believe it, Mercy. If *Papa Roi* had wanted me to talk to that creature he would have told me so himself.'

The ambassador tilts his head. 'Perhaps the king wishes to avoid a confrontation with you. Maybe he is too fond of you to want to cause you upset.'

Marie Antoinette flashes him a dubious look. 'Well, if that's his intention, he's made a fine job of it! How in heaven's name can *Papa Roi* expect me, the daughter of an empress, to accept a prostitute as my equal? Admit it, Mercy, it's too crazy for words. In fact, it breaches every rule of etiquette.'

The ambassador allows himself a broad smile. 'Protocol? I thought you had no time for such things!'

'Oh, Mercy, you know exactly what I mean. I could accept that person as a respectable countess only if I knew no better.'

'She is a countess, Madame.'

'A respectable countess, I said.'

'Madame, you have answered your own question. So long as

you can make others think you know no better than that the Comtesse du Barry is an honest woman, what is wrong with your speaking to her?'

Marie Antoinette lets his words sink in. 'The problem is, Mercy, that everyone knows she is a courtesan. What is more, Aunt Adélaïde has told me all about her. Am I supposed to set all that aside?'

'How do you know that what *Mesdames* have told you is the absolute truth? Haven't I had to confirm on a number of occasions that they weren't being completely candid with you? Aside from that, their father is King Louis XV. Is his word not law?'

By now completely confused, the Dauphine changes tack. 'Mercy, how am I supposed to be nice to the woman? After all, wasn't it she who made sure Choiseul had to leave court? Didn't she arrange for his place to be taken by that horrible d'Aiguillon?'

Mercy rubs his chin. 'I know that that is your conviction. But will you trust me if I tell you that the king had very different reasons for removing the Duc du Choiseul than those outlined by *Mesdames*?'

Marie Antoinette slumps down in a chair. 'How complicated it all is! Why is it that here the facts are always turned upside down?'

'That's a very good question. But you must please understand that your mother and the King of France have your best interests at heart. I am merely the bearer of their request, but I must stress that I entirely share their view.'

Marie Antoinette massages her temples. 'Very well, Mercy. I shall discuss it with Louis-Auguste,' she decides with a deep sigh. 'You'll hear from me.'

As usual, the Dauphin has no opinion on the matter and sends Marie Antoinette straight off to his aunts. They are only too pleased to give her their sound advice, but the Dauphine wavers. Mercy has quite clearly indicated his opinion of the sisters, and it isn't very bountiful. But who else can she consult? The Abbé Vermond shares Mercy's viewpoint. Lamballe always lends a listening ear, but then supports her friend in every decision without really venturing any opinion of her own. The Comte de Provence is too partial and will very probably speak up for *la favourite*. The same goes for his younger brother, the Comte d'Artois, who would be more than happy to slip into his grandfather's shoes when it comes to Madame du Barry. So that leaves the aunts as her only serious option.

'You do very well to come to us, child,' says Adélaïde, raising her voice over the fierce clicking of knitting needles. 'In all honesty, had this really been the king's wish, you would have known about it long ago. But you must understand that the king has much more important things on his mind. The reorganisation of the *parlements* demands a great deal of his attention. Do you really think he gives a fig whether or not you say hello to the *maîtresse en titre*? Huh! Whoever thinks that has no idea what a temporary fixture such a woman is! You needn't be surprised if next month she's thrown out of her apartment and sent back where she came from. Believe me, my child, we've seen it all before. My God, I can't bear to think of you humiliating yourself by descending to her level! What is the world coming to?'

Her cheeks flushing pink, Marie Antoinette nods and takes a sip of her hot chocolate. Adélaïde's words sound so very plausible. Whom should she believe? Privately struggling with her dilemma, the Dauphine relapses into superficial chatter, but without her usual animation. She yawns.

'Maybe you should have an early night, child,' says Adélaïde with apparent concern. 'You look a little feverish.'

'A little feverish,' echoes her sister Victoire affirmatively.

'Goodnight everyone,' mumbles the Dauphine, trailing off to her own apartment. All this conflicting advice has taken the ground from under her feet. Why can't they all just leave her in peace?

He is furious. What a stubborn little mule the girl is, after all! Why won't she simply listen to him? The Austrian ambassador's blood is simmering with rage – not at all a common occurrence. But, knowing that anger is a poor taskmaster, the Comte de Mercy with some difficulty swallows his fury.

'Once again, Madame, for reasons that I cannot yet divulge but which are so momentous that the alliance itself is in jeopardy, I beg you to give serious consideration to my request. I guarantee that this is your mother's most emphatic wish. Should you decide to ignore her desires and my request, I shall protect you from the consequences. But Madame, in all truth, I cannot stress forcefully enough how important this is.'

Tears well up in the Dauphine's eyes. She has hardly slept a wink all night and has given up trying to decipher whose advice she should follow. 'But Aunt Adélaïde told me herself that the king is not really concerned about this,' she sobs.

'Listen to me, Antoinette, please. I'm going to be frank with you. Not a soul takes *Mesdames* seriously. Not the court, and least of all their own father. Why do you think he dubbed Adélaïde '*Chiffe*', Victoire '*Coche*' and Sophie '*Graille*'? Rag, Sow and Grub – not very flattering names for the king to attach to his own daughters! No, Louis XV tolerates their presence, but that's about all. Why do you think he has personally instructed me to request this of you? As soon as the time is ripe, I shall explain the background. It is a truly weighty matter. More depends upon this than you could possibly imagine.'

'Why all the mystery? You said you were going to be honest with me – tell me, then, what is so important that I must humiliate myself?'

The ambassador takes a deep breath. Can he risk sharing a secret with her? He shuts his eyes and realises he cannot: she is still much too much of a chatterbox. In no time at all, the whole of Versailles would be in on it. Discussions concerning the partition of Poland are at far too early a stage, and when the time is right he must first inform Louis XV.

'Madame, some matters of State are so confidential that I myself am ignorant of the subtleties involved. All I know is that it directly concerns the survival of the alliance between France and Austria. I promise that the moment more news becomes available you will be the first to hear it from me.' Marie Antoinette blows her nose and dries her tears. She takes a deep breath. The time has come for a decision.

'Very well, Mercy. But you must help me. I'm finding all this really horrible. Where and when do I have to speak to the woman?'

Mercy breathes a sigh of relief. 'Madame, leave it all to me.'

The count wastes no time in informing the king that the Dauphine has understood what is expected of her. The next step is to organise the perfect opportunity, when the right people are assembled to witness the passing of a few words between Marie Antoinette and the Comtesse du Barry. The best time would obviously be during one of the Dauphine's card evenings. These gatherings are attended by all and sundry: the Dauphin, together with his brothers and the Comtesse de Provence; the aunts, of course; the Princesse de Lamballe and several aristocratic families, complete with their attendants and ladies in waiting. The arrangement is that at the end of the evening Mercy will escort the Comtesse du Barry into the room at the exact moment when Marie Antoinette is making her courtesy round of all the guests.

The Dauphine is nervous. 'What do I say, Mercy?'

'It doesn't matter. I will be standing next to the Comtesse du Barry and you will address me first. After that you can gradually include her in the conversation. A couple of words will do, but make sure it looks spontaneous. And I beg you, do not speak of this to anyone. Just let it happen naturally.'

Marie Antoinette nods as if in complete understanding.

The cards lie played out on the table. The busy salon is buzzing like a hive, at its centre the queen of the evening, moving from one group to another. A smile here, a few words there, all receive equal attention from Madame la Dauphine. Everything seems to be going swimmingly, but as Comte de Mercy enters with Madame du Barry on his arm, he at once feels the atmosphere charged.

From behind the fans there is whispering, peering and

speculation. It is instantly clear to Mercy that everyone knows what is to happen this evening. Everyone, including *Mesdames*, the target of whose radiantly innocent smiles he now finds himself. There can be no other explanation: Marie Antoinette has let her tongue run away with her. The Dauphine, however, is avoiding his eyes and, as always, ignoring the presence of *la créature*. But Mercy decides there is no going back, and plants himself and du Barry squarely in the middle of the salon, where everyone can see and hear them. The Dauphine inches nearer. Mercy feels Madame du Barry's grip tighten on his arm. Her fan trembles and her voice sinks to nothing.

'I am looking forward with pleasure to supper, Madame,' remarks the ambassador to Jeanne du Barry in a light tone, to reassure her. 'I feel certain the evening is going to be an excellent one,' he adds with a fatherly pat of her hand.

The Comtesse du Barry gives a nervous laugh, but her bosom is heaving. Little by little Marie Antoinette approaches; she has nearly finished talking to Mademoiselle d'Armont. Now, as if given the signal by an invisible master of ceremonies, everyone falls silent. The only sound in the salon is a frantic flapping of fans, as their owners vainly attempt to cool overheated brows. Marie Antoinette turns to the Comte de Mercy and the *maîtresse en titre* and draws herself up as if to dominate the duo with her towering presence. The empress's daughter swallows hard, and for the very first time her glance meets that of the uncrowned Queen of Versailles; it is a split-second encounter in which the two women share their mingled pride and fear.

The Dauphine takes a small step forward, moistening her dry lips with the tip of her tongue. Then, just as she is about to open her mouth to greet the Comte de Mercy, Aunt Adélaïde swoops upon them like a malicious harpy and plucks Marie Antoinette by the arm. 'Madame, make haste, it is already late!' instructs her aunt loudly. 'The king cannot begin supper without us.' And, without another word, she drags the totally bewildered Dauphine away with her, leaving the whole salon stunned in amazement and disbelief.

Jeanne du Barry stares, crushed, at the ambassador. She feels as though she is about to faint. Mercy puts his arm supportively around her waist and whispers in her ear, 'Keep smiling and follow me.' With as much dignity as he can muster, Mercy escorts his victim from the field of battle.

The moment they are gone, all hell breaks loose. Everyone begins talking at once. What a spectacle! Never in their lives have they seen such a thing! Reactions vary from one extreme to the other. 'How brave of Adélaïde to rush to the Dauphine's aid. It would be a fine thing were we to open up our ranks to the lower orders.'

But the Comte de Provence sees it very differently. 'Shameless behaviour! To think my own aunt can do this to us!' Louis-Auguste stares melancholically straight ahead of him and, as usual, says nothing.

Meanwhile, the ambassador has conducted Madame du Barry to her apartment, where he offers her his most heartfelt apologies. What an anticlimax! Never before in his entire career has he experienced such mortification. The weeping Madame du Barry withdraws.

Livid, the count goes in search of Marie Antoinette. He has to find out whether or not this was her idea. On the way he runs into the Comte de Provence, followed by his wife on the arm of the Duc d'Aiguillon. 'You will be joining us for supper, I suppose?' enquires the latter in a slightly mocking tone but with a deadly stare. 'Or has that too been cancelled for this evening?'

Mercy gives the minister a stiff little bow. 'You may expect me directly,' he flatly confirms, quickening his pace towards Adélaïde's salon. Just as he had expected, he finds there a tearful Marie Antoinette. The king, of course, is nowhere to be seen. Mercy shoots an incensed glance at Adélaïde, who looks less triumphant than he had anticipated. Perhaps it is only now dawning on her how badly she has violated all the rules of protocol. But the moment the king's eldest daughter claps eyes on the ambassador, she launches into a furious tirade against him.

'It's all your fault!' she screeches, jabbing an index finger at Mercy, who is amazed at this remarkable outburst.

'I'm afraid, Madame, you do not realise the damage you have done this evening,' responds the ambassador with suppressed rage.

'Damage?' gasps Adélaïde, as if she herself were the injured party.

'Leave Mercy alone,' reprimands Marie Antoinette, her voice terse with fastidious disgust at the whole situation. Adélaïde carries on grumbling away under her breath until Louis-Auguste quite unexpectedly brings her up short.

'You are quite in the wrong on this occasion, aunt,' he calmly rebukes her. 'In my view, the Comte de Mercy has the right end of the stick.' The Dauphin looks from Adélaïde to each of her sisters in turn, disapproval written all over his face. 'It was a great mistake, aunt. You are all entirely in the wrong.'

Adélaïde walks out in a huff, slamming the door behind her. Marie Antoinette tearfully embraces the Dauphin, unspeakably relieved that he has at last expressed a clear opinion of his own on the matter. It is now perfectly obvious to Mercy who was behind this evening's intervention. What a mess! He leaves the room, still shaking his head. There's no point whatsoever in reading Marie Antoinette the riot act now.

Instead, he strides as fast as his legs will carry him through the gallery to the king's apartment, in the hope that there might still be something to be redeemed there. But, in a quite uncharacteristic head-on engagement with reality, the king backs the Comte de Mercy almost literally into a corner, hissing like an aroused viper, 'So your so-called help has led precisely nowhere, ambassador. Do I have to do everything myself yet again?'

Before Mercy can give the king an answer, Louis XV has turned his back on him, to completely ignore the ambassador for the remainder of the evening. It doesn't escape Mercy's notice how easily the Comte de Provence and his wife get on with the now consoled Madame du Barry. Louis-Stanislas's wife has not become pregnant yet, but should she give birth to a royal heir, it would very probably turn the tables against Marie Antoinette.

Supper is a less prolonged affair than usual, but to Mercy it seems to last forever. For the first time in his life, he senses that he has fallen very far short of the mark indeed.

We're all terribly shocked – a stillborn child! The only good I can see coming of it is that the Duc de Chartres will be a bit kinder to her now. Might it save the marriage? Marie Adélaïde is strong, and I expect she will soon be back to her old self. I shall pray for her that the next pregnancy goes better.

From the journal of the Princesse de Lamballe,
12th October 1771

10

Marie Antoinette is more turned in on herself than ever and does her best to avoid the Comte de Mercy. You could cut the atmosphere in the palace with a knife. To her sorrow, the Dauphine is seeing far less of the king than she used to. Nowadays their conversation is confined to swapping polite formalities. The aunts are unbearable because their father refuses to visit them. Marie Antoinette still cannot decide who is in the right. If all this is really bothering the king, why doesn't *Papa Roi* demand that she adopt a tolerant attitude to the Comtesse du Barry?

Without a word, the Comte de Mercy hands Marie Antoinette the letter from Maria Theresa, Empress of the Holy Roman Empire. The wad of paper feels thicker than usual and the Dauphine breaks the seal with trepidation. Glancing up at Mercy, she finds that he has wandered off to the window and is staring vacantly outside. She could keep the letter for later, when she is alone. But curiosity gets the better of her and Marie Antoinette unfolds the pages and begins to read. The authoritarian tone hits the Dauphine like a body blow. Mama is infuriated. Wild with rage! The Comte de Mercy knows exactly what is in the letter; he read and sealed it himself. 'Is it perhaps a little too crudely put?' the empress had asked in her covering letter.

As far as Mercy is concerned, this time it cannot be put too strongly. Marie Antoinette has ignored his advice and been stupid enough to confide in the aunts. He had not for an instant imagined that Adélaïde would take such drastic action. What an indignity! No, such an incident must never be repeated. The Dauphine must learn, once and for all, what happens if she ignores his advice and goes her own way.

Mercy watches out of the corner of his eye the devastating effect of Maria Theresa's words upon her daughter. It's precisely as he had expected. The colour rises to Marie Antoinette's cheeks and tears well up in her eyes. Will this teach her to be less dependent on the aunts? Will she finally stop behaving in a way that offends people? Swallowing her sobs, Marie Antoinette catches a glimpse of her own reflection in the huge mirror above the fireplace. She looks awful. And that's exactly how she feels. The whole world has turned against her. Is there anybody who still loves her? She turns to the ambassador, waving the letter in her hand. Gulping for breath, she searches for the right words. 'It's not fair!' she splutters. Nothing more escapes her lips.

Mercy remains silent. He deeply regrets seeing her in this state, but has she not brought it upon herself?

The summer is almost over and quietly giving way to autumn. The days are shortening and the long dark evenings are largely taken up with turgid and extended card games. Marie Antoinette hates them. It seems to her that every evening's game goes more slowly than the last. Yet she continues to conduct herself impeccably, and even manages a few kind words to the old countesses, who sometimes join in a hand or two. Each day brings her birthday, her sixteenth already, a little closer. But she has no reason to celebrate. She is lulled nearly comatose by the tedious rhythm of the court, where gossip provides the only high point of the day. Her enthusiasm for the hunt is much tempered. The whole business surrounding Madame du Barry, her mother's constant criticism and the king's coolness towards her has broken something inside her.

Every evening she makes her way to bed with her mother's threats ringing in her ears: 'Where is the heir?' As if there is anything her daughter can do about it! Although her relationship with Louis-Auguste is improving all the time, he is still making no move to prolong the Bourbon dynasty. There is always some excuse. It saps Marie Antoinette's energy. She only has to feel unwell, her period be a day or two overdue, and the salons are buzzing with speculation. Could she be pregnant?

Actually, she would like nothing better herself, if only to put an end to all the fuss and speculation. She longs for the day when she can regale her mother with the news that she is expecting a child. But when will that be? Lately, she has been dreaming more and more about children, her own little ones. It must be because the Princesse de Lamballe talks incessantly about her sister-in-law, who is about to deliver any day now. 'Oh, I'm so looking forward to becoming an aunt,' croons Lamballe broodily, over and over again.

A nursery full of boisterous young savages and mischievous-looking little girls, chorusing 'Mama!' As she wakes and the shouts fade away, she realises once more that she is alone. Completely alone in the vast bed, and so very far from home.

Behind the scenes, the Comte de Mercy is working hard to get back into the king's favour. The best way of doing this is via the Comtesse du Barry, for Louis XV's faith in Mercy's diplomatic skills has suffered a severe blow. Madame du Barry, much less stiff-necked than the French monarch, is in no doubt that it is *Mesdames* who are at the root of the trouble. Exercising the utmost caution, the Austrian ambassador has managed to get round the countess, persuading her that it will not be long before Marie Antoinette respects her wish. The Dauphine just needs a little more time. To Mercy's great relief, Madame du Barry is able to accept this too, and Mercy takes advantage of the situation to make an ally of her. If he succeeds in getting Marie Antoinette to behave normally towards du Barry, he will be back in the good books of the *maîtresse en titre* and thus also the king. And that will be very necessary when it comes to breaking the news about Poland.

Adélaïde, Victoire and Sophie are complaining bitterly about their father's behaviour. For weeks now, they have been denied an opportunity to entertain the king in their salons. What is more, written requests submitted by *Mesdames* are either refused outright or go unanswered. All of this gives Marie Antoinette food for thought. Could Mercy and Mama be right after all?

The Dauphine warily raises the subject once more with the Abbé Vermond. The priest has his answer ready: of course they are right! Marie Antoinette gives a humble nod of the head. Yet surely she hasn't been mistaken all along? She still can't help wondering, even though Vermond has outlined in words of one syllable how the aunts have abused her trust.

One last time, the Dauphine fishes for her husband's opinion on the matter. After all, he did condemn the aunts at the time.

'You shouldn't go around wearing your heart on your sleeve all the time,' is his curt response. 'You ought to know by now how that can be used against you here. It's best not to let anyone know your real feelings.'

'That's easy for you to say,' she scoffs, 'but then you're a past master in those tactics anyway. Just tell me what I should actually do.'

The Dauphin shrugs. In his view, Marie Antoinette is more than capable of deciding for herself what is best for her. 'I wouldn't know,' he replies with candour.

'But you yourself barely speak to that woman. Surely that means you agree with my ignoring her?'

He gives his wife a glazed look.

'Take Provence, for instance,' persists Marie Antoinette: 'he does the opposite. He's regularly seen at *Papa Roi*'s table, getting on like a house on fire with the woman. You know your own brother better than I do, but he must have his reasons for that.'

The Dauphin nods. 'Oh, most certainly. Tartuffe still thinks he's destined for the throne of France. He reckons he's better cut out for the role of king than I am.' Louis-Auguste's tone is flatly devoid of emotion.

'But surely you don't let that get to you?' prompts the Dauphine.

Her husband smiles knowingly. 'Oh, I don't believe very much will come of it. *Papa Roi* is as fit as a flea. Just imagine, if he lives as long as his predecessor Louis XIV, I shall have to wait another fifteen years. No, all those machinations on my brother's part are a complete waste of his time and energy. I don't take them seriously. Only if I were to die would Tartuffe stand a chance.'

'But not if you had a son!' interjects Marie Antoinette, seizing her moment to remind him of the reason for their marriage.

'Exactly,' agrees Louis-Auguste. 'But as I've told you before, we have plenty of time. It's not wise to think of having children so young. After all, we're still children ourselves,' he adds precociously, opening his book again. As far as he is concerned, the subject is closed. Marie Antoinette continues to hover about his chair.

'But what am I supposed to do now about du Barry? What do you want me to do?' she asks despairingly.

The Dauphin looks up once more. 'If you want to please *Papa Roi*, say "hello" to her. It doesn't mean we have to take supper with them every evening.'

There is a certain amount of logic in this. If she just acknowledged that creature, what a huge burden of complaint would fall from her shoulders. But wouldn't that make her look a fool in front of all those who have encouraged and praised her disdain of the woman? What will people think of her if she changes tack? No, it doesn't feel right. She would end up thoroughly degraded. Why doesn't Papa consort with a real princess? Why didn't he marry Lamballe when he had the chance? Then none of this would have happened. What is she to do? Oh, but the pressure on her is becoming unendurable. Probing letters from Mama, paternal preaching from Mercy – and now from Vermond's mouth too. If only Mama knew what really went on here, then she would forgive her. But deep down Marie Antoinette knows that she may expect comfort from no quarter.

Her new *dame d'atours*, the Duchesse de Cossé, Mistress of the Robes, has come into the room looking tense, a note in her hand.

'What is it?' asks Marie Antoinette with a worried glance. Cossé casts her eyes down and dare not reply. The Dauphine accepts the note. She recognises the handwriting as belonging to the Princesse de Lamballe. Strange, she was to have been at Versailles this afternoon. Is her cousin indisposed again? The Dauphine quickly unfolds the message. It contains no more than a couple of lines.

'*Mon Dieu*,' gasps a shocked Marie Antoinette. She is trembling so violently that the paper falls from her grasp, as both hands fly spontaneously to her abdomen in panic, so closely has she identified with Lamballe's sister-in-law throughout her pregnancy.

'What's wrong?' asks the Dauphin, disturbed in his reading once again. Marie Antoinette looks distractedly at her husband. 'It's the Duchesse de Chartres, her baby ...' Weeping, she falls into the arms of her *dame d'atours*. 'Her little one is dead!'

Unbelievable! The Duchesse de Bracas, dame d'honneur to the Comtesse de Provence, has been relieved of her function by the king. We all know who is really behind it - that bitch du Barry, of course. Antoinette is even more afraid that she is next in line to go, but I don't think the king will allow himself to be brought so low. Still, I've promised Antoinette faithfully never to leave her side!

From the journal of the Princesse de Lamballe,
18th December 1771

11

Louis-Stanislas Xavier, Comte de Provence, could not be more certain that he, and not his elder brother, is the man to take over their grandfather's throne. He trumps the Dauphin in intelligence, style and gallantry. Despite his increasing frustration, however, the king shows no sign of setting aside the Dauphin. Since his marriage, the ambitious Provence has gathered about him a court that is nothing short of regal. It outshines that of the Dauphin, a man far less interested than his brother in outward appearance and stylish ceremony.

Today the Comte de Provence is in his element, for one of his little schemes is about to be realised. His frequent soirées and visits to Madame du Barry, and the access these give him to the listening ear of *Papa Roi*, are finally bearing fruit. Provence has engineered a post for himself at the head of the Swiss Guard, whose task it is to look after palace security. Until today this function had been in the hands of the Duc de Choiseul. The banished duke is desperately in need of the generous income that comes with the job to keep the debt collectors from his gate. The king, aware of the ex-minister's penury and having always had a soft spot for Choiseul, had never stripped him of the responsibility. But, a year on, feelings have changed.

From Choiseul's estate has come a constant sputtering of innuendo against Chancellor Maupeou, and the chateau hosts hordes of *Patriotes*. This has steadily undermined the king's sympathy for Choiseul. It only took a request to come in at the right moment for the king to make the simple gesture of transferring the command to the Comte de Provence. Louis XV is gratified to see his grandson so thankful. But the King of France has entirely failed to take into account the Dauphin's position.

Louis-Auguste has been told nothing of the move and thus, perhaps unconsciously, the king has passed him over. The Comte de Provence, on the other hand, is quite prepared for his brother's protests. He knows that as a rule they don't amount to much. At the most, Provence expects some blare and bluster, but once this has died down he looks forward to luxuriating in the position of Colonel-in-chief of the Swiss Guard and enjoying the vast honorarium.

Provence tries his best to pull in his stomach in while his tailor pins him meticulously into his new uniform. Without warning the door crashes open.

'What is the meaning of this?' roars Louis-Auguste, Dauphin of France. Provence, quickly recovering himself, stares at him without blinking.

'What an entrance, brother,' he calmly remarks. 'Your good manners aren't much in evidence these days. It's just as well mother isn't here to see it.'

The Dauphin circles his brother with a belligerent air. The tailor carries on as if nothing is happening, but does manage nervously to prick his finger on a pin. Both brothers are hefty, but Louis-Auguste is the only one with any muscle. His daily equestrian outings keep him in peak condition.

'Colonel-in-chief?' queries the Dauphin, giving his brother a devastating look. Provence feels his nerve ebbing a little. He has never seen his brother quite like this before. 'Let's hear it, Tartuffe: what are you up to now?'

Louis-Stanislas puts on a broad grin. 'Just ask Papa. It was his idea. Hadn't you heard anything about it, then?' He clicks his tongue in mock disapproval. 'How very careless of him not to have informed you.' With his left hand Provence sweeps the Dauphin nonchalantly aside so that he can view himself from top to toe in the mirror. 'Looks good, don't you think?'

Damn and blast it! Before Provence knows what is happening,

he is standing there in his singlet. In a flash Louis-Auguste has ripped the gaudy Swiss Guard's uniform from his brother's body and brass buttons are winking their way into every corner of the room. With a shriek, the tailor makes a swift exit.

'Forget it!' growls the Dauphin.

Comte de Provence gazes speechless into the mirror. He looks ridiculous in his tattered uniform. Angry tears spring to his eyes. 'How dare you!' he screams, mortified, and lashes out at the Dauphin with his fist.

But Provence is no match for his burly brother. His punch seems to bounce harmlessly off the Dauphin's chest. Louis-Auguste takes a step forward and gives his brother such a shove that the exalted military man literally takes to the air and lands against the far wall.

'And now I'm going to speak to Papa,' thunders the Dauphin, turning his back on the gasping Provence, who is still wondering what hit him.

Marie Antoinette has witnessed the whole spectacle from the gallery. How demeaning! But Louis-Auguste is right. What a mean trick on Provence's part! Marie Antoinette catches the Dauphin's flashing eye and quickly steps aside to let him pass. He heads for the king's apartment, taking such long strides that she can barely keep up with him.

'Halt! Who goes there?' The guards' warning cry rings through the hall. Looking back, she sees Provence waddling after them, foaming at the mouth.

The Dauphin does not slow his pace for a second, and soon breaks into a run. He must speak to the king. Marie Antoinette just manages to jump aside in time as her brother-in-law lumbers past like a charging rhinoceros, closely followed by the panic-stricken and whimpering Comtesse de Provence.

'Come on,' says Marie Antoinette, offering her a hand. The two women run after the brothers, closely followed by a growing train of curious courtiers attracted by the commotion. What can be going on?

As the panting Dauphine and Comtesse de Provence reach the Œil de bœuf, they see through the open door the king's astonished gaze as he faces his grandsons. Never before has the French sovereign known the brothers to indulge in public acrimony. Louis XV is especially astounded at the Dauphin. He had never thought to see the boy angry: he is normally so reserved and non-committal. What could have happened? The ministers who were in discussion with the king have stepped aside, sniggering. A new family drama unfolding?

'Sire,' announces the Dauphin, in a voice so loud that it silences everyone. The shy young man has never been known to adopt such a tone. 'Sire, it truly grieves me to have to disturb the king in the execution of his duties. He will be aware that I, of all people, have enormous respect for his daily efforts in governing this country.' The Dauphin's voice is still trembling with anger, but his usual reticence has vanished. It is apparent that he knows exactly what he wants to say.

Louis XV is having difficulty controlling himself at the hilarious sight of his grandson Provence, standing just behind Louis-Auguste in his singlet with the colours of the Swiss Guard unravelling across his shoulder. But the king soon forgets his laughter. A shameful family row in full view of the whole court is the last thing he wants. Why can't he be allowed to lead a quiet life?

'The king's well-considered decision to relieve the Duc du Choiseul of his function as Colonel-in-chief of the Swiss Guard will be respected by the whole court,' continues the Dauphin. His words spark renewed whispering in the corridor, which points to some division of opinion on this matter. Here at Versailles, too, Choiseul has many followers. 'The Most Christian King of France is fully entitled to take any decision that pleases him. But as Dauphin I must today register my protest at the course of events.'

The king raises his hand. What kind of nonsense is this? Louis XV wants to put a stop to the whole show. 'You are taking the part of the exile Choiseul?' he asks softly.

'No, Sire. I repeat, the King of France has every right, and his decision to transfer the command will be respected by all. It is only regrettable that the appointment of the new colonel-in-chief has taken place over my head. Naturally, the king is wholly entitled to appoint whomsoever he desires, and the Dauphin has no say in the matter. However, in this case, when my brother the Comte de Provence has been named behind my back, the king's complete lack of faith in the Dauphin appears quite inexplicable. It leaves the Dauphin seriously questioning his own position.'

No one speaks. Has the king indeed gone over the head of the crown prince? All those who have hitherto considered Louis-Auguste incapable of uttering two consecutive words are themselves struck dumb with amazement. The king, instantly grasping the nub of the matter, feels hugely relieved. Damn it all, Provence has led him well and truly by the nose! Idiot, fool that he is!

'My esteemed Dauphin. The whole thing is due to a dreadful misunderstanding,' says the king, going smilingly up to his eldest grandson. 'Shall we discuss this in private?' he adds in a low voice, surveying the curious faces straining to catch every word for the fleeting edification of this evening's salons. 'Come with me,' he orders, including the Comte de Provence in his invitation. Marie Antoinette and the Comtesse de Provence follow their husbands into the king's private chambers, leaving the court in a state of some excitement.

'My dear Louis-Auguste. As I see it, there has been a considerable miscalculation here. I have no idea how your brother has got it into his head that he might qualify for this function.' With this Louis XV gives Provence such a scowl that the younger brother casts his eyes to the ground. 'Yes, indeed I have considered bestowing this role on one of my grandsons. It brings with it a good income. And capital, a commodity becoming scarcer by the moment, is better kept circulating within the family. What do you think? Would you like the job yourself?'

Marie Antoinette stares at the king. Can Papa be serious? Now that his anger has died down, Louis-Auguste is his usual withdrawn self again. Of course he doesn't want the job. That is not at all what this is about.

'Sire, such a thing has never entered my head,' says the Dauphin. 'All that concerns me is that my existence was not acknowledged in your decision. As far as I'm concerned, my brother is welcome to the post. I'm sure he will take to it like a duck to water.'

The king hesitates a moment. He knows the written request from Provence is lying in his archive. But did he reply to it in writing? He cannot recall. Whatever, it has all turned into a very troublesome business. Provence had informed him that Louis-Auguste had no interest whatsoever in this function. Stupid of him not to have checked with the Dauphin personally.

'Fine. Now that the whole question has been thoroughly aired, I shall waste no time in making my official announcement concerning the appointment.'

The Comte de Provence stands bolt upright, already visualising himself inspecting the troops.

'It would seem to be to be a function eminently suited to your younger brother, the Comte d'Artois!'

The Dauphin nods in assent.

Louis-Stanislas emits a choking sound. 'But the boy is only just sixteen!' he splutters.

'This is the way I want it!' orders the king, clearly irritated. 'And let that be the end of the matter.'

Papa Roi is obviously in no mood for argument. Crushed, the Comte de Provence beats a sorry retreat, supported by his little wife.

Marie Antoinette takes Louis-Auguste's arm with pride. 'You were wonderful. I love you!' she tells him in a whisper, planting a kiss upon his cheek that makes him blush. Together they take their leave of the king, who, finding himself alone, mops his brow.

Another lesson learnt, he grimly tells himself. He has obviously underestimated the Dauphin, and from now on he will remember just how wily Provence can be. They'll be the death of him, these grandchildren of his!

It'll be lovely when Antoinette pays a visit to Paris at last. There's one ball after another, which means I get a chance to dance day after day. Marvellous! Papa still has a bad cold, but seems a bit better today. Just as well, because tomorrow I'm off to Versailles. I've seen nothing of Antoinette for days.

From the journal of the Princesse de Lamballe,
31st December 1771

12

Tomorrow is New Year's Day. Marie Antoinette wonders what 1772 will have in store for her. She has been at the court in Versailles for almost eighteen months now. Unbelievable! It seems centuries since the day she said her farewells to her mother. How she had looked forward to France, the court, her future husband and her own motherhood. And how little is left of all that happy anticipation!

Marie Antoinette is still not pregnant and, if things go on as they are, never will be. The threat of being sent back to Vienna still hangs over her. Her only comfort is that Comtesse de Provence is still not expecting a child. And recently the king has been being kind to his little Dauphine again, without giving the least sign of what he expects from her concerning Madame du Barry.

La favourite has been occupying Marie Antoinette's thoughts a great deal lately. Should she spring a New Year surprise on everyone and greet the *maîtresse en titre* as the king would like her to do? This afternoon the Dauphine has summoned the Comte de Mercy to her private boudoir.

'I shall speak to her,' Marie Antoinette tells him in a voice so subdued that he can barely make out her words.

'What did you say?' He cannot believe his ears.

'I shall speak to her, Mercy,' she repeats, louder this time.

The ambassador bows to the princess. 'Madame, that would be wonderful. May I ask whom you have informed of this?'

Nothing fills Mercy with more dread than the spectre of another Adélaïde ambush.

'No one, Mercy, no one. You are the only person I shall tell. Will you arrange for du Barry to be present at my reception tomorrow?'

Again Mercy bows. He takes a sip of his tea. But, for all his outward calm, inwardly he is jubilant. Has she finally given in? The lady of the chamber takes Mercy's cup with a friendly smile, and he excuses himself. From the Dauphine's boudoir he hastens straight to that of Jeanne du Barry.

The fire is nearly out, yet the room is still stifling hot. The salon is packed with guests on their annual visit to offer the Dauphine their best wishes for the New Year. Mercy has tucked himself well away in a corner. The long queue of waiting marquesses, impatient countesses and bored-looking duchesses edges its way forward like a torpid snake waking from long hibernation. Marie Antoinette has a few words for almost everyone, chatting longer with one than another. Some guests are seen off with a quick smile. The procession crawls agonisingly slowly past the Dauphine.

At last *la favorite* comes into view, firmly supported on both sides by the arms of the Duchesse d'Aiguillon and the Maréchale de Mirepoix. A flurry of excitement passes through the salon. Du Barry in the line! How dare she? The woman knows very well that the Dauphine will snub her. Or could something unexpected be about to take place? The news spreads like wildfire and those leaving the room turn around to hurry back in. What is going to happen next? Speculation is rife. Will the Dauphine accept or reject the *maîtresse en titre*'s New Year gesture? It is difficult to say; the Dauphine is giving nothing away. She carries on welcoming one and all with her usual flair, and seems not in the least unnerved by du Barry's approach.

But Marie Antoinette is not half as self-assured as she appears. Behind the regal smile, her heart is in her mouth. Again she experiences the familiar moment of dread, but the Dauphine is not going to be put off this time. With her unsuspecting aunts at a safe distance, she sees a golden opportunity to show everyone that she is more than capable of deciding things for herself.

The chattering threesome is making its way to the head of the queue, each woman ready to offer the Dauphine her respects. And for the second time in their lives the eyes of Marie Antoinette and Madame du Barry meet, however briefly. Humbly, the king's mistress casts her glance down, all her expectations of this encounter vanishing like summer snow.

Jeanne du Barry was overjoyed to hear Mercy's news. But what if Adélaïde should strike again? Perhaps it is nothing but a snare and *l'archiduchesse* will slight her by ignoring her New Year greeting. Oh, what a humiliation that would be! The very thought makes her so dizzy that she is glad of the support of her friends on either side. Imagine fainting here, in front of everyone! She only half hears what Marie Antoinette is saying to the Duchesse d'Aiguillon, standing beside her.

And then, my God! Jeanne du Barry feels the Dauphine's eyes directly upon her. The cool glance of the Austrian archduchess seems, despite her warm smile, to pass straight through du Barry. Then she sees Marie Antoinette's lips move.

'Il y a bien du monde aujourd'hui à Versailles.'

Madame du Barry gives a nervous giggle. Is she talking to me? What did she say again? That a great number of people are at Versailles today? But of course, it is New Year's Day! Suddenly Jeanne has to laugh. What does it matter what she said? The Dauphine is speaking to me!

The Comtesse du Barry inclines her head in gratitude as her eyes fill with tears. She tries to speak, but no words come. All she can think of is that the Dauphine has accepted her. Marie Antoinette continues calmly on her way, exchanging a greeting with the Maréchale de Mirepoix. But there could not have been a more sensational beginning to the year. The news is spreading through the salon like a shock wave, and yet the air is charged with doubt. Behind the quivering fans, those too far from the scene to have witnessed it shake their heads and ask 'Can it be true?' 'Really', comes the reply, 'I heard it with my own ears!' And so it goes for the remainder of the day and on through those that follow.

Back in her own boudoir, Marie Antoinette is reclining with her feet up on the sofa, exhausted. She has had more than enough of people for the moment. But even here they will not leave her alone. She knew she could expect a visit from the Comte de Mercy. The ambassador congratulates the Dauphine on the manner in which she has acknowledged the Comtesse du Barry. Marie Antoinette shrugs indifferently.

'I shall write to Mama about it immediately, Mercy. You will both be very pleased, no doubt,' she adds sullenly.

The whole night through, Madame du Barry haunts Marie Antoinette's dreams as time and again she steps forward to be spoken to by the Dauphine. The *maîtresse en titre*, gazing haughtily about her, seems more than ever to be the Queen of Versailles.

The next morning Marie Antoinette wakes up late, to find her nostrils filled with the aroma of freshly ground coffee beans. She opens her eyes and is astonished to behold the king, already in her chamber, humming a merry tune and peering into his bubbling coffee apparatus. Louis XV's face lights up even further.

'Ah, my daughter, my princess. Awake at last. Look, this is for you,' and he hands her a little cup of his fresh brew. She raises herself cautiously into an upright position. What is all this about? She throws the Comtesse de Noailles a quizzical glance, but can read nothing from the face of her Mistress of the Household, standing by and silently watching the scene. The king has poured himself some coffee and come to sit on the edge of her bed.

'Admit it, now,' banters Louis XV, 'there's no better way to start the day than with a fresh cup of coffee.'

Marie Antoinette gives him a sleepy look. She couldn't get a word in edgeways even if she tried, for the king is talking trivialities nineteen to the dozen. Although the name du Barry does not pass his lips, very slowly it dawns on the Dauphine what is going on. Despite the aunts' insistence that Louis XV cared not a jot how Marie Antoinette treated *la favorite*, that was clearly far from the truth. And just in case she needed any further evidence, the king produces two parcels and lays them at her feet.

'A little present, my child.'

Her tiny cup cradled in both hands, Marie Antoinette blows delicately across the surface of its hot contents. 'But what have I done to deserve all this, Papa?'

The king gestures airily. 'Oh, New Year,' he nonchalantly replies, 'and I haven't been paying you much attention lately. I wouldn't want you to think I didn't love you any more.'

Marie Antoinette is too bewildered to reply. On the one hand she is touched, but on the other it is now crystal clear how much du Barry really means to him. Yet how can the Most Christian King of France stoop so low as to fall in love with a common streetwalker? Mercy and Mama were right all along. Worse, the aunts have been lying to her. Why can nobody simply tell the truth? From now on she will see *Papa Roi* through very different eyes. He may appear all sweetness and light, but his true colours are never on show. Why hasn't he been honest with her?

She gives him a warm smile, so that the king resumes his blithe prattle. But the expression on the Dauphine's face is artificial. It is plainer to her than ever that she can trust no one, including the king. Henceforth she will be much more vigilant, watchful of every thought and word she utters.

Oh, what a relief it will be when she becomes Queen of France at last! Then she will be beholden to nobody, and there will come an end to all the treacherous plotting. But for now she has to persevere, play her part in the great pantomime of Versailles, in which her role remains confined to that of *seconda donna*.

It is two hours before the king finally makes a move to leave Marie Antoinette's boudoir. By now he has well and truly demonstrated the depth of his love for his mistress, for in addition to the gorgeous jewellery contained in the packages for the Dauphine, Louis XV has agreed to begin the New Year with two theatre performances a week. That at least makes for two fewer soporific card evenings to sit through, concludes Marie Antoinette with some relief. And, best of all, the Dauphine has the king's permission to continue giving her weekly ball.

February draws to a close, bringing an end to the dreariest month. In the palace grounds all is dull and leaden grey. Apart from the omnipresent crows, there is not a bird to be seen, let alone heard. Only the brown and shrivelled leaves in the beech hedges still hang on the branches; the trees in the park are bare and it seems as though the buds will never burst this spring. A bitter wind keeps everyone indoors, where the draughts keep blowing through corridors and apartments, although all the windows and most of the shutters are closed.

Marie Antoinette trails testily about the room. The Comtesse de Noailles is standing at her ease in the corner and two dogs are snoozing in front of the fire. The clock begins to chime the hour. Any minute now, the newly appointed Cardinal de la Roche-Aymon is due to call to pay his respects.

When the door opens, Marie Antoinette is astonished to see standing there not the cardinal, but the fleshy-faced Duc d'Aiguillon.

'Ah, Madame,' the duke begins in a most cordial and ingratiating tone, 'Your mother, the empress, how is she now?' He assumes an expression of consternation. 'Is Her Majesty feeling better?'

Maria Theresa's daughter gives d'Aiguillon a confused look. 'What do you mean precisely? As far as I know, Mama is in good health.'

'Oh, so you have not yet been informed?'

'What are you talking about, man? What is the matter with my mother?' demands Marie Antoinette in alarm.

The duke makes an apologetic gesture. 'I had no idea you had not been told of the situation, Madame. It would appear that your mother is seriously ill. Her Majesty's physicians have several times had to let blood.' He pulls a pessimistic face.

Wide-eyed with disbelief, the Dauphine returns his gaze. 'Let blood?' she whispers, terrified.

The Comtesse de Noailles chooses this moment to step forward and make her presence felt. 'Are you absolutely sure of this?' she sternly enquires of the young man.

'Absolutely,' swears d'Aiguillon, faintly insulted. How dare Noailles doubt his words!

'Oh, my God!' stammers Marie Antoinette in despair. And, tears welling, she flees into her own boudoir.

'What do you mean to achieve by this?' Noailles grimly demands of the young man. She still has her doubts as to the veracity of his message. Not without grounds, for were there anything wrong with the Empress Maria Theresa, Marie Antoinette would most certainly have heard it directly from the Austrian ambassador.

'Madame, what are you insinuating?' retorts the Duc d'Aiguillon. And he marches furiously out of the salon, practically mowing down the new cardinal in the process.

'Apologies, Your Eminence.' Noailles interrupts the cardinal's private speculation as to the absence of the Dauphine and briefly explains what has just occurred.

'I shall pray for her,' responds the dignitary solemnly, and makes an about-turn.

Marie Antoinette is resorting to the same measure. In her mind's eye she sees her mother on her deathbed. Wasted by fever, surrounded by family and priests offering a final prayer for her, the empress slips inexorably into the next world. Mama! Dear God, she will never again see her mother alive! Oh, how sorry she is that she was never able to present her with a grandchild. How she regrets her recalcitrant letters.

Through her unpractised fingers slips the rosary, a gift from the empress. If only she had prayed more for her! 'Holy Mary, Mother of God, pray for the soul of my mother. Have mercy upon her. Give her another chance of life.'

She prays for hours, until her knees are aching. Overwhelmed by the sense that it is already too late, she prays on.

Ambassador de Mercy, alerted in the meanwhile by the Comtesse de Noailles, is just as nonplussed as Marie Antoinette. He at once dispatches a courier and settles down to wait patiently for a response from Vienna. Days later comes the message that puts them all out of their misery. Mama is fit and well! It seems she had been suffering from nothing more than a bad cold. It was not even so severe that the empress felt it necessary to inform her family, but quite enough excuse for the Duc d'Aiguillon to scare the living daylights out of Marie Antoinette.

The Dauphine wonders what could be the motive behind his feigned concern. She has never much cared for d'Aiguillon, but this incident has shot him to the top of the list of her least favourite people. Mercy too hazards some guesses as to d'Aiguillon's machinations, but soon abandons the effort. In fact, the ambassador is rather pleased with the indirect consequences of d'Aiguillon's intervention. At least it forced Marie Antoinette to admit that she was afraid. Frightened that her mother had died and left her without the support of her family. Who else, in the last analysis, had she to lean upon? Marie Antoinette has now understood that all Mercy's advice and consolation in fact stems from her mother. From now on, the Dauphine will show much more respect for her mother's wishes.

At least, she solemnly promises Mercy, she will do her utmost in this direction.

The Comte de Mercy is well satisfied with Marie Antoinette's behaviour so far, and this spring finds him writing glowing reports to the empress. The Dauphine is spending more time each day with the Abbé Vermond. While she sits embroidering, the priest reads out loud to her from historical texts such as the *Mémoires de l'Estoile*. She is surprised to learn how little the French court has changed. The same scheming and intrigue was going on back in the days of Charles IX, Henri III and Henri IV. The Dauphine feels her ears reddening at the stories she hears about the forefathers of the Comtesse de Noailles and of the La Force, de Rohan and other established families. It's remarkable how some traits of character pass unmodified down through the generations.

'That bodes well for the future,' she remarks with a chuckle.

Every detail is effortlessly stowed away and slowly she builds up a full picture of the French aristocracy and the royal family.

The salon is quieter these days. The Dauphine has reached an age at which she considers it childish to cavort with the offspring of her ladies of the chamber – an opinion shared by her lapdogs, which are now allowed to spend most of the day sleeping peacefully. Marie Antoinette is taking a growing interest in music, and as well as having singing lessons she has taken up the harpsichord and cautiously strummed her first notes on the harp. She sees the aunts only when she is really stuck for something to do, and no longer takes any notice of their words of wisdom.

The Dauphin and Louis-Stanislas are more or less reconciled, and the two young couples spend a lot of time together. The Comte de Provence does his utmost to ingratiate himself, but Marie Antoinette keeps him at a polite distance. The Comtesse de Provence, who pretends to be dimmer than she really is, simply reiterates all her husband's opinions, which does not make for very exciting conversation. On such evenings Louis-Auguste usually manages to turn up late, the same ploy he resorts to for dances.

Up in the attic, where he has installed a workshop, the Dauphin finds it easy to lose track of time. Only his stomach acts as an alarm clock. Once or twice Marie Antoinette has followed him up to the top storey of the palace, where he has created his own world between the rafters: workbenches with vices, racks of strip metal and bronze plate, all ready for working. Louis-Auguste's favourite pastime is lock making. From raw materials he can fashion a finely decorated lock and key that fulfils its function noiselessly. The tiny windows up here afford the Dauphin a magnificent view, while he remains completely hidden from sight. In fine weather he even clambers out onto the roof to revel quietly in the still world about him.

Just looking down makes Marie Antoinette feel dizzy. She has no intention of climbing any higher and refuses his invitation to show her the superb vista. She isn't over-impressed with the workshop, either: it's far too dark and dirty. François Gamain, the locksmith from whom Louis-Auguste is learning the finer points of his craft, she likes even less. Grimy and sallow-skinned, he had regarded her silently, with sombre eyes. Absolutely devoid of manners! Well, those two won't talk the hind legs off one another, anyway, she thought on her way back down the little stepladder.

As long as he washes his hands afterwards, Marie Antoinette has no objection to her husband spending his time filing bits of metal. But Louis-Auguste has also, in his own way, been making more time for his wife. He is doing his absolute best to remedy his two left feet. With all the patience of a mother, the Dauphine goes over the dance steps time and again, leading him across the floor. He has almost begun to enjoy it.

The Austrian ambassador has not been feeling well lately. His stomach is playing up. It could be the pressure he is putting himself under, for Mercy sees the Polish problem looming larger by the day. The business will soon be an open secret, for fragments of news about the partition of Poland are starting to filter into the French court. What a mean trick on Austria's part! Initial reactions are nothing short of hostile. Mercy is not the only one holding his breath; in far-off Vienna, Marie Antoinette's mother is doing the same. But, despite widespread protest and heated discussions at court, Louis XV keeps a laconically cool head.

The Duc d'Aiguillon is astonished and affronted. The king, however, urges calm upon his minister. Louis XV has fought enough wars in his life, and what has he gained from them all? His defeat at Rossbach will remain with him as long as he lives. And the great realm of the Sun King – what is left of it? Louis XV well remembers being summoned as a five-year-old to the deathbed of Louis XIV, his great-grandfather. He had always been terrified of the old man, and even today the 'great' king haunts his nightmares.

'One day you will be a fine sovereign, my child,' the dying Sun King had told him. 'But do not do as I have done, led on by my passion for building. And certainly do not emulate my deeds of war. Try instead to live in peace with our neighbours.'

Wise words from a man whose lips had taken an entire lifetime to form them. But war could not always be avoided. Its powers of seduction were sometimes so great that the sirens of Odysseus paled in comparison. Yet where did it all lead? France had as good as lost all her overseas colonies and the Treasury was empty. No wonder Louis XIV pursued him relentlessly through his dreams, crying in a hollow voice, 'What have you done to my beloved France?'

'That's enough, d'Aiguillon,' Louis XV tells the duke, making no attempt to hide his irritation. 'I don't want to hear another word on the subject. We can and shall do nothing about it. Let well alone.' Stunned, the Duc d'Aiguillon stares at his king. How can he possibly adopt such a stance? He, who is himself married to a daughter of the Polish crown! Surely this is the moment for the full military force of France to descend like an avenging angel upon the Austrians and Prussians?

'Don't let it slip your mind why I unseated Choiseul,' Louis XV reminds him, a note of menace in his voice. The Duc d'Aiguillon bridles. As reality reasserts itself, he finds himself sharing the king's view, for even d'Aiguillon knows that the French army has been waiting months to be paid. Not the best starting point for winning a war.

It's ages since I've seen Antoinette so happy. She's her old self again. After three years' marriage, her sister Carolina is pregnant at last. It's such a relief to Antoinette and gives her renewed hope. Next year she will be almost three years married too. Who knows?

From the journal of the Princesse de Lamballe,
27th February 1772

13

Still in the dark as to how the king really feels about the partition of Poland, the Comte de Mercy brings Marie Antoinette up to date on the prickly situation. She finds it all very complicated, especially when she is asked to neutralise the hostile mood towards Austria.

'How in heaven's name am I to do that, Mercy?' asks the Dauphine helplessly, quickly re-reading the contents of the request passed to the ambassador by her mother.

'Make sure you do nothing that displeases the king. Remain, if you please, gracious to Madame du Barry.'

'What has she got to do with it?' the Dauphine promptly interrupts.

'Madame, do not underestimate her. Luckily, she is no Madame de Pompadour and, as far as I can make out, has no malicious intent. But if you get on the wrong side of the favourite it may have unfortunate repercussions for you and for the alliance. Too many factions have a grudge against Austria at the moment. That is not a pleasant state of affairs, but it may be reversed, as long as the king stays on your side. I cannot judge with confidence how far Louis XV might change his opinion, should Madame du Barry desire it of him. Be sure, therefore, not to make an enemy of her. And, though it pains me to have to say this, the continued absence of an heir gives great comfort to your opponents.'

'Thank you very much for the reminder, Mercy,' returns the Dauphine sharply. 'As if it's my fault! Look at my sister Carolina. Her husband does his very best to pay court to her – which is more than mine manages – and even so it has taken years for her to conceive. These things clearly happen in their own time. There's not a thing I can do about it. I'm not to blame.'

'No one is talking about blame, Madame,' replies Mercy in an attempt to soften his remark.

For a few minutes the only sound is the drumming of Marie Antoinette's fingers upon the mother-of-pearl inlaid surface of her dressing table. Her caustic expression has been replaced by a crestfallen look. 'Very well, Mercy, I understand. I shall do my utmost,' she relents with a sigh. But almost instantly a frown furrows her forehead. 'Mercy, just a moment. What if everything goes wrong? What if, despite my behaving impeccably, Mama and the king get into a dispute? What will happen to me then?'

Mercy hears the tremor of anxiety in her voice and fully understands her fear. In such a situation she would of course find herself caught fast between a rock and a hard place, crushed between two mighty opposing forces. Should he be honest with her?

Speaking as respectfully as he can, he tells her, 'Your Majesty, I shall always remain at your side, whatever happens. Have faith in me, and in your mother. Then all will be well.'

She gives him a wary look. Mercy is not altogether certain he has won her over this time.

So far, the king has shown no sign of any untoward change of mood; he is as cheerful as ever. Louis XV is his usual jocular self at the card table, plays his customary enthusiastic round of billiards and enjoys relaxing in front of a theatrical performance. The Dauphine seriously doubts whether the king knows anything about the partition of Poland, which will be settled by a treaty to be signed this summer in Saint Petersburg. The Comte de Mercy assures her that Louis XV is indeed well aware of events, but apparently has no desire to intervene. 'Thanks in great part to your own exemplary conduct, Madame,' he compliments her.

The Polish question is never mentioned in Marie Antoinette's presence. But, one evening during the royal family's summer retreat at Compiègne, Louis-Stanislas frightens the life out of everyone with a jibe about Poland. It is not meant at all seriously, but the word 'Poland' echoes long through the salon. Marie Antoinette looks thoroughly embarrassed, until the king bursts out laughing. 'For goodness' sake, let's not start on about Poland,' he says, grinning and beckoning to the Dauphine. She meekly takes her place upon his knee. Despite the sultry evening, the Comte de Provence has managed to give her goose pimples.

'No,' continues the king, his tone grave now, 'it isn't polite to discuss Poland in your presence. Your family, after all, has quite a different perspective on the matter. Were we to continue on this subject – who knows, we might find ourselves in disagreement, and then we'd have to send you packing, off back to Austria.'

Marie Antoinette holds her breath. You could hear a pin drop. Suddenly the king erupts into fresh gales of laughter and gives his granddaughter-in-law a hug. Nervously, she giggles along with him, until everyone joins in the hilarity.

The Dauphine is becoming more and more conscious of the peculiar world she inhabits, and it gives her an uncomfortable feeling. Sometimes she can see the funny side, such as when she takes part in private little theatrical performances with her sister-in-law and her brothers-in-law. For what is the difference between life at court and the characters of Molière? According to the Dauphin, who has no talent for acting and so takes his place as sole member of the audience, there is none.

The onstage antics of his brothers and the princesses keep Louis-Auguste in stitches. It is the Comte de Provence who steals every show. Though that is rather a foregone conclusion, since he who acts opposite Orgon and Elmire has only to play himself.

'I've always said it,' splutters the Dauphin as Tartuffe is carted off, unmasked by the king's officer: 'he's made for the part.' This time, the Comte de Provence takes it as a compliment.

But where does the acting stop and real life begin? Marie Antoinette finds this a very tricky question. Somehow the boundaries melt away and a Molière tragicomedy or some daft farce by Goldoni flows seamlessly into the repetitive court rituals of Versailles. It is gradually dawning on La Dauphine how dangerous are the games played here. Now over seventeen years old, she realises all too well that every day brings her own occupancy of the throne closer. That is, unless she is sent away in the meanwhile.

The Comte de Mercy subjects her to regular long diatribes in which he details the national predicament. Not that anyone will expect much of her when the time comes, for the task of the Queen of France is simply to provide the king with sufficient heirs. She has no political role assigned to her. It has always been thus. But Mercy has other ideas, for the Dauphin has still failed to make any real impression on him. The boy is not stupid; he is simply not made of the right stuff.

It is as clear as daylight to the ambassador that it is Marie Antoinette who wears the breeches in the marriage. Comte de Mercy cannot guess what consequences that will have when the Dauphin ascends the throne. Louis XV is getting old, as Mercy notes from the monarch's every move these days. The French king may like to think he is immortal, but all the signs point the other way. The lines in his face are deepening, for days at a time all the wind seems to be gone from his sails, and his memory is failing. Only God knows when the end will come.

It is not that either Mercy or the Empress Maria Theresa relishes the prospect; they certainly do not. The Dauphin and Dauphine are still far too young to carry the responsibilities of the monarchy. The more so at the present moment, when matters of State look so grim. On the other hand, it has crossed Mercy's philosophical mind that it is Louis XV who has made such a mess of everything. Might a new monarch turn the tide? But a single glance at Louis-Auguste is enough to show him that the reverse is true. With the best will in the world, this young man who spends too much time staring apathetically into space does not have it in him to put his country back on course.

The Comte de Mercy is a natural optimist, but these days his unease about the future is getting the better of him. It is with increasing anxiety that the ambassador follows the events unfolding around him. The reforms introduced by Chancellor Maupeou have borne little fruit. Unrest and civil disobedience may appear to have abated, but continue to simmer beneath the surface. Although the Princes of the Blood are returning to court one by one as the king buys back their favour, the aristocracy continues to insist that its privileges be upheld. Paying tax is the lot of the labouring class; the nobility stands above it! That is how things have always been – but will they forever remain so?

Mercy is familiar, too, with the works of Voltaire and Rousseau, and is perhaps more capable than most of reading between the lines. If these writers are to be believed, the values held by the common people and so firmly anchored in their mediaeval past are no longer taken for granted. The Enlightenment has brought in new ideas; people are learning to think for themselves. And that, as Mercy observes, is extremely perilous.

With knitted brow he sits down to read the latest publication to issue from Maupeou's pen, *Letters from the Provinces: A Study of the Origin, Constitution and Revolutions of the French Monarchy*. Underlining one passage after another with his pencil, the ambassador resolves to discuss the content with Marie Antoinette. Maupeou openly denounces all the scandals and misdeeds of the corrupt government and the previous *parlement*, and not wholly without reason. The examples he quotes are shocking in the extreme: corrupt judges and magistrates perverting the course of justice so that the innocent land in gaol, or worse.

Voltaire, himself only too familiar with the inside of the Bastille, is unsurprisingly lending his full support to the chancellor's plans. The disbanding of the *parlements* enraged the nobility and many asked themselves where things were heading. Voltaire may be cheering Maupeou on, but Diderot, editor-in-chief of the *Encyclopédie*, takes a very different view. And many agree with him that Louis XV is sliding towards the worst sort of despotism.

Yet, despite all the spluttering and muttering and the protests from the Princes of the Blood, Maupeou slowly but surely pursues his course. The man is on the right track, thinks Mercy, finishing the last page and placing the book down on the table. But will the chancellor have wind enough to follow through to the end? One moment of weakness is all it takes to lose momentum – and what if the king should choose today to pass away? Could the Dauphin hold the nobility at bay long enough for Maupeou to finish his work?

All the ambassador can do is ask Marie Antoinette to bring this book to the attention of the Dauphin. It can do no harm to stimulate the young man's awareness somewhat, for what is the alternative? To Mercy it is crystal clear. The forces Maupeou has let loose are too dangerous to be given free rein. Only an authoritative and powerful leader with the right vision is capable of steering the process of renewal along the right path. And, to his great regret and disquiet, the Austrian ambassador does not detect the desired characteristics in the Dauphin.

'He means well,' parries Marie Antoinette in response to Mercy's concerns.

'Madame, his good intentions are not in question. But determination, strong leadership, a clear will; these are the elements that concern me.'

She gives the ambassador a pensive look. She knows Mercy is right. But what is she to do about it? Can someone change character overnight? 'Whom might the Dauphin take as model, Mercy? The king?'

The diplomat meditates on his reply, hesitating to give voice to his thoughts. 'Madame, Louis XV is certainly not the cause of all the problems facing this country. To suggest so would be to oversimplify. But I am afraid that the present King of France will not go down in history as the greatest of monarchs.

'To try to answer your question; there is no single past personage who possessed all the characteristics that might serve as an example. Every human being, even a king, has his shortcomings. We must choose for ourselves which of our predecessors' deeds we wish to emulate. The Dauphin, if he wishes to be a successful king, must excel. I am convinced that, with your help, your husband will become a king who will live on in the memories of future generations.'

The compliment brings a smile to Marie Antoinette's lips, despite the undertone of anxiety. 'I can only do my best, Mercy,' she promises the ambassador solemnly, before returning to the book he has given her, the text dark with underlining.

Fired by Mercy's stories and intrigued by Maupeou's writings, the Dauphine forms a mental picture of a famished and tortured France. A land where farm labourers slave on their master's land for starvation wages. Where the poor and unemployed roam the streets in search of a crust of bread, and innocent wretches starve behind rusty bars, ridiculed by corpulent magistrates.

The ghastly image makes her shiver, so she puts it from her mind. She knows she has a vivid imagination, but this cannot be true. It is a world undreamed of even in her worst nightmares. No, this must be an exaggeration.

She remembers very well the one day she has spent in Paris. The festive crowds showered the Dauphin and herself with blessings, wishing them eternal happiness. Surely there were no sad faces among them? It was her wedding day, of course: everyone looked happy.

But she recalls too how, the same evening, the densely packed throng stampeded in the darkness, crushing hundreds to death. The event had cast a terrible shadow over the wedding festivities. The very memory makes the hair prickle on the back of her neck. Marie Antoinette has never been back to Paris since. But can it have changed so much? Can it really now be as Maupeou describes? Shutting the book, she pushes it away from her. Tomorrow she will see Lamballe again. She will ask her cousin how things really are in the city.

The king is sick. His doctors are not being very forthcoming about his true condition, but the rumour is that his days are numbered. It's making Antoinette nervous, but me even more so. Imagine, just a little while and Antoinette will be free to do whatever she likes. Every day a dancing day!

From the journal of the Princesse de Lamballe,
8th April 1772

14

Twenty-four hours later and Marie Antoinette has forgotten her weighty discussion with the Comte de Mercy. Carnival is nearly over and, now that the Princes of the Blood are back at court, evening balls are as busily attended as ever they were. The princes queue up to dance with the Dauphine. In their absence she has made a name for herself on the dance floor, and nowadays there is no one at Versailles who can match her for grace – not even a du Barry. She glides across the ballroom like an angel, by general assent a joy to behold.

But, as Carnival draws to an end, she finds she has had her fill of gazing into the same masks. A new diversion would be welcome. The Princesse de Lamballe has turned her head with stories of how Carnival is celebrated in the capital. They really know how to party there! Lamballe is aware of hardly any hunger or poverty. Naturally, there are always scroungers and beggars on the city streets – maybe a few more than formerly, but nothing to worry about. Chancellor Maupeou must be seeing things.

Marie Antoinette listens with mounting curiosity to Lamballe's reports of the Opéra ball. Might there be someone in Paris who is lighter on her feet than the Dauphine? Lamballe denies it, but Marie Antoinette knows that Marie-Thérèse has placed her on a pedestal. Oh, how she would love to accompany her cousin to Paris!

The next time she finds herself upon his knee, the Dauphine gaily asks the king's permission to attend the last evening of Carnival in Paris. She would like to take the Dauphin and the Comte and Comtesse de Provence with her.

'Of course, child. Why not?' replies Louis XV, to everyone's amazement. Before he can change his mind, Marie Antoinette plants a big kiss on *Papa Roi*'s cheek.

For hours they have danced undisturbed. But all that comes to an end when someone recognises the Dauphin. In no time the news spreads through the festive multitude of his and the Dauphine's presence among them, and people press excitedly around the pair. Philippe, Duc de Chartres and brother-in-law of Lamballe, is delighted and surprised to find himself in the company of family.

'Let's carry on dancing at my place,' shouts a rather worse for wear Chartres, who lives in the adjoining Palais Royal. But the Dauphin has had enough for this evening. He is not overly fond of his cousin and knows very well that the king would not appreciate his fraternising with Chartres; he and his arrogant father, the Duc d'Orléans, are the most unruly Princes of the Blood. Marie Antoinette is just as unenthusiastic, for she has heard only poor reports of Chartres from Lamballe. What is more, it is late enough already, and the journey back to Versailles will take them another hour and a half.

The palace is half shrouded in mist. Most of the torches have been extinguished, but the horses know exactly where to stop. Marie Antoinette, Louis-Auguste and the Comte and Comtesse de Provence step sleepily down from the coach. 'What an evening!' Marie Antoinette sighs with pleasure as she climbs the steps. The smiles on everyone's lips are answer enough. Even the Dauphin has stayed up all evening and enjoyed himself far into the night. Everyone is completely exhausted and longing for bed. But Louis-Auguste considers a logical antidote to the night's excesses is to attend early morning Mass. Yawning, the partygoers stumble along behind the Dauphin.

As Marie Antoinette slips between the sheets an hour later, dawn is already flushing the sky. For the first time in ages she falls straight asleep.

It is almost midday when Marie Antoinette wakes. She still feels a little light-headed, as if she has just come off the dance floor. What a wonderful evening that was! So full of merriment and free of intrigue. Reliving it all in her mind, she realises just how much pleasure it gave her, and she doesn't want to let the feeling go. Oh, what a shame they were discovered! The thrill of dancing incognito among all the masked partygoers was an experience in itself. But on top of that there was the bliss of being able to come and go unobserved and unadmonished. An indescribable sense of liberty! Almost as good as galloping wildly along on horseback, trying to shake off her outriders, with the wind tugging at her hair. But this was different. Last night she could waft across the floor as gracefully as in a dream, and when she turned about there was no one following on her heels. She was alone, despite the crowd. She was free!

Closing her eyes, Marie Antoinette imagines herself back at the Opéra. That sense of happiness that for so long has been out of her reach – she never wants to let it go. In the background the sweet tones of the dance music ... how lovely it all was! This afternoon she must try to recapture the melodies on her harp.

Slowly the days are lengthening and the birds are beginning to warble. The first fresh vegetables are appearing on the table. Delicious! Everyone is sick and tired of salted, bottled, pickled and dried produce. What is finer than to taste the first fresh lettuce from the field, crisp and crunchy between your teeth? There is a spring in every step. The blossom in the park invites the courtiers outside for a stroll, a welcome change from the long winter months spent cooped up in the palace.

For, apart from dances and the theatre, life has little to offer the many ladies of Versailles. The most popular occupation among the countesses is *parfilage*, which has become quite the rage of late. To Marie Antoinette it seems an inane pastime. Where is the fun in unravelling old epaulettes? The goldsmiths of Paris, never slow to exploit a good opportunity, make up for a shortage of epaulettes by fashioning intricate little figures from gold thread, which go down very well among the bored ladies of Versailles.

The hammering headache from which Louis XV has been suffering for days has done nothing for his mood. The King of France has not been sleeping well these past few nights, and is afflicted by regular bouts of violent coughing caused by an accumulation of tenacious mucus deep in his lungs. Even the presence of his mistress is too much for him. For whole days and nights on end she waits in her apartment for the sound of the king's approaching footsteps, but they do not come.

The Most Christian King of France is worried. He feels unwell and fears the end approaching. The most powerful man in France is realistic enough to face the truth. He has lost many a relative and friend much younger than he is now. Just last week, during a game of cards, his old comrade Louis Armand keeled over in his chair and was gone. A heart attack. And the poor fellow was winning too, for the first time in ages.

It gives the king food for thought. How long has he left? His priests look sombre, as do his doctors. The long hours out hunting and endless sessions of lovemaking with the *maîtresse en titre* are taking their toll on the monarch. One doctor has even had the temerity to intone, 'You ask too much of your body, Sire. There are limits!'

At such moments of vulnerability, Louis XV seems to heed his advisors. Does he really lead too dissipated a life? He is seriously beginning to wonder. Should he take a little distance from his mistress, and follow the hunt in a carriage from now on? Would it be an idea for him to attend Mass now and then, perhaps go to confession for the good of his eternal soul? Up to now he has always recovered just in time not to have to make any concessions to his mortality. Life without a woman is no life at all, certainly not if the woman in question is Jeanne du Barry.

But this time things feel different. The king is convinced his days are numbered. This brings with it another problem: his successor. Louis XV has three grandsons, after which the Bourbon dynasty fizzles out. Why do none of the boys get going and produce a child? The thought that the Orléans might take over the throne horrifies him. The sick king muses on, half dreaming. If he had been the Dauphin, he would have given Marie Antoinette at least two children. She has a sound constitution, after all.

Why doesn't the boy do his duty by her? Louis XV knows that the Dauphin has made hardly a move to make the daughter of the Austrian archduchess his wife. Unbelievable! The child gets more beautiful by the day. Her breasts are beginning to fill out, and oh, those buttocks! But mentally undressing his granddaughter only worsens the king's headache. With a sigh he struggles to redirect his thoughts. He turns over again and presses his hands against his temples. Might praying help after all?

Without being forced to have serious recourse to God, after two days the French sovereign feels sufficiently recovered to leave his bed. The court is surprised when Louis XV allows himself to be dressed. And, as on so many previous occasions, he disappoints his physicians and father confessors by once again picking up the threads of his old life, much to the joy of du Barry.

The king does, however, let it be known at court that he has decided to marry off the Comte d'Artois later that year to Marie-Thérèse, the Comtesse de Provence's sister. He then summons Jean-Marie Lassone, physician to Marie Antoinette. 'Well?' the king asks the doctor significantly. 'Have we still hope for the future?' The query is not devoid of sarcasm.

'Do not worry, Sire,' nods the physician. 'I have conducted lengthy discussions with the Dauphin and the Dauphine. From my enquiries I cannot deduce anything amiss. It is certainly not a matter of unwillingness. On the contrary, I have rather the distinct impression that Her Royal Highness greatly looks forward to a pregnancy. In so far as I can make a diagnosis, the continued absence of a child is more a question of inexperience.'

Louis XV frowns at the medical man. 'Inexperience?' repeats

the king, belligerence creeping into his voice. 'The clumsy oaf! Is it really that complicated? Are you quite sure my grandson knows what is expected of him? Or do I have to give him a demonstration?'

Doctor Lassone continues to fix the king with earnest eyes. 'Your Majesty, have a little more patience. It is merely a question of time.'

That's easy to say, thinks Louis XV to himself, but how much more time have I got? Anyway, all will be well once Artois is married, he reflects. The amorous adventures of his youngest grandson have not escaped the king's notice. It won't be long before the Comte d'Artois can turn his attention to making his bride into a wife, rather than keeping a smile on the face of every countess at court. There's something to be thankful for, chuckles the descendent of the Sun King with pride; at least I've bred one full-blooded Bourbon to add to the list!

'What a wonderful tale,' sighs Marie Antoinette, wiping a tear from the corner of her eye. 'Oh, I could read it all over again from the beginning,' and she presses her precious copy of *La Nouvelle Héloïse* lovingly to her breast. 'What else has this Rousseau written?' she asks avidly of the Abbé Vermond.

The priest cannot resist a sideways smile at his pupil. Not so long ago the Dauphine showed scarcely any interest in the written word. The brand new shelves in her library have since been filled, though mostly with imitation volumes. Their spines of Morocco leather, beautifully embellished with her insignia, carry the titles of well-known works of literature and lengthy theological and historical tracts. 'It looks lovely,' was the Dauphine's artless reaction when architect Gabriel unveiled the library.

But on a couple of occasions lately Marie Antoinette has been hoist by her own petard. Alighting on a title that appealed to her, she went to tilt the soft leather spine down from the shelf, only to find it stuck fast. The *faux livres* are very realistic. She laughed at herself, but instructed Vermond to order the relevant book immediately.

History remains her favourite subject: she is most inspired by tales of past kings and even more of queens. But now she has acquired a taste for the work of the philosopher Jean-Jacques Rousseau, and she is keen to read much more of his œuvre. Vermond is deeply satisfied. He had never dared hope to awaken any literary interest in the Dauphine, so he turns a blind eye when she indulges now and then in lighter reading. She much enjoys stories by Marie Jeanne Riccoboni and the more adventurous Thémiseul de Saint-Hyacinthe. Of course, these are slight narratives, written always to the same formula with an identical romantic plot. But Marie Antoinette devours the *Histoire du Prince Titi* just as hungrily as the tale of Claire and Julie.

'To what extent should France be concerned, ambassador?' asks the king testily of the Comte de Mercy, whom he has summoned for a personal interview. Mercy finds the absence of any other ministers encouraging. Apparently, Louis XV is not inclined to take the situation too seriously.

'In order to give a clear signal, Mercy, I must inform you that I have mobilised the fleet. I have one flotilla at anchor in Toulon and one in Brest, each ready to set sail.'

'Sire,' replies the Austrian ambassador in level tones, 'that will not be necessary. Austria's alliance with Russia comes a very poor second to maintaining friendly relations with France. There is absolutely no incentive at the present time for my sovereign to engage in armed struggle with your ally Turkey.'

Louis XV laughs ironically. 'Why, of course not, Mercy. The very idea of it!' mocks the King of France. 'For the rest, I am well pleased with the conduct of the Dauphine,' he continues, neatly changing the subject.

The Comte de Mercy bows in acknowledgement of the compliment. 'When, Sire, does it please you to formally introduce the Dauphin and Dauphine to Paris?' Mercy knows all about their nightly visits to the opera in the capital. In principle, there is no objection to them. But the ambassador has also heard the expressions of dissent. Why these clandestine visits to the city in the dead of night when there has never been an official royal entry? Traditionally, the wedding of a dauphin is followed by a State visit to Paris. Is it not about time, nearly three years after the wedding?

Mercy is also aware that Louis XV hardly ever shows his face in the capital, and the Comtesse du Barry even less. There is little love lost nowadays between the common folk and the French monarch they once dubbed 'Le Bien-Aimé'. For precisely this reason, Mercy wishes to prevent the future King and Queen of France becoming estranged from the people. His sources tell him that the charming Dauphine is adored in the capital, despite the fact that hardly a citizen of Paris has seen her in the flesh. It is high time this changed. Mercy is convinced that her smile will win over every heart in Paris. And that will be more than necessary, given the state into which Paris and the rest of the country is sliding.

The price of bread remains astronomical, and Maupeou's new *parlement* is far from popular. Frustration among the middle classes is increasing by the day, for while taxation rises the bourgeoisie are still denied a political voice. That the nobility, headed by an inviolable king, still has the last word, despite Maupeou's reforms, is a bitter pill for hard-working Parisians – craftsman and tradesman, baker and market trader – to swallow.

Louis XV knows there is no way out for him. The State entry of the Dauphin and Dauphine has to go ahead some time. But must he be there himself? He smiles inwardly. 'Very good, Mercy, thank you for reminding me. This should have happened long ago, of course. Let the Dauphine choose a date.'

The ambassador is stunned. Years of dithering and now he suddenly caves in without a murmur? That's the king all over.

But what Mercy doesn't yet know is that the king has no intention of accompanying his grandchildren. The Most Christian King of France is determined not to provide the Parisians with the slightest excuse for inflammatory words or offensive behaviour. That aside, Louis XV is hugely intrigued to see how the people will respond to the entry of the crown prince and princess. It's just that he would rather observe it from a safe distance.

I'm still trying to recover from yesterday. What an emotional whirlwind! Who would ever have thought it? Antoinette wants to come back as soon as possible. But won't Paris tire of her if she overdoes it? Only time will tell.

From the Journal of the Princesse de Lamballe,
15th June 1772

15

Harnessed and ready for off, the horses scrape their hooves impatiently on the cobblestones. They seem as excited as the human company taking its place in the carriages this sunny Tuesday morning in June. Marie Antoinette is wearing a light pink, delicately embroidered floral gown. She takes her place next to the Dauphin in a *calèche en gondole* that affords the couple protection from the sun while leaving them in clear view of all spectators.

The day is glorious: the heavens azure blue, with the lightest of breezes promising more warmth to come. As the procession of coaches gets underway, the clatter of hooves bounces off the palace walls and ascends to the open window from which Louis XV is keeping a close eye on the proceedings through his telescope.

The *calèche* carrying the royal pair is followed by a regiment of bodyguards, and behind them more carriages conveying the Princesse de Lamballe, the Comtesse de Noailles, ladies in waiting, Ambassador de Mercy and, last but not least, the aunts. Proudly bringing up the rear, the cavalry is decked out in its finest livery.

'Isn't it dangerous to go off to Paris in such an open carriage?' asks Madame du Barry in a lackadaisical show of concern, peering over the king's shoulder.

'Don't you worry,' growls the king, 'nothing untoward will happen today. Paris is in a good mood. For the occasion, I have granted an amnesty to a couple of hundred prisoners and arranged for a delegation of fishwives from *la Halle* to lunch at the Tuileries. Together with the appearance of the Dauphine, that should melt the heart of any Parisian.'

The king watches until the train of carriages has completely disappeared from sight. He wishes he could see all the way to Paris.

The nearer they get to the city, the greater the throng. People abandon their work to rush to the roadside, curious to catch a glimpse of the approaching retinue. The men respectfully doff their hats and stand on tiptoe to see over the heads of those in front. Youths run lanky-legged along behind the carriages, so that the procession soon turns into a thoroughgoing parade. As they near the city gates, the crowds pressing on every side prevent the horses from advancing any further.

The hordes make the Dauphin nervous. Marie Antoinette places a reassuring hand on his arm, waving with her other hand and bestowing her most charming smile on the farmers pressing about the carriage.

'Long live *Madame la Dauphine!*' is the constant chorus.

The ceremonial handing over of the keys to the city requires a brief halt, after which, accompanied by the Duc de Brissac, Governor of Paris, the cavalcade continues along the bank of the Seine.

The thunder of cannon summons everyone onto the streets and a mood of euphoria takes hold. Shopkeepers, workers, priests – they form a river pouring along every byway. Schools, poorhouses and hospitals too empty their occupants into the flow. Anyone and everyone capable of walking is making for the city centre. Even the market hall, usually bursting at the seams, is deserted as the *femmes de la Halle* rush out to find the royal couple. None wants to miss seeing the future queen with her own eyes.

The royal coach manages somehow to negotiate its way to Notre Dame, where the archbishop is to say a special Mass, the serenity and silence of the ancient cathedral in sharp contrast to the clamour outside.

The multitude that has gathered in the meanwhile begins cheering wildly as the Dauphin and Dauphine make their reappearance at the top of the cathedral steps. Firmly seated on their mounts and towering above the heads of the crowd, the bodyguards hold the Parisians at bay. The train of carriages moves off again. At walking pace, the horses climb the hill and pause, sweating and steaming, outside the unfinished church of Sainte Geneviève. Making a wide circuit through the city to avoid the worst of the mobs, the retinue trots past the Carmelite convent and via the Ile Saint-Louis reaches the opposite bank of the Seine. On past the town hall, *l'Hôtel de Ville*, the quay, streets and squares are crammed with swaying townsfolk joyfully cheering the grandchildren of the king.

From every wide-flung window and balcony, waving Parisians shout down to the procession: *'Vive Monsieur le Dauphin et vive Madame la Dauphine!'* There is not a thought in Paris today for the old king.

Once at the Tuileries Palace, brainchild of Catherine de Medici, the couple have a chance to draw breath. They are impressed.

'Oh, look at that!' cries Louis-Auguste ecstatically, catching sight of the laden dining table. He wastes no time in sitting down and tucking in. 'I'm dying of hunger,' he mumbles with a full mouth to Marie Antoinette as she takes her place next to him. 'So it would appear,' is her curt reply. The whole morning the Dauphin has hardly uttered a word or shown a spark of interest in anything they have seen or heard, but a full table is a different matter altogether, it seems. She hates it when he stuffs himself like this, especially since he ate a huge breakfast this morning.

Through the open doors comes the noisy prattle of the market fishwives invited in the name of Louis XV to lunch with the Dauphin and Dauphine. If their hilarity and loud toasts are anything to go by, they are thoroughly enjoying their royal repast. One by one they make a ludicrous gesture of respect to the Dauphine, who returns their greetings with a friendly smile. *Mes charmants vilains sujets*, she thinks naively, scooping up a spoonful of the lukewarm soup she has just been served. Far too salty!

At the far end of the room the doors stand open onto the

gallery, and swarms of Parisians are shuffling past, each peering in so that they can tell their friends they saw the Dauphin and Dauphine at lunch. Marie Antoinette hardly touches her food, she is so busy smiling sweetly at her audience. The crown prince presses on with his meal regardless. Some passers-by hungrily ogle the grilled dove and roast chicken gradually disappearing before their eyes. Others gaze just as avidly at the Dauphine, sitting there straight-backed and entrancing everyone with her angelic smile. Some males of the species find themselves completely bewitched – goodness, she is lovely!

The daughter of the Empress of the Holy Roman Empire does not know quite what to make of all these watching faces. Children staring at her in wide-eyed admiration and toothless old hags with their steady, respectful gaze, but also squinting spongers with unshaven faces and pockmarked women gaping sadly or enviously at the Dauphine's flawless complexion.

A group of *poissardes* approaches, preceded by their own shrill shrieks and a rancid stench of rotting fish. Don't they ever bathe? Marie Antoinette asks herself in bewilderment as the whiff of putrefaction assails her nostrils. The volume increases as the fishwives recognise their colleagues further down the hall. Oblivious of etiquette, the *poissardes* scream loud salutations at one another over Marie Antoinette's head in such crude accents that the Dauphine has no idea what they are saying or the reason for their raucous laughter. Thoughtfully she lays down her spoon, keeping her smile in place. And there it stays, even when one bright spark screeches out, 'When are you going to present us with an heir, Madame la Dauphine?'

Marie Antoinette cannot resist giving the Dauphin's ankle a gentle kick. 'Do you hear that?' she whispers so that no one else can hear. The Dauphin, deep in contemplation of a beautiful burgundy, looks up from his glass. 'What?' He gives her a sheepish look.

'Oh, never mind,' she sighs resignedly. 'It's nothing.'

Lunch over, the Duc de Brissac and the Comte de Mercy rejoin the party. The governor suggests treating the Parisians to an appearance on the grand balcony. Louis-Auguste would prefer a little nap, but understands that this is not in order. The huge windows are flung open to admit an inrush of stale and oppressive city air, but worse is to come.

A remarkable din meets Marie Antoinette's ears; a deep drone as of myriad flies trapped in a confined space. Then, just as she and Louis-Auguste are about to step out onto the balcony, she jumps back in alarm. 'Mon Dieu!' The terraces and gardens of the Tuileries have been transformed into a surging mass of people, rolling and roaring like a great sea monster: 'Vive Monsieur le Dauphin, vive Madame la Dauphine!'

Marie Antoinette looks aghast at the Dauphin, who blinks back, as appalled as she. 'Mon Dieu!' echoes the crown prince. Stammering and unnerved he adds, 'There are so many of them.'

As far as the eye can see, the green fields of Elysées are teeming.

Propelled more by curiosity than by courage, the Dauphine masters her diffidence and steps forward. The tumult grows as she raises her hand to wave to the enthralled populace. Hats and caps fly through the air; there is dancing, singing and applause. 'Hoorah!' cries the elated crowd. It is as if they cannot get enough of the princess. Still she graciously waves from on high. Convinced that the people's cheers are for his wife alone, the Dauphin steps back.

As she waves and smiles with increasing self-confidence, the Dauphine becomes aware of a strange new sensation spreading through her.

'You have a new admirer, Madame,' the enraptured Duc de Brissac shouts above the uproar. 'The whole of Paris lies at your feet.'

She hardly hears the governor's flattering words, so engrossed is she in her audience. With every breath she feels her stature increase, and for the first time she really begins to grasp how it would feel to be Queen of France.

Even the seasoned Austrian ambassador is impressed by this reception. Never before has the diplomat witnessed such a huge show of public feeling. Its effect upon the Dauphine's comportment has not escaped him either. Every flutter of her hand gives rise to louder cheering; she plays the people as a puppet master manipulates his marionettes on strings. Marie Antoinette may be thrilled by it all, but inwardly Mercy is deeply troubled.

He is afraid of this rabble. Frightened of the potential power that lies dormant in the beast. Today the Parisians are cheering, but what will be their mood tomorrow? Through his head resound Maupeou's words; written words they may be, but they shout as loud as the mob. What will happen when this vast army of citizens is no longer satisfied with a smile from Madame la Dauphine?

She is so touched that tears are pouring down her crimson cheeks. 'What a magnificent experience, what lovely people!' Marie Antoinette leans further forward as if to wrap herself in the warm mantle of their adulation. On and on she waves like one mesmerised, moistening her dry lips with her tongue. For the first time since she arrived in France, Marie Antoinette feels welcome here. Her whole body is trembling in response to the unconditional love of these people; surely she must be dreaming.

'*Vive la Dauphine!*' The princess wallows in their praise. Listen to them all! She longs to drown in the crowd, to drink in the warm affection of these true Parisians.

'Come with me, Louis,' she calls impulsively. 'We're going down.' Her husband gives her an uncomprehending stare. It always takes a minute or two for him to decipher the meaning of Marie Antoinette's words. 'We're going down to them, to the gardens.'

The Duc de Brissac wonders whether this is such a good plan. The Comtesse de Noailles splutters something about it being against protocol to walk among the common people. But the Dauphine, her proud head held regally erect, looks straight past her Mistress of the Household. The Marie Antoinette now leaving the balcony is a completely different person from the young Dauphine who ascended it.

Carried aloft on the cheers of the masses, the veils of childish innocence drift from her eyes forever. She is at home in France at last!

'Move! Make way there!' shout the bodyguards grimly, shoving the crowd before them. The first reaction from the mob is raised fists and outraged cries of 'Hey, what's all this about?' The answer comes in the form of Marie Antoinette appearing in person on the terrace with the Dauphin and their entourage.

'Vive Madame la Dauphine!' A roar goes through the masses as the news spreads. 'They're down here! The Dauphin and Dauphine are in the gardens!' The applause is deafening. Out from the undergrowth rush hordes of youngsters, abandoning their play to clamber on one another's shoulders for a better view of the royal pair. 'There they are!' comes the shout from high in the branches of a tree.

As fast as the bodyguards clear a path, it is blocked again, and very soon the crown prince and princess cannot take another step forward.

'Steady on,' cautions the Dauphin, as a bodyguard threatens to push an over-enthusiastic bystander to the ground. 'I don't want to see anyone getting hurt,' Louis-Auguste instructs the captain of the guard.

Mercy watches from his vantage point on the terrace, hardly daring to draw breath. It's absurd to mingle like that with the public. Asking for trouble. His instinct has told him to remain where he is. Like everyone else in the royal party, he is hoping against hope that nothing goes wrong, that no idiot out there takes it into his head to harm Marie Antoinette.

Mercy knows he will have a great deal of explaining to do in Vienna. On the terrace beside him stand the remaining members of the bodyguard, keeping an eagle eye on the situation and ready to spring into action at the first word of command. The Princesse de Lamballe stares down into the gardens, gnawing distractedly on a fingernail, her large eyes dark with concern. Please God, let everything be all right.

But the public behaves in an exemplary manner. People shout and cheer, but no one touches the Dauphine. They simply want to show their adoration, and it seems that nothing can break the spell she has cast this afternoon.

It is late afternoon before the Dauphin and Dauphine, exhausted but still flushed with excitement, set off on the journey back to Versailles. The caravan makes its way along the dusty road to meet the setting sun, leaving behind a city bubbling with euphoria.

Louis XV sees the horses approaching from afar. About time too! Slightly concerned by their long absence, he focuses his telescope on them. The misty image is transformed into a fresco of smiling faces. Are they so happy to have escaped Paris and be arriving safe and sound back at Versailles?

A little later he hears all from the lips of Marie Antoinette herself, as she rushes to him on dancing feet, her eyes still shining. 'Oh, Papa, you should have been there! It was so magnificent! You must be very greatly loved by the people, otherwise they would never have given us such a welcome.'

Mercy can hardly restrain himself from laughing, but diplomatic decorum prevails. The king knits his brow at the compliment. Louis XV is sanguine enough to know that his days as *Le Bien-Aimé* lie far behind him. With a broad smile, the old man embraces the princess, whispering gratefully in her ear, 'That's a very nice thing to say.'

Paris is buzzing with the *Joyeuse Entrée*. For the first time in many years, the royal family has offered a spark of hope to the common people, the vast majority of Parisians. The old king avoids the city, and who can still remember anything about the former Dauphin? The only picture in people's minds now is Marie Antoinette's fresh face, and they cannot find glowing words enough to do her justice. Her charm and grace are all that anyone can talk about.

Unbeknown to her, the Parisians now see the crown princess as the symbol of a future wherein everything is possible. They glimpse in her the dawn of a new age, one in which all the bitter memories of the old King Louis XV will be banished with his death. One in which taxes will come down and the price of bread will tumble. For anyone who shows such care for the common folk as the Dauphine did last Tuesday will be sure to look after them well.

Any remaining doubts vanish when the Dauphin and Dauphine pay another visit to the city two days later. Ovations for the royal couple ring out just as loud at the Opéra, the Comédie Française and the Italian theatre. Marie Antoinette has taken the city and its inhabitants to her heart. The combination of adulation and escape from the intrigues of Versailles makes for a heady mixture; it fills her with so much new energy that she grasps any chance to return to the capital.

Louis XV is delighted. Reports passed to him by his *lieutenant général de police* Sartine, detailing the public's response, fill him with optimism; such a pleasant change from the sombre news previously reaching him from Paris. The mood in the capital had seemed to be entirely dictated by Maupeou's reforms and the price of bread. But who cares about all that now? A breath of fresh air is blowing though the city and the French monarch takes grateful advantage of it. State visits to the various universities and museums in the capital are arranged. The Mint is on the list, as are hospitals, tapestry workshops and the Royal Library. The artists' studios surrounding the Louvre, the porcelain factories – all are honoured with a visit from Marie Antoinette and the Dauphin.

At first Louis-Auguste accompanies his wife on all her excursions, but the crown prince soon tires of them. He feels ill at ease among all these people making speeches and anxiously awaiting a response from the Dauphine. Marie Antoinette revels in it all. She loves seeing new faces and looks forward every day to encounters with people she has never met before, individuals who consider it an honour just to speak to her.

No intrigues, no double entendres. Just ordinary people who

love her! With her delicate smile and a few well-chosen words she touches the heart of everyone she meets. From the most tight-lipped and stringent professor to the weaver working fast and furious at his loom, she leaves all with a sense of blessedness, joy that this day in their life deserved the notice of the future queen.

Maupeou's work, meanwhile, proceeds unhindered.

I've ruined everything. How could I have been so stupid and thoughtless? I had no idea Antoinette could be so jealous but, to be fair, she had every reason. Will she ever forgive me?

From the journal of the Princesse de Lamballe,
23rd July 1772

16

'Oh, *cousine*,' exclaims Marie Antoinette to Marie-Thérèse, Princesse de Lamballe, 'how gorgeous! Turn around.' The smiling Lamballe makes a slow and sweeping pirouette. 'So daring!' the crown princess compliments her.

Lamballe's thick blond locks are piled high on her head in a fashion Marie Antoinette has never seen before. The whole effect is voluminous in the extreme, but it is the ostrich feathers that really set it off. Her exotic coiffure makes Lamballe tower above everyone else.

The cousins step into their carriage with some hilarity, for the interior is much too low to accommodate the hairdo. In the end Marie-Thérèse settles on the floor. There is room enough, after all, because the pregnant Duchesse de Chartres, normally inseparable from her sister-in-law Lamballe, is not feeling well and has decided to stay at home this evening.

They do not have far to drive. The two princesses arrive at the theatre to find a crowd already assembled at the entrance, all hoping for a close-up view of Madame la Dauphine. Loud applause as the footman opens the carriage door. As usual, Marie Antoinette takes the lead. She looks about her in some surprise, for where are the shouts of '*Vive Madame la Dauphine*'? Everyone is gazing at the Princesse de Lamballe, all eyes on her stunningly low-cut gown and the gently bobbing ostrich feathers.

In a flash Marie Antoinette realises what is going on, turns on her heel and stares speechless at her cousin. Still without a word, the Dauphine spins back and continues at a brisker pace than normal up the steps to the royal box. Marie-Thérèse is completely taken aback by her cousin's blazing eyes. This is not the Antoinette she knows and loves. It takes only a moment to uncover the reason, that people are applauding her and not the Dauphine. *Mon Dieu,* she thinks, what now?

She follows Marie Antoinette as quickly as she can without losing her dignity. Feeling faint and glad to reach her seat, Lamballe tries to catch the Dauphine's eye. But Marie Antoinette is staring stonily straight ahead of her, and Lamballe knows her cousin well enough to see that the smile upon her face is false.

Oh, how stupid of me. She will hate me for this, thinks Lamballe in a daze of embarrassment. Very carefully she shifts her chair backwards bit by bit until she is out of public view. She feels sick. If only she could just dismantle her coiffure here and now, for even breathing normally makes the ostrich features shudder as if begging for attention. Lamballe spends the remainder of the performance sitting dumb and dejected in the shadows at the back of the box, doing her best not to move a muscle.

Marie Antoinette jealous of her best friend! Who would have thought it possible? And how fair is her reaction? After all, Lamballe is goodness personified, and the only reason she would have had herself done up like that was to look her best for the evening. Knowing her, it could never have been her intention to upstage the Dauphine. Yet Marie Antoinette is devastated: the people clapped not her but Lamballe, as if the Dauphine was not there.

This evening has taught her just how addicted she has become to public adulation. She wants to be idolised by the Parisians and she wants the worship to go on forever. But how genuine is their love for her? The fact that they applaud a new coiffure worn by one of her entourage is not only humiliating for Marie Antoinette; it also shows her the Parisians' true face.

Apparently, the novelty of the Dauphine's presence in the city has worn off. If she wants to hold on to her popularity, Marie Antoinette will have to keep working hard for it. And the first step is to ensure that nobody in her train is better dressed or wears a more eye-catching hairstyle than does the future Queen of France.

With summer at its height, Marie Antoinette can temporarily set aside her concerns about her popularity. It is too hot for the city, and the royal family spends days at a time at Compiègne. The sweltering weather even precludes gallops in the forest behind the hunt. Lightly clad in a simple summer frock, Marie Antoinette holds the reins of her new cabriolet loosely in her hand. She is sitting comfortably in the little two-wheeled carriage, a vehicle that is coming more and more into fashion, and driving alone at a peaceful trot towards the chateau. In another hour the sun will reach its zenith, and by then she hopes to be indoors, protected by thick walls from the searing midday heat.

Nearing the stables, she finds a group of men busy at work. Naked from the waist up, they are heaving great slabs of paving stone into place to remake the path. Marie Antoinette finds their supple, muscular physique worthy of more than a passing glance. Two bare-armed young women are standing nearby, twittering encouragement at the men. The Dauphine smiles to herself at the sight of one pallid torso standing out conspicuously among the bronzed ones – and then the tingling in the pit of her stomach abruptly ceases. '*Mon Dieu*, it cannot be true!' she gasps.

'Louis!' she commands, tugging on the reins and bringing the cabriolet to a shuddering halt. 'What in heaven's name is the meaning of this?' she demands fiercely.

The Dauphin turns to face her with a bashful smile. The other men stop work too, and cast their eyes to the ground. One bows his head. 'We are repairing the footpath, Madame.' Her eyes are spewing fire. In recent weeks Louis-Auguste has been doing nothing but mending windows, oiling stiff doors and messing about for hours in his workshop. He has completely ignored her indignant remarks about this and carried on as if nothing had been said. But this is too much.

'Repairing the footpath? I can see that!' Her reply is vitriolic and addressed to her husband. 'But what are you doing helping with such a thing?'

Louis-Auguste does not reply. Slowly he wipes the sweat from his forehead with a dirty cloth. The two women are doing their best to keep their features composed out of respect for the Dauphine, but one is losing the battle to control her laughter. This infuriates Marie Antoinette even further. She'll soon find out the names of these two.

'Are you feeling a little neglected, perhaps? A little short of attention, that you find it necessary to show off half naked in front of a couple of kitchen maids?' She flicks her whip in the faces of the women, who have the sense to wipe the grins from their faces. 'When are you going to start behaving like a man?'

Her horse is growing impatient; maddened by the flies buzzing about his ears, he is straining for the shelter of the stable. The Dauphine pulls roughly on the reins again.

'I do believe, Madame, that my present occupation is a supreme example, in fact the epitome of masculine endeavour,' retorts the future King of France, pointing at the paving stones.

'Oh you do, do you? Well, I'm sure *Papa Roi* will be proud of you. I shall tell him all about it this evening, once you've sloped off for an early night as usual ... to recover from being a man. You think my report will please Papa, do you? You could try being just as much of a man in bed – my bed – as you are all day among the labourers. Try pulling your weight there for a change!'

She gives her horse an unnecessary crack of the crop that almost makes the animal rear up in fright. He gallops off as if to take cabriolet and all into the stable with him at full pelt. At the last moment, a stable lad manages to catch hold of the bridle, averting a ghastly accident that would certainly have smashed the carriage to smithereens.

Livid, Marie Antoinette springs from the *calèche* just in time to see Louis-Auguste walking away from the labourers, his shoulders bowed. She has obviously hit the mark. 'Good!' she thinks spitefully, and marches off to her apartment with head held high. A bath will cool her off.

But her usual remedy fails her today. Perhaps it's the dreadful heat, but her blood is still boiling. Actually, she should relay the whole sad story in a letter to her mother. That would show her once and for all what a lame duck of a son-in-law she has! Her endless nagging about the need for a grandchild, an heir whose veins flow with both Habsburg and Bourbon blood, is just about driving her daughter to distraction. And whose fault is it? Not hers, anyway!

That evening, Louis-Auguste sits yawning at supper. 'You look tired, my boy,' remarks the king with concern. 'You're not ill, are you?'

Louis-Auguste casts a guilty glance at his wife, who turns her nose up and looks the other way.

'Have you two been at loggerheads?' asks Louis XV, who has lived long enough to recognise female ire when he sees it. The Dauphin holds his tongue and dare not meet his grandfather's eyes. 'Or has the Dauphine been keeping you awake all night?' the king persists teasingly, transferring his attention to Marie Antoinette.

'Ha! That would be the first time,' she snorts. 'I'm afraid I am not a priority. My turn won't come until the whole chateau has been renovated.'

With a snigger the king turns to his grandson, who continues to avoid his glance. Louis XV has a notion how much pleasure the Dauphin gets from manual labour. To some extent he can understand it, too, for he himself greatly enjoys carving ivory. His own little workshop is an oasis of peace, a refuge from politics and the endless intrigue. But, in contrast to his grandson, his hobby never overshadows his appetite for the opposite sex. On the contrary! It must be his grandson's cool maternal Saxon blood, reflects Louis XV; it is plain to him that Marie Antoinette is sorely starved of attention, but what is he to do about it?

'I'm looking forward to the Artois wedding,' hints the king, hoping to prick the Dauphin's conscience. 'I'm pretty sure some fresh young Bourbon will see the light of day next summer. Don't you think it's about time you two got going on a new heir?'

By now Louis-Auguste is unable to look anywhere in the king's direction. Pettishly, Marie Antoinette tries to coax some cool air towards herself with the lovely Japanese fan that was a gift from her mother. The only other sound in the room is a moody background clicking of knitting needles. The aunts exchange silent, significant looks. The clock chimes.

'Good Lord, is it that time already?' The king sighs, getting to his feet. 'Goodnight, everyone.'

A moment later the Dauphin follows him from the room, still without a word, even to the aunts, who shake their heads at their young nephew's ill manners. Marie Antoinette is still seething, but who can she take her anger out on? Louis-Auguste has nothing to say for himself and the aunts are not worth talking to. With a muttered goodnight, she too retires to bed.

She should have known she wouldn't be able to sleep. It is far too muggy and the sheets are sticking annoyingly to her feet. Marie Antoinette has had the shutters opened, but there is no wind to send a cooling breeze through her bedchamber. Tired of trying in vain to rest, she slides out of bed and goes out onto the terrace. It is pitch dark, but cool, and the sweat between her shoulder blades quickly dries. Looking up at the palace façade she sees no lights burning. She must be the only one still awake. Slowly, her anger begins to subside.

Putting both hands behind her head, she gazes up into the starry heavens. The million tiny twinkling lights in the wide wastes of space seem to be beckoning to her. Ah, how lovely it would be to float up into the sky, high above this castle, far away from this land with all its idiocy; to drift back to the country of her childhood. Yet even as she stares upward, lost in imaginings, she knows has outgrown her dream of fleeing. For as long as the king permits it, her life is bound up with that of the Dauphin.

In some odd way relieved, she returns to bed. Actually, she is feeling a little cold. She half covers herself with the sheet. That's better, just warm enough.

How long has she been dozing she doesn't know. Perhaps she has even been asleep, but now something has awakened her. She lies as still as a mouse, her eyes open. She's too frightened to turn over, but why? All the doors and windows are standing wide and anyone could walk in, but who would want to harm her? It's so dark; it must still be the middle of the night.

Oh, no. There's the noise again. There is someone in her room! The hairs stand up on the back of her neck and every muscle in her body tenses. She feels someone sit down on the other side of the bed. Her heart begins to thump. An intruder! She turns violently onto her other side, only to find herself staring into the startled eyes of the Dauphin.

'Holy Mary, what a shock you gave me! What do you want?'

The Dauphin swallows hard. 'I thought ... I wanted to make up. I'm sorry about today.'

'Can't that wait until morning?' she hisses, to hide her fear.

Louis-Auguste shakes his head. 'I don't want Artois to be the father of the heir.'

'Oh.'

The crown prince hesitates, then gets up from the bed. 'You're right. It can wait till morning.'

Only now does Marie Antoinette realise what he means. 'Wait,' she says, taking hold of his arm. She draws him gently into the bed. He eases himself cautiously down beside her.

Now what? Louis-Auguste feels wretched. What in heaven's name is he doing here in her chamber? He knows it's too late now to beat a retreat, but he's damned sorry he ever came. The Dauphine moves closer, but still he has no idea where to begin.

Then Marie Antoinette sits up and pulls her nightdress over her head. He can make out the contours of her body in the darkness. He knows it should excite him, especially when she lies down again close to him and he feels her soft skin against his own. Her hand flutters uncertainly over his huge ribcage. His breathing becomes uneven ... how awful he feels!

'Come nearer, please,' his wife whispers in his ear, pressing herself even closer against him. A sudden rush of resolution, and he pushes up his own nightgown and turns to her. He hears her sigh deeply, like a little willing female animal.

Marie Antoinette is aroused. Is he going to make her his wife at last? Has the moment really arrived? She senses his hesitation and isn't sure what to do. The last thing she wants to do is scare him from her bed. She presses her hips encouragingly against him and is surprised when he then suddenly throws himself upon her, his heavy body forcing all the air out of her lungs.

My God! She lies beneath him, fighting for breath. This is the first time he has ever been so close. She feels trapped and the smell of his hair revolts her. Unnoticed, her lips brush his neck, but she is soon repulsed by his bitter-tasting, sweaty skin.

Where do they go from here? The Dauphin wriggles and tries to push inside her. But she resists! Why, she doesn't know, for this is the moment she has waited so long for. Her hips move instinctively, squirming aside in avoidance of him, but there's nowhere for her to go. Be strong, be brave, she tells herself. It's for Mama, for *Papa Roi*, for France! She shuts her eyes and tries to empty her mind. Is he there now?

Her lower body no longer feels part of her. He's lying motionless on top of her, breathing heavily. She lies there, stifled, frantic for air. Is this the much-sung act of love? Is this what has inspired people to commit crimes of passion, to serenade their muse? She feels sick, overwhelmed by the sour odour of his body. Placing her hands squarely beneath his shoulders, Marie Antoinette levers him away from her a little so that she can draw breath. Looking into the Dauphin's face, she sees that his eyes are tight shut, as if in pain. Slowly he withdraws from her and moves away to sit on the edge of the bed. Is that it?

Liberated from his weight, Marie Antoinette inhales deep breaths of fresh air. Her feelings are all over the place, ricocheting between disgust and relief. I'm his wife now. At last, after three years, I'm his wife! She starts sobbing and the Dauphin turns to look at her. 'What's the matter?' he asks with genuine concern.

'Nothing,' she weeps. 'I'm so happy.'

Louis-Auguste is probably even more confused than his young spouse. Happy? For him it was dreadful. He feels a little better now that his erection has gone, but while it lasted the pain was awful. It was only bearable as long as he didn't move, and luckily she kept still too. He can't imagine how she can be happy. But he's relieved to have finally made her his wife. With a bit of luck she's pregnant now and he has done his duty. 'Goodnight,' he says softly. And, righting his nightgown, he quietly disappears into the darkness.

'Will someone tell me what in heaven's name is going on?' demands the king, decapitating his soft-boiled egg with a single well-aimed swipe. 'Last night the pair of you were sitting there like a wet weekend, and this morning you look the sunniest couple I've ever clapped eyes on.' Louis XV sensuously licks the warm yolk from his spoon.

Marie Antoinette giggles. The Dauphin smiles.

'Louis-Auguste made me his wife last night,' announces the Dauphine with pride.

The last spoonful of egg hangs in the air.

'What was that?' asks the king, astounded, looking from one of his grandchildren to the other. 'No, surely, but I ...' Louis XV searches for the appropriate words. He wipes his mouth and puts the napkin back on the table. 'This is fantastic news!' Rising from the table, the king congratulates his grandson heartily, giving the Dauphin a comradely slap on his broad shoulder. Going over to Marie Antoinette, the monarch embraces her.

'You know what? This deserves a celebration.' He claps his hands. 'Make ready for a deer hunt!' He orders his gentleman of the chamber to pass the message to the stables. 'This may be the last time you can sit in the saddle, Madame. We must make the most of it.'

Half an hour later they are mounting their horses and the master of the hunt is marshalling the dogs.

The huntsmen indulge in plenty of whispering under their breath this morning, and each man comes forward to congratulate the Dauphin. It is remarkable to see the new respect the dukes are showing toward Louis-Auguste.

Trumpets sound, and they are off. The king is not showing his age today. He spurs on his steed and shouts to the Dauphin and Dauphine to follow him. A calm trot soon turns into a wild gallop as the hunt takes its lead from the royal trio. And, as in the old days, the rallying cry rings out: '*Tya-Hillaut!*'

I'm so touched by her sonnet. It's the loveliest birthday present I've ever had. And that's saying something, because yesterday was my twenty-fourth birthday. I'm getting old! Antoinette is always joking about it, but I never want to marry again. My life is perfect just as it is.

From the journal of the Princesse de Lamballe,
9th September 1773

17

Three weeks after the happy hunting party, Marie Antoinette gets her period. Ten days later than usual, it's true, but what is usual? She often misses a month for no apparent reason. So all hope of a pregnancy vanishes. Deeply disappointed, she stands before the window, soothing her aching abdomen with both hands.

She hasn't dared to tell the Dauphin yet, but knows she will have to. She has another full three months before Artois marries. Three months left in which to conceive. The last thing Marie Antoinette relishes is the prospect of her husband's corpulent body bearing down on her again. In fact, she had quite banished the thought, hoping that it would not be necessary, that she was pregnant already. All she can do now is try to convince herself that it will be better the second time around.

At the end of August Louis XV decides it is time to return to Versailles – quite a performance for the court, with only a couple of days left in which to get everything packed. Those who can be spared travel on ahead, for once the miniature emigration is underway the thoroughfare between Versailles and the hunting lodge will be rendered impassable by cartloads of bedding, clothing, pots and pans, and all the other paraphernalia of a pleasant summer break. Gentlemen of the chamber, cooks, servants, ladies in waiting, falconers, secretaries and everyone else, from kitchen maid to minister, will ride behind the king.

Marie Antoinette has been missing Paris. Versailles is much nearer the city than either Fontainebleau or Compiègne. She is looking forward to being reunited with the capital and its inhabitants, who have so taken her to their heart.

As soon as the court is reinstalled at Versailles, it settles back into the familiar pattern of its days. New ambassadors present their credentials, and more and more frequently the king asks his grandchildren to attend the receptions and State banquets on his behalf.

All the indications are that the approach of autumn is taking its toll on the king. As the dark evenings lengthen, Louis XV tires earlier, and the marks of fatigue can clearly be seen on his face. Sometimes the monarch repeats himself, and there are episodes when he seems scatterbrained. Yet nobody appears the least concerned about this – no one, that is, but the Comte de Mercy. Between Marie Antoinette's dance evenings and her singing lessons, the Austrian ambassador makes renewed efforts to focus her attention on the fact that the king will not live forever.

The Dauphine brushes aside his concerns. 'There's nothing to worry about, Mercy. The king is as strong as a horse and just as healthy. Just wait and see; he'll live as long as his great-grandfather Louis XIV. Yes, my dear Mercy, and by then I'll be more than thirty years old myself. A middle-aged lady.'

Mercy carries on staring gravely at her. 'Madame, you may joke about it, but you must be prepared for all eventualities.'

'But Mercy, how am I to prepare myself? You know there is no role for the French queen. My life will hardly change.'

Mercy's eyes narrow momentarily. 'I am afraid that is not the case, Madame. The character of the Dauphin is not sufficiently formed for him to be capable of strong government. He will require assistance. Unless you are able to stand by him, I am afraid that he will receive the wrong advice, with all the consequences thereof. It is your task to offer him leadership. For, with all respect, he will not be capable without you.'

Marie Antoinette shoots the ambassador a penetrating look. 'Those are dangerous words, Mercy.'

'I am fully aware of the implications of my remarks, Your Highness. But I also know to whom I address them.'

Marie Antoinette gets impatiently to her feet. 'The Dauphin is made of sterner stuff than you give him credit for, Mercy. He'll make a good sovereign when the time comes, and naturally I shall be at his side. But whether he really will have need of me is another matter.' With a smile Marie Antoinette turns back to the ambassador: 'I hope not, to be honest, for I hate politics and all that goes with it.'

'Do you think your mother feels any differently?' asks Mercy. 'Yet she has shown everyone what a woman can be made of.'

Marie Antoinette shakes her head. 'That's something else entirely. Her father relied upon her as the only heir. She had to do what she had to do. I'm quite sure that, had she had any choice in the matter, she would have avoided the throne.'

The Comte de Mercy doubts it. He cannot imagine Austria and Hungary without Maria Theresa. The empress knows how to stand her ground and has proved to the world what an effective and competent head of State a woman can be. Deep in his heart, the count can only hope that Marie Antoinette has inherited her mother's grit and determination, even if he has to bide his time to find out.

His audience with Marie Antoinette is brought to an abrupt close by the entry of a lady of the chamber announcing that it is time for her singing lesson.

Anyone who did not know better would think it was the wedding of another crown prince. Neither cost nor trouble has been spared, although many wonder why the nuptials of the king's third grandson need be celebrated quite so sumptuously. The list of guests is endless, and this time all the Princes of the Blood are also in attendance.

The huge banquet held in honour of the Comte d'Artois is going on far too long for the bridegroom's liking. Versailles's great theatre has been converted into a banqueting hall for the occasion. Seated round a vast dining table in the centre of the hall, the members of the royal family are doing justice to one course after another. The table features a breathtaking display by the king's own stage designer, who has surpassed himself. From the centrepiece springs a babbling brook that spills into a river, which in turn runs in a broad flood across the table. On the water float tiny yachts, their decks manned by miniature moving figures. The banks of the river are lined with willows and plumed reeds, beyond which the landscape turns into meadows full of grazing cattle.

As if this were an everyday spectacle, the Comtesse du Barry, smothered in diamonds, sits flirting unashamedly with her lover, the King of France, to the outrage of *Mesdames tantes*. There is only one thing they find more distasteful than her canoodling, and that is the way their father responds like a smitten teenager to his amorous *maîtresse en titre*.

The bride sits hunched her chair like a bird with a broken wing. She has not uttered a single word throughout the meal, although her older sister, the Comtesse de Provence, has been placed next to her. Artois sits staring at his new wife and calling repeatedly for his glass to be refilled. Marie-Thérèse, Princess of Sardinia, is at least two heads shorter than him. She has the same dark hair as her sister, but fortunately not the heavy eyebrows. Although not yet fully developed, the princess already has a nicely rounded young figure. All in all, he is far from dissatisfied with his new bride. Apart from her nose, that is, which might do better were it not quite so long. She seems very shy and has hardly said a word to him since they met. But what does he care? She's bound to come round in bed tonight. And what if she still won't talk? Well, he isn't in love. At least, not with her. And neither does he need to be. A royal heir: that's what it's all about.

Both his brothers are still childless, poor devils. If this is the competition, Artois scents the sweet smell of success! For as long as the marriages of Louis-Auguste and Stanislas remain barren, he, Artois, will father the new king of France. The very thought makes him want to hurl himself upon the Princess of Sardinia and impregnate her there and then.

He looks irascibly about him. All evening he has felt the

piercing stares of women in his back. The stares of mistresses now deprived of their royal lover and reduced to the status of jealous wedding guests. Will Artois ever return to their bed? So long as Louis-Auguste remains King of France, being his younger brother's mistress is no bad thing; it could bear fruit. But some are calculating enough to see how much more advantageous is the position of mistress to the king. The diamonds around du Barry's neck are proof enough of that. So far, however, Louis-Auguste hasn't shown the slightest interest in any woman. Artois surveys his brothers. Famished, but not for want of food!

His smiling eyes meet those of Marie Antoinette.

'A dance?' they seem to be asking one another. With one accord they get to their feet. Earlier in the evening, Artois took a turn around the floor with his new wife – at least, he attempted to. The Italian princess undoubtedly has her talents, but dancing is not among them. Ah, but his sister-in-law! No one in Versailles can match her grace on the dance floor. Artois has often wondered whether Marie Antoinette is as much in love with him as he with her. He has never declared his passion outright, although she always responds, within limits, to his playful flirting.

Marie Antoinette is almost certainly aware of his many amorous conquests at the court of Versailles. Artois knows his sister-in-law well enough by now to realise that she will never condescend to fall into his arms as long as they are still warm from some little duchess or, worse, a common chambermaid.

'Oh, I'm so happy for you, Artois,' laughs Marie Antoinette with sparkling candour as their dance ends. She has no fear of being displaced by the diminutive Italian princess. 'By tomorrow you will be a real man.'

With a smile, but a badly dented ego, Artois leads the Dauphine back to her chair. What can she have meant by that? She must know that this won't be the first night he has spent in a woman's bed! But there's no time to ponder her words further. Alluring luscious ladies block his way, all hungrily begging for a dance. Lapping up all the attention, Artois soon forgets Marie Antoinette. On he gaily dances, oblivious to his young wife's eyes upon him.

Marie-Thérèse is quite convinced now that her sister was right: Artois is a philanderer. But he is also an attractive man. She has more sympathy for her sister, for, good heavens, what a fat pig that Louis Stanislas is! The princess surveys the sea of unfamiliar faces. What remains for her to fear? Her sister has warned her about all the court politics and intrigue, but can it be any worse here than at home? What does dismay her is the conspicuous wealth and extravagance, the overabundance of food and wine, the sumptuous attire and glittering extravaganza of jewels. She had been led to believe that France's State coffers were empty, but that must be a myth, for each of this evening's guests seems to have outdone the next in sartorial elegance and splendour.

But many a partygoer will return home after tonight's masked ball to find a necklace or a purse missing. Dolled up to look like dukes and duchesses and so mingle effortlessly with the masked guests, the pickpockets have had the time of their lives this evening.

The year moves towards its end without any news of the Comtesse d'Artois having conceived. Artois is unconcerned; according to him it is only a matter of days before the announcement can be made. His younger brother's bragging appears to leave the Dauphin unmoved, but beneath the surface Louis-Auguste is awash with anger and grief. How can it be that his little brother manages to enjoy making love to his wife when the same act meant only agony for the Dauphin? And that despite the doctor's assurances that there is nothing the matter with him. Should he perhaps seek a second opinion? Louis-Auguste feels miserable and guilty in equal measure. Guilty towards Marie Antoinette, who for years has longed for a child whilst people pointed at her and whispered behind her back that she was incapable of conceiving. And saddened for himself, for he too has heard the rumour that the Dauphin is impotent. It isn't fair, but what is he to do?

I'm not sure if I did the right thing, talking so openly. She's very sweet to me, despite my having upset her. I've been able to forget about it all for a long time, but I think the silence and the snow must somehow have brought everything back. Last night I dreamt about him again. I truly thought he was standing by my bed. I daren't go back to sleep afterwards. I shall stay indoors all day today.

From the journal of the Princesse de Lamballe,
18th December 1773

18

As long as the Comtesse d'Artois does not conceive, Marie Antoinette can cherish some hope for herself. But she is increasingly driven to the wall by her husband's diffidence. Despite his promises, Louis-Auguste always has a new excuse: he is stuffed up with a bad cold, or his stomach is playing up again. Full of sincere regret, the Dauphin dutifully renews his faithful vow to pay his wife a visit soon. But how soon, wonders Marie Antoinette?

The freshly fallen snow offers her some welcome distraction. After days of persistent white-out, the wind has changed and Zephyros has swept the heavens clear. It is still very cold, the mercury remaining far below zero all day, but bright sunshine and azure skies have transformed the park into a fairyland. Marie Antoinette has had her sleigh prepared. The blacksmith, having fitted her horse with special shoes, is just driving the last sharp ice spikes into the iron.

The animal steps tentatively out onto the whiteness, snuffling nervously with dilated nostrils at what was once firm ground. Stableman Rogier has harnessed the sleigh and, as soon as he is confident that the horse has a secure enough footing on the slippery ice not to go staggering about like a delirious foal, he hands Marie Antoinette and the Princesse de Lamballe in. Snugly muffled up to the chin in fur, they look like a couple of Russian princesses.

'Off we go! Hurrah!' calls out the Dauphine, and laughing excitedly the two cousins set off across the snow, leaving Rogier shaking his head behind them.

The landscape is deserted. The only living creatures to be seen are a couple of deer trying in their hunger to tear the bark from some small trees at the forest edge. They gallop the length of the frozen Grand Canal, great clouds of steam billowing from the horse's nostrils. At the end of the frozen waterway Marie Antoinette guides the sleigh round in a semi-circle and lets her horse walk quietly back along the other bank to regain its breath. Now they are gliding close beneath the naked branches of the trees, with a curious robin hopping ahead of them from twig to twig. The two young women are chattering happily to one another, taking pleasure in everything, especially their privacy. Heavenly! No ladies in waiting, and no *Madame l'Etiquette*.

'If only it could always be like this!' sighs Marie Antoinette, completely at ease.

Before them the vast chateau nestles in the white landscape, shrouded in peace and tranquillity.

'It looks lovely from a distance,' murmurs the crown princess. 'Like another world.' The still serenity of the scene stands in such stark contrast to the raucous life of the court, driven as it is by jealousy and tainted with intrigue.

'The snow reminds me of home,' says Lamballe softly. 'I miss the mountains.'

'How strange you should say that, *cousine*. My happiest memories are always to do with snow. The hours and days spent sleighing with my sister. My God, how long ago that all seems!'

They travel on in silence, each warmly wrapped in her furs and her memories.

Lamballe breaks the silence. 'It's not just that it was long ago: it was another life. One of total innocence.' She shivers. 'Six years back I left Turin with my heart full of happy expectations. I was to marry Louis-Alexandre Stanislas de Bourbon, Prince de Lamballe, great-grandson of the Sun King and heir to the wealthiest man in France. I fell in love at first sight with my future husband. He was tall and slim and had the most wonderful dark blue eyes.'

Marie Antoinette listens spellbound to her cousin. Lamballe is usually so reserved; she has never spoken of her brief marriage before. In fact, until today she has always adeptly avoided the subject.

'He had beautifully proportioned hands, and his smile filled me with a warm glow. I was so in love with him – but that only lasted for a day. Our wedding night came as a terrible shock to me.'

'Ah,' interjects Marie Antoinette, herself lacking any experience of love. 'Did he not touch you at all?'

Lamballe stares at her, appalled. 'Not touch me?' she whispers. 'Mon Dieu, he took me like a wild beast and made me perform acts so hideous, so foul, I dare not name them.'

The Dauphine recoils in horror.

'His fascination with me lasted for nigh on ten days. After that I was utterly exhausted and had no stamina left to meet his perverse demands. Then it was over. He cursed and swore me into the ground. I was a useless woman, worthless in bed and an Italian whore. He struck me and abandoned me, and then went off in search of a woman who was capable of giving him the love that he called real.'

Lamballe swallows, and Marie Antoinette feels her eyes filling with tears. It is almost beyond her imagining that anyone might be capable of such deeds. 'What a ghastly man,' she murmurs.

Her companion nods in affirmation. 'A monster. Later it transpired that he kept several sweethearts. Cheap little actresses, tarts who were only after his money and so prepared to do anything and everything he asked of them to satisfy his bestial desires.'

'But his father, the Duc de Penthièvre, could he do nothing to restrain his son?' asks Marie Antoinette, her eyes slowly opening upon a world entirely new to her.

'My father-in-law didn't have the opportunity. Two such different characters as this father and son you couldn't imagine. Papa limited his income, but Alexandre could always find more money somehow, or rather steal it. Even the jewellery my father-in-law gave me as a wedding present wasn't safe from my husband.

'But the worst blow came with a visit from a heavily pregnant "mademoiselle" La Chassaigne, an actress who played some bit parts in the Comédie Française. There she stood, with a scornful smirk all over her face, announcing the imminent arrival of Lamballe's new prince. That was the last straw for me. Papa gave her a great deal of money in exchange for her promise never to see Alexandre again.

'I was amazed that I had never fallen pregnant by the animal myself, but to be confronted like that by one of his mistresses was simply unspeakable. So things went from bad to worse, and in the end Alexandre hardly set foot in the house. Papa did his best to shield me from the outside world. I couldn't show my face anywhere by then, of course.

'According to reports that reached my ears later, Alexandre took up with the Duc de Chartres and the Duc de Lauzun, joining in their drunken rampages from one orgy to the next. Oh, the shame of it! I no longer dared answer my parents' letters, I was so afraid Alexandre would want to divorce me. I felt so lonely, so utterly humiliated.' As if reliving it all, Lamballe stares into space with empty eyes.

'Before long I fell ill. The doctors couldn't make out what was wrong with me, but I couldn't swallow a mouthful of food without bringing it up again. Sleep eluded me. I'd lie awake in my bed night after night, for suddenly there he would be. Drunk, his eyes murderous, for I didn't know what I had to do to please him. Every move I made was wrong and only earned me more violence. Yes, I was petrified of him. I truly feared for my life. Horrendous, and we had been married barely a year.'

'I hardly know what to say, cousin,' whispers a stunned Marie Antoinette, blowing her nose to cover her confusion. 'I never imagined married life was so terrible for you.'

'No matter,' replies Lamballe. 'It's a relief to get it off my chest after all these years.' Then, as if awakening from a bad dream, she turns her huge eyes upon her cousin. 'Oh, my God, what am I saying? Why am I burdening you with all this?'

Sudden tears flood the cheeks of Marie-Thérèse, Princesse de Lamballe, and her whole body begins to shudder violently as if to escape the grip of her dreadful memories. The Dauphine places an arm tenderly about her cousin's shoulders and pulls the warm coverlet up to her chest.

'Shush, shush, my dearest. Your friend is here. You should have told me sooner. Didn't we promise to share everything?'

With a nod, the sobbing Lamballe rests her head on Marie Antoinette's shoulder like a child seeking the comfort of its mother.

'Are you glad he's dead?' asks the Dauphine gently, while pondering how absolutely unthinkable it is to wish someone dead and then rejoice over it.

Lamballe shrugs. 'Part of me died with him. I am no longer the Princesse de Carignan who left Turin with her head held high. His death was awful and he suffered terribly.'

'What happened?' asks Marie Antoinette, unable to contain her curiosity.

'The first day, after he had fallen from his horse and broken his leg, I felt relieved. It seemed like an act of God, because he couldn't move a muscle and had perforce to submit himself to my care. But Alexandre wanted none of that. He couldn't bear the sight of me. I prayed for him ceaselessly, especially as his condition worsened. He soon developed a fever, and the doctors seemed to have no idea how to treat the complicated fracture.

'Day by day the leg became more swollen, and gradually it turned black. Oh lord, I can still hear his screams during the amputation. Appalling! I think that was the moment when I forgave him everything. But it was already too late for that. The wound began to fester and its ghastly stench permeated every corner of his and every other room. There was not a physician who could stop the rot. His pain increased to the point where his moans could be heard all through the house. The screams ceased only with his death.

'Was I then glad it was over? I was totally and utterly exhausted. My mind was a blank. When I think about him now, it is without feeling. I don't miss him. On the contrary, my love for him was extinguished on our wedding night. After that night all he did was use, abuse and insult me. I was no more than a worthless rag to him; an instrument of pleasure that didn't require him to harness his inhibitions, upon which he could give full rein to his primitive passions.

'Was I glad? Relieved is, I think, more the word. Yes, relieved.'

Marie Antoinette nods in understanding.

'Why didn't you go home afterwards?' she asks Lamballe.

'I was in no state to travel. You should have seen me. I was a wreck, as thin as a rake and weeping all the time. Papa, my father-in-law, was ill too. He had lost his only son, after all. After the funeral my father-in-law placed me with the nuns at the convent of Saint-Antoine des Champs. It was the best thing for me and I'm not sure how I should have survived without the support of my friendship with the abbess, Gabrielle de Beauvau.

'Yes, I had planned to return to Italy. But my poor father-in-law ... It was pity for papa that held me back. He was so grief-stricken, I couldn't bear to leave him alone. The Duc de Penthièvre has always been very good to me; he looks on me as his daughter. So I decided to stay with him for the time being.'

'I shall miss you very much if you ever leave, Lamballe. You're my very best friend. You know that, don't you?'

The young widow's face lights up with a faint smile. 'I do know it, cousin, and I treasure our friendship. More perhaps than you can imagine, and I shall never desert you, never!'

Marie Antoinette responds with a warm kiss upon her cousin's cheek, followed by a click of her tongue to express disgust at all the misfortune that has befallen her. The horse, which was walking at a stately pace, is alerted by the sound and at once accelerates into a canter.

'Time for hot chocolate,' announces Marie Antoinette, with a gay wave at all the faces peering through the iced-up windows of the palace.

Only late that evening, once she is in bed, does the Dauphine find the peace and quiet to fully contemplate Lamballe's frank confession. Playing absent-mindedly with the bed-warmer between her feet, the only company that she can expect tonight, Marie Antoinette considers Lamballe's suffering at the hands of her husband. Why did he have to hit her? Naive as she is, Marie Antoinette has no concept of what might have taken place in her cousin's marriage bed.

The Dauphine rubs her stomach with both hands, trying to massage away the ache and nausea slumbering there in anticipation of her menstrual period. What is worse? A husband who mistreats you horribly, or one who never touches you, so that the whole world accuses you of being incapable of bearing a child?

With her feet she manoeuvres the bed-warmer up past her legs until it lies against her abdomen. It alleviates the pain there. But not the gnawing sadness in her heart at another monthly harbinger of disappointment.

A new year, and what a start to it! Antoinette thought I hadn't noticed, but it was so obvious! I'm really thrilled for her, although she will have to be careful. She denies everything, of course, but she doesn't ool me! It seems an age ago, but I too have been in love.

From the journal of the Princesse de Lamballe,
1st January 1774

19

The bells of Versailles joyously ring in the New Year. A night's newly fallen snow does not prevent the ambassadors from finding their early way to court. The first arrived in Versailles yesterday, in good time to deliver New Year greetings to the king, only to find all the hotels fully booked in the nearby village of the same name. No one can afford to be late, far less fail to appear at court at all.

The huge square in front of the palace has been cleared of snow to allow the guests to dismount safely from horse and carriage. The sun is breaking through as though heaven itself is shining down upon the palace of King Louis XV. The sparkling light turns each arrival into a radiant spectacle, for every guest is gorgeously arrayed in all his finery.

Rival countries do their best to steal a march on one another, their emissaries each sporting their most elegantly cut waistcoat or their most magnificently towering coiffure. Gathering at the entrance to the palace, the State representatives of Europe swap formalities and idle chatter. It all looks amiable enough, but between courtesies the Prussians are casting a suspicious eye over the Turks, the Russian delegation glowering mistrustfully at the Saxons, and the Spaniards throwing the Austrians disdainful glances. It falls to the experienced diplomats among them, those who know how to hide their feelings with a cool smile and a curt nod of the head, to maintain the appearance of harmony.

Behind the English ambassador and his entourage comes the coach carrying the Swedish delegation. The ambassador, Count Creutz, clambers laboriously down from the carriage, blinking and shielding his eyes from the fierce sunlight. His head is thumping.

He should have gone to bed much earlier last night, but ... well, it was an entertaining evening and the wine improved with drinking.

Count Creutz scours the assembled faces but can see no sign of the boy. And he damned well gave his word to get here on time, too! The ambassador has to make way for the following carriage, so he begins to climb the steps in any case. At that moment, with a wild clatter of hooves, another carriage flies through the gate at full gallop, so that the coachman has quite some difficulty bringing it to a halt. The footman gives him a dirty look for his trouble. Manners maketh man!

Before the carriage has come fully to a standstill, the door swings open and the young Count Hans Axel von Fersen leaps energetically down. In a few long strides he reaches the Swedish ambassador.

'Why so late, Fersen?' demands Count Creutz.

A mischievous smile plays across the young man's features as, with a laconic gesture of pride, he lifts the collar of his new fur coat. 'It wasn't ready until this morning.'

The ambassador shakes his head. Meanwhile, Fersen's mentor has stepped down from the carriage. 'Ah, Bolémany,' continues Creutz. 'So you've decided to attend the reception after all?' Bolémany mumbles an excuse, and the threesome make their way together up the steps.

Axel Fersen, standing a head higher than his two compatriots, minutely takes in his surroundings. He has visited the court on a couple of occasions over the past month, but this is the first time he has seen so many high-ranking officials assembled. His mastery of languages allows him to understand with ease all that is said, whether in Italian, French or German. What he finds difficult is keeping his face straight as he picks up the remarks swapped by these foreigners behind one other's backs.

Strolling through the gallery, his admiring and respectful glance takes in every detail of the palace: the magnificent frescoes, the marble, the superb moulded plasterwork. Versailles must be far and away the finest edifice that he has had the honour of viewing in the three years he has been travelling Europe.

In the Hercules Hall Fersen has more eyes for the splendid ceiling than for the king now accepting New Year salutations from the foreign diplomats. The many guests filling the hall, along with the fire blazing in the enormous hearth, make for a pleasantly warm atmosphere. Count Creutz does some swift calculations and reckons it will be a little while before his turn comes to present himself to King Louis XV. To his regret, he cannot spot a free chair. Renewing his pious vow never again to touch a drop of drink, he resolutely refuses the glass a manservant holds out to him.

Fersen and Bolémany, however, each lighten the tray by another glass and raise them to the New Year. Once Axel has looked his fill at the magnificent interior, he turns his attention to its occupants. There is no one here he knows. Fortunately he is tall enough to see over most of their heads. A couple of metres away, the king is engaged in amiable conversation; near him stands the Comtesse du Barry, whom Fersen recognises from his one other encounter with her. He has heard enough stories about her to be astounded at the sight of a line of diplomats bending the knee and proffering gifts. She looks an attractive enough woman, obviously much younger than the king, but what makes her so worthy of attention?

'I understand she's no more than a courtesan,' whispers Axel in his mentor's ear.

'Absolutely, just that,' replies Bolémany confidentially in Swedish. 'But quite an unusual one! She's the gateway to the king, so it's no wonder everyone's so keen to confide in her.'

Fersen raises an arched eyebrow. That would not be his manner of government. He watches her chatting flirtatiously with each admirer, including the Duc d'Aiguillon himself, one of the king's most important ministers. The Swedish count keeps his eye on her. With a childlike show of pleasure she accepts the gifts showered upon her, passing each one to her servant, a little tramp from Bengal dressed up as the King of Siam. What an exhibition! But it goes without saying that Fersen will make his feelings known to no one: France is Sweden's most important ally.

Axel takes a sip of wine and surveys the company on the king's other flank. He at once recognises the unmistakable figure of the Dauphin, for whom he can muster little respect. The crown prince is a year older than he, but what a difference there is between them. Blubbery and bored, the heir to the French throne gazes vacantly around the room. 'What a shame for his wife,' thinks Fersen, just as he realises with a shock that the Dauphine's eyes are directly upon him.

Abashed, as if she had read his thoughts, he casts his gaze to the ground. But when he looks up at her curiously a second later she is in conversation with one of the ambassadors. Perhaps it was just coincidence. He scrutinises her. Taller than average, she seems to carry herself so as to make the most of her height, setting off her figure to great advantage. The way she holds her head a little averted at first gives the impression of arrogance, but this is soon offset by the charm of her smile. A greater contrast between this poised and proud Archduchess of Austria and her dull consort would be difficult to imagine.

'Well, what do you make of her?' asks Bolémany inquisitively.

Axel Fersen turns to the man standing next to him. The count has no liking for such direct questions. 'I know nothing of her, but she would seem to me to be an interesting woman.'

Bolémany smirks, but does not pursue the matter.

Slowly the queue crawls forward. Axel feels strangely drawn to Marie Antoinette; to her aura, her gestures and her smile. Yet she ignores him. It is precisely as though he does not exist for her. He wonders if she knows who he is. If she were to know that he was the son of Marshal Fersen, would she still look past him then? He could tell her about his visit to the court of her brother, Leopold the Great, Duke of Tuscany. Might that win her attention?

But then, why should the future Queen of France be the least bit interested in some Swedish count? It would be better to put her out of his head. After all, Paris has plenty of fascinating women to offer, and much more accessible than the Dauphine.

The tall figure with the dark hair and youthful face stands out noticeably among the greying diplomats in the queue before her. Marie Antoinette cannot recall ever having seen him before. She would certainly not have forgotten him. His dark and eloquently arched eyebrows emphasise the large and expressive eyes, currently fixed with grave interest upon the Deification of Hercules.

Between one exchange of greetings and the next, the Dauphine nudges her lady in waiting. 'Who is that young man, Adrienne?' she enquires.

Mademoiselle de La Ferté is quite a lot shorter than her mistress and has to stand on tiptoe to see who she is referring to. 'I have no idea, Your Highness, but he's certainly very handsome.'

'Thank you very much, Adrienne.' The Dauphine's tone is both aloof and possessive.

Marie Antoinette notes how Axel's gaze shifts to the king and then to that woman du Barry. Why doesn't he look at her? The Dauphine takes a small and unobtrusive step forward; perhaps she has been standing too much in the shadow. Slowly the young man moves down the line and turns his eyes upon her. She feels the full effect of his glance; how her blood stirs, her breath falters.

Then he casts his eyes to the ground. Is he shy? She can hardly tear her gaze away from him, and yet she must. Out of the corner of her eye she sees him taking her in. Should she respond to his fleeting glance? The oddest sensation comes over her, and she tries instead to ignore his presence. But when she averts her own eyes she can still feel his upon her like a soft caress. Oh lord, how impossibly tight is this corset! She can hardly breathe.

The next time Marie Antoinette finds the courage to look in his direction is when the dark-haired young man is being introduced to her.

'Comte Axel von Fersen.' She hears his voice as if from afar, soft and friendly.

She nods and does not know what to reply. Two beautiful eyes regard her. A whiff of scent reaches her, too ethereal even to identify, and yet enough to touch her senses. A warm wave sweeps over her.

'Your Highness,' declares Fersen in farewell, moving on to let the Swedish ambassador introduce him to the Comtesse du Barry.

As if awaking from a dream, Marie Antoinette scolds herself back into reality. What a disaster! Has she lost the power of speech? She pictures herself as she stood before him, like some silly teenage girl, lost for words. What a missed opportunity! And now, of course, that creature is busy flirting with him. How dare she be so insolent! Out of the corner of her eye she sees Madame du Barry lay her hand on Count Fersen's arm, smiling at something he says, and they are out of earshot! He seems to be quite taken in, thinks Marie Antoinette with a stab of jealousy.

Adrienne is digging her gently in the ribs, and the Dauphine composes herself and smiles at the next guest. But inside she is boiling with rage at herself for having acted so inanely. Mad that du Barry has worked her black magic on Fersen, but most of all incensed that he is no longer looking at her, the Dauphine. The best thing she can do is forget this Swede as fast as possible.

But the count is not so easily banished from her thoughts. His eyes keep appearing before the Dauphine. The more she tries to put Fersen out of her head, the more vividly he manifests himself to her. Her food is like ashes in her mouth; she can no longer bear to sit quietly at the card table all evening. And things are not much better once she gets to bed. His perfume seems to envelop her in the darkness and, half asleep, she thinks she hears his voice. He is beside her! She raises herself in bed to embrace him. He has come to her! Axel Fersen!

The bitter taste of sweat provides a rude awakening.

'Well, well, that's a passionate welcome,' mumbles Louis-Auguste, more than amazed and kicking off his slippers.

As if caught in some forbidden act, she loosens her embrace upon the Dauphin and, biting her lip, slides back down among the pillows with a sinking heart. She feels like weeping. The warm sensation that filled her a moment ago is gone. With a deep intake of breath she dutifully half-raises her nightdress. She knows it will not take long and tries to dwell instead on the slender physique of the Swedish count.

But the leaden weight of the Dauphin seems to pulverise all thoughts of Fersen. Struggling for breath, she counts the minutes and fights the urge to thrust her husband from her. It seems an eternity.

'I think that's done it,' announces Louis-Auguste in triumph.

Marie Antoinette fills her lungs with air. 'I think so too.'

And, offering her a heartfelt 'Goodnight', he creeps from the room, slippers in hand.

Marie Antoinette turns onto her other side and lets the tears flow. The splendid-eyed Swedish count, however, is nowhere to be found.

No partying for me today; I'm going to rest instead. Yesterday was another hectic evening. I got tired out and nearly fainted. Whether from the warmth or the tension I don't know, but I hope Antoinette understands.

From the journal of the Princesse de Lamballe,
14th January 1774

20

For the fourth time since her arrival at Versailles, Marie Antoinette is celebrating Carnival at the palace. This year, like last, two masked balls are held each week, on Monday evening in the Dauphine's apartment and on Wednesday in the Comtesse de Noailles's salon. But in fact it matters little where the festivities take place, for every time the same masks appear, behind them the same faces.

'How nice it would be, Lamballe, to meet some new people now and then,' remarks Marie Antoinette, still trembling slightly from her latest outburst. 'They're supposed to be adults,' she adds, with a lancing look at the corner where the boys are standing. The three brothers have been at each other's throats as usual and she has had to intervene on several occasions to prevent them from tearing one another apart.

The Dauphin leans sulkily against the wall and the Comte de Provence is slouching in his armchair looking bored, while at a nearby table the Comte d'Artois, with a pained expression, rubs his shin. The swelling slowly turning blue there marks the spot where Louis-Auguste has just landed a hefty kick.

'Why don't we invite some mature gentlemen here on Saturday evening?' suggests the Dauphine to her cousin.

Lamballe blinks. 'Who do you have in mind, cousin?'

Marie Antoinette flicks open her fan. 'I've no idea; a few grown men who know how to conduct themselves. Perhaps my husband and his little brothers are in need of role models. I'm sick and tired of playing mother to them all.'

'So it isn't to make Louis-Auguste jealous?'

'I beg your pardon, Lamballe? Whatever are you saying, *chère cousine*? That would be quite superfluous, surely! Jealousy isn't exactly in short supply here. Oh, and while we're on the subject, I have some news for you – you won't believe it!'

Expectantly, Marie-Thérèse, Princesse de Lamballe, shifts her chair a little closer to her cousin's. 'Tell me.'

'You know how that dreadful du Barry woman is itching to attend my ball evenings?' Lamballe nods. 'Well, I've already explained to Papa that, were I to invite her, it would only insult the aunts. But now the silly baby thinks she's found a new answer to the problem.'

'Surely not!' reacts Lamballe, outraged.

'Of course not, *ma chère*. But you'll never guess what she dreamt up. Du Barry approached Noailles and asked her if I might be interested in a pair of exclusive diamond earrings! And I really do mean exclusive, for these trinkets appear to be valued at around seven hundred thousand livres.'

Some quick mental arithmetic tells Lamballe that this represents nearly twenty-five times her annual allowance. An exclusive sum indeed.

'And then ... and then she presses them into Noailles's sweaty little palm with the request that she show me the earrings; if I liked them, I was to keep them, and du Barry would arrange for me to receive them as a special gift from the king. Her only condition – and here's the crunch – would be her presence henceforth as a guest at my weekly ball.'

'Unbelievable!' exclaims Marie-Thérèse in disgust. She leans closer to her cousin and whispers, 'Have you seen the earrings?'

'Oh yes, I most certainly have. They're really magnificent. The most gorgeous ones I've ever seen. But do you think I'd fall for a cheap trick like that? I'd be bringing myself right down to her level, where love and friendship can simply be bought for money and jewellery. And apart from that, Lamballe, can't you just see her strutting about here? Head held high in triumph, as if she were the queen herself? Oh no, *ma chère*. I'm the one who is first in line for the title of Queen of France. And when that moment arrives there'll be no more room here for persons of du Barry's sort!'

'Oh, good for you! Goodness, she'll be livid. Have you heard anything since?'

Marie Antoinette gives a shrug of contempt. 'Do you think I care what happens?'

Lamballe leans back in her chair and stares straight ahead of her. 'Actually, I feel quite sorry for her.'

'You what?'

'Well, I mean, where *is* she welcome? I understand she no longer dare show her face in Paris. The last time she was there, they stoned her carriage. And it seems the king has been seeing less and less of her lately. Haven't you noticed? What will happen when Louis XV has had enough of her? What then?'

'Good grief, Lamballe! I had no idea what a sensitive flower you were. Hasn't she brought it all upon herself? Don't forget it was she who had the poor Duc de Choiseul banished. It's thanks to her that the Duc d'Aiguillon got into power. The very fact that she's in a position casually to offer me a costly present says it all! My ladies in waiting, let alone the rest of my household, are owed months of salary and can't be paid, apparently, because the money's all gone. Just you tell me how such a woman manages to carry on the way she does under the circumstances!'

Marie-Thérèse finds herself forced to think deeply. 'Indeed, it's not a very pretty picture that you paint. I think you must be right, *cousine*,' admits the young widow with a serious face. 'But I still find it a shame for her.'

'Oh Lamballe, you're such a soft-hearted little lamb!' declares her cousin, tapping her very gently on the cheek with her fan and bursting out laughing.

A second later, the Dauphine's tone changes dramatically. 'Louis!' she bawls fiercely, getting to her feet.

The Dauphin has found a way to relieve his boredom by grabbing a servant by the arm and challenging him to a wrestling match. This is not the first time he has gone in for such a diversion.

It is usually over pretty quickly, as Louis-Auguste is not only large and heavily built, but also strong as an ox. As the Dauphin's arm tightens about his neck like a vice, the unfortunate manservant begins to turn crimson in the face and his pleading eyes pop nearly out of his head. His cry for help, however, is strangled at birth.

'Louis, for goodness' sake, stop that!'

Taken aback, the Dauphin lets his man go. The servant drops onto his hands and knees, wheezing noisily.

'Help the poor man up. Have you gone crazy?' roars Marie Antoinette. Louis-Auguste gapes at her, thunderstruck. Help a servant to his feet? The poor man claws his own way upright, and, still gasping, straightens his waistcoat. Before anyone can say another word, he staggers from the room. Everyone's eyes are on the royal pair.

'Just a joke,' mumbles Louis-Auguste in excuse.

Behind their fans, people are sniggering and murmuring.

'And there we have the future King of France,' mocks the Comte de Provence.

In a flash Louis-Auguste turns on his brother, but Marie Antoinette grabs her husband, her eyes blazing. 'Get to bed!' she hisses, shoving him away from her.

The Dauphin gives her a bewildered look, his eyes filling with humiliated tears. He surely can't allow himself to be dismissed like a little boy. 'So you're on Tartuffe's side,' he whines.

'Get to bed,' she repeats, but now in such a threatening tone that the Dauphin turns on his heel and is gone. Oh mother, thinks Marie Antoinette, if only you could see how things really are here. Perhaps you would have more compassion for me.

The room begins to buzz again and the music restarts. The Dauphine takes her seat, embarrassed and subdued, next to the Princesse de Lamballe. Marie Antoinette feels the consoling touch of her cousin's hand upon her shoulder, while Mercy's warning echoes in her ears. Might the old fox be right about her husband after all?

Lost in thought, the Dauphine feels a fleeting chill upon the nape of her neck. Yet all the windows and shutters are firmly fastened. She turns her head a little. It must be her imagination, for the air is warm and the fire carefully tended. There is no shortage of logs here, although the Comte de Mercy has told her that things are very different in Paris. The cold weather has meant that the huge stockpiles of fuel have dwindled much more quickly than expected. Prices keep on rising, and even flour is growing scarce. There are rumoured to have been sporadic outbreaks of unrest, provoked by empty stomachs.

Marie Antoinette finds it hard to believe Mercy's worrying reports. For Lamballe, whose residence is in the heart of Paris, has told her that the hearths of the Hôtel de Toulouse burn as brightly as ever and the stock-cupboard shelves are just as amply filled with provisions. Could Mercy be exaggerating a little? The Dauphine thinks with regret of her dispatched husband. Was she right to send him off like that with his tail between his legs? Is she being fair to Louis-Auguste?

Suppose Mercy is justified in his assessment; how would Louis-Auguste respond to hungry stomachs? What would he do about the situation if he were king?

'Do you want to play cards or dance?' Lamballe breaks in upon her thoughts.

It takes a moment for her cousin's question to sink in. Then Marie Antoinette sheds her sombre expression. 'Dance, Lamballe!' The Dauphine's smile is back. 'Do let's dance, if you'd like to.'

Jeanne du Barry is deeply disappointed at the Dauphine's rejection of her offer of the costly earrings. She has obviously badly underestimated 'la petite rousse' and cannot immediately think of another way to win over Marie Antoinette. Of course, all this has nothing to do with her attending the Dauphine's ball evenings. It has to do with her future!

For two whole weeks the Comtesse du Barry has seen nothing of the king. The old monarch hasn't paid her a single visit. She daren't go to him herself, and so the *maîtresse en titre* is reduced to waiting restlessly in her salon for him to appear. Now and then she thinks she hears a creaking on the small staircase that heralds his arrival, but it's just her imagination playing tricks again.

For fourteen days Jeanne du Barry has cancelled all her engagements and waited, terrified in case the king ascends the stairs only to find her bed empty. Jeanne is worried. Her position feels extremely insecure, for what will happen to her when the king dies? Jeanne du Barry cherishes no illusions as to Marie Antoinette's feelings towards her. Completely undeserved, of course, but still. Jeanne is quite prepared to be banished from the palace the instant the King of France draws his last breath, and cruelly stripped of all the gifts she has received over the years. The very thought sickens her.

She stares at the great canvas bearing Anthony van Dyck's portrait of the English King Charles I, a work she has always loved. But, in her heart of hearts, she loved even more the moment at the auction when she outbid the Russian ambassador. Over recent days, though, the English monarch, a distant ancestor of Louis XV, has seemed to look down upon her with disdain.

It is as if the sovereigns are closing ranks and shutting her out, telling her she doesn't belong among them. And neither can she expect any mercy from the Dauphin. The great fat lump is entirely under his wife's thumb. Jeanne sees plainly that in order to assure her future she must make a friend of the future king of France. But isn't it already too late for that? She collapses on the bed, sobbing.

Jeanne du Barry no longer has eyes for her vast art collection or her priceless porcelain. She feels friendless and alone, wretchedly and miserably alone.

In his apartment on the floor below, the King of France sits hunched in his bed, staring out from sombre eyes. Almost everyone is celebrating Carnival at Versailles, apart from Louis XV. Just after New Year he caught a cold. Nothing to make a fuss about, for the king's temperature fortunately remains normal. But despite the optimism of his personal physicians, there would seem to be more amiss than a mere cold. No one can find a reason for it, but the king's depression is deepening by the day.

Louis XV has let it be known that he has no interest in attending yet another ball. Withdrawing to his private quarters he begins, remarkably enough, to occupy himself with the state of his immortal soul. It has not helped that he has lost three of his oldest and closest associates recently – and, what is more, it happened in his presence. The Marquis de Chavelin, the Abbé de la Ville, and even the Maréchal d'Armentières, always so robust – all of them as dead as a doornail from one moment to the next. Three in a row; is that not a sign of God's divine providence?

The king has been accustomed to enjoying rude good health, yet he has been struck down by sickness a couple of times over the past year. According to his father confessor, the Abbé Maudoux, this is a very clear sign from God that the king must repent. Repent of his extremely dubious lifestyle. Up until now Louis XV has always dismissed his confessor's advice. What, after all, has he ever done wrong?

Louis XV is a lonely widower; surely he is entitled to keep a mistress? The forbidding face of Maudoux, a man ill-inclined to make the slightest concession, has the French sovereign doubting himself. And his youngest daughter Louise is always happy to oblige when it comes to piling on the pressure. She too is convinced that her father's life is nearing its end. No one, including the King of France himself, escapes God's fury for having lived so profane a life. Nevertheless, Louise, who for years has shut herself away in the Carmelite convent in Paris, promises piously to pray every day for her father's soul.

'The mercy of even God Himself is finite,' warns the Abbé Maudoux sharply. 'Might I remind His Majesty of Marie-Anne, Duchesse de Châteauroux, one of his former *maîtresses en titre* of long ago? Might I revive his memory of his sickbed at Metz? It is indeed thirty years ago, but you can surely never forget, Sire, how you looked death in the eye? How all the letting of blood and purging proved futile, and how even the ceaseless prayers of your people seemed unable to elicit God's mercy?'

Louis shuts his eyes and relives the moment when he hovered on the brink of death.

'Only when you were at the utmost extremity and the Bishop of Soissons was preparing to administer the final sacraments, once you had sent Mademoiselle Châteauroux away, did the miracle take place.'

The father confessor pauses to let his words hit home. Louis XV is staring mournfully straight ahead, but then looks up suddenly. 'I thought I had the secret potion prescribed by Doctor du Moulin to thank for that,' he quietly remarks.

This proves almost too much for Maudoux.

'When are you finally going to accept the mercy of God?' demands the priest. 'Do you really want to wait until the very last moment ... when it is actually too late and there is no further opportunity for you to be cleansed of sin?'

The Abbé Maudoux makes the sign of the cross and at once begins to pray.

The mere sight of this plunges Louis XV even further into despondency. He knows very well that he cannot live forever, but is there really life after death? Does God truly exist? Is there any sense in changing his way of life at this late stage? It was indeed only by a miracle that he escaped the jaws of death last time. In that moment he had believed in a divine being, and he had derived great strength from the reaction of his loyal subjects, as for days on end they celebrated his triumph over the grave. It was then that his jubilant people had endowed him with the nickname *Le Bien-Aimé*.

Louis XV laughs contemptuously at himself. *Le Bien-Aimé* indeed – what is there left of him? Self-doubt gnaws away at his soul. Was it truly God who cured him that time? And did that same God contrive the sudden and completely unexpected death, a couple of days later, of his dismissed *maîtresse en titre*? Was it out of vengeance against the Almighty, or solely due to human weakness, that within a year he had installed Mademoiselle Le Normant d'Etioles in her vacated position?

While he was still young, Louis XV could not have cared less about the advice of his counsellors and priests. Things feel different to him now. The threat of impending death, as he experienced it so long ago on his sickbed in Metz, is once more a palpable presence in his room. He cannot see it, but he knows it is there. Lurking, awaiting the arrival of his last day.

'What am I to do, Maudoux?' murmurs the king, his voice trembling slightly.

A triumphant smile appears on the face of the abbé. 'Repent of all your sins,' declaims the confessor solemnly, 'and seek full absolution.'

'Is that all?' responds the king in surprise.

Maudoux stares aghast at the king.

'In the present instance, Your Majesty,' he replies, 'that is a very great deal.'

Outraged, Louis XV lets himself fall back on his pillows and shuts his eyes.

'I shall consider the matter, Maudoux,' he tells the abbé, with a dismissive wave of the hand.

The confessor, sensing that there is little to be gained from prolonging his stay further, prepares to take his leave of the royal bedroom.

'Just a moment, Maudoux,' the king calls after him.

Ever hopeful, the priest turns back to his monarch. The king purses his lips and sighs.

'Cancel the carriage I have ordered for Madame du Barry.'

The priest bows more deeply than he is accustomed to do. It is a start!

'Most certainly, Your Majesty.'

What can I say? It's her life, after all, but is she behaving sensibly? I think the same person is involved as on New Year's Day. I'm sorry Antoinette won't talk about it. It's as if someone has come between us. I think I must be jealous! Anyway, time to go to Mass now.

From the journal of the Princesse de Lamballe,
21st February 1774

21

It is a grey and overcast Saturday afternoon as the carriage carrying the Dauphine reaches Paris. But today the sky, still laden with snow, seems to have told the clouds to hold on to their burden. Marie Antoinette briefly considered making the journey by sleigh. There was plenty of snow still lying, but once she arrives at the Rue Saint-Honoré she sees how the pristine covering has been trampled into sludge.

Drenched, the horses trot on though the yellowish slush en route for the Hôtel de Toulouse, the town house of Marie-Thérèse, Princesse de Lamballe. This evening there is a masked ball at the Opéra, which is just round the corner from Lamballe's mansion, next to the Palais Royal.

Practical considerations have led Marie-Thérèse to invite the Dauphine to come and dress for the ball at her residence. There would be little left of the princess's costume and coiffure were she to make the two-hour journey from Versailles this evening in a jolting carriage, muffled up in warm rugs. The Dauphin is to come direct to the Opéra later on, accompanied by his brothers and their wives.

'Oh, *ma chère* Lamballe, I should do this more often,' smiles Marie Antoinette happily, carving herself off a tiny slice of quail breast.

'You're always welcome, *cousine*, absolutely always,' Lamballe replies, glowing with pleasure at the sight of her cousin's happy face.

'What costume are you wearing this evening?' returns the Dauphine.

'I have a choice of Mary Queen of Scots or Catherine the Great. But I'm not sure which will suit me better. What do you think?'

The crown princess takes a sip of water. 'Hmm ... I think, *cousine*, that Mary Queen of Scots would be most appropriate.'

Lamballe nods in agreement.

'Only you must make sure not to lose your head!' adds Marie Antoinette, collapsing into a fit of giggles. 'Actually,' she resumes, 'I should most like to go as King Henry IV. Or even as Louis XIV! But I'm afraid I should be so conspicuous that people would immediately recognise me. And that's the last thing I want.'

Marie-Thérèse dabs her lips carefully with her napkin and lays it back in her lap. 'Why should you want to remain incognito?' she asks in amazement. 'After all, you're the darling of Paris.'

Marie Antoinette has to laugh. 'Maybe that's exactly why. I think it would be so lovely just to mingle with people without them knowing who I was, and then I'd hear what they really had to say about the Dauphine!'

'I don't see that it would make any difference, *cousine*. Everyone adores you.'

'We'll see, *ma chère*, we shall see.'

The carriages come to a halt as near as possible to the awning-covered entrance, so that the masked guests can step down onto dry ground. It is a bitter night, even for the notorious beggars who haunt the foot of the steps on such evenings with their ingratiating grins and pleas for alms, in the hope of milking the rich. From the windows pour streams of golden light, and through the open doors come the strains of music and laughter.

Once in the foyer, the snowy world is forgotten. As on a lovely summer afternoon, in here everything seems to radiate its own light. The richly coloured costumes make every heart sing, helped by the freely flowing wine. Husbands and wives, arriving separately so as to preserve their cover, peek from behind their masks in an attempt to identify their own spouse. Most soon give up the effort and abandon themselves to the party, so packed with adventurers, so seething with temptation.

The great hall is pulsating to the rhythms of dancing and flirtation, the swapping of vicarious nonsense and kisses. In the seclusion of dimly lit vestibule and curtained box the most outrageous encounters take place. It is the best Carnival party ever, and one that only Paris could play host to. Admiral, cardinal, king, empress, milkmaid and mischievous marchioness – all ogle one another to their hearts' content, without fear of being recognised. A romance here may last no more than a couple of minutes, at the price of a lifetime's attachment. But then, that is the way of the masked ball.

'You must be the Dauphin,' says the half-seas-over cardinal, pawing the ample belly of a gaudily dressed young man. The cardinal gives the paunch another poke. 'Is that all real?'

The corpulent 'king' pulls in his stomach and says nothing.

'What's that? Is the Dauphin here? Where?' croons a nun who has rather overdone the rouge.

'Here,' bellows the cardinal cheerfully, pointing with his glass.

The nun throws her arms around the podgy young man, who sets his crown straight again.

'How lovely,' babbles the nun. 'You do look quite like the Dauphin, only he's a lot fatter! Come on! What's your name?'

Debating with himself whether he should lower his mask, the young man responds, 'Madame, I am the Dauphin.'

After a pensive look, the nun bursts into laughter. 'I knew it! But I won't tell a soul!' She gives him a big kiss on the cheek, takes an even bigger gulp of wine and asks, 'Do you want to know who I am?'

'Do tell.'

She embraces him again, this time whispering in his ear, 'I may look like a nun, but really I'm Marie Antoinette, the Dauphine! Shall we dance?'

'Perhaps later.'

She slides her arms away from him, disappointed, her face

crestfallen. But not for long. A couple of seconds later she is prattling with a tall man posing unmistakably as the great Voltaire.

The warmth of overheated bodies ascends towards the gorgeously decorated ceiling of the Opéra, its aesthetic beauty entirely disregarded by this evening's revellers. From one of the boxes, Marie Antoinette and Lamballe, newly joined by the Duchesse de Chartres, gaze down upon the seething masses. It is very hard to make out friends and acquaintances from up here, especially if they are masked. And yet, to her utter amazement, one tall figure is instantly recognisable to the Dauphine.

There is no doubting it. Despite his mask, she identifies the slender, dark-haired young man who has just made his entry into the hall. She had almost forgotten him, but the moment she claps eyes on him again Marie Antoinette feels the stirring effect of his presence. He glances momentarily upward at the painted ceiling and the gilded stucco dome. But he too is soon distracted from the magnificent architecture by this evening's deeply plunging necklines and the rise and fall of softly rounded bosoms.

'I'm going down,' declares Marie Antoinette, getting to her feet. The Duchesse de Chartres and Lamballe rise too, preparing to accompany the Dauphine, but she gestures to them to wait here.

'I'd rather go alone. If all three of us go down together, everyone will recognise us directly ... what with you and your amazing hair, my sweet Lamballe. Believe me, there isn't a mask or costume capable of disguising you!'

Marie-Thérèse smiles briefly at the compliment, but resumes her seat with some dejection as her cousin leaves the box without her.

Marie Antoinette descends the stairs almost at a run, terrified she will lose him in the bustle. Her heart hammering, she enters the hall and weaves her way through the crowds. Where is he? This is the spot where he was standing, but he's gone. Surely he can't have left the ball already? Distracted, she stands and stares about her.

'Ah, Madame!' A deep voice addresses her and she feels a strong arm about her waist. 'We haven't yet been introduced this evening.'

Marie Antoinette turns quickly, shocked that anyone dare grasp hold of her in such a way. Her immediate impulse is to lash out with her fan, but just in time she remembers where she is.

'Who are you?' she sharply demands.

'The Admiral of the French fleet,' comes the arrogant reply. 'And with whom have I the pleasure?' His huge hand is already gliding down from her waist towards her buttocks.

Marie Antoinette looks stonily past him, calculating how to rid herself of the filthy slob. Then she puts an arm about his neck and, planting a quick, soft kiss there, whispers playfully in his ear, 'I'm your wife's best friend.'

'Ah,' smiles the man, a little less sure of himself. 'A mere jest,' he adds, now subdued, and removes his hand. Without another word the admiral sets course for a safer shore.

The Dauphine gulps a deep breath of relief and moves on through the throng. A hunchback bumps into her, grinning from ear to ear. Marie Antoinette smiles back and tries to circumvent the man, who is dressed as a humble peddler. The hunchback blocks her way.

'Hey, little sweetheart, where're you off to this fine evening?'

She recoils from the foul stench of decay that envelops her with each word.

'When was the last time you took a bath?' replies the Dauphine haughtily.

'Come, come, have pity on poor Jacques and give him a kiss,' begs the peddler, reaching into her bosom and clumsily pinching her there.

'*Mon Dieu!*' cries the princess in horror, this time unhesitatingly striking out with her fan and hitting him full in the face.

'Ow! What's the matter with you?' he shouts. 'Who do you think you are?' Rubbing his nose with one hand, the hunchback confronts her, his other fist raised in threat. As the Dauphine stands trembling with rage and ready to drop her disguise, the brandished arm disappears suddenly behind the peddler's back and his body twists to avoid a broken limb.

'Monsieur almost made a wrong move, did he not?' comes the cool voice of Axel Fersen, who has the hunchback's arm bent almost double. The man gives a moan of pain. 'It would do you no harm to apologise to the lady, and then I could rid us both of you.'

The peddler makes the best of a bad job. He is no match for the man in Swedish regimental uniform. As Axel loosens his hold, the pathetic creature finds himself able to turn round and stammer out some sort of apology.

Marie Antoinette is shaking all over. Not so much at the threat from this dirty little monster – she could have dealt with him – but more in response to Count Fersen's chivalry in coming to her rescue. Can he have recognised her? Axel lets go of the hunchback, who is soon lost in the crowd.

'Is Madame unharmed?' enquires Fersen with concern.

The Dauphine nods her head, holding her mask securely in place as she does so. 'I am greatly indebted to you, Monsieur. You intervened just in time.'

Fersen smiles. 'It was nothing, Madame. Tell me, are you here unaccompanied this evening?'

'That is rather a bold question, sir,' laughs Marie Antoinette.

'I ask only to ascertain whether there is anyone looking after you. I should find it most regrettable were the man who bothered you just now, or another of his ilk, to upset you again.'

'In that case, I should much appreciate it if you stayed by my side a little longer,' she tells him.

'Madame, that will be a great pleasure. Would you like to dance, or perhaps you prefer to take a seat?'

'Dance!' she declares with gusto, taking his arm as he leads her out onto the floor.

Axel is surprised. Gliding in step with the lady, he reflects on the evening. He hadn't known what to expect of it, although it was plain to him from the outset that there were plenty of female guests willing to engage in more than a dance. But he found most not to his taste. Too heavily made up, too old, or simply already too merry. He isn't a heavy drinker himself. His spirits are high enough without the need of wine to raise them. But to what extent is his cheerfulness just a façade? His friends always find him rather on the serious side, but then not all of them share his interests.

Hmm, this woman is very singular, though. As light as a feather on her feet! He scrutinises his partner more closely still. She's taller than average, her figure unimpeachable. And what a ravishing smile! Axel cannot see her eyes properly behind the mask, but that smile alone would sink a thousand ships. And tender too, like a homecoming.

'You dance truly wonderfully, Madame. Might I know your name?' asks Axel delicately.

Marie Antoinette laughs, thrilled to discover how beautifully he too moves around the floor. Far better even than Artois, and that's saying something. Oh, he's perfect! Shall I tell him who I am?

'My name is Julie d'Etange.' She introduces herself with a slight bow of the head.

'Ah, Julie. From *La Nouvelle Héloïse* by Monsieur Rousseau.'

'Very good!' she exclaims, delighted to find he knows the romantic novel from which her character comes. 'Now that you know who I am,' teases Marie Antoinette, 'I should very much like to learn your name.'

The Swede gives a little cough. 'I am Axel, Count von Fersen, of Sweden.'

'Ah, hence the uniform.'

'Er, no. I borrowed that from a friend, an officer in the *Royal-Suédois*.'

'So you're not a soldier, but truly a Swedish count?' she laughs.

With a shrug, Fersen replies, 'Nobody knows me here, so why

should I trouble to disguise myself and assume another identity?'

'Don't you know anyone here, then?'

'Hardly anyone. I haven't been in Paris long.'

'When did you arrive?'

'At the end of November.'

'Straight from Sweden?'

'Oh, no. I've been travelling for three years and seen half of Europe.'

'Oh my goodness! Then you are indeed a man of the world.'

Fersen makes a wry mouth, as if to modify this impression.

'Where are you staying, my good count?'

'In the Hôtel d'York, on the Rue du Colombier.'

'Ah,' responds Marie Antoinette in a neutral tone. She has no idea where the street is.

'On the other bank. Near the abbey of Saint-Germain des Prés.'

'Oh, of course,' laughs Marie Antoinette, feeling the blood rise to her cheeks. There is a lull in the conversation, but still they float together in perfect harmony across the dance floor.

'You aren't from Paris yourself?' asks Axel Fersen, attempting to verify his own conclusion.

'I live nearby,' replies the Dauphine, vague and non-committal.

'Do you know many people here yourself?' persists Fersen.

'To be honest, I hardly know a soul. But if they removed their masks, I would most likely recognise one or two faces.'

This young woman is beginning seriously to intrigue him. Who can she be? What is her real name? She definitely belongs to the nobility, but is she married? She must be, for she is far too young and beautiful to attend a Carnival ball unchaperoned. The scent of roses surrounds her; too ethereal for an expensive fragrance, but nonetheless sweet to his senses. She says she doesn't live in Paris. Is she perhaps a lady in waiting at the court of Versailles?

'Have we met before, at the palace of Versailles?' asks he suddenly.

Marie Antoinette feels her cheeks flush once more. Has he realised who I am?

'What makes you think that?'

'Well, you say aren't from here, yet you live nearby. Why then not at Versailles?'

'Do you think you've seen me on a previous occasion?'

'It's difficult to say, so long as you remain unwilling to remove your mask.'

Marie Antoinette giggles. Should she do so, or prolong this delicious moment of pleasure?

'Have you met someone at court, then, whose acquaintance you would like to renew?' she enquires, with mischief in her voice.

A frown flits across Fersen's brow. That's a dangerous question. He clears his throat. 'Madame, there is one woman who has made an impression upon me. You greatly resemble her, but I don't expect her to be present this evening.'

'Is she beautiful?'

'Almost as lovely as yourself, Madame,' responds Fersen gallantly.

'Do I know her, count?'

Axel laughs out loud. 'Everyone knows her. That's why she cannot be here this evening.'

'Oh, and why not?'

'The lady to whom I refer, Madame, is the Dauphine. I'm afraid that, were she to show herself here, the guests would overwhelm her with adoration like bees their queen.'

'Is Madame la Dauphine aware of the effect she has had upon you?'

Fersen sighs. 'I fear not, Julie. For a brief moment, on New Year's Day, she glanced in my direction. Afterwards I felt she was avoiding looking at me. I don't think she really noticed me. But what can I expect? I'm only a foreign count, after all.'

'Why so self-deprecating? She's a foreigner herself, is she not? Perhaps she's simply faithful to her husband, and doesn't make eyes at every handsome young man she meets.'

Fersen is indignant. 'Do you really think that? A less compatible pair I cannot imagine! But whatever, Madame la Dauphine is inaccessible to me. I can only worship her in my dreams.'

'Ah, you're a true romantic! But tell me, then, how do you feel about Madame du Barry? Does she too grace your dreams with her presence?'

Axel shrugs once more, this time with indifference. 'The Comtesse du Barry seems very charming, but I'm afraid that I wouldn't have much to say to her.'

'Come, come. Most men aren't so terribly interested in talking,' laughs Marie Antoinette.

'That's true. Perhaps I would also disappoint you in that respect. I very much enjoy good conversation.'

The Swedish count and Julie have meanwhile been gathering a crowd around them. It begins to dawn on Axel that people are watching him and pointing at Julie. Holding her fan so as to hide her face, Marie Antoinette realises that too many prying eyes have already seen through her disguise. Looking up, she catches Lamballe beckoning from their box. Julie is unmasked! Marie Antoinette stops dancing in mid step.

'Would you like to meet Madame la Dauphine again?' she asks, her tone now earnest.

'Madame, I may cause you offence by saying so, yet I would be belying my own nature were I to deny it. But if I'm to make such an admission, I should like to know to whom I am baring my soul.'

In the background the Dauphine hears her name being whispered from mouth to mouth. Oh, what a pity!

'Count Fersen, I should like to invite you to attend my ball this coming Monday, as my special guest.'

Fersen gazes questioningly at her, his puzzlement intensifying as she casts about impatiently for an escape route.

'Your name, Madame?' insists Fersen uncertainly.

It's remarkable how the crowds of excited faces have gathered around them.

'I have to go,' she whispers.

Did he imagine her lips brushing his ear? Aroused, he puts his hand to his neck as she passes. She turns swiftly back to face him.

'My name,' says she, articulating each word with tantalising slowness, '... is Marie Antoinette.'

For a brief moment she lowers her fan and Fersen stares stupefied into the loveliest pair of eyes in the world. Her face, her smile are so ... so perfect.

'*Mon Dieu!*' His lips can form no other sound. Her radiant eyes have disappeared once more behind the fan.

'Until Monday!' is the last thing he hears her say, as she slips her supple way through gaps in the crowd and vanishes into the shadow of the gallery. Like Orpheus watching his Eurydice swallowed up by the underworld, Count Fersen feels rooted to the spot.

He is incredulous. How can he possibly have been so dim as not to recognise her? My God, I hope I didn't say anything too idiotic! He tries to replay the conversation mentally word for word, but finds he cannot. Her face is still too fresh in his mind. And then there are people tapping him on the shoulder and demanding his attention.

'Well, was that really the Dauphine you were talking to just now?'

The sea of inebriated faces awaiting an answer quickly restores Fersen to his senses.

'Madame la Dauphine, you say?' he replies with feigned surprise. 'I think she was just another gorgeous Parisienne.'

Disappointed, his audience of eavesdroppers disperses, with murmurs of 'Still, I could have sworn it was Madame la Dauphine,' to resume their excesses.

And yet the rumour will not die, and it is only a matter of time before the rest of the royal family is also identified and the Dauphin and Provence are forced to present their artificial smiles to an enthusiastic public.

Marie Antoinette casts a final glance down from her box on the spectacle below: the crowd cheering '*Vive Monsieur le Dauphin, Vive Madame la Dauphine*' and among them her Swedish count. She will not return to the dance floor this evening. For many a long hour

Axel lingers, refusing the invitations to dance from blushing countesses, hungry only for another glimpse of her. But it seems he will have to contain himself until Monday.

I've won her back completely! I could hardly fail to, because Rose Bertin is the crème de la crème! This is the first time Marie Antoinette has shown any real interest in fashion, and I think she was truly taken with the sketches and the gorgeous fabrics. If I'd only known, I'd have introduced her to Rose Bertin far sooner.

From the journal of the Princesse de Lamballe,
6th March 1774

22

The floor is strewn with balls of screwed-up paper. Fersen stares outside, heavy-eyed and still searching fruitlessly for the right words. He has spent the whole afternoon seated behind his desk opposite the huge window, making tireless attempts to compose a single letter. Outside the light is failing, earlier than usual, thanks to an impenetrable blanket of cloud obscuring the heavens. It must be time to light the lamps. Not that they will shed any light on his present task. Why, oh why do the words continue to elude him?

Axel has to find a way of making his feelings known without violating any unwritten law. How far can he confide in her without causing offence? A servant comes in and lights the lamps. Without saying anything, the man proceeds to pick up the discarded paper.

'Leave that,' instructs Axel, thanking him nonetheless.

Count Fersen gets to his feet, stretches and begins gathering up the balls of paper and consigning them one by one to the fire. The pages full of his warm words and declarations of love for her instantly go up in flames. He knows that nothing could be worse than a letter to Madame la Dauphine falling into the wrong hands. For days now he has written hardly a single entry in his diary, his thoughts are so entirely filled with her. Oh God, how desperately in love he is!

In recent weeks Axel Fersen has been attending the regular balls given by Marie Antoinette. There has been little opportunity for talking; mostly they have danced and danced, content simply to gaze into one another's eyes. In the brief moments between dances it quickly became evident how closely their musical taste coincided.

In their enthusiasm Marie Antoinette promised to sing for Axel, and he to play some songs for her.

There were few, if any, disapproving looks from the Dauphin. The king's grandson seems rather to have been quite taken with Count Fersen, who hardly left the dance floor. The Comte d'Artois, himself seething with jealousy, remarked on one occasion that Louis-Auguste should keep a closer watch on his wife. But he was soon silenced by a furious look and a kick under the table from the Dauphin.

And now it is all over. Carnival is finished for this season and the weeks of festivities are at an end. Only behind the closed doors of Paris does the partying continue in secret.

The news that Marie Antoinette had found a favourite in Axel Fersen circulated at lightning speed. As a result, Axel has become a welcome guest in all the numberless salons of Paris. People hang on his every word to glean the latest news about Marie Antoinette, but Axel is no gossipmonger. Nothing passes his lips that might cause the Dauphine embarrassment, and every snippet of a romantic nature he resolutely smothers at birth.

'We make good dance partners,' is his bland response, 'and nothing more.'

Axel is deeply conscious that he is playing with fire, an inferno that can offer him no warmth but only badly burnt fingers. How long can things go on like this? She is the future Queen of France, not a little country bumpkin of a countess who can carry on an extramarital affair without considering the consequences. He may worship the Dauphine from afar, but he knows that this is all he can do.

There is a knock at the door. Opening it, Axel is surprised to find Count Creutz, the Swedish ambassador, standing there. Creutz steps quickly inside as Axel scans the corridor.

'I'm alone, Count Fersen,' the ambassador reassures him. 'I should like a few words with you in private.'

The two men walk over to the hearth, where Count Creutz

extends his cold hands to the glow.

'Might I offer you a drink?' Axel politely enquires.

'Thank you, no, Fersen. I shan't be staying long.'

'Has something happened?'

Count Creutz stares into the blaze and shakes his head. 'No, no. Nothing to worry about. Tell me, Fersen, how are you enjoying your stay in Paris so far? You're looking rather tired, my boy.'

Axel knows exactly what the ambassador has to say to him.

'My stay here is almost at an end, Your Excellency. You need have no fear.'

Creutz draws a deep breath of relief. 'Our country's relationship with France is an important one, Fersen. A scandal would not be good for the alliance.'

Fersen gives the diplomat a cool, appraising look.

'It's said that she will soon be Queen of France,' Creutz continues. 'Sweden will more than benefit from sound relations with the royal household, but the frontier between good understanding and something more is easily crossed.'

'Have I done anything to jeopardise the alliance?' asks Fersen curtly.

'Why no, Fersen, of course not. I'm not accusing you of anything.'

'Or do you mean to imply that the future queen comports herself rather too frivolously towards others?'

Creutz gives Axel a penetrating look, arrested by his accusatory tone.

'My dear Fersen, you must understand me. I'm entirely satisfied with you and your conduct at court. The cordiality with which the royal family has welcomed you is a source of great pleasure to me. If indeed you are soon to resume your travels, both countries may look back upon a pleasant episode that has provided an opportunity for members of the French and Swedish courts to become better acquainted. I'm certain that our King Gustav III will greatly appreciate that. It's merely regrettable to note how evil tongues are contending that more lies hidden behind certain encounters and ball evenings.'

Fersen, his heart lifting at the memory of letters recently safely ablaze, stares fixedly at Creutz. 'I don't feel myself to be at fault in any way, and I dare speak for Madame la Dauphine when I say that her behaviour is impeccable. A scandal is thus completely out of the question.'

Count Creutz smiles with satisfaction. 'I'm pleased to see that you are aware of the issues involved, Fersen. I shall make a favourable report of you to King Gustav. What are your plans on your return to Sweden?'

'I have no idea, as yet, Your Excellency. I shan't be able to make any decisions about the future until I've seen my father again.'

The ambassador gives a nod of approval. 'Should you ever return to France, you will find yourself most welcome!' Count Creutz shakes Fersen heartily by the hand and gives him a comradely slap on the shoulder.

Alone again, Axel ponders the ambassador's words. The sooner he gets away from Paris, the better. But will he be able to forget her? Can he put Marie Antoinette out of his mind?

The Comte de Mercy and the Abbé Vermond are sitting uncomfortably in the rocking carriage on the road to Versailles. Outside the rain pours down. It is not often that the two men travel together, but Mercy is using this rare opportunity to extract from Vermond the content of Marie Antoinette's outpourings in the confessional.

The Comte de Mercy is in an agony of doubt. How much about Marie Antoinette's jaunty exploits should he report to her mother? For weeks now, the hottest topic of gossip has been how, during a *bal d'Opéra*, the Dauphine conversed with a foreigner and was even seen to reach out her hand and touch him.

'Has she said anything of this matter, or mentioned Count Fersen in any way?' enquires Mercy with a grave face.

Vermond shakes his head.

As is his wont, Mercy is busy mentally totting up the pros and cons. There have been some positive reactions to the way the *l'archiduchesse* has been conducting herself. Just see how close Madame la Dauphine is to the people! To some extent this has rubbed off on the Dauphin, who was also seen talking freely to ordinary people on the same occasions. True, it was Carnival, but nevertheless the rules were certainly overstepped at times. The older generation is particularly scandalised and has been voluble in saying so. Mercy is not over-concerned as yet, for the future King and Queen of France will be in great need of their popularity with the people.

The muttering among the populace against the old king and his ruthless chancellor is assuming worrying proportions. And it is not entirely without reason, of course. Mercy has never fully understood the motives underpinning Maupeou's policy, for, as an ambassador, he has no inside knowledge of France's financial situation. But if the Treasury is run along anything like the same lines as Marie Antoinette's personal finances, there is surely reason enough for concern.

Having once dethroned the Duc de Choiseul, the new chancellor Maupeou lost no time in embarking upon his reform of the *parlement*. 'The corruption and injustice of the magistrates shall finally be addressed,' declared the ambitious chancellor.

But what has the man achieved so far? A great deal of unrest, while corruption remains the order of the day. Censorship is stricter than ever and Sartine, head of the secret police, and his minions are working overtime. Despite his well-intentioned efforts to end vice and corruption, Maupeou has turned himself into a laughing stock. Naturally, that was not his aim at all, but no one seems capable of repressing the publication of Beaumarchais's pamphlets.

The watchmaker and playwright Caron de Beaumarchais has made it his business to describe with his inimitable wit how the barrister Louis Valentin Guzman and his wife are being just as blithely bought as ever they were in pre-Maupeou days. 'All those men have their price' is the message relayed from one Paris salon to the next by the redoubtable playwright. Whatever the truth of the matter, *tout Paris* is revelling in the allegations and the implication that Maupeou's incorruptible legal eagles after all have feet of clay.

The pamphlets appear in instalments and are so popular that no dealer is able to order and stock more than a few copies at a time. Even Louis XV, in a serious breach of loyalty to his own chancellor, has been known to split his sides with laughter as Madame du Barry reads episodes out loud to him.

At first Marin, editor-in-chief of the *Gazette de France*, did his best to intervene on Guzman's behalf and whitewash the whole affair. A court case followed which found against Guzman, resulting in his being disbarred.

Beaumarchais too has ended up on the wrong side of the law, but this hardly seems to bother him. The court case turned into a battle between his David and the Goliath of Maupeou's reforms. The playwright has since gathered the support of all those who backed the old *parlement*, and no lesser personages than the Prince de Conti and the Duc de Chartres, both Princes of the Blood, have embraced his cause. The only inconvenience is that the premiere of his new play, *The Barber of Seville*, has been postponed.

All in all it is a bad business, a long-running farce that Mercy fears is far from over.

The Princesse de Lamballe's dressmaker has recently begun supplying the Dauphine with her creations. But the innovative Rose Bertin takes her art further than the design of sumptuous gowns. She is also the originator of the *pouf*, a fantastic coiffure never before seen in Paris, variations of which rejoice in all sorts of exotic names. Inspired by Beaumarchais and a pronouncement by editor Marin, she has now come up with a style entitled the *Quesaco*, designed exclusively for the Dauphine.

'What do you think of Marie Antoinette's new toilette?' Mercy interrogates the priest.

The Abbé Vermond chuckles. 'I know nothing about such things, Your Excellency, but it can't be bad, for I understand that within a couple of days all the ladies in Paris had followed her example. The one person who will certainly be less than charmed is Monsieur Maupeou.'

Mercy nods assent. He takes antics of this sort far more seriously than any Carnival flirtation. By wearing such a coiffure the Dauphine sends out a clear political message. Yet, as always, Louis XV says and does nothing. It would be a good thing for the country if the king were to abdicate. But are the Dauphin and Dauphine up to the enormous task he would leave behind him? Mercy only has to think for a moment to answer his own question.

'By the way, Vermond, have you any notion how the Dauphin stands with regard to the Guzman affair?'

Vermond shrugs. 'How should I know? The young man has never addressed a word to me in his life, let alone confided his thoughts in me.'

Mercy closes his eyes in exasperation. When will the boy grow up? 'Has Marie Antoinette given no hint of his thoughts on the matter?' the ambassador continues.

'None, Your Excellency. The only thing that exercises her is the childish behaviour the boys indulge in among themselves. The Comte d'Artois shoots his mouth off at everyone and looks askance when the Dauphine reproves him. Artois may be the youngest, but since he got married he's been drinking more than both the others put together. He's well and truly changed his colours from the pretty princeling he once was. The Comte de Provence regularly lets the Dauphin know how unsuited he is for the throne and says Louis-Auguste should step aside and make room for him. It's plain that neither of his brothers have any respect for the Dauphin. They're always scrapping, and Marie Antoinette feels she has had to act as mediator for far too long.'

Mercy shakes his head sadly. What hope is there with such a family? What would happen if Louis XV were to die suddenly? He can envisage a thousand scenarios, none with a positive outcome.

Meanwhile, the carriage has arrived in the palace square. It is still raining and the gutters are overflowing. Where midnight revellers have made off with the valuable lead drainpipes, torrents of water cascade straight onto the cobblestones or run down the palace walls. Like a river in flood, the rainwater seeps its way indoors through every nook and cranny, a most unwelcome incursion.

'And does our Dauphine still read?' asks Mercy as the coach comes to a halt in front of the covered entrance.

'Oh most certainly, Your Excellency, more and more. At the moment she is mesmerised by the lives of the French queens.'

'Which ones, Vermond?' asks Mercy in consternation.

'Marguerite de Valois and Isabeau de Bavière.'

'Just as I feared.' The ambassador sighs despondently and steps down from the carriage as the door is held open for him.

How much water can fall from the skies? It's unbelievable. Papa says there will be problems sowing the crops - yet another blow for the farmers. The road is too bad for travelling, and I'll just have to sit out the days at Versailles. Everyone is wandering around with a long face and it's making me melancholy. When is something nice going to happen for a change?

From the journal of the Princesse de Lamballe,
25th March 1774

23

'I'm bored, Lamballe,' sighs Marie Antoinette, drawing patterns with her finger in the condensation on the windowpane. The rain hasn't stopped for days, and it's far too cold for the time of year. 'Where is spring?' complains the Dauphine. 'This time last year we were walking in the gardens. Do you remember, Lamballe?'

Marie-Thérèse, Princesse de Lamballe, looks up from her embroidery and smiles at the Dauphine. Of course she remembers. She noted it in her diary.

Marie Antoinette wipes the window clean with her hand. Once she would have dried her fingers on her skirt, but now she takes a napkin from the table, where the empty teapot still stands, and meticulously dries her fingers one by one.

'Oh, what a shame Carnival is over. It went by so quickly this year, don't you agree, *cousine*?'

Lamballe sticks her needle into her work and lays it in her lap. 'Do you miss him?' she asks the Dauphine gently.

Marie Antoinette takes a deep breath, giving herself time to think carefully before answering. She knows she cannot keep a secret from her cousin. And there has to be someone she can talk to, after all.

'Yes, I miss him,' she admits with some relief. 'But I mustn't think about him any more. Now that the party season is over, he'll set out on his travels again. There's a good chance he'll be given some appointment at the Swedish court, and if that happens I'll never see him again.'

Marie Antoinette walks over to the hearth and, turning round, feels the warmth of the fire embrace her back and shoulders, as if she were in the arms of her Swedish count again. She steps quickly away from the blaze, to take a seat on a sofa at the far side of the room. She has to consciously erase the soft shawl of memories.

'Has he written?' asks Lamballe inquisitively.

'No!' comes the reply, tinged with offence. 'I have to put him out of my mind, Lamballe. It's impossible, and also dangerous. Even Mercy has broached the subject with me. Oh, that man drives me mad sometimes – as if I weren't capable of thinking things out for myself! I know as well as he does that *Papa Roi* could still send me home, and I'm well aware that it doesn't take much, living in this palace, for one's imagination to run away with one. It's all to the good that he hasn't written to me; all the easier for me to forget him.'

Lamballe nods in approval. It is better so. 'Shall we do something amusing?' suggests the princess gaily.

'What have you in mind?' returns Marie Antoinette rather petulantly.

A long silence follows, broken only by the clatter of rain against the high windows.

'I don't know,' Lamballe sighs sadly.

'Madame,' announces her lady in waiting Madeleine excitedly, 'Monsieur Gluck has arrived. May I let him in?'

Marie Antoinette springs from her seat at once. 'But of course! That's great news.' The Dauphine glances in the mirror and passes her hand quickly over her curls.

'Your Highness!' Christoph Willibald von Gluck does his best to inject a note of cheer into his deep bass voice. The light tone is in sharp contrast to his sombre and badly pockmarked face.

The German composer acknowledges the Princesse de Lamballe and then accepts Marie Antoinette's invitation to sit down. The composer, who is approaching sixty, has been in the French capital for a couple of months now, busily preparing for performance of his new opera.

'I'm so pleased to see you again, Monsieur. How long is it since you were my teacher?'

The old man ponders for a moment. 'Not so very long, surely, Madame. About five years, by my estimation.'

'That's right,' confirms Marie Antoinette. 'But it seems much longer to me. I was still at home in Vienna. Oh, Monsieur, do tell, how is my mother?'

Gluck blows his nose while Madeleine serves their tea. After a moment he replies: 'It's some time since I saw your imperial mother. But all is well with her, as you must be aware.'

Marie Antoinette paces restlessly up and down the salon. 'Of course, Monsieur. But I'm pleased to hear it from someone who has seen her for himself. How are things otherwise? With the other members of my family, I mean?'

The composer takes long, quiet draughts of warm tea, feeling the stimulant reviving him as it goes down. 'Madame, be assured that all are well, and everyone misses you.'

A sudden frisson passes over Marie Antoinette. She takes her handkerchief from her sleeve and dabs the corners of her eyes in an attempt to hide her tears from her visitor.

'Just look, Monsieur,' says the Dauphine, recovering herself enough to point at a lovely vase gracing the mantelpiece. 'Mama gave me this, along with a painting of Laxenburg Castle. You know, I can never have my fill of looking at them. If I gaze very hard I can hear my little sister's voice and the birds whistling. Sometimes, on very rare occasions, I can even imagine my father calling my name.'

Marie Antoinette falls silent, her eyes fixed on the summer residence of the Habsburgs. She blows her nose quietly. 'Oh, I miss them so. How I miss them all!'

A tidal wave of homesickness sends tears coursing down her cheeks. As usual, Lamballe immediately responds in kind, and, before Gluck knows where he is, he finds himself saddled with two weeping women.

Good grief, what is he doing in Paris at all? It had seemed a fine idea at the time, despite his lack of faith in the management of the

Opéra. The Empress Maria Theresa had promised the composer that he would be welcome in Paris, especially if her daughter, Madame la Dauphine, lent him her support. And indeed he found himself badly in need of it, for those in charge of the Paris Opéra had made it subtly but patently clear to him that his presence there was not wanted. Nothing new had been seen on the French operatic stage since Rameau.

'I have discovered a musical language independent of nationality or culture. My music is universal!' had been Chevalier Gluck's public declaration. But the Parisians were unimpressed.

A humble request to *Papa Roi* from Marie Antoinette had, as expected, worked wonders, and in no time Monsieur Gluck found himself officially welcomed. But his real problems were only just beginning.

The composer plans to put on six operas in Paris, the first based on an early play by Jean Racine. But an opera in French? And, what is more, set to music by a non-Frenchman? Unheard of!

In a couple of weeks' time, on 13th April to be precise, the premiere of *Iphigénie en Aulide* is due to take place. But the composer is showing an obstinate side to his nature. The rehearsals are never-ending, for the German doesn't always see eye to eye with his French colleagues. Artistes, musicians, ballet master and set builders feed him a constant stream of criticism and torment him with impossible demands. But Gluck remains full of grim determination and refuses to budge one iota. He'll show Paris a thing or two – if he ever manages to cajole *Iphigénie* as far as the first night, that is.

The support of Madame la Dauphine is vital. She is the only member of the French royal household from whom he can expect any help. At least, that is what he has felt up until now, but after this little episode he is beginning to have his doubts on this score too. For what has he here? Two hysterical young ladies who burst into tears whenever they think of home.

Mademoiselle Madeleine begs to know whether Monsieur

Gluck would like some more tea? The composer nods and lets out a deep sigh. Patience, he knows, is the better part of valour.

'My apologies for having upset you, Your Highness.'

Marie Antoinette sniffs again. 'I do beg your pardon, Monsieur Gluck. But it's so lovely to hear a voice from home again. It's rare occurrence, and I would certainly suffer far less from homesickness were I to have more contact with my homeland.'

Gluck nods, but deftly avoids pursuing the subject. 'How are your music lessons progressing, Madame?'

The Dauphine stows away her handkerchief. 'Very well, Monsieur. I have harp lessons too, now, from Monsieur Grétry. A most kind man. He has also started to give me vocal instruction.'

Gluck nods again, although personally he hardly knows André Grétry. 'You will attend the opening night, Your Highness?' he enquires hopefully.

Privately, it pains him to have to depend upon the presence of his ex-pupil, a mere slip of a girl in his eyes, for the success of his opera. Not that there's anything amiss with his work. On the contrary, it's sublime! But Gluck knows he is in no position to triumph unaided over French complacency.

Her tears forgotten, Marie Antoinette gives him a sparkling smile. 'I'll be there, Monsieur, and I'll bring the whole royal family with me!'

'Surely not the king as well?' exclaims Gluck in astonishment.

'I'm not sure as yet,' replies Marie Antoinette, knowing that the king has no desire to be seen anywhere in public. And just as well, for then that *créature* would be clinging to his side too. And does she wish to share the royal box with that woman? Of course not, not for all the tea in China! 'But in any case the Dauphin will be there,' continues the Dauphine, 'his brothers the Counts of Provence and Artois, together with my sisters-in-law, and naturally my best friend, the Princesse de Lamballe.'

'That will be a great honour, Your Highness.'

'Oh, I'm looking forward to it immensely,' Marie Antoinette sighs. 'Are the rehearsals going as you would wish?'

Gluck clears his throat with a fixed smile. It is, of course, all too easy to wash one's dirty linen in public. Perhaps a discreet word would be enough to effect a few changes in personnel. But it's far too late for that. He will just have to make do with the singers and musicians allotted to him.

'Perfection, Madame, is an impossible goal. But your presence at the premiere will give me the strength I need to make it an unforgettable evening for you.'

Day in, day out, it goes on raining. Dark banks of cloud, now and then broken by shafts of mercurial light, shear across the skies above Versailles. Daffodils hang their drowned heads sadly towards the earth. It seems impossible to shake off the wet and the chill, and everyone is bad-tempered and miserable at the prospect of yet another long grey day. There are far fewer visitors than usual at the palace, and sometimes hardly any onlookers even at the *Grand Couvert*.

This is more like it, thinks Marie Antoinette happily, taking a bite herself for once. Once I am queen, this will be the first piece of nonsense to be got rid of.

Madame du Barry is more desolate than ever. The king is peevish because the rain has meant calling off the hunt, and for days his mistress has sat shut up in her apartment. The only diversion was Easter Mass, although that could hardly be described as having cheered her up. Droning on and on about the fall of Nineveh, the priest seemed to be preaching to her personally. And, despite herself, his words keep bubbling back up from her subconscious. She has read in one of this year's new almanacs that April would see an eminent woman playing the last act of her role at a great court. She is perturbed.

For hours at a time Jeanne sits before the mirror, ensuring that her appearance is perfect. Every wrinkle is smoothed away with oils and fragrant ointments, but each morning the lines seem to be back, deeper and clearer than ever. Nevertheless, the *maîtresse en titre* is still, by day and by night, the most beautiful woman in France for Louis XV. Despite his sullen quirkiness, she still knows how to bewitch him.

Lying on his back, sated, the Most Christian King of France listens to the relentless patter of rain upon the tiled roof. The pleasure of a moment ago is soon gone, giving way to nervous irritation at the eternal gurgling of the gutters.

'Will that infernal row never cease?' he roars, throwing the bedclothes off him and glowering towards the window.

'Shall we go to Marly?' suggests du Barry.

'It's raining there too,' snaps the king, struggling into his undershirt.

She knows it's best to leave him to his own devices when he is in this mood. Wrapping herself in her peignoir, she watches as her lover makes his escape. Sometimes it is days before she sees him again. But he stops in his tracks, his hand upon the doorknob.

'Listen,' he says in a low voice.

'What is it?' quavers du Barry, sitting bolt upright in alarm, her brain clamouring with the words of the almanac. An intruder? She pulls her dressing gown close around her.

'Listen,' repeats the king, pointing towards the ceiling. A broad grin spreads across his features. 'It's quiet.'

Baffled, du Barry resorts to fluttering her long eyelashes. 'What do you mean?'

'Quietness, my little goose. The rain has stopped!'

The king steps swiftly back to the window and throws it wide. The rain has indeed abated. The gutters give forth a final rattling sound, like a bath emptying, and that's that. In the west, the clouds break open and sunshine streams down upon the sodden earth.

'Ha!' shouts the king, overjoyed. 'Spring is coming. You mark my words, spring is really on the way now!'

And, hopping and skipping like a foal let out after months in the stable, Louis XV disappears down the stairs.

Du Barry leans back against the pillows, her heart thumping.

Dear God, that was the fright of her life! She must stop thinking about that priest and she should never have opened the almanac. You see? Spring is on the way. Everything is going to come right after all!

Antoinette was the star of the evening. The whole hall paid homage to her in a way that surpassed anything I'd ever seen before. Personally, I found it all a little long-winded, but that's probably just me. Everyone was so entranced that I found myself clapping along as enthusiastically as the rest. Personally, though, I still prefer Monsieur Grétry's music.

From the journal of the Princesse de Lamballe,
20th April 1774

24

What a difference a bit of good weather can make! One sunny day has brought a smile back to everyone's face. Even the Comte de Mercy is radiant, although that is more likely due to his relations with the king. It seems that Mercy has been worrying about nothing for weeks. Louis XV is as one reborn, riding to the hunt through the forests of Versailles like a young cavalier.

'You see,' says Marie Antoinette to the ambassador with a laugh, 'that's the king for you. Believe me, Mercy, Papa will live to at least eighty! He's made of the same stuff as the Maréchal de Richelieu, and he's fourteen years older!'

The Comte de Mercy flashes her a smile at the mention of that old rogue of a womaniser. Come to think of it, God's reward for a profane life would seem to be eternal youth. The Duc de Richelieu, at least, is a notorious example of a veteran charmer who is still adept at capturing young female hearts. But, that aside, Mercy is once again disappointed at Marie Antoinette's apparent incapacity to appreciate how drastically her own life might change at any moment. Her naturally optimistic nature leads the Dauphine to shelve the notion that she might find herself Queen of France tomorrow. She barely takes in Mercy's advice to encourage Louis-Auguste to prepare himself better for the throne.

Deep down, Louis-Auguste would be more than happy to do so; it is Papa who keeps him at arm's length from all matters politic. An absolute monarch in heart and soul, Louis XV has no intention whatsoever of sharing the task of government with his grandson. Let the boy get to work on ensuring the future of the Bourbon dynasty; that's what he's there for.

This is a question that greatly exercises the French king. According to his spies, the Spanish ambassador, the Comte d'Aranda, has managed to infiltrate the Dauphine's inner court with his own secret informants. Louis XV is not unduly impressed. His spies can tell the Comte d'Aranda no more than all Versailles knows: Madame la Dauphine is not yet pregnant. More worrying is the fact that not one of his granddaughters seems capable of producing a male heir to safeguard the future of the French branch of the Bourbons. If the dynasty dies out, the throne will pass to the Orléans, and that will be unacceptable to the King of Spain, Carlos III.

It is almost half a century since the Spanish Bourbons were forced to relinquish their rights to the French throne. But the fact that the Orléans branch of the family is junior to the Bourbons gives Carlos III, also a great-grandson of the Sun King, sufficient excuse to make a claim for Spain. The clash of weaponry is already in the air. Louis XV has invested all his hopes in the Comtesse d'Artois, but so far, alas, and despite her husband's assiduous ardour, no welcome news of a Bourbon pregnancy is forthcoming.

It is late afternoon when the Dauphin and Dauphine, with an enormous train of carriages from Versailles in their wake, make their appearance at the doors of the Opéra. Instead of the formal welcome that normally awaits them, they find the foyer ringing with the sound of raised voices and a red-faced director of the Opéra gesticulating wildly at an apparently calm and collected Monsieur Gluck.

'Who do you think you are?' screams the director. 'You can't do such a thing! We're talking about a royal premiere here, you know, and it emphatically must go ahead.'

Chevalier Gluck, with folded arms and closed eyes, allows the director's fury to wash over him. He knows he will stand his ground no matter what, and if they can't accept that, well, that's their problem; he'll hotfoot it straight back to Vienna, never more to return.

A bystander taps the director nervously on the shoulder and indicates the newly arrived guests. Almost choking, the director bows his way towards the royal couple.

'A thousand pardons, Your Highness,' stammers the man, stumbling along with his knee to the ground.

Louis-Auguste maintains his customary muteness.

'What's wrong?' asks Marie Antoinette impatiently, unable to make head or tail of this remarkable scene.

'It's nothing, Madame. A small matter that has already been resolved, as a matter of fact.'

At this Gluck steps forward with a face like thunder. 'Resolved, did you say?'

The director draws himself up with a forced smile. The poor man sees his whole world falling apart before his eyes.

'Of course, Monsieur Gluck,' responds the mortified director with a hysterical laugh. 'We shall not disappoint Monsieur le Dauphin and Madame la Dauphine this evening.'

'Indeed you shall not,' confirms the composer,' and that is precisely why the performance cannot go ahead.'

The director of the Opéra gasps and turns more crimson still. What is this foreigner thinking of?

'Will someone explain all this to me?' demands Marie Antoinette, clearly irritated.

'Monsieur Gluck wishes to postpone the performance,' replies the director with an exaggerated sigh and an expression intended to convey complete innocence on his own part.

'And what might be his reason for that?' enquires the Dauphine.

Gluck re-enters the conversation. 'Madame, the tenor has caught a cold and is quite incapable of performing his role satisfactorily.'

The director, with a gesture that indicates his desire to strangle the composer, intervenes. 'Madame, forgive me, but we have an understudy for this part. There is nothing to stop the performance going ahead.'

Marie Antoinette shoots the composer a questioning look.

'No question of it,' Gluck resolutely declares. 'The man may think he has studied the role, but he's a mere amateur and doesn't understand the first thing about it. He'll wreck the whole performance. No, the only option is postponement.'

'Impossible,' bleats the director again.

'Listen to me, man, and listen well,' says Gluck in a threatening tone, completely impervious to the presence of royalty: 'I haven't been rehearsing for hours on end for nothing. Joseph Legros has mastered the role like no other. In a couple of days his cold will be gone and he'll treat everyone to a unique evening. But don't pressure me to go on stage this evening! I'd rather throw my score onto a bonfire than expose it to mutilation by a bunch of amateurs. If you disagree, just say so, and I'll pack my trunk immediately!'

Nobody in the foyer has ever seen a scene like it. Tears spring to the director's eyes. What a disaster! He may as well say goodbye to his job here and now. What on earth will His Highness think of him? In a fresh bid to rescue the situation, he turns to the Dauphin with his hands folded, like one of the faithful invoking Sainte Geneviève.

'Your Highness, I beg you,' implores the man despairingly, 'instruct us in this matter. Just give your orders and we will obey your command.'

The Dauphin emits a deep sigh and stares blankly at his wife.

Marie Antoinette does not hesitate for a moment. She has heard the gossip circulating over recent weeks: despairing vocalists running to their patrons with complaints; accusations of authoritarianism on the part of the German composer, who keeps telling them that they cannot sing and are hopeless dancers. Yes, dancing and singing simultaneously – that was Gluck's new prank! Never before had a singer been made to dance at the same time. Wasn't that what the ballet was for?

The ballet master and musicians had also put up with weeks of purgatory. Every rehearsal had apparently turned into a trial by fire. And neither, alas, had Gluck himself escaped unscathed: he had regularly been reduced to tearing off his wig in fury and frustration and threatening to walk out on the whole business.

Marie Antoinette has some empathy with the artistes, for she can still recall the strict taskmaster that lurks just beneath the surface in Gluck. But she also has enormous respect for this composer, whose standards of perfection are all and everything to him. She knows how much it will please her mother if she can report that Monsieur Gluck has enjoyed a profitable stay in Paris, and she knows that Mama will never forgive her if the premiere is a flop.

The Dauphine beckons the director over with her fan. 'A postponement of a couple of days,' she whispers, 'or perhaps even a week, will suit the Dauphin and Dauphine very well.'

Gluck pricks his ears but cannot catch a word. What is his former pupil up to?

The director is gazing at her in wonderment. What now? Is Madame taking sides with the foreigner?

'We must have eaten something that does not agree with us this afternoon,' she calmly continues, thus saving face for the Opéra. '*Monsieur le Directeur*, if you choose to be of real service to Monsieur le Dauphin, we shall not readily forget it.'

The man draws a deep sigh of relief.

'I trust that the news of our indisposition will not be trumpeted abroad,' adds Marie Antoinette for the avoidance of all doubt.

'Madame!' exclaims the director with a shocked air, once again bowing to the ground before the Dauphin and Her Highness.

Louis-Auguste gives him a cursory nod and turns to leave, catching a glimpse as he does so of Count Fersen among the bystanders.

'So we made the whole trip here for nothing,' complains the Dauphin. They are in the carriage on their way back to Versailles.

'At least you can get an early night,' snaps his wife.

The Comte de Provence chortles. Marie Antoinette stares at the Comtesse de Provence's lap and wonders why her thoughts have alighted upon pregnancy.

She too had caught sight of Count Fersen, but avoided any eye contact with him. There is no future for the two of them, so what is the point in letting her thoughts run wild? Yet she can still feel the flutter of butterflies in her stomach. Marie Antoinette turns her hopeless gaze upon her husband, who has meanwhile fallen asleep and is sprawled across the seat, open-mouthed and snoring. How and when in heaven's name will I ever conceive a child?

A week later, on 19th April, Marie Antoinette and Louis-Auguste take their places in the royal box to loud cheering and applause. All the rest of the family, with the exception of the king, is also present at the Opéra. The enormous hall, capable of seating an audience of three thousand, has never been so full. Every box is packed with aristocrats and dignitaries like a cattle pen on a busy market day. The increasingly close air is fanned from one hot face to another and then rises to join the incandescence of a thousand wax candles, burning in the massive chandeliers.

Every eye in the humming auditorium is fixed expectantly upon the stage, where the curtain is about to rise. The fact that the premiere has been postponed for a full week has been good for ticket sales. At first there had been little interest in the show, for who was Gluck, anyway? A foreigner and, what was more, a *bourgeois*, who had apparently enjoyed some success in Rome and Vienna. But when did music worth listening to ever come out of Vienna?

Most Parisians labour under the conviction that Italy is the only cradle of good music. Others are convinced that no one will ever again equal the compositions of Rameau and Lully. Only a tiny minority of the audience has any faith in the Chevalier, so it is really quite remarkable that, despite all the cynicism, every seat is filled.

The truth is that ever since last week the Paris salons have been buzzing to the news of how Gluck managed to have a royal premiere cancelled, and this achievement has thoroughly whetted appetites in the city. People have been queuing patiently all day on the Rue Saint-Honoré. The opening night is sold out, with some tickets going for three times their face value. Expectations are sky high – for if the royal family allowed themselves to be kept waiting for a week for the first performance, then this *Iphigénie en Aulide* must be really something.

The musicians tune their instruments and at last the curtain goes up. As usual, there is a mixed reaction to the stage set, but the first aria from Agamemnon leaves most of the audience firmly under the spell of the Trojan War. During the first act, the audience politely follows the Dauphine's enthusiastic lead, applauding whenever she does. But eyebrows are raised. Is Madame la Dauphine's response not a touch exaggerated? Although *haute-contre* Joseph Legros has certainly fully recovered his voice and plays the role of Achilles with style and panache.

'It's time she retired,' hisses Rosalie le Vasseur in her lover's ear.

Iphigénie is in the middle of her aria. Florimond, Comte de Mercy-Argenteau, lays his hand softly upon that of his mistress.

'Seriously, that Sophie Arnould has had her day,' persists Rosalie grumpily. 'Just listen to that!' She pulls a wry face.

'Shhh!' Mercy places a finger on her pouting lips. 'Contain yourself, little one. Your time will come.'

The Comte de Mercy returns his full attention to the music. He likes it, and he sets aside his sweetheart's remark. He knows by now that she submits the soprano to the same treatment at every performance. Perhaps things will change when Rosalie is given a lead role of her own to sing.

A good five hours later, Achilles finally rescues Iphigénie from the hands of High Priest Calchas. A storm of applause announces the triumph of Chevalier Gluck. The clapping and cheering is deafening, striking dumb all those still wallowing in prejudice, who are forced to eat their words. How can the audience react like this? Surely the Paris Opéra is not going to resound to the music of

Gluck for years to come?

As the applause dies away, Mercy and Rosalie join the mass exodus from the auditorium. He has enjoyed the show in more ways than one. He found it fascinating to witness how Marie Antoinette set the tone for the auditorium from the moment the curtain went up. How would things have gone for Gluck had the royal box remained empty? Does Marie Antoinette herself realise the power she has over public opinion? Mercy doubts it: she is still too naive. But she must be made aware of the fact that she wields such influence and must learn to manage it.

In Mercy's eyes, the Paris public is a two-faced monster, as capricious as it is fantastic, a freakish beast capable at any moment of turning upon its master. The more he thinks about it, the more peril Mercy perceives. Before he and Rosalie have reached the door of the Opéra, the Austrian ambassador has added another worry to his already long list.

What a lot of fuss about nothing! Gluck this, Gluck that – no one can talk about anything else at the moment. His music is a sensation, and the whole of Paris is living and breathing the Opéra. And close behind Gluck comes Rose Bertin: her fantastic designs amaze us all.

From the journal of the Princesse de Lamballe,
27th April 1774

25

Paris has entirely forgotten Beaumarchais and his pamphlets. The talk now is of Chevalier Gluck and his *Iphigénie en Aulide*. The heated debate among those for and against the composer reminds older Parisians of the *Querelle des Bouffons* twenty years earlier. In those days, literary Paris did battle in the salons with word and pen over the pros and cons of traditional French opera as opposed to the popular comic variety newly arrived from Italy.

History appears to be repeating itself, and emotions are once more running high. Opponents of Gluck have even suggested inviting Niccolò Piccinni here to persuade Paris audiences once and for all of the superiority of Neapolitan opera. The opera, meanwhile, is thriving on all the controversy, and every Tuesday and Thursday the Trojan War, given fresh life by Gluck, plays to a full house.

Louis XV has heard the conflicting views about the German composer and read the ensuing discussion in the pages of the *Gazette*. The whole business suits him down to the ground: the busier folk are quarrelling among themselves, the less they bother him. The brouhaha surrounding Gluck has distracted everyone from the fact that Beaumarchais's plays have disappeared from the stage. Their author's current whereabouts are known only to a handful of people, among them the king, but he has in fact gone to England.

Precisely because he has been officially outlawed, no one will suspect that the king has entrusted Beaumarchais with a secret mission. The playwright has an appointment in London with a renowned blackmailer, Théveneau de Morande. This individual, who no longer dare show his face in France, is in possession of a fluent pen and an extremely fertile imagination. Fantastic tales flow unstoppably from his nib onto the printed page. But not, of course, in France, where his work would never survive the present censorship. No, Théveneau de Morande has his 'sensational revelations' printed safely in England and the Netherlands. The publications are then cunningly smuggled into France, where an eager market awaits them.

Three years ago Morande 'made his name' with his *Anecdotes Scandaleuses de la Cour de France*. This juicy publication, since sold out, exposed the entire court of Versailles to ridicule, with Madame du Barry bearing the brunt of it. Now Morande has sent the *maîtresse en titre* an advance proof copy of his latest work – beautifully written, in his view. But the Comtesse du Barry is appalled at the obscenities and lies littering every page of *Les Mémoires Secrets d'une Femme Publique*, from first to last. The only way to prevent its publication is to buy the author off with a huge sum of money.

Two weeks later, in London, Beaumarchais reaches an agreement with the crafty Théveneau. Backed by Louis XV, the playwright has been able to reduce the ransom significantly. On 27th April, three thousand books vanish into the oven of a brick factory in Saint Pancras. His fingers a-tremble, the blackmailer counts his money, while the charred shreds of pages that once bore his fictional account of du Barry's life spew from the sooty chimney. Slowly the black snow drifts down upon London: ashes, singed flakes and snippets, unreadable and destined only for the gutter.

At the same moment, still ignorant of the success of Beaumarchais's mission, Louis XV is gazing out from the Petit Trianon over his botanical gardens. But he has no eyes for the exotic plants diligently collected over decades to grace the greenhouses. The king feels unwell, as if he has eaten too many oysters.

A persistent headache forced him to return earlier than usual from the hunt this afternoon, and to avoid the hustle and bustle of the palace he has decided to retire to the Petit Trianon. Far enough removed from all the comings and goings, here he can rest and recover. The small mansion offers him the space he needs to be himself and, freed from the demands of protocol, to crawl under the swansdown quilt without more ado. He is bound to feel better by tomorrow.

As soon as the king has undressed, Madame du Barry comes to his side. Sitting on the bed, she strokes his cheek. 'I think you may be feverish,' she remarks at the touch of his hot, dry skin.

'Nonsense,' splutters the king, turning onto his other side. 'I want to sleep.'

She withdraws her hand, knowing that he wants to be left alone. 'Shall I close the shutters?'

The king growls something that his mistress takes as assent. It is still light outside, but with the shutters drawn the room is plunged into the darkness of night. Louis XV is already emitting a continuous droning sound. Madame du Barry slips out on tiptoe, leaving the door open a crack. She is not completely happy with the situation; she will come and listen every now and then. His regular snoring is reassuring, but the warning words of the almanac are still echoing in her mind.

Another three days, just three more full days, and April will be at an end. Oh, if only they can manage to stick it out here for a little longer! As long as they are hidden away in the peace of Trianon, far from the court, surely nothing untoward can befall them. How happy she will be when May arrives in all its brightness and glory!

It is still dark when Jeanne du Barry wakes with a jolt. She pricks up her ears, but all is quiet. Gliding noiselessly in her silken slippers, she feels her way from her room to listen again with bated breath at his door.

The snoring has made way for stuttering and sighing, and she can hear the king turning restlessly on the bed. Worried now, du Barry pushes the door fully open and creeps over to Louis XV.

He wakes up and gazes around in confusion until he makes out her figure in the gloom.

'Oh, I still feel awful,' he sighs, rubbing his head and trying to sit up.

'Come, I'll plump up your pillows.'

'I've such a pain in my back,' grumbles the monarch.

'Shall I rub it for you?

Louis XV seems to be considering her offer, then shakes his head slowly. 'Call Le Monnier,' he orders.

Du Barry stands up and, without arguing, goes into the next room, where the king's gentleman of the chamber is sleeping. On being told of the king's state of health and that the doctor must be summoned, the man runs off downstairs in his nightshirt to carry out the order.

Outside, the first cock is crowing and the world is slowly awakening to a new day.

'A slight fever,' the physician confidently diagnoses. 'Nothing to worry about, Sire. Stay put, rest today and tomorrow you'll be back to your old self.'

With a taciturn grunt, Louis XV lies down again.

'I haven't felt this bad for years,' he whimpers, sipping the warm honeyed milk that Madame du Barry holds to his lips.

Doctor Monnier refuses to take the bait. He knows the king all too well by now. Every little sniffle and cough is enough to convince Louis XV that he is on his deathbed. 'If I were you, I should spend the rest of the day here at Trianon, Sire,' he advises reassuringly.

Meanwhile, the Comtesse du Barry has sent word to the Duc d'Aiguillon that the king does not wish to receive visitors. By midday the news has trickled into Adélaïde's boudoir.

'Is it serious, or is he just making a nuisance of himself again?' she asks her lady in waiting spitefully. The lady doesn't know, but she will make further enquiries. When teatime arrives with the news that the king is still keeping his bed, Adélaïde begins to fret.

'I wish Doctor La Martinière to call on Papa directly,' she commands in resolute tones.

The physician-in-chief at Versailles had not expected to find his sovereign in this state. Louis XV lies huddled under the blankets, trembling feverishly in every limb.

'This is more than a simple fever,' La Martinière whispers to his junior colleague, who has to hide his blush of shame.

'What do you think, doctor?' asks du Barry anxiously.

'Get the king's carriage ready; we are going straight back to the palace.'

Louis XV blinks his eyelids and groans. 'Can't I stay here?'

'Out of the question,' replies the chief physician in a voice low with concern.

Evening is approaching as Louis XV emerges into the fresh air. It bites his throat. Supported by a manservant on either side, he steps quaking into the coach, followed closely behind by du Barry, who tucks extra rugs firmly in around him. They leave the Petit Trianon at a gallop, to arrive a couple of minutes later at the palace.

Here they are met by a worried Duc d'Aiguillon, *Mesdames*, and everyone else who desires to see with their own eyes how the king is looking. Muttering confusedly under his breath about a headache and pain in his back and joints, the king is conveyed to his bedchamber.

Everyone makes of it what they will. Is His Majesty playing them all along again, or is he really sick this time? The best the doctors can do for the King of France this evening is to prescribe him a generous dose of opium.

Shocked by the news, upon arriving back at the palace from the theatre the Dauphin and Dauphine rush straight to their grandfather's bedside. But the opium has done its work and for the moment the king is sleeping peacefully. The doctors do not want him disturbed; in all probability he will be better by tomorrow. So all will be well, after all. As Marie Antoinette and Louis-Auguste re-emerge, reassured, into the anteroom, the assembled courtiers take their cue to disperse, each to their own apartment.

The Dauphin is peckish after spending a long evening out and about in Paris. Marie Antoinette is still enjoying in retrospect their visit to the Théâtre Italienne, but she is looking forward even more to tomorrow, to hearing Gluck's music. She lets her fingers wander over the keys of her harpsichord, humming one of the arias from *Iphigénie*. Chevalier Gluck has told her that he is hard at work on a new composition. Oh, what a wonderful sense of anticipation!

Tomorrow she is also expecting Monsieur Léonard, the hairdresser recommended by Mademoiselle Bertin. Rose Bertin has designed a special *pouf*, the *coiffure à l'Iphigénie*, sketches of which she has proudly shown to the Dauphine. It looks fantastic! She yawns. It's so late already. Oh dear, she wonders how Papa is. Tomorrow she will tell him all about the rapturous applause the audience gave her this evening. The Parisians are so sweet. She knows that Papa loves to hear this sort of thing. It will do him good, she's sure of it.

Marie Antoinette shuts her eyes and falls asleep at once. The blissful smile upon her lips betrays her dream of Achilles rushing to her rescue, just in time. Together they sing the loveliest duet of the evening. The applause goes on and on forever.

Neither Antoinette nor I have slept for days. I'm like a cat on hot bricks. All the questions are driving me mad. As if I know what's going on! We've been looking forward to this moment for so long, yet now that it's here it's really frightening. Shall I be allowed to remain friends with her? Or will everything change?

From the journal of the Princesse de Lamballe,
5th May 1774

26

The bedchamber of the Most Christian King of France is crowded with those who have the right to be there, all holding their breath while a grave-faced Doctor Le Monnier takes the monarch's pulse. Louis XV looks extremely ill. His fever and pain are unabated, and are beginning to cause Le Monnier real concern. The king is always catching a chill and blowing it up to huge proportions, but this seems altogether more serious.

'I should like to hear the opinion of my colleague Lassone,' says Le Monnier, in as neutral a tone as he can find.

There is whispering in the background. The king's daughters seem shocked. Madame du Barry and the Duc d'Aiguillon exchange glances. Lassone is physician to the Dauphine and has nothing whatsoever to do with the king.

'In that case,' remarks the wily d'Aiguillon, I should like Bordeu and Lorry to be in attendance too.'

Le Monnier, who steers as clear as he can of all court intrigue, gives an indifferent shrug of the shoulders. He couldn't care less, but it strikes him as strange that Madame du Barry and d'Aiguillon should be showing such suspicion.

Lassone and Le Monnier quickly agree that the case is serious. To reduce the king's temperature as swiftly as possible, the two doctors decide to let blood immediately.

'Is that really necessary?' moans Louis XV.

Slowly the hours tick away.

'The fever should have subsided by now,' Le Monnier whispers to Lassone.

'Might a second letting help matters?' responds the physician who normally ministers to Marie Antoinette.

'Most certainly. If that doesn't work, we'll carry out a third this evening.' Le Monnier speaks decisively.

'What are you saying?' calls out the king in fear and trembling, having caught the end of the doctors' exchange. 'A third bloodletting? Am I that sick? A third time could be the end of me. Forget it! I do not wish it!'

By now four medical men are standing by the bed, each doing his best to pacify the king.

'A third will not be required, Sire,' says Le Monnier, setting out his instruments. He will tap off enough now to render another letting unnecessary. As the basin fills with the royal lifeblood, Bordeu and Lorry swap silent, significant looks.

Soon the king begins to sweat so copiously that the bedsheets have to be changed. The gentlemen of the chamber help the doctors to raise the king and lay him on a camp bed nearby. The king groans softly at every movement, but nevertheless seems to be enjoying all the attention.

The patient now has assembled around him six doctors, five surgeons and three pharmacists. Outside the bedchamber, a growing crowd passes on the first of a spate of rumours. The king is really ill!

The physicians, who can do little more than look earnest, take turns to count the king's pulse, percuss his abdomen and inspect the royal tongue. The learned gentlemen spend the rest of their time scrutinising the contents of the chamber pot with extraordinary interest, studying the colour of the urine, consulting one another under their breath and guessing at a plausible diagnosis.

The king had smallpox as a young man, so that can be eliminated. Apart from the fever and pains, the sick king shows no other visible signs or symptoms. The rising anxiety of the people outside the door is soothed by the news that the King of France's urine looks perfectly healthy. This is enough excuse for some to withdraw, for they have already been standing here for hours and their legs are aching. And from past experience they know that the whole show is quite likely to be a false alarm.

Doctors Bordeu and Lorry reassure du Barry. 'You have really nothing to fear, Madame.'

Lassone is less convinced, but keeps his doubts to himself, even when pressed by the Dauphine for his opinion. Marie Antoinette debates with herself whether or not she should go to this evening's performance, the Dauphin having let it be known that he will remain at Versailles. A good excuse for him not to have to attend the theatre!

'If I may make so bold, Madame, it would be wiser to remain here,' advises the Comte de Mercy. Lassone nods in affirmation.

'You surely don't think Papa is going to die?' asks Marie Antoinette, taken aback and still unaware of the gravity of the situation.

'I am not a doctor and do not wish to speculate in any direction, Madame. It is for God to decide,' replies Mercy.

Marie Antoinette flashes Lassone an interrogative glance, upon which he gestures in support of the ambassador. 'May I see Papa?' she enquires of her physician.

Lassone gives a lukewarm nod of the head; he cannot forbid it outright, not until he knows the truth of the situation. 'If that is the king's wish, Madame,' he replies.

Louis XV feels himself sinking very fast. There has not been the slightest improvement in his condition since the bloodletting. An enema is the next measure decided upon by the physicians. Their eyes fixed somewhat sheepishly upon the imperial posterior, they supervise Forgeot, the chief pharmacist, as he delicately introduces an elixir of herbs infused with honey.

This seems to bring about some improvement in Louis XV. Forgeot beams from ear to ear with satisfaction: that's definitely one up on the quacks.

It is late in the evening, and one of the doctors is attempting to get the sick man to drink something. Only a couple of candles are burning in the bedchamber, for the king cannot tolerate much light. The patient raises himself in the bed and takes a sip. The physician almost jumps out of his skin with fright. Is he seeing aright?

'Bring some light over here,' he abruptly orders the gentleman of the bedchamber, who is leaning against the wall, yawning. 'The king cannot see the glass properly.'

The doctor does not want to worry the king. As the light from the candle reaches him, the physician bends over. Now he can see clearly. He beckons his colleagues, finger on lips. The learned gentlemen, bowing silently over the prostrate king, see it too. The monarch's face is covered in characteristic red spots, unmistakable forerunners of much worse misery to follow. Le Monnier nods over his shoulder towards the door and his fellow doctors follow him silently from the bedchamber. It takes a moment or two for them to find a quiet corner, away from any eavesdroppers.

'I don't know who made the original diagnosis,' whispers Le Monnier, 'but it can't have been what people thought it was at the time.'

The doctors all shake their heads in sorrowful assent.

'Gentlemen,' sighs Le Monnier, 'the King of France has smallpox.'

Marie Antoinette, who is just on her way to see Papa, is detained at the door. In a soft voice, Lassone explains the situation to her.

'*Mon Dieu!*' she shrieks and runs sobbing back the way she came, arousing the suspicions of the old Maréchal de Richelieu, who only just manages to avoid bumping into her. The *premier valet de chambre* can see the doctors huddled together in a corner, whispering like conspirators. He strides over to them.

'What is going on here?' demands Richelieu grimly.

Le Monnier explains the diagnosis. The marshal's face falls.

'We must inform the king,' decides Le Monnier.

'Out of the question!' retaliates Richelieu instantly. 'Give him this news and he'll die of fright straight away. I know the man. Say nothing for the time being. What are his chances? He can recover from this, can he not?'

The doctors look round at one another.

'Indeed,' says Lassone, 'the king is strong and can survive the disease. But the outcome lies in God's hands. Only His mercy can save the king.'

The old marshal bends over the physician from his great and etiolated height and looks him straight in the eye. 'In that case, my good gentlemen, you had better do your best to lend God a helping hand!'

No one dare answer back, for this grand old man is the elder statesman of France and a personal friend of the king.

Remarkable as it may seem, it occurs to no one to consult the successor to the throne. At this moment, Maréchal Louis François Armand, Duc de Richelieu, *premier valet de chambre*, has the reins entirely in his own hands and is revelling in it.

'What is your plan?' Doctor Lorry meekly enquires.

'Under no circumstances may any of the royal family come near,' decides Richelieu.

'And his daughters?' stammers Lassone. 'For days now *Mesdames* have been nursing the king!'

The old marshal's features break into a chilly grin. 'They no longer count anyway.'

Within a couple of hours, everyone in Versailles – with the exception of the king himself – knows what is really wrong with him. Reactions vary greatly. Followers of Choiseul see the sun rising above the horizon again. Conversely, nervousness breaks out among the Barriens and some even pack their trunks. But the Duc d'Aiguillon reassures as many of his friends as possible that all will certainly be well. The king has an iron constitution. Pray to God and have faith!

The next day, as soon as he is thoroughly awake, Louis XV sees the spots on his hand for himself. To his horror, they slowly transform themselves into blisters as the day progresses. Following Richelieu's orders, the doctors stick to their story that it is nothing more than an innocent eruption of fever rash. The aunts, though aware of the risk of contagion, dutifully nurse their father through the daylight hours. All night Madame du Barry stays at his bedside, ministering to him as lovingly as though he were her sick child.

Evening draws in, and the *maîtresse en titre* prepares to go downstairs. She doesn't feel well herself. It is the last day of April, and the only thing that can happen tonight to make the almanac's prophecy come true is for the king to die. That will spell the end for her anyway, for Jeanne knows that she cannot expect a grain of sympathy from the Dauphin or Dauphine. Lying on her stomach, she flicks through the almanac, searching for a single sentence, some reference to the death of a king. But she can find no reassuring word. Should Louis XV fail to survive this sickness, she would do well to follow him to the grave. Calmly, she gets to her feet and descends the stairs to her lover's bedchamber. Still her lover, but for how long?

The crowds in the stairwell are gathering force. The impatient among them pray, chatter and wait hopefully for their sovereign to recover. Despite the Duc d'Aiguillon's confident message, each hour that passes strengthens people's expectation that the Most Christian King of France will die. Nervousness is apparent even among the ministers. Naturally, they have every reason to be anxious. What will the new king do?

Chancellor Maupeou, realistically enough, fears the worst. The people hate him. The easiest way for the new king to get the Parisians eating out of his hand would be to divest the loathed chancellor of his powers. That would of course set a precedent, for thus far no chancellor has ever been sacked. Maupeou is also aware of the Dauphine's displeasure at the banishment of the Duc de Choiseul. How vindictive will Marie Antoinette prove to be in her dealings? It's far too late in the day for him to worm his way into her good books. The contemptuous glance she throws him says everything. In any case, all he can do is wait and see.

A new visitor announces himself. It is Christophe de Beaumont, Archbishop of Paris. Too old and infirm to climb the stairs, the cleric is carried up on a sedan chair. Richelieu stands waiting at the top and orders the carriers to a halt. The marshal opens the little side door in the litter and stares into the pale face of an ailing man. Richelieu chuckles. Who will be first to go?

'Alas, I cannot admit you, Monseigneur,' he tells the cleric. 'All *entrées* have already been halted.'

The archbishop blinks his tired eyes. Has he understood correctly? Richelieu's hostile tone displeases him, but he is too weak to rebuke the man.

'I should merely like to know whether or not my presence would be appreciated.'

The marshal hovers like an eagle about to perform the *coup de grâce* upon its prey. 'When the time comes for the last rites, you will be the first to know,' hisses Richelieu. But even as he speaks, the marshal feels a tap on his shoulder and turns, to be waved aside by the Dauphin.

Louis-Auguste addresses himself directly to the archbishop. 'You hereby have my permission,' he says, 'to speak with the king.'

Richelieu is struck dumb. What does the young calf think he's up to? Protocol forbids him to contravene the orders of the Dauphin, but he grabs his chance to take advantage of the situation.

'Monseigneur.' Furtively addressing him by his title, the marshal extends his arm to the cleric for support. Step by step, the two men shuffle into the bedchamber, leaving the Dauphin safely behind in the hall. 'You've got your way,' whispers Richelieu, 'but I warn you: one word about a final confession and I'll throw you out of the window.'

The poor old man gives a quavering nod as he is placed in a

chair beside the king. Richelieu takes a couple of steps backwards and stands by the casement, his arms provocatively crossed.

Louis XV manages a smile. The men talk, inaudibly for the rest of the room. The aunts look on tensely from a corner. Will Papa confess and show remorse for his sins? That had been his salvation once before. But is the king prepared to distance himself from du Barry now? Does he have the willpower to send her away forever? After a quarter of an hour chatting with the king, Christophe de Beaumont beckons to Richelieu.

'You may take me back to my litter,' announces the old man contentedly.

Feeling himself a little above such a lowly task, the marshal clicks his fingers for the nearest manservant.

Louis XV looks satisfied. 'I feel a great deal better,' he tells Richelieu.

'I'm pleased to hear it, Sire,' replies his old friend with suspicion. 'What did you talk about?'

Louis XV casts a glance heavenward. 'Don't be so nosy, Maréchal.'

Richelieu bites his tongue, his eyes on the figure of the archbishop shambling his way out of the room.

'It's a good job I've already had smallpox,' announces Louis XV. 'But take a look at this, Richelieu,' continues the king, sticking his hand out. 'If I knew no better, I'd have sworn these pustules were the pox!'

The marshal gives his monarch a level look. 'I suggest we leave the diagnosing to the doctors, Sire. They're trained for it, after all.'

Louis XV sinks back on the pillows, scratching his forehead fretfully. 'I reckon it's the pox, all the same,' he mumbles under his breath.

Everyone continues to withhold the truth from the king, each fooling himself in the process. Hardly a soul can imagine the immediate future without Louis XV and the Comtesse du Barry. This, however, is in sharp contrast to the rest of the nation. Priests are being paid to offer up prayers in church for the sick king. But who is paying any attention? The special services held in the churches and cathedrals of France, to pray for the return to health of their 'beloved' sovereign, attract hardly a single worshipper. Why should God Himself be listening?

Camille the bookseller stares glumly at the piles of printed *Masses for the King*. Thirty years ago, when the monarch lay dying in Metz, his father had sold six thousand copies. Yet so far he has managed to shift just three copies across the counter. By their thousands, the people are distancing themselves from Louis XV and anticipating ever more impatiently the news of his death.

The Comte de Mercy has already sent an urgent message to the Empress of Austria. Prepared for the worst outcome of the king's illness, he tries his best to persuade Marie Antoinette to accept his prognosis.

'The first thing we need to take account of is that Madame du Barry may pay you a visit at any moment. She will undoubtedly try to ascertain your and the Dauphin's attitude towards her. May the Comtesse remain at court after the king's demise?'

'Mercy, how can you ask such a thing?' replies Marie Antoinette aghast. 'If she's got any sense in her head, she will know that she is no longer welcome.'

'Correct,' nods Mercy. 'And that is exactly why you must tread carefully. Imagine if you were to be asked this question while the king still lives. Imagine, even, what would happen were the king to recover.'

'But Mercy, you've said yourself that the chances of that are negligible.'

The ambassador raises a warning forefinger, schoolmaster fashion.

'Madame, you must always consider the unthinkable. How painful would your position be if Madame du Barry were dispatched and the king subsequently returned to health? Who would explain to him that the *maîtresse en titre* had been sent away? How would

Louis XV react were he to learn that the Dauphine, who, what is more, has so far failed to provide him with an heir, had a personal hand in the matter? Madame, I shouldn't be surprised if in that event it were you who were banished.'

Marie Antoinette feels the blood rise to her face. 'You're right, Mercy. Good grief, I hadn't thought it through.' She fans some cool air towards her. 'But Mercy, what am I to say if she knocks at my door?'

'Madame, so long as the king lives, however sick, it is up to him to decide whose company he keeps.'

Marie Antoinette nods in understanding.

'Oh, Mercy, you must remain by my side. I hardly dare imagine what might happen.'

'Madame, you must take seriously the possibility that you may at any moment find yourself Queen of France.'

Marie Antoinette nervously massages her wrist. She mustn't allow herself to be taken by surprise. She knows that Mercy has insisted time and again that she must be prepared for a change in her situation. But then, what then? Then she will be Queen of France. Hasn't she looked forward to that for long enough? Nobody will then be able to send her away, apart from Louis-Auguste himself. And she knows him well enough by now not to have any great worries on that score. Oh, how wonderful it will be to have that horrible creature gone from the palace. No more intrigues!

But the other side of the medallion shines less bright. Mercy has drawn her attention to it on many an occasion. Has Louis-Auguste the courage to reign? He will have to be decisive. Obviously he will have to dispatch Maupeou, and that dreadful d'Aiguillon. And of course Choiseul must be brought back. Yes, there is the man to support Louis-Auguste!

Oh, she feels hot all over at the thought of it all. But wait, she mustn't count her chickens before they are hatched. Perhaps Mercy is far too pessimistic in his outlook.

The fever continues to rise and one by one the pustules break open,

I'm overjoyed! Antoinette has asked me to come straight to Choisy. The Queen of France misses me and doesn't want anything to change between us! Oh, I'm so happy that we can just stay friends. What a beautiful future awaits us!

From the journal of the Princesse de Lamballe,
11th May 1774

27

Eyes closed, Marie Antoinette inhales deeply through her nose. The spring air is laden with the scent of fruit blossom. She adores its sweet bouquet, wafted to her on a soft breeze from the orchard nearby. The sun is high in the sky above Choisy-le-Roi, the country retreat of Louis XV – or rather that of Louis XVI, as the new king has announced he will be called.

All is still but for the twittering of birds. It is almost midday. Marie Antoinette slept solidly right through the night, arising only late this morning. Queen of France: the words repeat themselves again and again in her head. No one can forbid her anything any more. Never more will she have to ask the king's permission to visit the theatre. And, best of all, she will never again have to suffer the presence of that du Barry woman!

Only yesterday, in the carriage speeding away from the disease-ridden palace, did it really begin to dawn upon her. Freedom, real liberty at last! She has seen Louis-Auguste only very briefly this morning. The young man is still terribly upset, and she thinks he will probably spend the rest of the day in the chapel again. The new king looks haggard and fragile, and Marie Antoinette is not sure whether he is mourning *Papa Roi* or the heavy responsibility of his new role.

'I'm the unhappiest man in the world,' he had sobbed in the coach yesterday.

There has been hardly a peep out of his two brothers. Will Provence and Artois show more respect for Louis-Auguste now? Will it be the end of their infantile fighting at last? Marie Antoinette strolls with a light heart along the bank of the rushing Seine. The skipper of a great barge raises a friendly hand to her as he drifts quietly past, apparently unaware that he is waving to the Queen of France. Laughing, Marie Antoinette returns his greeting.

She has left her ladies in waiting chatting beside the lake. The new queen wants to be alone for a moment, to set her thoughts in order. Oh, what will she change first? Her mind is racing: so many ideas, too many to make sense of, all jostling for position. But for now she will have to stay here at Choisy, until it is safe to return to the palace. How will she bear it? If she had her way, Marie Antoinette would rush back today, for Versailles needs a complete overhaul. Everyone will be looking to her. To the true Queen of France, rather than that *créature*. She is desperately curious to see the apartment the woman occupied until so recently. Whatever will she find there?

Between the trees, Marie Antoinette can make out the contours of the *petite maison*, temporary home to the aunts. The three sisters are in quarantine, confined to the house because of the danger of contagion, and the king has forbidden Marie Antoinette to visit them. The poor old aunts! She wonders how they are, vividly recalling how upset she was at the news of her own father's sudden death, so many years ago. At first she had refused to believe it. Marie Antoinette was her father's darling, and she had gone on missing him terribly for a long time.

The aunts are much older, of course. She was a mere child when she lost her own father. And there is also the indisputable fact that *Papa Roi* was not always kind to his daughters.

Marie Antoinette notices that she is far less sad than she had expected to be. Louis XV was always good to her, but she had never come to terms with the hypocrisy of the Most Christian King of France. She had never been able to reconcile herself to the fact that Papa had publicly consorted with a prostitute.

Yet she had been moved yesterday to find her own portrait, given to Louis XV by her mother, hanging in a place of honour. The likeness of the then future Dauphine had brought back memories of her early days in France; her first meeting with the king, and with a surly Dauphin. Goodness, what a child she had been back then!

This afternoon she will write to Mama. Oh, how thrilled she will be to hear that her daughter, her youngest daughter, is Queen of France! The Austrian princess leans merrily over the embankment wall and laughs at the sight of some ducklings, cheeping madly as they swim, watched over by a vigilant mother duck. Marie Antoinette picks up a handful of pebbles and throws them into the water. The little bundles of fluff rush over, hoping for a bite to eat. She's sorry she hasn't brought a few crusts with her. How lovely to have a river like this flowing past the palace! It's a shame Versailles lies so far from the Seine.

Marie Antoinette wonders how things are with Lamballe. She has sent a messenger to her cousin, asking Marie-Thérèse to make her way to Choisy as soon as she can. She misses her friend and hopes against hope that Lamballe won't feel she must distance herself from the new Queen of France. Surely nothing has changed between them?

She picks up a stick, throws it as far as she can into the middle of the stream, where the current will bear it onwards, and watches happily as it disappears from sight.

It will be a while before her twig sails under the bridges of Paris. And nobody will notice it in any case, for everyone is too busy celebrating. People dressed in black, or simply wearing a back ribbon in their hair or on their arm, are running and dancing through the streets, singing and yelling: 'Le Roi est mort, vive le Roi!'

Countless church bells toll their tidings across the rooftops of Paris. The city is like a beehive whose colony is preparing to swarm. Printers are working overtime: the moment the ink is dry, portraits of the young royal couple are rushed through the city and hung in every shop window. With remarkable alacrity, people are removing from view anything and everything that reminds them of Louis XV.

The entire population is convinced that a new era is dawning, for have the Parisians not seen with their own eyes how sweet and charming are the young pair? And it is not a magnanimous gesture on the part of the new king that he has reduced the price of bread?

There's no end to the good news! Louis XVI has told his people that he is waiving his right to the *joyeux avènement*, the extra tax that a newly crowned king is entitled to impose. Will the king also get rid of Maupeou? Is it possible that the corrupt d'Aiguillon will be sent packing? He's bound to be! Only the most outright pessimist could doubt that France faces the rosiest of futures!

A sombre Axel Fersen turns his back on the French coast. Overhead, gulls screech and swoop insolently low over the railing. It's just as though they're laughing at me, reflects Axel morosely. The news of the death of the King of France was for him the defining moment, the signal for him to take his leave. Becoming Queen of France renders Marie Antoinette as inaccessible as the moon. Time and again Axel had postponed his decision to leave for England. He hadn't really known why. Had he cherished a quiet hope that she might still give him a chance?

Actually, it's all to the good that Louis XV is gone. It clarifies everything and Axel need no longer feel that his own future hangs in the balance. A future without her! He stares at the horizon with a heavy heart. A wave of white spume crashes up and over the railing in his face. Upon his tongue he tastes the briny water, bitter as tears.

Fate will always be against me, he muses unhappily.

Marie Antoinette is sitting in the sunny salon. The King of France has just come in and taken a seat opposite her.

'You look a lot better,' she remarks brightly.

'Thank you very much,' he mumbles absent-mindedly in return.

'What are your plans?' enquires Marie Antoinette with interest.

Louis-Auguste gives her a puzzled look and says nothing. His thoughts are still too preoccupied with the contents of the document the aunts have handed over to him. His father's papers, full of good advice and warnings, drawn up on his supposed deathbed years before.

'Have you issued instructions for the Duc de Choiseul to be permitted to return?' she asks hopefully.

Louis looks up with an appalled expression.

The queen is taken aback by the hostility in her husband's glance. This look in his eyes is new to her. Slowly, he empties his cup of tea.

'Have I said something wrong?' she asks, her tone now cool. 'Listen, Louis. I want to help you, to support you through these difficult times. Mercy has explained to me the sad state the country finds itself in, and I feel you can use all the assistance available.'

The gentleman of the chamber does not even get a chance to remove the king's cup. With a crash Louis-Auguste slams it down upon the table and makes for the door without a word, in the process almost knocking over the lady in waiting.

'Louis!' exclaims Marie Antoinette, deeply insulted.

The new King of France gives his wife a cold glance over his shoulder, contempt written all over his face. In his head echo the words of his old mentor, but even more those of his deceased father. 'Watch out for the Austrians. Before you know it, those Habsburgs will have us under their thumb!' Could the Duc de Vauguyon be proved right after all these years? Did father also have such foresight? Better to be safe than sorry; he will keep Marie Antoinette at arm's length. There is only one occupant of the French throne, after all – it has always been so!

Louis XVI slams the door shut behind him.

Marie Antoinette is livid. What right has he to treat me like this? She will go after him. No, her pride forbids it. But he will regret this! What is he thinking of? That he can rule without her? She throws a furious glance at her lady in waiting, who is acting as if nothing has happened.

The more Marie Antoinette thinks about it, the more uncertain she becomes. It's all so unexpected! He has always seemed so submissive, listening to her advice in everything. What in heaven's name has changed? The fact that he has assumed the throne must have awakened something dormant in his personality.

His angry look said everything, and now the pieces begin to fall into place. Marie Antoinette begins to realise that Louis-Auguste intends to rule in the absolute manner of his 'divine' forefathers, without the queen. Louis XVI, the Most Christian King of France and Navarre, has no need of her!

Cold shivers run through Marie Antoinette as the consequences of this come home to her. *Mon Dieu!* Her hands begin to tremble and she realises that this cup of tea will be the last of her previously envisioned existence; her future suddenly looks very different from the one that she has been imagining for years. And, given the absence of an heir, her role might already have played itself out. She allows the cup to be removed from her hands and gets to her feet.

Feeling faint, she goes over to the window and stares down over the sun-drenched gardens, where only this morning she was strolling with her head still full of ideals. Tears well up in her eyes. Her stomach contracts with the familiar cramping pains and she feels lonelier than ever. Oh, Lamballe, where are you? For God's sake, don't you desert me too!

Historical Notes

Aiguillon, Emmanuel Armand de Wignerod du Plessis de Richelieu, Duc d' (1720–82), was the nephew of the Maréchal de **Richelieu**. He entered the army at the age of seventeen and later served in the War of the Austrian Succession. His marriage in 1740 to Louise Félicité de Brehan, coupled with his connection with the Richelieu family, gave him an important place at court. He was appointed *Commandant* (Governor) of Brittany in 1753 and soon became unpopular in that province, which had retained a large number of privileges. He finally alienated the Parlement of Brittany by violating the province's privileges (1762). In June 1764 the king, at the instance of d'Aiguillon, quashed a decree of the parlement forbidding the levying of new imposts without the consent of the estates, and refused to receive the parlement's remonstrations against the duke. In 1768 the duke returned to court, where he resumed his intrigue with the *parti dévot* and finally obtained the dismissal of Foreign Minister **Choiseul**. When **Louis XV** reorganised the government with a view to suppressing the resistance of the parlements, d'Aiguillon was made Minister of Foreign Affairs, **Maupeou** and the Abbé **Terray** also obtaining places in the ministry. The new ministry, although a reforming one, was very unpopular and was styled the 'triumvirate'. All the failures of government were attributed to the mistakes of these ministers. After Louis XV's death he dismissed (1774).

Ancien Régime is the name given to the absolute monarchy of France before the Revolution of 1789.

Artois, Charles, Comte d' (1757–1836), youngest brother of Louis XVI, reigned as Charles X, King of France, 1824–30.

Barriens were the supporters of Madame du Barry.

Barry, Jeanne, Comtesse du (1743–93), was **Louis XV**'s official mistress from 1769 until his death in 1774. Although she exercised little political influence at the French court, her unpopularity contributed to the decline in prestige of the Crown during the early 1770s. She was born Marie-Jeanne Bécu, the illegitimate daughter of lower-class parents. After a convent education she became a shop assistant, under the name Jeanne Vaubernier, in a fashion house in Paris. While there she became the mistress of Jean du Barry, a nobleman who had made a fortune as a war contractor. He introduced her into Parisian high society and her beauty captivated a succession of nobly born lovers before she attracted Louis XV's attention in 1768. She could not qualify as official royal mistress, a position vacant since the death of Madame de Pompadour in 1764, unless she was married to a noble. Hence du Barry arranged a nominal marriage between Jeanne and his brother, Guillaume du Barry; in April 1769 she joined Louis XV's court.

Beaumarchais, Pierre-Augustin (Caron de) (1732–99), was a watchmaker and harp teacher to the four daughters of Louis XV, but is principally remembered as the writer of the stage comedies Le Barbier de Séville and Le Mariage de Figaro. He was also a spy and supplier of arms to both the American and the French Revolutions.

Bourbon, Elisabeth de (1764–94), sister of Louis XVI.

Bourbon-Penthièvre, Louis Jean Marie de: see **Penthièvre**, Duc de.

Bourbon-Penthièvre, Louise Marie Adélaïde de (1753–1821), was the daughter and sole heir of one the richest men in France, the Duc de **Penthièvre**. In 1769 she married the Duc de **Chartres**, heir of the

Duc d'Orléans. She was the sister-in-law (and close friend) of the Princesse de **Lamballe**.

Bourgeois means one who enjoys the rights of citizenship, or the whole body of those who do so; derivatively, 'the middle class.' It does not necessarily have the pejorative connotations of the adjective 'middle-class'.

Brunswick-Lüneburg, Charles William Ferdinand, Duke of (1735–1806), was a Prussian field marshal. In the early summer of 1792 Ferdinand was poised with military forces at Koblenz. Following France's declaration of war on Austria on 20 April 1792, the Catholic **Holy Roman Emperor**, Leopold II, and the Protestant King of Prussia, Frederick William II, had combined their armies under Brunswick's command.

Catherine II (1729–96), born Sophie Friederike Auguste, Prinzessin von Anhalt-Zerbst (Germany), was Empress of Russia 1762–96. She led her country into full participation in the political and cultural life of Europe. With her ministers she reorganised the administration and law of the Russian Empire and extended Russian territory, adding the Crimea and much of Poland.

Chartres, Louis Philippe Joseph, Duc de (1747–93), son of the Duc d'Orléans, was married to Louise Marie Adélaïde de **Bourbon-Penthièvre**, daughter of the Duc de **Penthièvre**.

Choiseul, Etienne-François, Duc de (1719–85), was the French Foreign Minister who dominated the government of King **Louis XV** from 1758 to 1770. His appointment came at a critical moment, when French forces were being defeated by the Prussians on the European continent and by the British in North America and India. In August 1761 he concluded with Spain a military alliance that was known as the *'Pacte de Famille'* because both countries were under Bourbon rule. The subsequent entry of Spain into the war (1762) gave Choiseul leverage in his negotiations with the British. By the Treaty of Paris (1763) France surrendered most of its North American and Indian colonies to Great Britain, but Choiseul's diplomatic manoeuvres had enabled France to avoid even more humiliating terms. Choiseul immediately began to rebuild French military power, with the intention of striking back at the British. While serving as naval minister (1761–66) he dramatically increased the number of French warships, and as minister of war (1766–70) he initiated a period of army reforms that continued until the outbreak of the Revolution. In 1768 Louis XV brought the Duc d'**Aiguillon** and **Maupeou** into the Foreign Ministry. The latter was eager to take the offensive against Choiseul and the parlements, and when Choiseul called for war against Great Britain (1770) Maupeou convinced the king that the government was too heavily in debt to finance such a venture. Louis dismissed Choiseul from office on December 1770 and exiled him to his estates at Chanteloup. Although allowed to return to Paris in 1774, after the death of Louis XV, Choiseul never regained political power.

Coinage: see **Livre**.

Cordon Bleu (Blue Ribbon) originally referred to *l'Ordre des Chevaliers du Saint Esprit* (Knights of the Holy Ghost), an elite order of French knights created in 1578. Members wore the Cross of the Holy Ghost, which hung from a blue ribbon.

Corvée was a system of forced labour. It was one of the oldest of French taxes, possibly inherited from Roman times.

l'Etiquette, Madame: see Anne-Claude-Louise d'Arpajon, Comtesse de **Noailles**.

Gabelle was an indirect tax levied on salt. Everyone over eight years of age was compelled to buy a certain amount of salt at prices fixed by the State. The vast difference in prices from one district to another made smuggling irresistible, and every year 3,500 people were punished for the offence. A third of the prisoners in the galleys were there for salt-smuggling.

Gabriel, Ange-Jacques (1698–1782), was trained in architecture by his father, Jacques Gabriel V, Premier Architecte at Versailles, and by Robert de Cotte. He became a member of the Académie Royale de l'Architecture in 1728 and in 1735 principal assistant to his father, whom he succeeded as Premier Architecte in 1742. The principal royal architect for most of **Louis XV**'s reign, Gabriel promoted the transition from Rococo to Neoclassicism through the development of the Louis XVI Style.

Gluck, Christoph Willibald, Chevalier von (1714–87), was a German composer best known for his operas, including *Orfeo ed Eurydice* (1762), *Alceste* (1767), *Paride ed Elena* (1770), *Iphigénie en Aulide* (1774), the French version of *Orfeo* (1774) and *Iphigénie en Tauride* (1779). He was knighted by the Pope in 1756. In Paris Gluck made both friends and enemies, who formed two opposing parties: his adherents, the Gluckists, led by the French writers and music critics François Arnaud and Jean-Baptiste-Antoine Suard, and his opponents, called Piccinnists after the Italian composer Piccinni.

Grétry, André-Ernest-Modeste (1741–1813), was the most famous composer in France, before, during and after the Revolution. Born in Liège (Belgium), he became a pupil of Félix Leclerc. It was not without the help of his friend, the Swedish ambassador Count Creutz, that Grétry dominated the musical scene of Paris. Grétry wrote more than seventy operas, which were generally very popular, the best known being *Zémire et Azir* (*Beauty and the Beast*), *Le Huron* and *Richard Cœur de Lion*. In 1774 Marie Antoinette appointed him her music director, but which instrument he taught her is uncertain.

Gustav III (1746–92), King of Sweden from 1771, assassinated in 1792.

Héloïse, La Nouvelle: see **Rousseau**.

Holy Roman Emperor was the elected monarch ruling over the Holy Roman Empire, a union of territories in Central Europe during the Middle Ages and the Early Modern period. Until the 16th century, popes were crowned by the Holy Roman Emperors. Holy Roman Emperor was the inheritor of the title of Emperor of the Western Roman Empire, left unclaimed in the West after the death of Julius Nepos in 480. The title of emperor (*imperator*) carried with it an important role as protector of the Catholic Church.

Lamballe, Marie-Thérèse Louise de Savoie-Carignan, Princesse de (born 8 September 1749, murdered 3 September 1792), was the fourth daughter of Louis-Victor of Savoy, Prince of Carignan. In 1767 she married Louis-Alexandre de Bourbon, Prince de Lamballe, the only surviving son of the vastly wealthy Duc de Bourbon-**Penthièvre**. She is best remembered as the most loyal friend of Marie Antoinette.

Legros, Joseph (1739–93), was a French singer and composer, best remembered for his association with the composer **Gluck**. Legros is usually regarded as the most prominent of his generation of *hautes-contres* (counter-tenors).

Lettres de cachet were, under the **ancien régime**, sealed orders bearing the authority of the Crown and signed by the Secretary of State for the King's Household.

Lit de Justice was a session of the Parlement at which the king presided and personally ordered registration of a law. (See also **Parlement**.)

Livre was the name of the basic currency unit. The standard coins before the Revolution were in gold. The Louis d'or' had a value of 24 livres, the 'écu' a value of three livres. The 'sou' or 'sol' was one-twentieth of a livre. It is difficult to give an exact equivalent in today's currency, but a loaf of bread weighing four pounds cost on average eight sols and the best seat in the opera around ten livres. A skilled worker's family might live on 1,000 livres a year if he was regularly employed.

Louis XV (1710–74), King of France 1715–74. His ineffectual rule contributed to the decline of royal authority that led to the outbreak of the French Revolution in 1789. Louis was the great-grandson of King Louis XIV (ruled 1643–1715) and the son of Louis, Duc de Bourgogne, and Marie-Adélaïde of Savoy. Because his parents and his only surviving brother had all died in 1712, he became king at the age of five on the death of Louis XIV (1 September 1715). Until he attained legal majority in February 1723, France was governed by a regent, Philippe II, Duc d'Orléans. In 1721 Orléans betrothed Louis to the infanta Mariana, daughter of King Philip V of Spain. After the death of Orléans (December 1723), Louis appointed as his first minister Louis-Henri, Duc de Bourbon-Condé, who cancelled the Spanish betrothal and married the King to Marie Leszczy ska, daughter of the dethroned King Stanis aw I of Poland. Louis's tutor, Bishop (later Cardinal) André-Hercule de Fleury, replaced Bourbon as chief minister in 1726, and the dynastic connection with Poland led to French involvement against Austria and Russia in the War of the Polish Succession (1733–38).
Louis XV's personal influence on French policy became perceptible only after Fleury's death in 1744. Although he proclaimed that he would henceforth rule without a chief minister, he was too indolent and lacking in self-confidence to coordinate the activities of his secretaries of state and give firm direction to national policy. While his government degenerated into factions of scheming ministers and courtiers, Louis isolated himself at court and occupied himself with a succession of mistresses, several of whom exercised

considerable political influence. In September 1745 the king took as his **maîtresse en titre** Jeanne-Antoinette Poisson, Marquise de Pompadour, whose political influence lasted until her death in 1764.

Louis was not, however, a totally passive monarch. His desire to determine the course of international affairs through intrigue caused him to set up, in about 1748, an elaborate system of secret diplomacy known as 'le *Secret du Roi*'. He stationed French secret agents in major European capitals and ordered them to pursue political objectives that were frequently opposed to his public policies. At first Louis employed his secret diplomacy in an unsuccessful attempt to win the elective Polish crown for a French candidate (a goal he officially renounced). Soon he expanded the network of agents, intending to form an anti-Austrian alliance with Sweden, Prussia, Turkey and Poland. Because his official ministers knew nothing of 'le *secret*', Louis's foreign policy became paralysed by confusion. In 1756, prompted by Madame de Pompadour, the king temporarily abandoned the objectives of his secret diplomacy and concluded an alliance with Austria. France and Austria then went to war with Great Britain and Prussia (Seven Years' War, 1756–63), but Louis's continental commitments to the Austrians prevented him from concentrating his country's resources on the crucial colonial struggle with Great Britain, a country with greater maritime power and overseas resources. As a result, by 1763 France had lost to the British almost all her colonial possessions in North America and India. Although Madame de Pompadour's favourite, the Duc de **Choiseul**, restored France's military strength, the failure of Louis's secret diplomacy in Poland enabled Russia, Austria and Prussia to partition Poland (1772) and virtually eliminate French influence in Central Europe.

During the later years of his reign an attempt was made to strengthen the waning authority of the Crown by withdrawing from the **parlements** the privilege of obstructing royal legislation. This privilege, suspended by Louis XIV, had been restored to the parlements during the regency. The parlements stood resolutely in the way of financial reform. In 1771 Chancellor **Maupeou** determined to strike at this abuse by restricting the Parlement of Paris to purely judicial functions. In spite of some popular opposition, the new judicial system functioned effectively until the king's death. Apart from this reform, Louis XV's long reign had been marked by a decline in the Crown's moral and political authority, as well as by reverses in foreign and military affairs.

Louis XVI (1753–93), King of France from 1774, deposed and executed in 1793. In 1770 he married Marie Antoinette.

Lully, Jean-Baptiste (1632–87), was an Italian-born French court and operatic composer who from 1662 completely controlled French court music.

Marie Antoinette (1755–93), Queen of France from 1774, married **Louis XVI** in 1770.

Marie Christine (1742–98), Archduchess of Austria, sister of Marie Antoinette, was married to Albert, Prince of Saxony, Duke of Teschen, Regent of the Austrian Netherlands in Brussels.

Maria Theresa (1717–80), Archduchess of Austria, Holy Roman Empress and Queen of Hungary and Bohemia, was the mother of Marie Antoinette.

Maîtresse en titre was the officially appointed royal mistress of **Louis XV**.

Maupeou, René Nicolas Charles Augustin de (1714–92), former President of the **Parlement** of Paris, became Chancellor of France in September 1768. After the death of **Louis XV**, Maupeou was replaced. Maupeou aimed at securing absolute power for Louis XV, but the way he handled the separation of the judicial and political functions and the reform of the abuses attaching to a hereditary magistrature was a serious blow to the monarchy. Although the 'Maupeou revolution' did not result in any important permanent political or social changes, France became a different nation. The literate elite in particular were preoccupied with the problems facing the country and with the 'battle' between king and parlement. Growing awareness of the country's political and social problems after the replacement of Maupeou led France steadily and inescapably towards revolution.

Mercy-Argenteau, Florimond Claude, Comte de (1727–94), was, in his capacity of Austrian Ambassador in Paris, appointed as Marie Antoinette's guardian by **Maria Theresa**. The Comte de Mercy embarked on his diplomatic career in Paris before becoming Minister at Turin and St Petersburg and returning to Paris in 1766. His primary aim was to strengthen the alliance between France and Austria. In 1792 Mercy was nominated Governor General and Minister Plenipotentiary of the Austrian Netherlands. In July 1794 he was appointed Austrian Ambassador to Great Britain, but he died a few days after his arrival in England.

Molière (1622–73), born Jean-Baptiste Poquelin, was a French actor and playwright, the greatest of all writers of French comedy. Although the sacred and secular authorities of 17th-century France often combined against him, the genius of Molière finally emerged to win him acclaim. Molière employed most of the traditional forms of comedy, but he also succeeded in inventing a new style based on a double vision: the normal and the abnormal seen in relation to each other, the comedy of the true opposed to the specious, the intelligent contrasted with the pedantic. While living in an age of reason, his own good sense led him not to proselytise but rather to animate the absurd, in such masterpieces as **Tartuffe**, *L'École des femmes, Le Misanthrope* and many others.

'Most Christian King of France and Navarre'. This title, *Rex christianissimus* or *Roi Très-chrétien*, owed its origins to the long and distinctive relationship between France and the Roman Catholic Church. France was the first modern state recognised by the Church and was known as the 'Eldest Daughter of the Church'; Clovis, King of the Franks, had been recognised by the papacy as a protector of Rome's interests. Accordingly, this title was frequently given to French kings, until it became recognised as a hereditary and exclusive title of the Kings of France.

Noailles, Anne-Claude-Louise d'Arpajon, Comtesse de (1729–94), was first lady of honour to Marie Antoinette, who nicknamed her 'Madame l'Etiquette'. The Comtesse de Noailles was guillotined on 27 June 1794.

Noblesse is the name of the French aristocracy or nobility. Its core was formed by the original *noblesse d'épée* (nobility of the sword), who derived their traditional privileges from military service to the Crown. More recent additions were the *noblesse de robe* (magistral nobility), created by the sale of public offices, mainly since Louis XIV's time; and the less numerous *noblesse de cloche*, formed by the privileged holders of municipal offices.

Parlement of Paris was established in the 13th century and became the most prestigious law court in France, sitting at the Palais de Justice on the Ile de la Cité. As well as being the highest court of appeal, the Parlement also shared responsibility for a host of judicial and administrative functions, including upholding public order, censorship, provisioning of bread and firewood and overseeing the guilds, corporations and hospitals of Paris. It was the duty of the Parlement to register new laws, after they had been checked against existing statutes and precedents. If the Parlement and the king disagreed about new or amended laws, the king had the power to command obedience by holding a **lit de justice**, when the king personally attended the Parlement, accompanied by the **Princes of the Blood**, and imposed his sovereign will.

Patriotes were supporters of **Parlement** and opponents of **Maupeou**.

Penthièvre, Louis Jean Marie de Bourbon- (1725–93), was the son of Louis-Alexandre de Bourbon, Comte de Toulouse. As such, he was the grandson of Louis XIV and Madame de Montespan. He was born at the Château de Rambouillet and was known from birth as the Duc de Penthièvre. He succeeded to his father's military and government titles and posts, among many others that of Grand Admiral of France in the French navy. In 1744 the Duc de Penthièvre married Marie Thérèse Félicité d'Este-Modène (1726–54), the daughter of Francesco III d'Este, sovereign Duke of Modena and Reggio. His only surviving son, Louis-Alexandre de Bourbon, Prince de Lamballe, died in 1768, leaving Princesse Marie-Thérèse Louise de **Savoie-Carignan** a widow. His only surviving daughter and eventual heir was Louise Marie Adélaïde de **Bourbon-Penthièvre**.

Prince of the Blood (*prince du sang*) was a rank accorded to all legitimate descendants of a French sovereign in the direct male line. The term dates from the 14th century. The Princes of the Blood all had seats on the *Conseil du Roi* (Royal Council) and in the Paris **Parlement**. In the 17th and 18th centuries it became customary to restrict the term *prince du sang* to those who were not members of the royal family itself, i.e. male children or grandchildren of the reigning sovereign, who became known as the *enfants* and *petits-enfants de France*.

Provence, Louis Xavier, Comte de (Monsieur) (1755–1824), brother of Louis XVI, reigned as Louis XVIII, King of France, 1814–24.

Querelle des Bouffons (War of the Comic Actors) was the name given to a battle of musical philosophies in France, which took place between 1752 and 1754. The controversy concerned the relative merits of French and Italian opera. It was sparked by the reaction of literary Paris to a performance of Giovanni Battista Pergolesi's short opera buffa *La Serva Padrona* at the Académie royale de musique in August 1752. This was performed by an Italian troupe of itinerant comic actors known as 'buffoni' ('*bouffons*' in Fench, hence the name of the quarrel). In the controversy that followed, critics such as Jean-Jacques **Rousseau** and Friedrich Melchior Grimm, together with other writers associated with the *Encyclopédie*, praised Italian opera buffa. They compared it favourably with French lyric tragedy, a style originated by Jean-Baptiste **Lully** and promoted by contemporary composers including Jean-Philippe **Rameau**.

Racine, Jean-Baptiste (1639–99), was a French dramatic poet and historiographer renowned for his mastery of French classical tragedy. His reputation rests on the plays he wrote between 1664 and 1677, notably *Andromaque* (1667), *Britannicus* (1669), *Bérénice* (1670), *Bajazet* (1672) and *Phèdre* (1677).

Rameau, Jean-Philippe (1683–1764), was a French composer of the late Baroque period, best known today for his harpsichord music, operas and works in other theatrical genres.

Richelieu, Louis François Armand du Plessis, Duc de (1696–1788), was a Marshal of France and a great-nephew of Cardinal Richelieu. King Louis XIV was his godfather. In his early days he was imprisoned in the Bastille three times. Despite a deplorably defective education and a reputation for exceptionally loose morals, he attained distinction as a diplomat and general. He served in the Rhine campaign in 1733–4. He fought with distinction at Dettingen and Fontenoy, where he directed the grapeshot on the English columns, and three years later made a brilliant defence of Genoa. In 1756 he expelled the English from Minorca by capturing the stronghold of San Felipe and in 1757–8 concluded his military career with pillaging campaigns against Hanover. His public career began ten years after his service in the Rhine campaign, when he plunged into court intrigue. He was initially the closest friend of King **Louis XV**, whom he had known since the king was a child, but their relationship later cooled a little when he opposed Louis's mistress, Madame de Pompadour. After her death in 1764 his position at court was restored and he developed a friendship with the King's last mistress, Madame du **Barry**. Richelieu was so renowned as a lover that Choderlos de Laclos is said to have based the character of Valmont in *Les Liaisons Dangereuses* on him.

Rousseau, Jean-Jacques (1712–78), was a philosopher, theorist and composer, born in Geneva (Switzerland). He moved to Paris in 1742. His first operatic success came in 1752 with *Le Devin de Village*. Diderot entrusted Rousseau with the articles on music in the *Encyclopédie*. Rousseau's aesthetic thinking permeates all his work. His epistolary novel *La Nouvelle Héloïse*, published in 1761, was enormously popular.

Smallpox is an acute infectious disease caused by infection with variola major, a virus of the family Poxviridae. It begins with a high fever, headache and back pain and proceeds to an eruption on the skin that leaves the face and limbs covered with cratered pockmarks, or pox. For centuries smallpox was one of the world's most dreaded plagues, killing as many as 30 per cent of its victims, most of them children. Those who survived were permanently immunised against a second infection. A huge pandemic spread from Europe to the Middle East in 1614 and epidemics arose regularly in Europe throughout the 17th and 18th centuries. Though infectious organisms such as viruses were still unknown to medical science, it was understood that smallpox was somehow a contagious disease and that its victims had to be separated from the general populace. Little could be done for the victims. In the early 18th century European doctors began to publicise the value of inoculation and the practice was soon adopted by royalty and people of means in Europe and America.

Taille was the most important of all French taxes on the unprivileged. It was arbitrarily assessed upon the supposed income of the peasant. Any sign of improvement or mark of enterprise produced an increase in the *taille*. Even punctuality of payment was dangerous, for it might be interpreted as a sign of easy circumstances.

Tartuffe, a comedy by **Molière**, dramatises an attempt by an irredeemable hypocrite to destroy the domestic happiness of a citizen who, hoodwinked by his apparent piety, has received him as a prominent guest.

Taxation under the **ancien régime** was extremely complicated. The population of France was basically divided into the privileged and the unprivileged, leading to huge injustice in the assessment of taxes, for they were for the most part imposed by those who did not pay them. The taxes were either direct (**taille**, *capitation*, *vingtième* and **corvée**) or indirect (**gabelle**, *aides*, *octroi* and customs duties). Direct taxes were collected by the agents of the Crown; indirect taxes were farmed out to individuals or private companies. (See also **Terray**.)

Terray, Joseph-Marie (1715–78), was Controller General of Finances during the last four years of **Louis XV**'s reign. After entering the priesthood, in 1736 Terray became an ecclesiastical counsellor in the Parlement of Paris, where he specialised in financial matters. Louis XV's chancellor, **Maupeou**, secured his appointment as Controller General in December 1769. A year later Terray helped to bring about the downfall of the powerful Minister of Foreign Affairs, the Duc de **Choiseul**, by demonstrating to Louis XV that the government was too heavily in debt to support Choiseul's plans for war with Great Britain. Terray then began to stabilise the finances by repudiating part of the debt, suspending payments of the interest on government bonds and levying forced loans. His measures aroused vigorous opposition among the nobles and wealthy bourgeoisie and even from the mass of the population. Terray and Maupeou both realised that any further attempts at fiscal reform would be blocked by the parlements. Maupeou took the offensive, depriving the parlements of their political powers in a drastic overhaul of the judicial system in 1771. Terray then proceeded with his reforms. He made the collection of the *vingtième* (five per cent tax on income) less arbitrary, reorganised assessment of the Paris *capitation* (poll tax) and concluded more lucrative agreements with the farmers general, the financiers who purchased the right to collect indirect taxes. These measures dramatically increased the government's revenue.

Tourzel, Louise-Elisabeth-Felicité, Marquise de (1764–1832), was the governess of Marie Antoinette's children.

Vauguyon, Antoine-Paul-Jacques de Quelen de Stuers et de Caussade, Duc de La (1706–72), was the *gouverneur des enfants de la Maison de France*, teacher of Louis-Auguste (Louis XVI) and his brothers, the Comtes de **Provence** and d'**Artois**.

Victor Amadeus III (1726–96), reigned as Savoyard king of Sardinia (Piedmont-Sardinia) 1773–96.

Voltaire was the pseudonym of François-Marie Arouet (1694–1778), one of the greatest of all French writers. Although only a few of his works are still read, he continues to be held in worldwide repute as a courageous crusader against tyranny, bigotry and cruelty.

ILE DE FRANCE

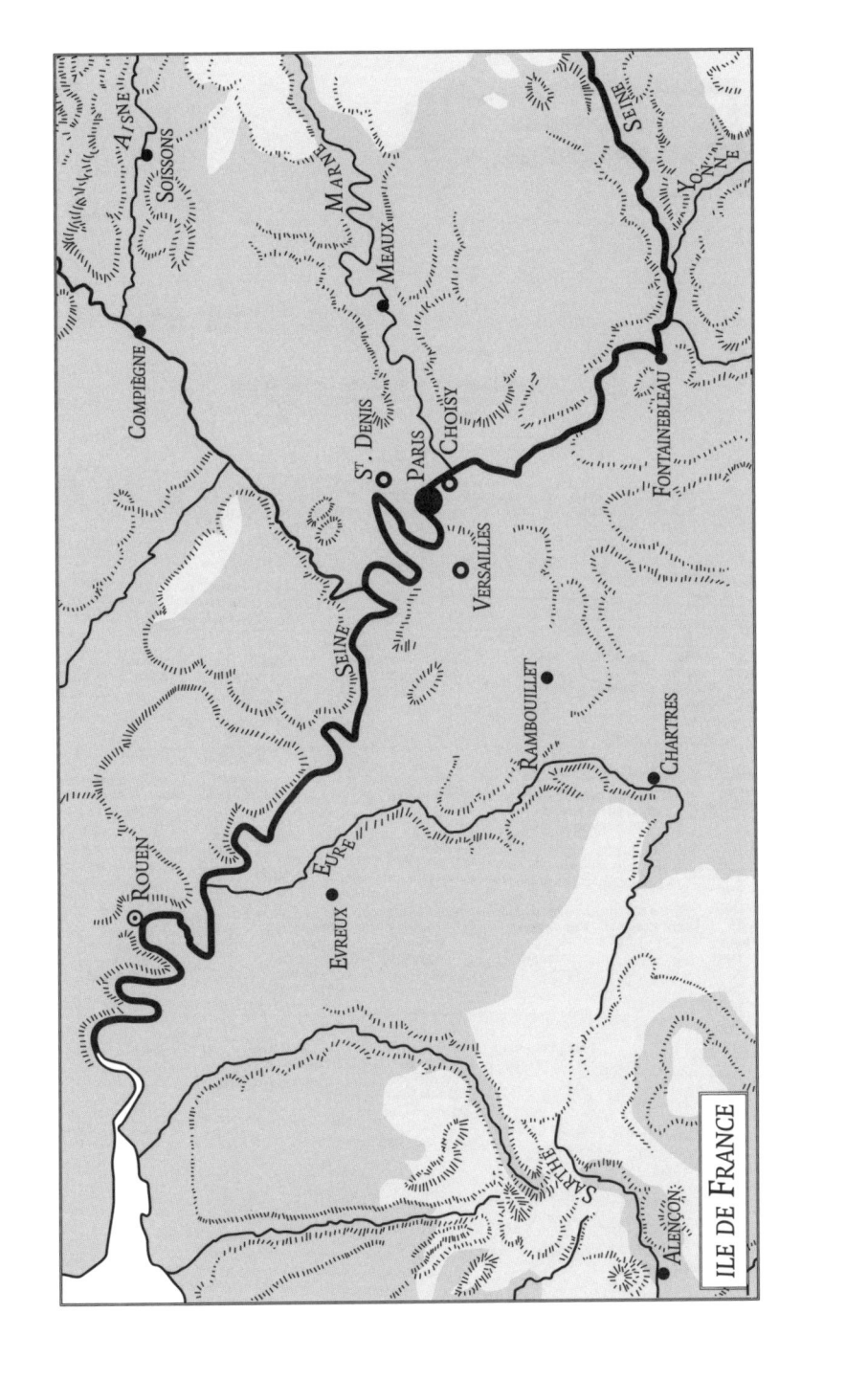

House of Bourbon

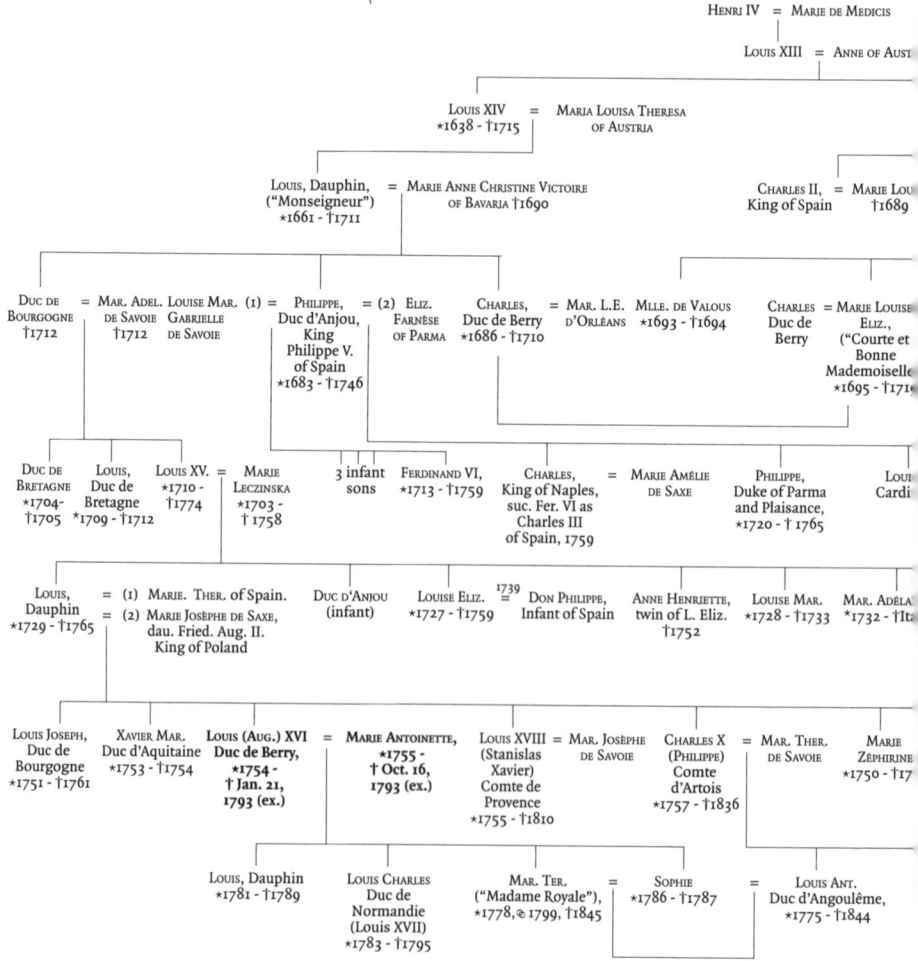

Henri IV = Marie de Medicis

Louis XIII = Anne of Austria

Louis XIV = Maria Louisa Theresa of Austria
*1638 - †1715

- Louis, Dauphin, ("Monseigneur") = Marie Anne Christine Victoire of Bavaria †1690
  *1661 - †1711
- Charles II, King of Spain = Marie Lou... †1689

- Duc de Bourgogne †1712 = Mar. Adel. Louise Mar. de Savoie †1712
- Louise Mar. Gabrielle de Savoie
- (1) = Philippe, Duc d'Anjou, King Philippe V. of Spain *1683 - †1746 = (2) Eliz. Farnèse of Parma
- Charles, Duc de Berry *1686 - †1710 = Mar. L.E. d'Orléans
- Mlle. de Valous *1693 - †1694
- Charles Duc de Berry = Marie Louise Eliz., ("Courte et Bonne Mademoiselle" *1695 - †171...

- Duc de Bretagne *1704 - †1705
- Louis, Duc de Bretagne *1709 - †1712
- Louis XV. *1710 - †1774 = Marie Leczinska *1703 - †1758
- 3 infant sons
- Ferdinand VI, *1713 - †1759
- Charles, King of Naples, suc. Fer. VI as Charles III of Spain, 1759 = Marie Amélie de Saxe
- Philippe, Duke of Parma and Plaisance, *1720 - †1765
- Loui... Cardi...

- Louis, Dauphin *1729 - †1765 = (1) Marie. Ther. of Spain. = (2) Marie Josèphe de Saxe, dau. Fried. Aug. II. King of Poland
- Duc d'Anjou (infant)
- Louise Eliz. *1727 - †1759 =1739 Don Philippe, Infant of Spain
- Anne Henriette, twin of L. Eliz. †1752
- Louise Mar. *1728 - †1733
- Mar. Adéla... *1732 - †It...

- Louis Joseph, Duc de Bourgogne *1751 - †1761
- Xavier. Mar. Duc d'Aquitaine *1753 - †1754
- Louis (Aug.) XVI Duc de Berry, *1754 - †Jan. 21, 1793 (ex.) = Marie Antoinette, *1755 - †Oct. 16, 1793 (ex.)
- Louis XVIII (Stanislas Xavier) Comte de Provence *1755 - †1810 = Mar. Josèphe de Savoie
- Charles X (Philippe) Comte d'Artois *1757 - †1836 = Mar. Ther. de Savoie
- Marie Zéphirine *1750 - †17...

- Louis, Dauphin *1781 - †1789
- Louis Charles Duc de Normandie (Louis XVII) *1783 - †1795
- Mar. Ter. ("Madame Royale"), *1778, ⚭ 1799, †1845 =
- Sophie *1786 - †1787 =
- Louis Ant. Duc d'Angoulême, *1775 - †1844

---

* Birth
† Death
⚭ Married

Henrietta Anne, (1)	=	Philippe I,	=	(2) Elizabeth Charlotte					
(dau. Charles 1)		Duc d'Orléans		of Bavaria					
*1644 - †1670		*1640 - †1701		*1652 - †1722					

Victor Amadée II, = Anne Marie   Philippe II, Regent = Françoice Marie
Duc de Savoie   *1674 - †1723   De Bourbon,
                                   Duc de Chartres   ("Mlle. de Blois")
                                   till 1701   (dau. Mme. de Montespan)

                            1730   1722   BETROTH.
                                                                                                    TO
Louise Adel, Fran. Marie = Char. Aglaé, Aug. Mar. = Louis,   Louis I, = Louise Eliz., Charles, Phillippine Louis de = Louise
Mlle. De   d'Este,   Mlle. de Valois, Jeanne Duc d'Orléans, King of   Mlle. de   King of   Eliz.   Bourbon,   Diane
Chartres,   Prince of   *1700 - †1761. of Baden Duc de Chartres Spain   Montpensier   Sicily   ("Mlle. de   Prince de   Mlle. de
Abbesse   Modena   till 1723.   *1709 - †1742   Beaujolais") Conti   Chartres
de Chelles   1714   *1716 - †1736

              1729   1745
Mar. Ann. = Prince of Brazil, Mar. Ther. = Louis,   Mar. Ant. = Vic. Amadée,   Louise Henriette = Louis Philippe
Vic.   aft. King of   Ant.   Dauphin   Duc de Savoie De Bourbon Conti   (Duc de Chartes
*1716   Portugal,   *1726 - †1745   †1759   til 1752)
              as Joseph I   *1725 - †1785

M.L. Victoire Sophie,   Ther. Fel.   Louise,   Louis Philippe   = Lou. Mar.   Lou. Hen. Joseph = Lou. Mar.
*1733 - †1799, *1734 - †1782 *1736 - †1744 *1737 - †1787 Joseph ("Egalité"), Adélaïde de   Duc de Bourbon   Ther. Bathilde
Trieste   (religieuse, 1771) (Duc de Chartres   Bourbon-   *1755 - †1830   *1750 - †1822
                                                               till 1785)   Penthièvre   (strangled)   (suddenly)
                                                               Duc d'Orléans,   *1753 - †1821
                                                               *1747 - †1793 (ex.)

Mar. Adel. = Charles Emman, Philippine   Louis Philippe = Mar. Amé.   Antionio Phil,   Alph. Léodgar, Lou. Mar. Louis Ant. Henri
Clotilde   Prince de   Mar. Hel.   procl. King 1830, de Naples Duc de   Comte de   Adel. Eug. de Bourbon
*1759 - †1802 Piémont,   Eliz.   *1773, ⚭ 1809   *1782   Montpensier   Beaujolais   Condé, Duc
               King   *1764 -   Niece of   *1775 - †1807   *1779 - †1808   d'Enghien
               of Sardinia   †1794 (ex.)   Marie   (d. unm.   (d. unm.   *1772 - †1804
                                                           Antoinette   in London)   in Malta)   (shot)

"Mademoiselle"   Chas. Ferdin.   10 children
*1776 - †1783   Duc de Berry
                 *1778

                 Duc de Bordeaux,
                 *1820 (Henri V),
                 Comte de Chambord,
                 †1870 (ass.)

House of Austria

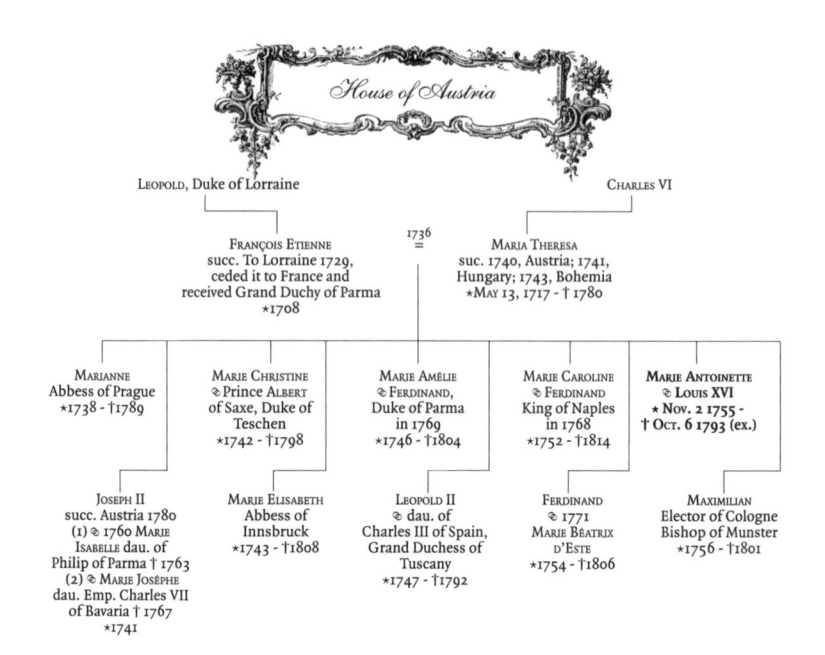

Leopold, Duke of Lorraine — **Charles VI**

François Etienne succ. To Lorraine 1729, ceded it to France and received Grand Duchy of Parma *1708

= 1736 =

Maria Theresa suc. 1740, Austria; 1741, Hungary; 1743, Bohemia *May 13, 1717 - †1780

Marianne Abbess of Prague *1738 - †1789

Marie Christine ⚭ Prince Albert of Saxe, Duke of Teschen *1742 - †1798

Marie Amélie ⚭ Ferdinand, Duke of Parma in 1769 *1746 - †1804

Marie Caroline ⚭ Ferdinand King of Naples in 1768 *1752 - †1814

Marie Antoinette ⚭ Louis XVI * Nov. 2 1755 - † Oct. 6 1793 (ex.)

Joseph II succ. Austria 1780 (1) ⚭ 1760 Marie Isabelle dau. of Philip of Parma † 1763 (2) ⚭ Marie Josèphe dau. Emp. Charles VII of Bavaria † 1767 *1741

Marie Elisabeth Abbess of Innsbruck *1743 - †1808

Leopold II ⚭ dau. of Charles III of Spain, Grand Duchess of Tuscany *1747 - †1792

Ferdinand ⚭ 1771 Marie Béatrix d'Este *1754 - †1806

Maximilian Elector of Cologne Bishop of Munster *1756 - †1801

---

* Birth
† Death
⚭ Married

House of Savoy

CHARLES III, Duke of Savoy
⚜ 1504 - 1553

EMMANUEL PHILIBERT
⚜ 1553 - 1580

CHARLES EMMANUEL I
⚜ 1580 - 1630

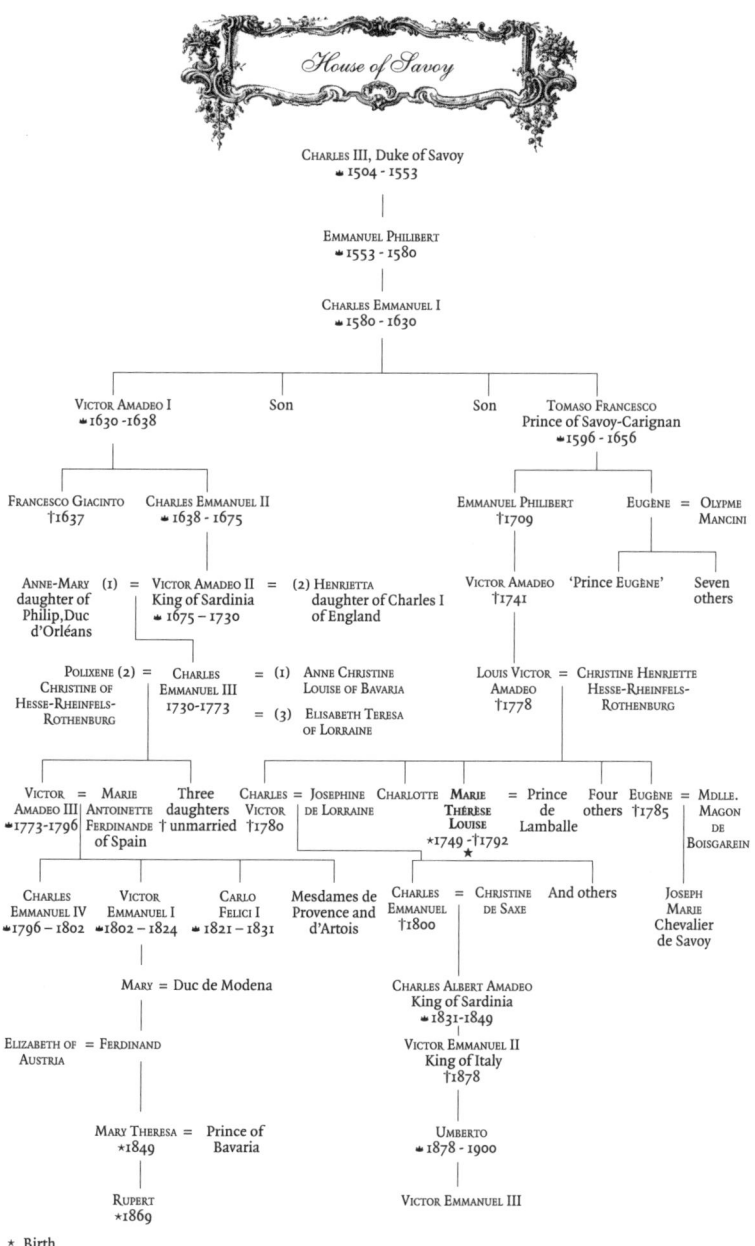

- VICTOR AMADEO I ⚜ 1630 -1638
- Son
- Son
- TOMASO FRANCESCO Prince of Savoy-Carignan ⚜ 1596 - 1656

From Victor Amadeo I:
- FRANCESCO GIACINTO †1637
- CHARLES EMMANUEL II ⚜ 1638 - 1675

ANNE-MARY (1) = VICTOR AMADEO II = (2) HENRIETTA
daughter of   King of Sardinia   daughter of Charles I
Philip, Duc   ⚜ 1675 – 1730   of England
d'Orléans

POLIXENE (2) = CHARLES = (1) ANNE CHRISTINE
CHRISTINE OF   EMMANUEL III   LOUISE OF BAVARIA
HESSE-RHEINFELS- 1730-1773   = (3) ELISABETH TERESA
ROTHENBURG   OF LORRAINE

From Tomaso Francesco:
- EMMANUEL PHILIBERT †1709
- EUGÈNE = OLYMPE MANCINI

- VICTOR AMADEO †1741
- 'Prince EUGENE'
- Seven others

LOUIS VICTOR = CHRISTINE HENRIETTE
AMADEO   HESSE-RHEINFELS-
†1778   ROTHENBURG

VICTOR = MARIE   Three   CHARLES = JOSEPHINE   CHARLOTTE   MARIE   = Prince   Four   EUGENE = MDLLE.
AMADEO III ANTOINETTE daughters   VICTOR   DE LORRAINE   THÉRÈSE   de   others   †1785   MAGON
⚜1773-1796 FERDINANDE † unmarried †1780   LOUISE   Lamballe   DE
           of Spain   ★1749 -†1792   BOISGAREIN
                                                                          ★

CHARLES   VICTOR   CARLO   Mesdames de   CHARLES   = CHRISTINE   And others   JOSEPH
EMMANUEL IV EMMANUEL I   FELICI I   Provence and EMMANUEL   DE SAXE   MARIE
⚜ 1796 – 1802 ⚜1802 – 1824 ⚜1821 – 1831 d'Artois   †1800   Chevalier
                                                                                             de Savoy

              MARY = Duc de Modena   CHARLES ALBERT AMADEO
                                                    King of Sardinia
ELIZABETH OF = FERDINAND   ⚜ 1831-1849
AUSTRIA
                                                    VICTOR EMMANUEL II
                                                    King of Italy
                                                    †1878

MARY THERESA = Prince of   UMBERTO
★1849   Bavaria   ⚜ 1878 - 1900

RUPERT   VICTOR EMMANUEL III
★1869

★ Birth
† Death
⚜ Crowned

Stewart Descent of Louis XVI

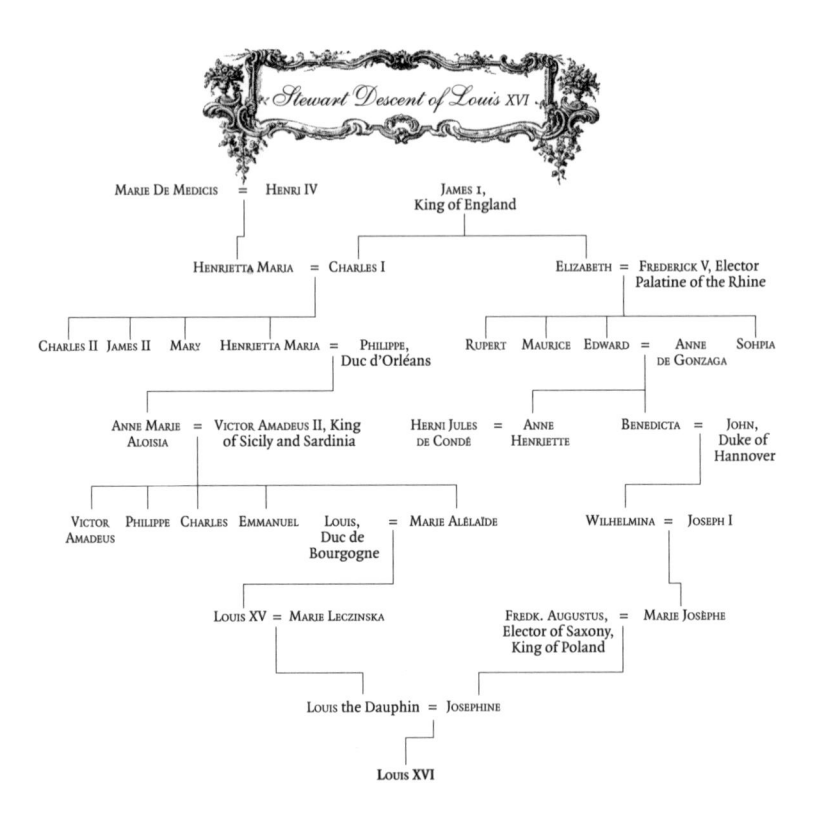

```
Marie De Medicis = Henri IV            James I,
                      |              King of England
                      |                    |
        ┌─────────────┴──┐        ┌────────┴────────────┐
   Henrietta Maria = Charles I   Elizabeth = Frederick V, Electorr
                │                            Palatine of the Rhine
   ┌─────┬─────┬──┴──────────────┐      ┌────┬────┬────┴──┬─────────┐
Charles II James II Mary Henrietta Maria = Philippe,  Rupert Maurice Edward = Anne    Sohpia
                                Duc d'Orléans                          de Gonzaga
                    ┌───────────┴──────┐                       ┌──────┴────┐
              Anne Marie = Victor Amadeus II, King    Herni Jules = Anne    Benedicta = John,
                Aloisia    of Sicily and Sardinia     de Condé    Henriette              Duke of
                                                                                         Hannover
   ┌────────┬────────┬─────────┬──────────┐                          ┌──────┴─────┐
Victor   Philippe  Charles  Emmanuel   Louis,    = Marie Alélaïde  Wilhelmina = Joseph I
Amadeus                               Duc de
                                     Bourgogne
                        ┌──────────────┴──┐                  ┌──────────────┴──┐
                    Louis XV = Marie Leczinska        Fredk. Augustus, = Marie Josèphe
                            │                         Elector of Saxony,
                            │                         King of Poland
                            └──────────┬──────────────────────┘
                                Louis the Dauphin = Josephine
                                                │
                                           Louis XVI
```

Genealogical Table of the Spanish Succession

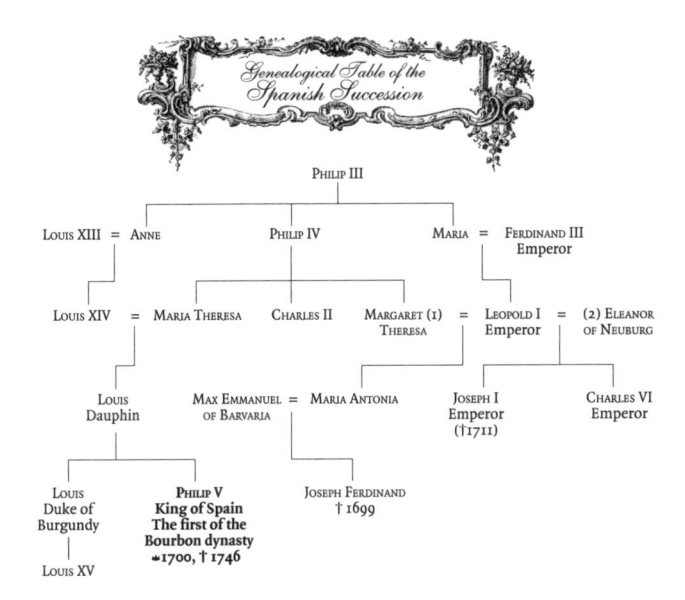

```
                                    PHILIP III
         ┌──────────────────────────────┼──────────────────────────────┐
   LOUIS XIII = ANNE              PHILIP IV                    MARIA = FERDINAND III
                                                                         Emperor
         │               ┌──────────────┼──────────────┐           ┌──────────┴──────────┐
   LOUIS XIV = MARIA THERESA      CHARLES II     MARGARET (1) = LEOPOLD I = (2) ELEANOR
                                                    THERESA      Emperor        OF NEUBURG
         │                      ┌──────────────────────┤              │               │
      LOUIS              MAX EMMANUEL = MARIA ANTONIA          JOSEPH I        CHARLES VI
     Dauphin             OF BAVARIA                             Emperor          Emperor
         │                              │                       (†1711)
    ┌────┴────┐                         │
   LOUIS              JOSEPH FERDINAND
  Duke of              PHILIP V             † 1699
 Burgundy            King of Spain
    │              The first of the
  LOUIS XV         Bourbon dynasty
                    ♛ 1700, † 1746
```

♛ Crowned

filling the air of the bedchamber with an insufferable stench. Even the incense burners hastily brought through from the chapel prove incapable of vanquishing the pestilent atmosphere.

It is a long time since Louis XV last smiled. Now and then he relapses into delirium. The doctors, but also all the priests present, are finding it more and more difficult to avoid telling the truth. Every time the king, in a moment of 'lucidity', cries out in a wavering voice, 'These blisters surely are the pox!', it is left to Madame du Barry's physician to deny it.

And yet the truth will out, and that night, as Jeanne du Barry watches by his bed, the French king knows what awaits him.

'I am very sick and probably dying,' he tells his beloved.

Shocked, Madame du Barry claps her hand to her mouth. The dreaded moment has arrived at last.

'Listen, I have been here before and do not desire another scandal. Tomorrow morning you must leave Versailles. Retreat to Rueil, as d'Aiguillon's guest, and ask him to be here at ten o'clock tomorrow.'

Jeanne du Barry lets out a sob. 'But I don't want to leave you. I love you.'

He raises his hand. Weak as he is, the king will tolerate no contradiction. As if realising their predicament for the first time, he turns away to hide his mortification from her. His own salt tears bite venomously into his open sores.

Controlling herself, the *maîtresse en titre* walks in as dignified a manner as possible from the room. Shutting the door softly behind her, she runs up the stairs. But once in her bedchamber, she throws herself onto the bed, burying her head in the pillows. There, unheard by the outside world, she gives free rein to her grief, weeping as never before in her life.

It is the end. Her end! *Incroyable!* It is the fourth of May. That bloody almanac had it almost to the day!

It is the eleventh day of the king's illness, a crucial moment, for this is when most smallpox sufferers breathe their last. The king's respiration is shallow, and he grimaces in pain every time he swallows. His tongue and mucous membranes are covered in blisters. Everything hurts. His face is black and swollen, the sheets strewn with dark, dry scabs scratched off by the sick sovereign in his fits of unbearable itching. Louis XV keeps sprinkling himself with holy water to keep the evil spirits at bay.

It costs him a huge effort to speak, but he has just told Richelieu that he wishes to receive the last rites. A triumph for the clerics; the king is to make his confession! But their victory is incomplete as yet. The fact that Madame du Barry has departed the palace to reside an hour from Versailles is considered inadequate. She needs to withdraw at least a hundred and fifty miles distant.

In the ensuing heated debate, d'Aiguillon manages to fix it so that the former *maîtresse en titre* may remain where she is, provided the king publicly relinquishes his scandalous way of life. The ceremony is due to begin at six o'clock in the morning. The priests and the old Archbishop of Paris take their places next to the Cardinal de La Roche-Aimon. Around them kneel d'Aiguillon, Richelieu and the aunts. Praying for the soul of the king in the next chamber are the *cabinet du conseil*, Marie Antoinette and the Comtesse de Provence. A little way away, at the top of the stairs, the Dauphin mutely folds his hands.

Having administered the sacraments, the cardinal walks over to the door and opens it. All eyes are upon La Roche-Aimon. Standing in the doorway, he announces in a loud voice: 'Gentlemen, the king has instructed me to inform you that he has asked God's forgiveness. Absolution for his misconduct in relation to God and the inconvenience this has caused his people.'

La Roche-Aimon pauses to allow his words to sink in. The cardinal is partial to a little drama. 'If God in His mercy grants the King recovery, he will devote himself to remorse, reinstitution of the faith and the welfare of his subjects.'

Everyone crosses himself; Richelieu swallows a curse. The marshal knows the king better than anyone, and he is sure that the cardinal's words have nothing whatsoever to do with any sentiment held by Louis XV.

Later that morning Richelieu is sitting bolt upright by the bedside of his old comrade, whose face and torso are now unrecognisable; the king has mutated into a repulsive monster. Only the eyes remain those of Louis XV, although the light is almost gone from them. Grief strikes at the old marshal's heart. The two men gaze at one another and both know what lies ahead. Wordlessly, they take their leave of one another.

'Du Barry?' whispers Louis XV a few minutes later, audible only to Richelieu. A tear negotiates its way with difficulty over the disfigured cheek.

'Have no fear,' Richelieu replies in a low voice.

Wearily, the king closes his eyes. The atmosphere in the airless room is tense. The priests, barely able to tolerate the stench, missay their prayers. The candlelight flickers and is dimmed and disseminated through the clouds of incense.

Outside the bedchamber hums the court, now more and more clearly divided into two camps. The followers of du Barry and the paladins of d'Aiguillon are pacing restlessly to and fro, hopefully awaiting news of the king's recovery. Spurred on by burgeoning optimism, Choiseul's supporters hungrily anticipate the power that now seems within reach, and look down contemptuously upon those who for years have suppressed and thwarted them. Huh, their days are numbered now!

On Monday evening the King of France receives the last rites. Anyone who still believes in the king's recovery is fooling only himself. It could all be over at any moment. Scores of bored messengers and couriers loaf around the courtyard in front of the palace. But again tonight the candle burning in the king's window remains alight.

Everyone's patience has been tested to the limit. As dawn breaks, fresh horses are harnessed and the carriages held ready.

The palace is preparing to abandon the house of plague directly upon the announcement of the death of their king. Marie Antoinette has withdrawn to her own quarters. The Dauphin came upstairs in the early hours and has spent the time since then pacing restlessly up and down. All the windows have been thrown open to admit fresh air. But the putrid miasma of the sickroom has reached even this far, a dreadful odour of rotting flesh, despite the bunches of freshly picked scented violets in every room.

A manservant of the Dauphin arrives quarter-hourly with the latest bulletin. Each time, Marie Antoinette looks expectantly over at her husband, to be met by a sombre stare and shake of his head. No news.

She has hardly slept a wink for days, but has spent hours in prayer with the Dauphin and the Abbé Vermond. It feels better to be back here in her own apartment, out of sight of the jealous glances. To Marie Antoinette, the internecine rivalry among the courtiers is so palpable and so ubiquitous that it threatens to overwhelm her.

The Comtes de Provence and d'Artois have, mercifully, kept themselves in the background. Their usual sibling squabbling would be considered extremely inappropriate at such a time. Louis-Auguste has let his brothers know that they must be ready to depart from one moment to the next. As soon as Papa has breathed his last, the whole family will leave the infected palace.

The Comte de Mercy waits patiently in a corner. He has read the *Gazette* through twice. There is nothing more he can do for the time being. He observes the Dauphin and wonders how the boy will behave when the time arrives. How much room will he give Marie Antoinette to think and rule alongside him?

Until now the role of the Queen of France has been negligible, but France has never before been confronted with a king who cannot or dare not express an opinion. A king who prefers to keep his mouth firmly shut. Who in heaven's name is to rule the country? It is a question he has asked himself a thousand times but has never yet been able to answer.

Mercy has made Marie Antoinette promise to persuade the Dauphin – if, that is, he asks her advice – not to make any changes in the government for the time being.

'Let him first familiarise himself with the current set-up, so that he is able to form a judgement. What he should do right away is bring down the price of bread.'

Once more the manservant appears and whispers something to the Dauphin. His expression unchanging, Louis-Auguste again shakes his head. Marie Antoinette sighs in discomfiture and goes over to the open window. 'This is driving me mad!'

Mercy excuses himself. In the antechamber the guards are engaged in a lack-lustre game of cards. Mercy makes a way for himself through the landing at the top of the stairs, where people are leaning against the walls or lying asleep on the floor. Every stair, too, is occupied by people waiting. Waiting for death.

'Mon Dieu!' calls out one of the couriers; he has just seen the candle snuffed out. Swiftly tightening the girth on his saddle, he sets off at a gallop for Paris.

'Le Roi est mort!' announces a servant without emotion. For a split second all is still. The Most Christian King of France and Navarre has passed away.

Then people fall on one another's necks, whether in sympathy or in joy. Some are silent, stunned at the king abandoning them. Quietly they wander off, now that Versailles has nothing more to offer them.

'Vive le Roi!' shouts the horde, seeing before them a golden future.

'Where is the king?'

The Comtesse de Noailles knows the whereabouts of the Dauphin, or rather the King of France. She runs to Marie Antoinette's apartment, in her wake a train of folk keen to swear allegiance to their new king. Throwing etiquette to the wind, the Comtesse de Noailles pushes open the door and is the first to reach the astounded couple.

Panting like a hunted deer, Noailles throws herself at the feet of the King of France. Within a couple of seconds the apartment is teeming with subjects greeting their new sovereign, or failing to do so. Louis-Auguste recoils from the throng, terrified that someone will infect him. But the pressure is too great; more and more courtiers are flooding in.

It is all too much for Louis-Auguste. Never in his life has he found himself at the centre of attention like this. Weeping, he accepts the pledges of loyalty. But he remains clear-headed enough not to shake anyone by the hand.

Then people turn to the queen.

'Vive la Reine!'

And she too finds herself overwhelmed.

The guards, obviously taken by surprise, abandon their card game and eventually force their way through the masses. Reimposing some modicum of discipline, they create a space between the royal couple and their cheering courtiers.

The king raises a trembling hand. Silence falls and all bow before their monarch.

The king's *valet de chambre* steps forward. 'Sire, your carriage is prepared. You must depart immediately.'

Louis-Auguste nods.

'Make way for the king!' shouts the bodyguard. The crowds of adoring courtiers part.

Marie Antoinette wonders whether or not she should take his hand, for the new king stands rooted to the spot. She understands that she must not treat him like a child. Drawing herself up to her full height, Marie Antoinette takes her place at her husband's side, whispering, 'Take my arm.'

He does precisely as she instructs and she leads him, just as on the dance floor, without this being evident to anyone else's eyes. The cheers of the people bring tears to her own. Scurrying quickly down the stairs, the couple step into the big carriage.

The Comtes de Provence and d'Artois and their countesses have already taken their places. To the cracking of the coachman's whip, the royal carriage gets underway, slowly clearing a path for itself through the chaos of sedan chairs, calèches and people running as fast as their feet will carry them away from the palace.

The King of France is on his way from Versailles to Choisy. The aunts will follow in their own coach.

Never before has the palace been so swiftly evacuated. For the coming ten days the windows will be left standing open and the palace scrubbed and disinfected. In the King's Bedchamber lie the remains of Louis XV. As soon as possible the corpse, already decomposing as a result of his final illness, was laid to rest in a lead coffin. The smell is unbearable, despite the coffin being topped up with wine.

Two days later it is conveyed without ceremony to the crypt of Saint-Denis. On its way, the funeral procession is pelted with stones and obscenities, so that the officiators are only too relieved to heave the leaden colossus that was once Louis XV into the crypt between his forefathers.

Just as drenched in wine as their deceased monarch, France celebrates his passing. The bastard is gone at last and a new era is at hand. Singing and dancing Parisians throng the streets. Everything will be better from now on, you'll see.

'*Vive le Roi et vive la Reine!*